HOLY TEMPLE
JIMETA
N
OMBE
ORON
KADUNA
LOKOJA
BENIN CITY

TOMI ADEYEMI

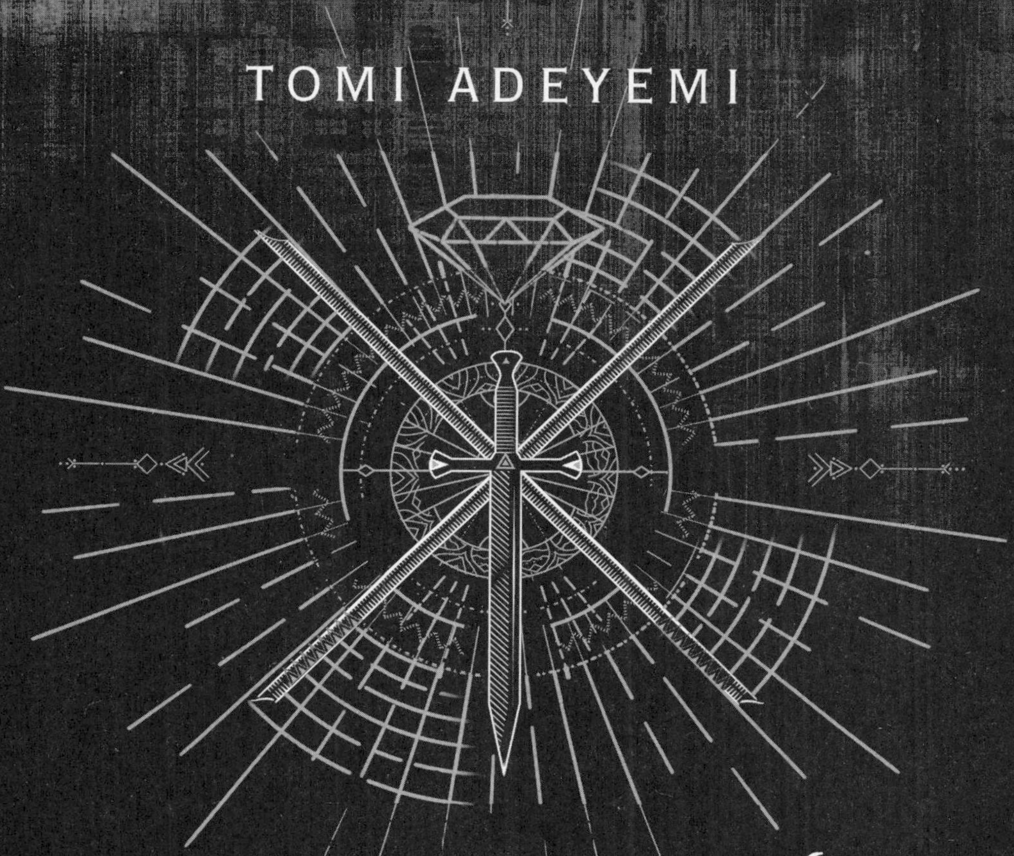

CHILDREN OF BLOOD AND BONE

HENRY HOLT AND COMPANY ✦ NEW YORK

Henry Holt and Company, *Publishers since 1866*
Henry Holt® is a registered trademark of Macmillan Publishing Group, LLC
175 Fifth Avenue, New York, NY 10010 • fiercereads.com

Library of Congress Control Number: 2017945039

First edition, 2018 / Designed by Patrick Collins
Map illustration by Keith Thompson
Printed in the United States of America

ISBN 978-1-250-17097-2 (hardcover)
10

ISBN 978-1-250-29544-6 (special edition)
1 3 5 7 9 10 8 6 4 2

ISBN 978-1-250-19412-1 (international edition)
1 3 5 7 9 10 8 6 4 2

To Mom and Dad—

who sacrificed everything to give me this chance

&

To Jackson—

who believed in me and this story long before I did

THE MAJI CLANS

IKÚ CLAN

MAJI OF LIFE AND DEATH

MAJI TITLE: REAPER

DEITY: OYA

ÈMÍ CLAN

MAJI OF MIND, SPIRIT, AND DREAMS

MAJI TITLE: CONNECTOR

DEITY: ORÍ

OMI CLAN

MAJI OF WATER

MAJI TITLE: TIDER

DEITY: YEMỌJA

INÁ CLAN

MAJI OF FIRE

MAJI TITLE: BURNER

DEITY: SÀNGÓ

AFÉFÉ CLAN

MAJI OF AIR

MAJI TITLE: WINDER

DEITY: AYAO

....

AIYE CLAN

MAJI OF IRON AND EARTH

MAJI TITLE: GROUNDER + WELDER

DEITY: ÒGÚN

....

ÌMỌ́LÈ CLAN

MAJI OF DARKNESS AND LIGHT

MAJI TITLE: LIGHTER

DEITY: OCHUMARE

....

ÌWÒSÀN CLAN

MAJI OF HEALTH AND DISEASE

MAJI TITLE: HEALER + CANCER

DEITY: BABALÚAYÉ

....

ARÍRAN CLAN

MAJI OF TIME

MAJI TITLE: SEER

DEITY: ORÚNMILA

....

ẸRANKO CLAN

MAJI OF ANIMALS

MAJI TITLE: TAMER

DEITY: OXOSI

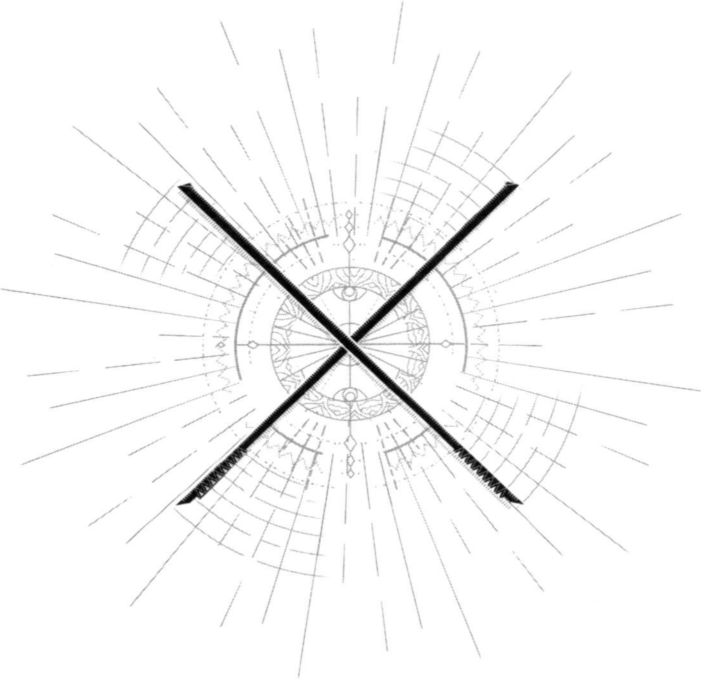

I try not to think of her.

But when I do, I think of rice.

When Mama was around, the hut always smelled of jollof rice.

I think about the way her dark skin glowed like the summer sun, the way her smile made Baba come alive. The way her white hair fuzzed and coiled, an untamed crown that breathed and thrived.

I hear the myths she would tell me at night. Tzain's laughter when they played agbön in the park.

Baba's cries as the soldiers wrapped a chain around her neck. Her screams as they dragged her into the dark.

The incantations that spewed from her mouth like lava. The magic of death that led her astray.

I think about the way her corpse hung from that tree.

I think about the king who took her away.

CHAPTER ONE

ZÉLIE

Pick me.

It's all I can do not to scream. I dig my nails into the marula oak of my staff and squeeze to keep from fidgeting. Beads of sweat drip down my back, but I can't tell if it's from dawn's early heat or from my heart slamming against my chest. Moon after moon I've been passed over.

Today can't be the same.

I tuck a lock of snow-white hair behind my ear and do my best to sit still. As always, Mama Agba makes the selection grueling, staring at each girl just long enough to make us squirm.

Her brows knit in concentration, deepening the creases in her shaved head. With her dark brown skin and muted kaftan, Mama Agba looks like any other elder in the village. You would never guess a woman her age could be so lethal.

"Ahem." Yemi clears her throat at the front of the ahéré, a not-so-subtle reminder that she's already passed this test. She smirks at us as she twirls her hand-carved staff, eager to see which one of us she gets to defeat in our graduation match. Most girls cower at the prospect of facing Yemi, but today I crave it. I've been practicing and I'm ready.

I know I can win.

"Zélie."

Mama Agba's weathered voice breaks through the silence. A collective exhale echoes from the fifteen other girls who weren't chosen. The name bounces around the woven walls of the reed ahéré until I realize Mama Agba's called me.

"Really?"

Mama Agba smacks her lips. "I can choose someone else—"

"No!" I scramble to my feet and bow quickly. "Thank you, Mama. I'm ready."

The sea of brown faces parts as I move through the crowd. With each step, I focus on the way my bare feet drag against the reeds of Mama Agba's floor, testing the friction I'll need to win this match and finally graduate.

When I reach the black mat that marks the arena, Yemi is the first to bow. She waits for me to do the same, but her gaze only stokes the fire in my core. There's no respect in her stance, no promise of a proper fight. She thinks because I'm a divîner, I'm beneath her.

She thinks I'm going to lose.

"*Bow*, Zélie." Though the warning is evident in Mama Agba's voice, I can't bring myself to move. This close to Yemi, the only thing I see is her luscious black hair, her coconut-brown skin, so much lighter than my own. Her complexion carries the soft brown of Orïshans who've never spent a day laboring in the sun, a privileged life funded by hush coin from a father she never met. Some noble who banished his bastard daughter to our village in shame.

I push my shoulders back and thrust my chest forward, straightening though I need to bend. Yemi's features stand out in the crowd of divîners adorned with snow-white hair. Divîners who've been forced to bow to those who look like her time and time again.

"Zélie, do not make me repeat myself."

"But Mama—"

"Bow or leave the ring! You're wasting everyone's time."

With no other choice, I clench my jaw and bow, making Yemi's insufferable smirk blossom. "Was that so hard?" Yemi bows again for good measure. "If you're going to lose, do it with pride."

Muffled giggles break out among the girls, quickly silenced by a sharp wave of Mama Agba's hand. I shoot them a glare before focusing on my opponent.

We'll see who's giggling when I win.

"Take position."

We back up to the edge of the mat and kick our staffs up from the ground. Yemi's sneer disappears as her eyes narrow. Her killer instinct emerges.

We stare each other down, waiting for the signal to begin. I worry Mama Agba'll drag this out forever when at last she shouts.

"Commence!"

And instantly I'm on the defensive.

Before I can even think of striking, Yemi whips around with the speed of a cheetanaire. Her staff swings over her head one moment and at my neck the next. Though the girls behind me gasp, I don't miss a beat.

Yemi may be fast, but I can be faster.

When her staff nears, I arch as far as my back will bend, dodging her attack. I'm still arched when Yemi strikes again, this time slamming her weapon down with the force of a girl twice her size.

I throw myself to the side, rolling across the mat as her staff smacks against its reeds. Yemi rears back to strike again as I struggle to find my footing.

"Zélie," Mama Agba warns, but I don't need her help. In one smooth motion, I roll to my feet and thrust my shaft upward, blocking Yemi's next blow.

Our staffs collide with a loud crack. The reed walls shudder. My weapon is still reverberating from the blow when Yemi pivots to strike at my knees.

I push off my front leg and swing my arms for momentum, cartwheeling in midair. As I flip over her outstretched staff, I see my first opening—my chance to be on the offensive.

"Huh!" I grunt, using the momentum of the aerial to land a strike of my own. *Come on*—

Yemi's staff smacks against mine, stopping my attack before it even starts.

"Patience, Zélie," Mama Agba calls out. "It is not your time to attack. Observe. React. Wait for your opponent to strike."

I stifle my groan but nod, stepping back with my staff. *You'll have your chance*, I coach myself. *Just wait your tur*—

"That's right, Zél." Yemi's voice dips so low only I can hear it. "Listen to Mama Agba. Be a good little maggot."

And there it is.

That word.

That miserable, degrading slur.

Whispered with no regard. Wrapped in that arrogant smirk.

Before I can stop myself, I thrust my staff forward, only a hair from Yemi's gut. I'll take one of Mama Agba's infamous beatings for this later, but the fear in Yemi's eyes is more than worth it.

"Hey!" Though Yemi turns to Mama Agba to intervene, she doesn't have time to complain. I twirl my staff with a speed that makes her eyes widen before launching into another attack.

"This isn't the exercise!" Yemi shrieks, jumping to evade my strike at her knees. "Mama—"

"Must she fight your battles for you?" I laugh. "Come on, Yem. If you're going to lose, do it with *pride*!"

Rage flashes in Yemi's eyes like a bull-horned lionaire ready to pounce. She clenches her staff with a vengeance.

Now the real fight begins.

The walls of Mama Agba's ahéré hum as our staffs smack again and again. We trade blow for blow in search of an opening, a chance to land that crucial strike. I see an opportunity when—

"Ugh!"

I stumble back and hunch over, wheezing as nausea climbs up my throat. For a moment I worry Yemi's crushed my ribs, but the ache in my abdomen quells that fear.

"Halt—"

"No!" I interrupt Mama Agba, voice hoarse. I force air into my lungs and use my staff to stand up straight. "I'm okay."

I'm not done yet.

"Zélie—" Mama starts, but Yemi doesn't wait for her to finish. She speeds toward me hot with fury, her staff only a finger's breadth from my head. As she rears back to attack, I spin out of her range. Before she can pivot, I whip around, ramming my staff into her sternum.

"*Ah!*" Yemi gasps. Her face contorts in pain and shock as she reels backward from my blow. No one's ever struck her in one of Mama Agba's battles. She doesn't know how it feels.

Before she can recover, I spin and thrust my staff into her stomach. I'm about to deliver the final blow when the russet sheets covering the ahéré's entrance fly open.

Bisi runs through the doorway, her white hair flying behind her. Her small chest heaves up and down as she locks eyes with Mama Agba.

"What is it?" Mama asks.

Tears gather in Bisi's eyes. "I'm sorry," she whimpers, "I fell asleep, I—I wasn't—"

"Spit it out, child!"

"They're coming!" Bisi finally exclaims. "They're close, they're almost here!"

For a moment I can't breathe. I don't think anyone can. Fear paralyzes every inch of our beings.

Then the will to survive takes over.

"Quickly," Mama Agba hisses. "We don't have much time!"

I pull Yemi to her feet. She's still wheezing, but there's no time to make sure she's okay. I grab her staff and rush to collect the others.

The ahéré erupts in a blur of chaos as everyone races to hide the truth. Meters of bright fabric fly through the air. An army of reed mannequins rises. With so much happening at once, there's no way of knowing whether we'll hide everything in time. All I can do is focus on my task: shoving each staff under the arena mat where they can't be seen.

As I finish, Yemi thrusts a wooden needle into my hands. I'm still running to my designated station when the sheets covering the ahéré entrance open again.

"Zélie!" Mama Agba barks.

I freeze. Every eye in the ahéré turns to me. Before I can speak, Mama Agba slaps the back of my head; a sting only she can summon tears down my spine.

"Stay at your station," she snaps. "You need all the practice you can get."

"Mama Agba, I . . ."

She leans in as my pulse races, eyes glimmering with the truth.

A distraction . . .

A way to buy us time.

"I'm sorry, Mama Agba. Forgive me."

"Just get back to your station."

I bite back a smile and bow my head in apology, sweeping low enough to survey the guards who entered. Like most soldiers in Orïsha, the shorter of the two has a complexion that matches Yemi's: brown like worn leather, framed with thick black hair. Though we're only young girls, he keeps his hand on the pommel of his sword. His grip tightens, as if at any moment one of us could strike.

The other guard stands tall, solemn and serious, much darker than his counterpart. He stays near the entrance, eyes focused on the ground. Perhaps he has the decency to feel shame for whatever it is they're about to do.

Both men flaunt the royal seal of King Saran, stark on their iron breastplates. Just a glance at the ornate snow leopanaire makes my stomach clench, a harsh reminder of the monarch who sent them.

I make a show of sulking back to my reed mannequin, legs nearly collapsing in relief. What once resembled an arena now plays the convincing part of a seamstress's shop. Bright tribal fabric adorns the mannequins in front of each girl, cut and pinned in Mama Agba's signature patterns. We stitch the hems of the same dashikis we've been stitching for years, sewing in silence as we wait for the guards to go away.

Mama Agba travels up and down the rows of girls, inspecting the work of her apprentices. Despite my nerves, I grin as she makes the guards wait, refusing to acknowledge their unwelcome presence.

"Is there something I can help you with?" she finally asks.

"Tax time," the darker guard grunts. "Pay up."

Mama Agba's face drops like the heat at night. "I paid my taxes last week."

"This isn't a trade tax." The other guard's gaze combs over all the divîners with long white hair. "Maggot rates went up. Since you've got so many, so have yours."

Of course. I grip the fabric on my mannequin so hard my fists ache.

It's not enough for the king to keep the divîners down. He has to break anyone who tries to help us.

My jaw clenches as I try to block out the guard, to block out the way *maggot* stung from his lips. It doesn't matter that we'll never become the maji we were meant to be. In their eyes we're still maggots.

That's all they'll ever see.

Mama Agba's mouth presses into a tight line. There's no way she has the coin to spare. "You already raised the divîner tax last moon," she argues. "And the moon before that."

The lighter guard steps forward, reaching for his sword, ready to strike at the first sign of defiance. "Maybe you shouldn't keep company with maggots."

"Maybe you should stop robbing us."

The words spill out of me before I can stop them. The room holds its breath. Mama Agba goes rigid, dark eyes begging me to be quiet.

"Divîners aren't making more coin. Where do you expect these new taxes to come from?" I ask. "You can't just raise the rates again and again. If you keep raising them, we can't pay!"

The guard saunters over in a way that makes me itch for my staff. With the right blow I could knock him off his feet; with the right thrust I could crush his throat.

For the first time I realize that the guard doesn't wield an ordinary sword. His black blade gleams in his sheath, a metal more precious than gold.

Majacite . . .

A weaponized alloy forged by King Saran before the Raid. Created to weaken our magic and burn through our flesh.

Just like the black chain they wrapped around Mama's neck.

A powerful maji could fight through its influence, but the rare metal is debilitating for most of us. Though I have no magic to suppress, the proximity of the majacite blade still pricks at my skin as the guard boxes me in.

"You would do well to keep your mouth shut, little girl."

And he's right. I should. Keep my mouth shut, swallow my rage. Live to see another day.

But when he's this close to my face, it's all I can do not to jam my sewing needle into his beady brown eye. Maybe I should be quiet.

Or maybe he should die.

"*You* sh—"

Mama Agba shoves me aside with so much force I tumble to the ground.

"Here," she interrupts with a handful of coins. "Just take it."

"Mama, don't—"

She whips around with a glare that turns my body to stone. I shut my mouth and crawl to my feet, shrinking into the patterned cloth of my mannequin.

Coins jingle as the guard counts the bronze pieces placed into his palm. He lets out a grunt when he finishes. "It's not enough."

"It has to be," Mama Agba says, desperation breaking into her voice. "This is it. This is everything I have."

Hatred simmers beneath my skin, prickling sharp and hot. This isn't right. Mama Agba shouldn't have to beg. I lift my gaze and catch the guard's eye. A mistake. Before I can turn away or mask my disgust, he grabs me by the hair.

"Ah!" I cry out as pain lances through my skull. In an instant the guard slams me to the ground facedown, knocking the breath from my throat.

"You may not have any money." The guard digs into my back with his knee. "But you sure have your fair share of maggots." He grips my thigh with a rough hand. "I'll start with this one."

My skin grows hot as I gasp for breath, clenching my hands to hide the trembling. I want to scream, to break every bone in his body, but with each second I wither. His touch erases everything I am, everything I've fought so hard to become.

In this moment I'm that little girl again, helpless as the soldier drags my mother away.

"That's enough." Mama Agba pushes the guard back and pulls me to her chest, snarling like a bull-horned lionaire protecting her cub. "You have my coin and that's all you're getting. Leave. Now."

The guard's anger boils at her audacity. He moves to unsheathe his sword, but the other guard holds him back.

"Come on. We've got to cover the village by dusk."

Though the darker guard keeps his voice light, his jaw sets in a tight line. Maybe in our faces he sees a mother or sister, a reminder of someone he'd want to protect.

The other soldier is still for a moment, so still I don't know what he'll do. Eventually he unhands his sword, cutting instead with his glare. "Teach these maggots to stay in line," he warns Mama Agba. "Or I will."

His gaze shifts to me; though my body drips with sweat, my insides freeze. The guard runs his eyes up and down my frame, a warning of what he can take.

Try it, I want to snap, but my mouth is too dry to speak. We stand in silence until the guards exit and the stomping of their metal-soled boots fades away.

Mama Agba's strength disappears like a candle blown out by the wind. She grabs on to a mannequin for support, the lethal warrior I know diminishing into a frail, old stranger.

"Mama . . ."

I move to help her, but she slaps my hand away. "*Òdẹ̀!*"

Fool, she scolds me in Yoruba, the maji tongue outlawed after the

Raid. I haven't heard our language in so long, it takes me a few moments to remember what the word even means.

"What in the gods' names is wrong with you?"

Once again, every eye in the ahéré is on me. Even little Bisi stares me down. But how can Mama Agba yell at me? How is this my fault when those crooked guards are the thieves?

"I was trying to protect you."

"Protect me?" Mama Agba repeats. "You knew your lip wouldn't change a damn thing. You could've gotten all of us killed!"

I stumble, taken aback by the harshness of her words. I've never seen such disappointment in her eyes.

"If I can't fight them, why are we here?" My voice cracks, but I choke down my tears. "What's the point of training if we can't protect ourselves? Why do this if we can't protect you?"

"For gods' sakes, *think*, Zélie. Think about someone other than yourself! Who would protect your father if you hurt those men? Who would keep Tzain safe when the guards come for blood?"

I open my mouth to retort, but there's nothing I can say. She's right. Even if I took down a few guards, I couldn't take on the whole army. Sooner or later they would find me.

Sooner or later they would break the people I love.

"Mama Agba?" Bisi's voice shrinks, small like a mouse. She clings to Yemi's draped pants as tears well in her eyes. "Why do they hate us?"

A weariness settles on Mama's frame. She opens her arms to Bisi. "They don't hate you, my child. They hate what you were meant to become."

Bisi buries herself inside the fabric of Mama's kaftan, muffling her sobs. As she cries, Mama Agba surveys the room, seeing all the tears the other girls hold back.

"Zélie asked why we are here. It's a valid question. We often talk of *how* you must fight, but we never talk about why." Mama sets Bisi down and motions for Yemi to bring her a stool. "You girls have to remember that the world wasn't always like this. There was a time when everyone was on the same side."

As Mama Agba settles herself onto the chair, the girls gather around, eager to listen. Each day, Mama's lessons end with a tale or fable, a teaching from another time. Normally I would push myself to the front to savor each word. Today I stay on the outskirts, too ashamed to get close.

Mama Agba rubs her hands together, slow and methodical. Despite everything that's happened, a thin smile hangs on her lips, a smile only one tale can summon. Unable to resist, I step in closer, pushing past a few girls. This is our story. Our history.

A truth the king tried to bury with our dead.

"In the beginning, Orïsha was a land where the rare and sacred maji thrived. Each of the ten clans was gifted by the gods above and given a different power over the land. There were maji who could control water, others who commanded fire. There were maji with the power to read minds, maji who could even peer through time!"

Though we've all heard this story at one point or another—from Mama Agba, from parents we no longer have—hearing it again doesn't take the wonder away from its words. Our eyes light up as Mama Agba describes maji with the gift of healing and the ability to cause disease. We lean in when she speaks of maji who tamed the wild beasts of the land, of maji who wielded light and darkness in the palms of their hands.

"Each maji was born with white hair, the sign of the gods' touch. They used their gifts to care for the people of Orïsha and were revered throughout the nation. But not everyone was gifted by the gods." Mama Agba gestures around the room. "Because of this, every time new maji were born, entire provinces rejoiced, celebrating at the first sight of their white coils. The chosen children couldn't do magic before they turned thirteen, so until their powers manifested, they were called the *ibawi*, 'the divine.' "

Bisi lifts her chin and smiles, remembering the origin of our divîner title. Mama Agba reaches down and tugs on a strand of her white hair, a marker we've all been taught to hide.

"The maji rose throughout Orïsha, becoming the first kings and queens. In that time everyone knew peace, but that peace didn't last. Those in power began to abuse their magic, and as punishment, the gods stripped them of their gifts. When the magic leached from their blood, their white hair disappeared as a sign of their sin. Over generations, love of the maji turned into fear. Fear turned into hate. Hate transformed into violence, a desire to wipe the maji away."

The room dims in the echo of Mama Agba's words. We all know what comes next; the night we never speak of, the night we will never be able to forget.

"Until that night the maji were able to survive because they used their powers to defend themselves. But eleven years ago, magic disappeared. Only the gods know why." Mama Agba shuts her eyes and releases a heavy sigh. "One day magic *breathed*. The next, it died."

Only the gods know why?

Out of respect for Mama Agba, I bite back my words. She speaks the way all adults who lived through the Raid talk. Resigned, like the gods took magic to punish us, or they simply had a change of heart.

Deep down, I know the truth. I knew it the moment I saw the maji of Ibadan in chains. The gods died with our magic.

They're never coming back.

"On that fateful day, King Saran didn't hesitate," Mama Agba continues. "He used the maji's moment of weakness to strike."

I close my eyes, fighting back the tears that want to fall. The chain they jerked around Mama's neck. The blood dripping into the dirt.

The silent memories of the Raid fill the reed hut, drenching the air with grief.

All of us lost the maji members of our families that night.

Mama Agba sighs and stands up, gathering the strength we all know. She looks over every girl in the room like a general inspecting her troops.

"I teach the way of the staff to any girl who wants to learn, because in this world there will always be men who wish you harm. But I started this training for the divîners, for all the children of the fallen maji. Though your ability to become maji has disappeared, the hatred and violence toward you remains. That is why we are here. That is why we train."

With a sharp flick, Mama removes her own compacted staff and smacks it against the floor. "Your opponents carry swords. Why do I train you in the art of the staff?"

Our voices echo the mantra Mama Agba has made us repeat time and time again. "It avoids rather than hurts, it hurts rather than maims, it maims rather than kills—the staff does not destroy."

"I teach you to be warriors in the garden so you will never be gardeners in the war. I give you the strength to fight, but you all must learn the strength of restraint." Mama turns to me, shoulders pinned back. "You must protect those who can't defend themselves. That is the way of the staff."

The girls nod, but all I can do is stare at the floor. Once again, I've almost ruined everything. Once again, I've let people down.

"Alright," Mama Agba sighs. "That's enough for today. Gather your things. We'll pick up where we left off tomorrow."

The girls file out of the hut, grateful to escape. I try to do the same, but Mama Agba's wrinkled hand grips my shoulder.

"Mama—"

"Silence," she orders. The last of the girls give me sympathetic looks.

They rub their behinds, probably calculating how many lashes my own is about to get.

Twenty for ignoring the exercise . . . fifty for speaking out of turn . . . a hundred for almost getting us killed . . .

No. A hundred would be far too generous.

I stifle a sigh and brace myself for the sting. *It'll be quick*, I coach myself. *It'll be over before it—*

"Sit, Zélie."

Mama Agba hands me a cup of tea and pours one for herself. The sweet scent wafts into my nose as the cup's warmth heats my hands.

I scrunch my eyebrows. "Did you poison this?"

The corners of Mama Agba's lips twitch, but she hides her amusement behind a stern face. I hide my own with a sip of the tea, savoring the splash of honey on my tongue. I turn the cup in my hands and finger the lavender beads embedded in its rim. Mama had a cup like this—its beads were silver, decorated in honor of Oya, the Goddess of Life and Death.

For a moment the memory distracts me from Mama Agba's disappointment, but as the tea's flavor fades, the sour taste of guilt seeps back in. She shouldn't have to go through this. Not for a divîner like me.

"I'm sorry." I pick at the beads along the cup to avoid looking up. "I know . . . I know I don't make things easy for you."

Like Yemi, Mama Agba is a kosidán, an Orïshan who doesn't have the potential to do magic. Before the Raid we believed the gods chose who was born a divîner and who wasn't, but now that magic's gone, I don't understand why the distinction matters.

Free of the white hair of divîners, Mama Agba could blend in with the other Orïshans, avoid the guards' torture. If she didn't associate with us, the guards might not bother her at all.

Part of me wishes she would abandon us, spare herself the pain.

With her tailoring skills, she could probably become a merchant, get her fair share of coin instead of having them all ripped away.

"You're starting to look more like her, did you know that?" Mama Agba takes a small sip of her tea and smiles. "The resemblance is frightening when you yell. You inherited her rage."

My mouth falls open; Mama Agba doesn't like to talk of those we've lost.

Few of us do.

I hide my surprise with another taste of tea and nod. "I know."

I don't remember when it happened, but the shift in Baba was undeniable. He stopped meeting my eyes, unable to look at me without seeing the face of his murdered wife.

"That's good." Mama Agba's smile falters into a frown. "You were just a child during the Raid. I worried you'd forget."

"I couldn't if I tried." Not when Mama had a face like the sun.

It's that face I try to remember.

Not the corpse with blood trickling down her neck.

"I know you fight for her." Mama Agba runs her hand through my white hair. "But the king is ruthless, Zélie. He would sooner have the entire kingdom slaughtered than tolerate divîner dissent. When your opponent has no honor, you must fight in different ways, smarter ways."

"Does one of those ways include smacking those bastards with my staff?"

Mama Agba chuckles, skin crinkling around her mahogany eyes. "Just promise me you'll be careful. Promise you'll choose the right moment to fight."

I grab Mama Agba's hands and bow my head, diving deep to show my respect. "I promise, Mama. I won't let you down again."

"Good, because I have something and I don't want to regret showing it to you."

Mama Agba reaches into her kaftan and pulls out a sleek black rod. She gives it a sharp flick. I jump back as the rod expands into a gleaming metal staff.

"Oh my gods," I breathe out, fighting the urge to clutch the masterpiece. Ancient symbols coat every meter of the black metal, each carving reminiscent of a lesson Mama Agba once taught. Like a bee to honey, my eyes find the *akofena* first, the crossed blades, the swords of war. *Strength cannot always roar*, she said that day. *Valor does not always shine.* My eyes drift to the *akoma* beside the swords next, the heart of patience and tolerance. On that day . . . I'm almost positive I got a beating that day.

Each symbol takes me back to another lesson, another story, another wisdom. I look at Mama, waiting. Is this a gift or what she'll use to beat me?

"Here." She places the smooth metal in my hand. Immediately, I sense its power. Iron-lined . . . weighted to crack skulls.

"Is this really happening?"

Mama nods. "You fought like a warrior today. You deserve to graduate."

I rise to twirl the staff and marvel at its strength. The metal cuts through the air like a knife, more lethal than any oak staff I've ever carved.

"Do you remember what I told you when we first started training?"

I nod and mimic Mama Agba's tired voice. " '*If you're going to pick fights with the guards, you better learn how to win.*' "

Though she slaps me over the head, her hearty laughter echoes against the reed walls. I hand her the staff and she rams it into the ground; the weapon collapses back into a metal rod.

"You know how to win," she says. "Just make sure you know when to fight."

Pride and honor and pain swirl in my chest when Mama Agba places the staff back into my palm. Not trusting myself to speak, I wrap my hands around her waist and inhale the familiar smell of freshly washed fabric and sweet tea.

Though Mama Agba stiffens at first, she holds me tight, squeezing away the pain. She pulls back to say more, but stops as the sheets of the ahéré open again.

I grab the metal rod, prepared to flick until I recognize my older brother, Tzain, standing in the entrance. The reed hut instantly shrinks in his massive presence, all muscle and strain. Tendons bulge against his dark skin. Sweat rains from his black hair down his forehead. His eyes catch mine and a sharp pressure clamps my heart.

"It's Baba."

CHAPTER TWO

ZÉLIE

The last words I ever wanted to hear.

It's Baba means it's over.

It's Baba means he's hurt, or worse—

No. I stop my thoughts as we sprint across the wooden planks of the merchant quarter. *He's okay*, I promise myself. *Whatever it is, he's going to live.*

Ilorin rises with the sun, bringing our ocean village to life. Waves crash against the wooden pillars that keep our settlement afloat, coating our feet with mist. Like a spider caught in the web of the sea, our village sits on eight legs of lumber all connected in the center. It's that center we run to now. That center that brings us closer to Baba.

"Watch it," a kosidán woman yells as I sprint past, almost knocking a basket of plantain off her black hair. Maybe if she realized my world is falling apart, she'd find the heart to forgive.

"What happened?" I pant.

"I don't know," Tzain rushes out. "Ndulu came to agbön practice. Said Baba was in trouble. I was headed home, but Yemi told me you had a problem with the guards?"

Oh gods, what if it's the one from Mama Agba's hut? Fear creeps into my consciousness as we zip through the tradeswomen and craftsmen crowding the wooden walkway. The guard who attacked me could've gone after Baba. And soon he'll go after—

"Zélie!" Tzain shouts with an edge that indicates this isn't his first attempt to grab my attention. "Why'd you leave him? It was your turn to stay!"

"Today was the graduation match! If I missed it—"

"Dammit, Zél!" Tzain's roar makes the other villagers turn. "Are you serious? You left Baba for your stupid stick?"

"It's not a stick, it's a weapon," I shoot back. "And I didn't abandon him. Baba overslept. He needed to rest. And I've stayed every day this week—"

"Because I stayed every day last week!" Tzain leaps over a crawling child, muscles rippling when he lands. A kosidán girl smiles as he runs past, hoping a flirtatious wave will break his stride. Even now, villagers gravitate to Tzain like magnets finding their way home. I have no need to push others out of my way—one look at my white hair, and people avoid me like I'm an infectious plague.

"The Orïshan Games are only two moons away," Tzain continues. "You know what winning that kind of coin could do for us? When I practice, *you* have to stay with Baba. What part of that's so hard to understand? Dammit."

Tzain skids to a stop before the floating market in the center of Ilorin. Surrounded by a rectangular walkway, the stretch of open sea swells with villagers haggling inside their round coconut boats. Before the daily trades begin, we can run across the night bridge to our home in the fishermen's sector. But the market's opened early and the bridge is nowhere to be seen. We'll have to go the long way.

Ever the athlete, Tzain takes off, sprinting down the walkway surrounding the market to make it back to Baba. I begin to follow him but pause when I see the coconut boats.

Merchants and fishermen barter, trading fresh fruit for the best of that day's catch. When times are good, the trades are kind—everyone accepts a little less to give others a little more. But today everyone bickers, demanding bronze and silver over promises and fish.

The taxes . . .

The wretched face of the guard fills my mind as the ghost of his grip burns my thigh. The memory of his glare propels me. I leap into the first boat.

"Zélie, watch out!" Kana cries, cradling her precious fruit. Our village gardener adjusts her headwrap and scowls as I hop onto a wooden barge teeming with blue moonfish.

"Sorry!"

I yell apology after apology, leaping from boat to boat like a red-nosed frogger. As soon as I land on the deck of the fishermen's sector, I'm off, relishing the sensation of my feet pounding against the wooden planks. Though Tzain trails behind me, I keep going. I need to reach Baba first. If it's bad, Tzain'll need a warning.

If Baba's dead . . .

The thought turns my legs to lead. He can't be dead. It's half past dawn; we need to load our boat and sail out to sea. By the time we lay out our nets, the prime catch will have passed. Who'll scold me for that if Baba's gone?

I picture the way he was before I left, passed out in the emptiness of our ahéré. Even asleep, he looked worn, like the longest slumber couldn't grant him rest. I had hoped he wouldn't wake until I returned, but I should've known better. In stillness, he has to deal with his pain, his regrets.

And me . . .

Me and my stupid mistakes.

The crowd gathered outside my ahéré makes me stumble to a halt.

People block my view of the ocean, pointing and shouting at something I can't see. Before I can push my way in, Tzain barrels through the crowd. As a path clears, my heart stops.

Almost half a kilometer out at sea, a man flails, his dark hands thrashing in desperation. Powerful waves ram against the poor soul's head, drowning him with each impact. The man cries out for help, voice choked and weak. But it's a voice I'd know anywhere.

The voice of my father.

Two fishermen row toward him, frantic as they paddle in their coconut boats. But the force of the waves pushes them back. They'll never reach him in time.

"No," I cry in horror as a current pulls Baba below the water. Though I wait for him to surface, nothing breaks through the vengeful waves. We're too late.

Baba's gone.

It hits me like a staff to the chest. To the head. To the heart.

In an instant the air vanishes from my world and I forget how to breathe.

But while I struggle to stand, Tzain launches into action. I scream as he dives into the water, cutting through the waves with the power of a dual-finned shark.

Tzain swims with a frenzy I've never seen. Within moments he overtakes the boats. Seconds later he reaches the area where Baba went under and dives down.

Come on. My chest tightens so much I swear I feel my ribs crack. But when Tzain reemerges, his hands are empty. No body.

No Baba.

Panting, Tzain dives again, kicking harder this time. The seconds without him stretch into an eternity. *Oh my gods . . .*

I could lose them both.

"Come on," I whisper again as I stare at the waves where Tzain and Baba have disappeared. "Come *back*."

I've whispered these words before.

As a kid, I once watched Baba haul Tzain from the depths of a lake, ripping him from the seaweed that had trapped him underwater. He pumped on his fragile chest, but when Baba failed to make him breathe, it was Mama and her magic who saved him. She risked everything, violating maji law to call on the forbidden powers in her blood. She wove her incantations into Tzain like a thread, pulling him back to life with the magic of the dead.

I wish Mama was alive every day, but never more than this moment. I wish the magic that coursed through her body ran through mine.

I wish I could keep Tzain and Baba alive.

"Please." Despite everything I believe, I close my eyes and pray, just like I did that day. If even one god is still up there, I need her to hear me now.

"Please!" Tears leak through my lashes. Hope shrivels inside my chest. "Bring them back. Please, Oya, don't take them, too—"

"Ugh!"

My eyes snap open as Tzain bursts out of the ocean, one arm around Baba's chest. A liter of water seems to escape Baba's throat as he coughs, but he's here.

He's alive.

I fall to my knees, nearly collapsing on the wooden walkway.

My gods . . .

It's not even midday, and I've already risked two lives.

SIX MINUTES.

That's how long Baba thrashed out at sea.

How long he fought against the current, how long his lungs ached for air.

As we sit in the silence of our empty ahéré, I can't get that number out of my head. The way Baba shivers, I'm convinced those six minutes took ten years off his life.

This shouldn't have happened. It's too early to have ruined the entire day. I should be outside cleaning the morning's haul with Baba. Tzain should be returning from agbön practice to help.

Instead Tzain watches Baba, arms crossed, too enraged to throw a glance my way. Right now my only friend is Nailah, the faithful lionaire I've raised since she was a wounded cub. No longer a baby, my ryder towers over me, reaching Tzain's neck on all fours. Two jagged horns protrude behind her ears, dangerously close to puncturing our reed walls. I reach up and Nailah instinctively brings her giant head down, careful to maneuver the fangs curved over her jaw. She purrs as I scratch her snout. At least someone's not angry with me.

"What happened, Baba?"

Tzain's gruff voice cuts through the silence. We wait for an answer, but Baba's expression stays blank. He gazes at the floor with an emptiness that makes my heart ache.

"Baba?" Tzain bends down to meet his eyes. "Do you remember what happened?"

Baba pulls his blanket tighter. "I had to fish."

"But you're not supposed to go alone!" I exclaim.

Baba winces and Tzain glares at me, forcing me to soften my tone. "Your blackouts are only getting worse," I try again. "Why couldn't you just wait for me to come home?"

"I didn't have time." Baba shakes his head. "The guards came. Said I had to pay."

"What?" Tzain's brows knit together. "Why? I paid them last week."

"It's a divîner tax." I grip the draped fabric of my pants, still haunted by the guard's touch. "They came for Mama Agba, too. Probably hitting every divîner home in Ilorin."

Tzain presses his fists to his forehead as if he could smash through his own skull. He wants to believe that playing by the monarchy's rules will keep us safe, but nothing can protect us when those rules are rooted in hate.

The same guilt from earlier resurfaces, squeezing until it sinks into my chest. If I wasn't a divîner, they wouldn't suffer. If Mama hadn't been a maji, she'd still be alive today.

I dig my fingers through my hair, accidentally ripping a few strands from my scalp. Part of me considers cutting all of it off, but even without my white hair, my maji heritage would damn our family all the same. We are the people who fill the king's prisons, the people our kingdom turns into laborers. The people Orïshans try to chase out of their features, outlawing our lineage as if white hair and dead magic were a societal stain.

Mama used to say that in the beginning, white hair was a sign of the powers of heaven and earth. It held beauty and virtue and love, it meant we were blessed by the gods above. But when everything changed, magic became a thing to loathe. Our heritage transformed into a thing to hate.

It's a cruelty I've had to accept, but whenever I see that pain inflicted on Tzain or Baba, it cuts to new depths. Baba's still coughing up salt water, and already we're forced to think about making ends meet.

"What about the sailfish?" Tzain asks. "We can pay them with that."

I walk to the back of the hut and open our small iron icebox. In a bath of chilled seawater lies the red-tailed sailfish we wrangled yesterday, its glistening scales promising a delicious taste. A rare find in the Warri Sea, it's much too valuable for us to eat. But if the guards would take it—

"They refused to be paid in fish," Baba grumbles. "I needed bronze.

Silver." He massages his temple like he could make the whole world disappear. "They told me to get the coin or they'd force Zélie into the stocks."

My blood runs cold. I whip around, unable to hide my fear. Run by the king's army, the stocks act as our kingdom's labor force, spreading throughout all of Orïsha. Whenever someone can't afford the taxes, he's required to work off the debt for our king. Those stuck in the stocks toil endlessly, erecting palaces, building roads, mining coal, and everything in between.

It's a system that served Orïsha well once, but since the Raid it's no more than a state-sanctioned death sentence. An excuse to round up my people, as if the monarchy ever needed one. With all the divîners left orphaned from the Raid, we are the ones who can't afford the monarchy's high taxes. We are the true targets of every tax raise.

Dammit. I fight to keep my terror inside. If I'm forced into the stocks, I'll never get out. No one who enters escapes. The labor is only supposed to last until the original debt is worked off, but when the taxes keep rising, so does the debt. Starved, beaten, and worse, the divîners are transported like cattle. Forced to work until our bodies break.

I push my hands into the chilled seawater to calm my nerves. I can't let Baba and Tzain know how frightened I truly am. It'll only make it worse for all of us. But as my fingers start to shake, I don't know if it's from the cold or my terror. How is this happening? When did things get this bad?

"No," I whisper to myself.

Wrong question.

I shouldn't be asking when things got this bad. I should ask why I ever thought things had gotten better.

I look to the single black calla lily woven into the netted window of our hut, the only living connection to Mama I have left. When we lived in Ibadan, she would place calla lilies in the window of our old home to honor her mother, a tribute maji pay to their dead.

Usually when I look at the flower, I remember the wide smile that came to Mama's lips when she would inhale its cinnamon scent. Today all I see in its wilted leaves is the black majacite chain that took the place of the gold amulet she always wore around her neck.

Though the memory is eleven years old, it's clearer to me now than my own vision.

That was the night things got bad. The night King Saran hung my people for the world to see, declaring war against the maji of today and tomorrow. The night magic died.

The night we lost everything.

Baba shudders and I run to his side, placing a hand on his back to keep him upright. His eyes hold no anger, only defeat. As he clings to the worn blanket, I wish I could see the warrior I knew when I was a child. Before the Raid, he could fight off three armed men with nothing but a skinning knife in hand. But after the beating he got that night, it took him five moons before he could even talk.

They broke him that night, battered his heart and shattered his soul. Maybe he would've recovered if he hadn't woken to find Mama's corpse bound in black chains. But he did.

He's never been the same since.

"Alright." Tzain sighs, always searching for an ember in the ashes. "Let's get out on the boat. If we leave now—"

"Won't work," I interrupt. "You saw the market. Everyone's scrambling to meet the tax. Even if we could bring in fish, whatever spare coin people have is gone."

"And we don't have a boat," Baba mutters. "I lost it this morning."

"What?" I didn't realize that the boat wasn't outside. I turn to Tzain, ready to hear his new plan, but he slumps to the reed floor.

I'm done. . . . I press into the wall and close my eyes.

No boat, no coin.

No way to avoid the stocks.

A heavy silence descends in the ahéré, cementing my sentence. *Maybe I'll be assigned to the palace.* Waiting on spoiled nobles would be preferable to coughing up coal dust in the mines of Calabrar or the other nefarious channels stockers can force divîners into. From what I've heard, the underground brothels aren't even close to the worst of what the stockers might make me do.

Tzain shifts in the corner. I know him. He's going to offer to take my place. But as I prepare to protest, the thought of the royal palace sparks an idea.

"What about Lagos?" I ask.

"Running away won't work."

"Not to run." I shake my head. "That market's filled with nobles. I can trade the sailfish there."

Before either can comment on my genius, I grab parchment paper and run over to the sailfish. "I'll come back with three moons' worth of taxes. And coin for a new boat." And Tzain can focus on his agbön matches. Baba can finally get some rest. *I can help.* I smile to myself. I can finally do something right.

"You can't go." Baba's weary voice cuts into my thoughts. "It's too dangerous for a divîner."

"More dangerous than the stocks?" I ask. "Because if I don't do this, that's where I'm headed."

"I'll go to Lagos," Tzain argues.

"No, you won't." I tuck the wrapped sailfish into my pack. "You can barely barter. You'll blow the entire trade."

"I may get less coin, but I can protect myself."

"So can I." I wave Mama Agba's staff before tossing it into my pack.

"Baba, please." Tzain shoos me away. "If Zél goes, she'll do something stupid."

"If I go, I'll come back with more coin than we've ever seen."

Baba's brow creases as he deliberates. "Zélie should make the trade—"

"*Thank* you."

"—but Tzain, keep her in line."

"No." Tzain crosses his arms. "You need one of us here in case the guards come back."

"Take me to Mama Agba's," Baba says. "I'll hide there until you return."

"But Baba—"

"If you don't leave now, you won't be back by nightfall."

Tzain closes his eyes, stifling his frustration. He starts loading Nailah's saddle onto her massive back as I help Baba to his feet.

"I'm trusting you," Baba mutters, too quiet for Tzain to hear.

"I know." I tie the worn blanket around his thin frame. "I won't mess up again."

CHAPTER THREE

AMARI

"Amari, sit up straight!"

"For skies' sake—"

"That's more than enough dessert for you."

I lower my forkful of coconut pie and push my shoulders back, almost impressed by the number of critiques Mother can hiss under her breath in one minute. She sits at the top of the brass table with a golden gele wrapped snug around her head. It seems to catch all the light in the room as it shimmers against her soft copper complexion.

I adjust the navy gele on my own head and try to appear regal, wishing the servant hadn't wrapped it so tight. As I squirm, Mother's amber eyes scan the oloyes dressed in their finest, searching for the hyenaires hiding in the flock. Our female nobility paste on smiles, though I know they whisper about us behind our backs.

"I heard she's been pushed to western quarters—"

"She's far too dark to be the king's—"

"My servants swear the commander's carrying Saran's child—"

They wear their secrets like glittering diamonds, embroidery woven through their lavish buba tops and wrapped iro skirts. Their lies and lily-scented perfumes taint the honeyed aroma of sweet cakes I am no longer allowed to eat.

"And what is your opinion, Princess Amari?"

I snap my head up from the heavenly slice of pie to find Oloye Ronke studying me expectantly. Her emerald iro sparkles bright along her mahogany skin, chosen precisely for the way it shines against the white stucco of the tearoom walls.

"I beg your pardon?"

"On a visit to Zaria." She leans forward until the fat ruby hanging from her throat grazes the table. The garish jewel serves as a constant reminder that Oloye Ronke wasn't born with a seat at our table. She bought her way in.

"We would be honored to have you stay at our manor." She fingers the large red gem, lips curving as she catches me staring. "I'm sure we could even find a jewel like this for you as well."

"How kind of you," I stall, tracing the path from Lagos to Zaria in my mind. Far past the Olasimbo Range, Zaria sits on the northern end of Orïsha, kissing the Adetunji Sea. My pulse quickens as I imagine visiting the world beyond the palace walls.

"Thank you," I finally speak. "I would be honored—"

"But unfortunately Amari cannot," Mother cuts in, frowning without the slightest hint of sadness. "She is in the thick of her studies and she's already fallen behind in arithmetic. It would be far too disruptive to stop now."

The excitement growing in my chest deflates. I poke at the uneaten pie on my plate. Mother rarely allows me to leave the palace. I should have known better than to hope.

"Perhaps in the future," I say quietly, praying this small indulgence will not incite Mother's wrath. "You must love living there—having the sea at your feet and the mountains at your back."

"It's just rocks and water." Samara, Oloye Ronke's eldest daughter, wrinkles her wide-set nose. "Nothing compared to this magnificent palace." She flashes a smile at Mother, but her sweetness disappears when she turns back to me. "Besides, Zaria's over*run* with divîners. At least the maggots in Lagos know to stick to their slums."

I tense at the cruelty of Samara's words; they seem to hang above us in the air. I glance over my shoulder to see if Binta heard as well, but my oldest friend does not appear to be here. As the only divîner working in the upper palace, my chambermaid has always stood out, a living shadow forever by my side. Even with the bonnet Binta secures over her white hair, she's still isolated from the rest of the serving staff.

"May I assist you, Princess?"

I turn over my other shoulder to see a servant I don't recognize: a girl with chestnut skin and large, round eyes. She takes my half-empty cup and replaces it with another. I glance at the amber tea; if Binta were here, she would've snuck a spoonful of sugar into my cup when Mother wasn't looking.

"Have you seen Binta?"

The girl draws back suddenly; her lips press together.

"What is it?"

The girl opens her mouth, but her eyes dart around the women at the table. "Binta was summoned to the throne room, Your Highness. A few moments before the luncheon began."

I frown and tilt my head. What could Father possibly want with Binta? Of all the servants in the palace, he never summons her. He rarely summons servants at all.

"Did she say why?" I ask.

The girl shakes her head and lowers her voice, choosing each word with care. "No. But guards *escorted* her there."

A sour taste crawls onto my tongue, bitter and dark as it travels down my throat. The guards in this palace do not escort. They take.

They demand.

The girl looks desperate to say more, but Mother shoots her a glare. Mother's cold grip pinches my knee under the table.

"Stop talking to the help."

I snap around and look down, hiding from Mother's gaze. She narrows her eyes like a red-breasted firehawk on the hunt, just waiting for me to embarrass her again. But despite her frustration, I cannot get the thought of Binta out of my head. Father knows of our closeness—if he required something from her, why wouldn't he go through me instead?

I stare out the paneled windows at the royal gardens as my questions grow, ignoring the empty laughter of the oloyes around me. With a lurch, the palace doors fly open.

My brother strides through.

Inan stands tall, handsome in his uniform as he prepares to lead his first patrol through Lagos. He beams among his fellow guards, his decorated helmet reflecting his recent promotion to captain. Despite myself, I smile, wishing I could be a part of his special day. Everything he ever wanted. It's all finally happening for him.

"Impressive, is he not?" Samara fixes her light brown eyes on my brother with a frightening lust. "Youngest captain in history. He will make an excellent king."

"He will." Mother glows, leaning in closer to the daughter she cannot wait to have. "Though I do wish the promotion was not accompanied by such violence. You never know what a desperate maggot might try with the crown prince."

The oloyes nod and dispense useless opinions as I sip my tea in silence. They speak of our subjects with such levity, as if they were discussing the diamond-stitched geles sweeping Lagos's fashion. I turn back to the servant who told me about Binta. Though she is far away from my table, a nervous tremble still rocks her hand. . . .

"Samara." Mother's voice breaks into my thoughts, pulling my focus back. "Have I mentioned how regal you look today?"

I bite my tongue and drain the rest of my tea. Though Mother says "regal," the word "lighter" hides behind her lips. Like the regal oloyes who can proudly trace their lineage back to the royal families who first wore Orïsha's crown.

Not *common*, like the farmers who toil the fields of Minna, or Lagos's own merchants bartering their wares in the sun. Not *unfortunate* like me, the princess Mother is almost too ashamed to claim.

As I peek at Samara from behind my cup, I'm struck by her new, soft brown complexion. It was only a few luncheons ago she shared her mother's mahogany coloring.

"You are too kind, Your Majesty." Samara looks down at her dress in false modesty, smoothing nonexistent wrinkles.

"You must share your beauty regimen with Amari." Mother places a cold hand on my shoulder, fingers light against my dark copper skin. "She lounges in the gardens so often she's beginning to look like a farmhand." Mother laughs, as if a horde of servants don't cover me with sunshades whenever I step outside. Like she didn't coat me with powder before this very luncheon began, cursing the way my complexion makes the nobility gossip that she slept with a servant.

"That is not necessary, Mother." I cringe, remembering the sharp pain and the vinegar stench of her last cosmetic concoction.

"Oh, it would be my pleasure." Samara beams.

"Yes, but—"

"Amari." Mother cuts me off with a smile so tight it could split her skin. "She would love to, Samara, especially before courting begins."

I try to swallow the lump in my throat, but the very act almost makes me choke. In that moment, the smell of vinegar becomes so strong I can already feel the searing on my skin.

"Do not worry." Samara grips my hand in her own, misreading my distress. "You will grow to love courting. It really is quite fun."

I force a smile and try to pull my hand away, but Samara tightens her hold, as if I am not allowed to let go. Her gold rings press into my skin, each band set with a special stone. One ring feeds into a delicate chain, connecting to a bangle adorned with our monarchy's seal: a diamond-studded snow leopanaire.

Samara wears the bangle with pride. No doubt a gift from Mother. In spite of myself, I admire its beauty. It has even more diamonds than min—

Skies . . .

Not mine. Not anymore.

Panic floods me as I remember what happened to my own bangle. The one I gave to Binta.

She did not want to take it; she feared the price of a gift from the throne. But Father raised the divîner taxes. If she didn't sell my bangle, she and her family would've lost their home.

They must have found out, I realize. *They must think Binta is a thief.* That's why she's been summoned to the throne room. That's why she needed to be *escorted*.

I jump out of my seat. The legs of my chair screech against the tiled floor. I can already see the guards holding out Binta's delicate hands.

I can see Father swinging down his sword.

"Pardon me," I say as I step back.

"Amari, sit down."

"Mother, I—"

"Amari—"

"Mother, please!"

Too loud.

I know it the instant the words leave my mouth. My shrill voice bounces along the tearoom's walls, quieting all conversation.

"M-my apologies," I sputter. "I feel ill."

With all eyes burning into my back, I scurry toward the door. I can feel the heat of Mother's coming wrath, but I do not have time for that now. The moment the door shuts, I take off, hiking up my heavy gown. My heeled slippers clack against the tiled floors as I sprint through the halls.

How could I be so foolish? I chastise myself, swerving to avoid a servant. I should have left the moment that girl told me of Binta's summoning. If the roles were reversed, Binta would not have wasted a heartbeat.

Oh skies, I curse, pushing myself past the slender vases of red impala lilies in the foyer, past the portraits of my royal ancestors glaring at me from generations past. *Please be okay.*

I hold on to the silent hope as I round the corner into the main hall. The air is thick with heat, making it even harder to breathe. My heart beats in my throat as I slow before Father's throne room, the room I fear most. The first place where he ordered Inan and me to spar.

The home of so many of my scars.

I grip the velvet curtains hanging outside the black oak doors. My sweat-covered hands soak into the rich fabric. *He may not listen.* I gave up the bangle. Father could punish me in Binta's stead.

A pulse of fear travels down my spine, numbing my fingers. *Do this for Binta.*

"For Binta," I whisper out loud.

My oldest friend. My *only* friend.

I have to keep her safe.

I take a deep breath and wipe the sweat from my hands, savoring my last few seconds. My fingers barely graze the handle glistening behind the curtains when—

"What?"

Father's voice booms through the closed doors like the roar of a wild gorillion. My heart pounds against my chest. I have heard Father yell before but never like this. *Am I too late?*

The door swings open and I jump back as a stream of guards and fanners sprint from the throne room like thieves on the run. They grab the remaining nobles and servants milling around the main hall and pull them away, leaving me all alone.

Go. My legs throb as the door starts to close. Father's mood has already soured. But I have to find Binta. For all I know, she could be trapped inside.

I can't let her face Father alone.

I lunge forward, catching the door just before it slips shut. I wedge my fingers into the frame and pull the door open a crack, peering through the slit.

"What do you mean?" Father shouts again, spittle flying onto his beard. Veins pulse under his mahogany skin, stark against the red agbada he wears.

I pull the door open a hair wider, fearing I'll catch sight of Binta's slender frame. But instead I see Admiral Ebele cowering before the throne. Beads of sweat gather on his bald head as he stares at everything except Father. Beside him, Commander Kaea stands tall, her hair falling down her neck in a tight, glossy braid.

"The artifacts washed ashore in Warri, a small village off the coast of the sea," Kaea explains. "Their proximity activated latent abilities in a few of the local divîners."

"Latent abilities?"

Kaea swallows; her muscles tense against her light brown skin. She gives Admiral Ebele a chance to talk, but the admiral stays silent.

"The divîners transformed." Kaea winces, as if the words cause her physical pain. "The artifacts awakened their powers, Your Highness. The divîners became maji."

I gasp but quickly cover my mouth to stifle the sound. *Maji? In Orïsha? After all this time?*

A dull spike of fear travels up my chest, making each breath tight as I open the door a hair wider to get a better view. *That cannot be*, I wait for Father to say. *That would be—*

"Impossible," he finally says, voice barely above a whisper. He grips the pommel of his black majacite blade so hard his knuckles crack.

"I am afraid not, Your Highness. I saw it with my own eyes. Their magic was weak, but it was there."

Skies . . . What does this mean for us? What shall happen to the monarchy? Are the maji already planning an attack? Will we have any chance of fighting back?

Memories of Father before the Raid play in my head, a paranoid man with grinding teeth and forever graying hair. The man who ordered Inan and me into the palace cellar, placing swords in our hands though we were far too young and weak to lift them.

The maji will come for you, he warned. The same words every time he forced us to spar. *When they do, you must be prepared.*

The memory of pain stabs my back as I study Father's blanched face. His silence is more intimidating than his rage. Admiral Ebele all but trembles.

"Where are the maji now?"

"Disposed of."

My stomach clenches and I hold my breath, forcing the luncheon's tea back down. Those maji are dead. Slaughtered.

Tossed to the bottom of the sea.

"And the artifacts?" Father presses, unfazed by the maji deaths. If he had his way, he'd probably "dispose" of the rest of them.

"I have the scroll." Kaea reaches into her breastplate and pulls out a weathered parchment. "Once I discovered it, I took care of the witnesses and came straight here."

"What of the sunstone?"

Kaea shoots Ebele a gaze so sharp it could draw blood. He clears his throat deeply, as if stretching out every last second before he delivers the news.

"The stone was stolen from Warri before we arrived, Your Highness. But we are tracking it. We have our best men on its path. I have no doubt we will recover it soon."

Father's rage simmers like heat rising through the air.

"You were tasked to destroy them," he hisses. "*How* did this happen?"

"I tried, Your Highness! After the Raid, I tried for moons. I did everything I could to destroy them, but the artifacts were hexed." Ebele's eyes dart to Kaea, but she stares straight ahead. He clears his throat again. Sweat pools in the folds beneath his chin.

"When I ripped the scroll, it pieced itself back together. When I burned it, it formed again from the ashes. I had my strongest guard take a mace to the sunstone, and it did not even sustain a scratch! When those wretched artifacts wouldn't break, I locked them in an iron chest and sank them in the middle of the Banjoko Sea. They could never have washed up on the coast! Not without mag—"

Ebele catches himself before uttering the word.

"I promise, Your Highness. I did what I could, but it would appear the gods have other plans."

The gods? I lean in. Has Ebele's mind gone to the skies? Gods don't exist. Everyone in the palace knows that.

I wait for Father to react to Ebele's foolishness, but his face remains even. He rises from his throne, calm and calculating. Then quick as a viper, he strikes, grabbing Ebele by the throat.

"Tell me, Admiral." He raises Ebele's body into the air and squeezes. "Whose plans do you fear more? The gods'? *Or mine?*"

I flinch, turning away as Ebele chokes for air. This is the side of Father I hate, the side I try so hard not to see.

"I—I promise," Ebele wheezes. "I will fix it. I promise!"

Father drops him like a rotten piece of fruit. Ebele gasps and massages his neck, bruises already darkening his copper skin. Father turns back to the scroll in Kaea's hand.

"Show me," he commands.

Kaea gives a signal, motioning to someone outside my line of sight. Boots clank against the tiled floor. That's when I see her.

Binta.

I clutch my chest as she's dragged forward, tears gathering in her wide silver eyes. The bonnet she takes so much care to tie every day sits askew, revealing locks of her long white hair. Someone has gagged her with a scarf, making it impossible for her to shout. But if she could, who would help her? She's already in the guards' grasps.

Do something, I order myself. *Now.* But I cannot bring my legs to move. I cannot even feel my hands.

Kaea unrolls the scroll and walks forward slowly, as if approaching a wild animal. Not the sweet girl who has wiped my tears for so many years. The servant who saves all her palace rations so her family can enjoy one good meal.

"Raise her arm."

Binta shakes her head as the guards yank up her wrist, her muffled cries breaking through the scarf. Though Binta resists, Kaea pushes the scroll into her grip.

Light explodes from Binta's hand.

It coats the throne room in its magnificence—brilliant golds, shining purples, sparkling blues. The light arcs and shimmers as it cascades, a never-ending stream erupting from Binta's palm.

"Skies," I gasp, terror at war with the awe bubbling inside my chest.

Magic.

Here. After all these years . . .

Father's old warnings of magic bloom inside my head, tales of battle and fire, darkness and disease. *Magic is the source of all evil*, he would hiss. *It will tear Orïsha apart.*

Father always taught Inan and me that magic meant our deaths. A dangerous weapon threatening the existence of Orïsha. As long as it existed, our kingdom would always be at war.

In the darkest days following the Raid, magic took hold inside my imagination, a monster without a face. But in Binta's hands, magic is mesmerizing, a wonder like no other. The joy of the summer sun melting into twilight. The very essence and breath of life—

Father strikes fast. Quick like lightning.

One moment Binta stands.

In the next, Father's sword plunges through her chest.

No!

I clasp my hand to my mouth before I can scream, nearly falling onto my back. Nausea rises to my throat. Hot tears sting my eyes.

This isn't happening. The world starts to spin. *This isn't real. Binta is safe. She's waiting with a loaf of sweet bread in your room.*

But my desperate thoughts do not change the truth. They do not bring back the dead.

Scarlet seeps through the scarf binding Binta's mouth.

Crimson flowers stain her light blue dress.

I choke back another scream as her corpse thuds to the ground, heavy like lead.

Blood pools around Binta's innocent face, dyeing her white locks red. Its copper smell wafts through the crack in the door. I stifle a gag.

Father yanks off Binta's apron and uses it to clean his sword. Completely at ease. He doesn't care that her blood stains his royal robes.

He doesn't see that her blood stains my own hands.

I scramble backward onto my feet, tripping over the hem of my dress. I rush up the stairwell at the corner of the main hall, my legs shaking with every step. My vision blurs as I fight to make it to my quarters, but it's all I can do to rush over to a vase. I grab onto the ceramic rim. Everything inside me comes back up.

The bile stings something fierce, bitter with acid and tea. The first sob breaks free as my body collapses. I clutch my chest.

If Binta were here, she would be the one to come to my rescue. She would take my hand and guide me to my quarters, sit me on my bed, and wipe my tears. She would take all the shattered pieces of my heart and find a way to make them whole again.

I choke back another sob and cover my mouth, salty tears leaking through my fingers. The stench of blood fills my nose. The memory of Father's blade stabs again—

The throne room doors slam open. I jump to my feet, fearing it's Father. Instead, one of the guards who restrained Binta leaves.

The scroll sits in his hands.

I stare at the weathered parchment as he climbs the stairs toward me, recalling how just one touch made the world explode with light. Light trapped inside my dear friend's soul, unbelievably beautiful, eternally bold.

I turn away as the soldier nears, hiding my tearstained face.

"Forgive me, I'm unwell," I murmur. "I must have eaten some rotten fruit."

The guard barely nods, distracted as he continues ascending. He grips the scroll so hard his knuckles darken, as if afraid of what the magical parchment will do if he doesn't. I watch as he walks to the third floor and pushes a painted black door open. Suddenly I realize where he's headed.

Commander Kaea's quarters.

Seconds ache by as I watch the door, waiting, though I do not know why. Waiting will not bring Binta back. It shall not allow me to enjoy her melodic laugh. But still I wait, freezing when the door reopens. I turn back to the vase and retch once more, not stopping until the guard passes me again. His metal-soled boots clink as he heads back down to the throne room. The scroll is no longer in his grip.

With shaking hands, I wipe my tears, no doubt smearing the paints and powders Mother forced onto my face. I run my palm over my mouth, taking any remnants of vomit away. Questions fill my mind as I rise and approach Kaea's door. I should continue to my quarters.

Yet I step inside.

The door shuts behind me with a loud thud and I jump, wary that someone will seek out the source of the sound. I have never set foot in Commander Kaea's quarters. I don't even think the servants are allowed in here.

My eyes comb the burgundy walls, so different from the lavender paint that covers my own. A royal cloak lies at the foot of Kaea's bed. *Father's cloak . . .* He must have left it behind.

On another day the realization that Father was in Kaea's quarters would've made my throat tight, but I can barely feel anything now. The discovery of Father's cloak pales in comparison to the scroll sitting on Kaea's desk.

I step toward it, legs throbbing as if approaching the edge of a cliff.

I expect to feel some aura in the scroll's presence, yet the air surrounding it remains dead. I reach out, but pause, swallowing the fear that begins to swell. I see the light that exploded from Binta's hands.

The sword that pierced through her chest.

I push myself, reaching out again with the very ends of my fingertips. When they brush the scroll, I close my eyes.

No magic comes forth.

The breath I did not realize I was holding rushes out as I pick up the wrinkled parchment. I unroll the scroll and trace the strange symbols, trying in vain to make sense of them. The symbols look like nothing I have ever seen, no language ever covered in my studies. Yet they are symbols that maji died for.

Symbols that might as well be written in Binta's blood.

A breeze flutters from the open windows, stirring the locks of hair that have fallen out from my loosened gele. Underneath the flowing curtains, Kaea's military supplies sit: sharpened swords, panthenaire reins, brass chest plates. My eyes settle on the spools of rope. I knock my gele to the floor.

Without thinking, I grab Father's cloak.

CHAPTER FOUR

ZÉLIE

"Are you really not going to talk to me?"

I lean to the side of Nailah's saddle to get a look at Tzain's stone face. I expected the first hour of silence, but now it's hour three.

"How was practice?" I try instead. Tzain can never resist a conversation about his favorite sport. "Is M'ballu's ankle okay? Do you think she'll be healed in time for the games?"

Tzain's mouth opens for a split second, but he catches himself. His jaw clamps shut and he smacks Nailah's reins, riding her faster through the towering jackalberry trees.

"Tzain, come on," I say. "You can't ignore me for the rest of your life."

"I can try."

"My gods." I roll my eyes. "What do you want from me?"

"How about an apology?" Tzain snaps. "Baba almost died! And now you want to sit here and pretend like it never happened?"

"I already said sorry," I snap back. "To you, to Baba."

"That doesn't change what happened."

"Then I'm sorry I can't change the past!"

My yell echoes through the trees, igniting a new stretch of silence between us. I run my fingers along the cracks of worn leather in Nailah's saddle as an uncomfortable pit forms in my chest.

For gods' sakes, think, Zélie, Mama Agba's voice echoes in my mind. *Who would protect your father if you hurt those men? Who would keep Tzain safe when the guards come for blood?*

"Tzain, I'm sorry," I say quietly. "Really. I feel awful, more than you can know, but—"

Tzain releases a sigh of exasperation. "Of course there's a but."

"Because this isn't just my fault!" I say, my anger reaching a boiling point. "The guards are the reason Baba went out on the water!"

"And you're the reason he almost drowned," Tzain shoots back. "*You* left him alone."

I bite my tongue. There's no point in arguing. Strong and handsome kosidán that he is, Tzain doesn't understand why I need Mama Agba's training. Boys in Ilorin try to be his friend, girls try to steal his heart. Even the guards flock his way, singing praises of his agbön skills.

He doesn't understand what it's like to be me, to walk around in a divîner's skin. To jump every time a guard appears, never knowing how a confrontation will end.

I'll start with this one. . . .

My stomach clenches at the memory of the guard's rough grip. Would Tzain yell at me if he knew? Would he shout if he realized how hard it was for me not to cry?

We ride in silence as the trees begin to thin and the city of Lagos comes into view. Surrounded by a gate crafted from the heartwood of the jackalberry trees, the capital is everything Ilorin isn't. Instead of the calming sea, Lagos is flooded with an endless horde of people. Even from afar, so many swell within the city walls it's impossible to understand how they all live.

I survey the layout of the capital from atop Nailah's back, noting the white hair of passing divîners along the way. Lagos's kosidán outnumber its divîners three to one, making them easy to spot. Though the space between Lagos's walls is long and wide, my people congregate along the city's fringe in slums. It's the only place they'd allow divîners to live.

I settle back in Nailah's saddle, the sight of the slums deflating something in my chest. Centuries ago, the ten maji clans and their divîner children were isolated all over Orïsha. While kosidán populated the cities, the clans lived along the mountains and oceans and fields. But with time, maji ventured out and clans spread across Orïsha's lands, curiosity and opportunity driving their migration.

Over the years maji and kosidán began to marry, creating families with divîners and kosidán like mine. As the blended families multiplied, the number of Orïsha's maji grew. Before the Raid, Lagos housed the biggest maji population.

Now those divîners are all that's left.

Tzain pulls on Nailah's reins, stopping her when we near the wooden gate. "I'll wait here. It'll be too crazy for her in there."

I nod and slide off, giving Nailah's dark, wet nose a kiss. I smile as her rough tongue licks my cheek, but the smile fades when I glance back at Tzain. Unspoken words hang in the air, but I turn and keep moving forward all the same.

"Wait."

Tzain slides off Nailah, catching up to me in a single bound. He places a rusted dagger into my hand.

"I have a staff."

"I know," he says. "Just in case."

I slide the weapon into my worn pocket. "Thanks."

We stare at the dirt ground in silence. Tzain kicks a rock by his feet. I don't know who will break first until he finally speaks.

"I'm not blind, Zél. I know this morning wasn't all your fault, but I need you to do better." For a moment Tzain's eyes flash, threatening to reveal everything he holds back. "Baba's only getting worse, and the guards are breathing down your neck. You can't afford to slip right now. If you make another mistake, it could be your last."

I nod, keeping my gaze on the ground. I can handle a lot of things, but Tzain's disappointment cuts like a knife.

"Just do better," Tzain sighs. "Please. Baba won't survive if he loses you. . . . I won't, either."

I try to ignore the tightness in my chest. "I'm sorry," I whisper. "I'll do better. I promise."

"Good." Tzain pastes a smile on his face and ruffles my hair. "Enough of this. Go sell the hell out of that fish."

I laugh and readjust the straps on my pack. "How much do you think I can get?"

"Two hundred."

"That's it?" I cock my head. "You really think that lowly of me?"

"That's crazy coin, Zél!"

"I bet you I can get more."

Tzain's smile widens, gleaming with the shine of a good bet. "Get above two hundred and I'll stay home with Baba next week."

"Oh, you're on." I grin, already picturing my rematch with Yemi. Let's see how she does against my new staff.

I rush forward, ready to make the trade, but when I reach the checkpoint, my stomach churns at the sight of the royal guards. It's all I can do to keep my body still as I slide my collapsible staff into the waistband of my draped pants.

"Name?" a tall guard barks, keeping his eyes on his ledger. His dark curls fuzz in the heat, collecting the sweat dripping down his cheeks.

"Zélie Adebola," I answer with as much respect as I can muster. *No screwups.* I swallow hard. *At least, no more today.*

The guard barely spares me a glance before writing the information down. "Origin?"

"Ilorin."

"Ilorin?"

Short and stout, another guard wobbles as he approaches, using the giant wall to keep himself upright. The pungent smell of alcohol wafts into the air with his unwelcome presence.

"Wha'sa maggot like you doin' s'far from 'ome?"

His words slur just before incomprehension, dripping from his mouth like the spittle on his chin. My chest clenches as he nears; the drunken glaze in his eyes turns dangerous.

"Purpose of visit?" the tall, thankfully sober guard asks.

"Trading."

At this, a disgusting smile crawls onto the drunk guard's face. He reaches for my wrist, but I back away and raise the wrapped package.

"Trading *fish*," I clarify, but despite my words, he lunges forward. I grunt as he wraps his pudgy hands around my neck and presses me against the wooden wall. He leans in so close I can count the black and yellow stains on his teeth.

"I can see why you're sellin' the fish." He laughs. "What's the goin' rate for a maggot these days, Kayin? Two bronze pieces?"

My skin crawls and my fingers itch for my hidden staff. It's against the law for maji and kosidán to so much as kiss after the Raid, but it doesn't keep the guards from pawing at us like animals.

My anger twists into a black rage, a darkness I sensed in Mama whenever the guards dared to get in her way. With its rush, I want to shove him back and snap each of the soldier's fat fingers. But with my rage comes Tzain's concern. Baba's heartache. Mama Agba's scolding.

Think, Zélie. Think of Baba. Think of Tzain. I promised not to mess this up. I can't let them down now.

I repeat this again and again until the brute unhands me. He laughs to himself before taking another swig from his bottle, proud. At ease.

I turn toward the other guard, unable to hide the hatred in my eyes. I don't know who I despise more—the drunk for touching me or this bastard for letting it occur.

"Any other questions?" I ask through my teeth.

The guard shakes his head.

I move through the gate with the speed of a cheetanaire before either can change his mind. But it only takes a few steps away from the gates before the frenzy of Lagos makes me want to run back outside.

"My gods," I breathe, overwhelmed by the sheer number of people. Villagers, merchants, guards, and nobles fill the wide dirt roads, each moving with precision and purpose.

In the distance, the royal palace looms—its pristine white walls and gilded arches gleam in the sun. Its presence is a stark contrast to the slums lining the city's fringe.

I marvel at the rustic dwellings, breath catching at the towering shacks. Like a vertical labyrinth, the shanties sit atop one another, each starting where another stops. Though many are brown and fading, others shine with bright paints and colorful art. The vibrant protest defies the title of slum, an ember of beauty where the monarchy sees none.

With tentative steps, I begin walking toward the city center. As I pass the slums, I notice the vast majority of the divîners roaming its streets aren't much older than me. In Lagos, it's almost impossible for any divîner children who lived through the Raid to reach adulthood without being thrown in prison or getting forced into the stocks.

"Please. I didn't mean to—*agh!*" A sharp cry rings out.

I jump as a stocker's cane strikes down in front of me. It cuts through the flesh of a young divîner, leaving bloodstains on the last clean clothes the boy will ever wear. The child falls into a pile of broken ceramics, shattered tiles his thin arms probably couldn't hold. The stocker raises his cane again, and this time I catch the gleam of its black majacite shaft.

Gods. The acrid smell of burning flesh hits me as the stocker presses the cane into the boy's back. Smoke rises from his skin as he struggles to crawl to his knees. The vicious sight makes my fingers numb, reminding me of my own potential fate in the stocks.

Come on. I force myself forward though my heart sinks. *Move or that'll be you.*

I rush toward the center of Lagos, doing my best to ignore the smell of sewage leaking from the slum streets. When I enter the pastel-colored buildings of the merchant quarter, the odor shifts to sweet bread and cinnamon, making my stomach growl. I brace myself for the barter as the central exchange hums with the sounds of endless trading. But when the bazaar comes into view, I'm forced to stop in my tracks.

No matter how often I trade big catch here with Baba, the madness of the central market never ceases to amaze me. More tumultuous than the streets of Lagos, the bazaar is alive with every Orïshan good imaginable. In one row alone, grains from the vast fields of Minna sit alongside coveted ironworks from the factories of Gombe. I walk through the crowded booths, enjoying the sweet smell of fried plantain.

With ears perked, I try to catch the pattern of the barter, the speed of every trade. Everyone fights, using words as knives. It's more cutthroat than the market of Ilorin. Here there's no compromise; only business.

I pass wooden stalls of cheetanaire cubs, smiling at each tiny horn that protrudes from their foreheads. I have to wade past carts of patterned textiles before finally reaching the fish exchange.

"Forty bronze pieces—"

"For a tigerfish?"

"I won't pay a piece above thirty!"

The shouts of hagglers at work ring so loud I can barely hear myself think. This isn't the floating market of Ilorin. A regular barter won't work. I bite the inside of my cheek, surveying the crowd. I need a mark. A fool, some—

"Trout!" a man shrieks. "Do I look like I eat trout?"

I turn to the plump noble clad in a dark purple dashiki. He narrows his hazel eyes at the kosidán merchant like he has just received a grave insult.

"I have searobin," the merchant offers. "Flounder, bass—"

"I said I want swordfish!" the noble snaps. "My servant says you refuse to sell it."

"They aren't in season."

"Yet the king eats it every night?"

The merchant scratches the back of his neck. "If a swordfish is caught, it goes to the palace. That's the law of the land."

The noble's face turns red and he pulls out a small velvet purse. "What does he offer?" He jingles the coins. "I'll pay double."

The merchant stares at the purse longingly but stays firm. "I can't risk it."

"I can!" I shout.

The noble turns, eyes narrowed with suspicion. I wave him toward me, away from the merchant's stand.

"You have swordfish?" he asks.

"Better. A fish no one else in this market can sell you."

His mouth falls open, and I feel the same rush I get when a fish circles my bait. I unwrap the sailfish with care and move it under a ray of light so that its scales gleam.

"Skies!" The noble gapes. "It's magnificent."

"It tastes even better than it looks. Red-tailed sailfish, fresh from the coast of Ilorin. They're not in season, so you can be sure even the king's not eating this tonight."

A smile crawls onto the noble's face, and I know I've made my own catch. He holds out his purse.

"Fifty silver pieces."

My eyes widen, but I grit my teeth. *Fifty* . . .

Fifty gets us by this tax, maybe leaves us enough for a new boat. But if the guards raise the taxes next quarter moon, fifty won't keep me out of the stocks.

I let out a loud laugh and start rewrapping the fish.

The noble's brow furrows. "What are you doing?"

"Taking this jewel to someone who can afford it."

"How dare you—"

"Forgive me," I interrupt. "I don't have time for a man who bids fifty on a prize worth ten times that much."

The noble grumbles, but he reaches into his pockets and pulls out another velvet purse.

"You won't get a piece above three hundred."

My gods! I dig my feet into the dirt to keep myself from wobbling. That's more than we've ever seen in our lives. At least six moons of taxes, even if they're raised!

I open my mouth to take the deal, but something in the noble's eyes makes me hesitate. If he folded so quickly on the last offer, maybe he'll fold again. . . .

Take it, I imagine Tzain warning. *It's more than enough.*

But I'm far too close to stop now.

"I'm sorry." I shrug and finish wrapping the sailfish. "I can't waste a meal for a king on someone who can't afford it."

The noble's nostrils flare. *Gods.* I may have gone too far. I wait for him to break, but he only seethes in silence. I'm forced to walk away.

Each step lasts an eternity as I crumble under the weight of my mistake. *You'll find another one*, I try to calm myself. *Another noble desperate to prove his worth.* I can do better than three hundred. The fish is worth more than that . . . right?

"Dammit." I almost ram my head against a shrimp stall. What am I going to do now? Who's going to be stupid enough to—

"Wait!"

As I turn, the plump noble shoves three jingling purses into my chest.

"Fine," he grumbles in defeat. "Five hundred."

I stare at him in disbelief, which he mistakes for doubt.

"Count them if you must."

I open one purse and the sight is so beautiful I nearly cry. The silver shines like the scales of the sailfish, its weight a promise of things to come. *Five hundred!* After a new boat, that's almost a year's worth of rest for Baba. *Finally.*

I've done something right.

I hand the fish to the noble, unable to hide my glowing smile. "Enjoy. Tonight you'll eat better than the king."

The noble sneers, but the corners of his mouth twitch up in satisfaction. I slide the velvet purses into my pack and start walking, heart buzzing so quickly it rivals the insanity of the market. But I freeze when screams fill the air. This isn't the sound of haggling. *What the—*

I jump back as a fruit stand explodes.

A troop of royal guards charges through. Mangoes and Orïshan peaches fly through the air. Second by second, more guards flood the market, searching for something. Someone.

I stare at the commotion in bewilderment before realizing I have to move. There are five hundred silver pieces in my pack. For once, I have more than my life to lose.

I push through the crowd with a new fervor, desperate to escape. I'm almost past the textiles when someone grabs my wrist.

What in gods' names?

I whip out my compacted staff, expecting to meet the arm of a royal guard or a petty thief. But when I turn, it's neither a guard nor a crook who's grabbed me.

It's a cloaked amber-eyed girl.

She pulls me into a hidden opening between two stalls with a grip so tight I can't fight my way free.

"Please," she begs, "you have to get me out of here!"

CHAPTER FIVE

ZÉLIE

FOR A MOMENT, I can't breathe.

The copper-skinned girl shakes with a fear so visceral it leaks into my skin.

Shouts grow louder as the guards thunder by, getting closer with each passing second. They can't catch me with this girl.

If they do, I'll die.

"Let me go," I order, almost as desperate as she is.

"No! No, *please*." Tears well in her amber eyes and her grasp tightens. "Please help me! I have done something unforgivable. If they catch me . . ."

Her eyes fill with a terror that is all too familiar. Because when they catch her, it's not a matter of whether she'll die, it's only a question of when: On the spot? Starving in the jails? Or will the guards take turns passing her around? Destroy her from within until she suffocates from grief?

You must protect those who can't defend themselves. Mama Agba's words from this morning seep into my head. I picture her stern gaze. *That is the way of the staff.*

"I can't," I breathe, but even as the words leave my mouth, I brace myself for the fight. *Dammit.*

It doesn't matter if I can help.

I won't be able to live with myself if I don't.

"Come on." I grab the girl's arm and barge into a clothing stall larger than the rest. Before the cloth merchant can scream, I put my hand over her mouth and press Tzain's dagger to her neck.

"Wh-what are you doing?" the girl asks.

I inspect her cloak. How did she even make it this far? The girl's copper skin and thick robes scream of noble blood, rich with velvet and golden hues.

"Put on that brown cloak," I order her before turning back to the merchant. Beads of sweat drip down her skin; with a divîner thief, one wrong move could be her last. "I'm not going to hurt you," I promise. "I just need to make a trade."

I peek out the front of the stall as the girl changes into the muted cloak, tightening my grasp when the merchant lets out a muffled yelp. The market's crawling with enough guards to fill an army. The scrambling traders and villagers add to the chaos. I search for a way out of this madness, but no escape route emerges. We have no choice.

We'll just have to test our fortune.

I duck back into the stall as the girl pulls the hood of her new cloak low over her forehead. I grab the fine robe she was wearing and shove it into the merchant's hands. The fear in the trader's eyes dims as the soft velvet passes through her fingers.

I lower the dagger from her neck and grab a cloak of my own, hiding my white hair under its dark hood.

"Are you ready?" I ask.

The girl manages a nod. A hint of determination flashes in her eyes, but I still detect a paralyzing terror.

"Follow me." We exit the stall and step into the pandemonium. Though guards stop right in front of us, our brown cloaks act as a shield. They're searching for noble blood. *Thank the gods.*

Maybe we actually have a chance.

"Walk quickly," I hiss under my breath as we move through the spaces between the textile stalls. "But don't—" I grab her by the cloak before she goes too far. "Don't run. You'll draw attention. Blend into the crowd."

The girl nods and tries to speak, but no words come out. It's all she can do to tail me like a lionaire cub, never more than two steps behind.

We push through the crowd until we reach the market's edge. Though guards cover the main entrance, there's an opening on the side manned by only one guard. When he steps forward to interrogate a noble, I spot our chance.

"Quick." I squeeze behind a stock trader's stall to slip from the crowded market down the stone streets of the merchant quarter. I breathe a sigh of relief as the girl's petite frame breaks free, but when we turn, two hulking guards block our path.

Oh gods. My feet skid to a stop. The silver coins jingle in my pack. I glance at the girl; her brown skin has lost most of its color.

"Is there a problem?" I ask the guards as innocently as I can.

One crosses his treelike arms. "Fugitive's on the loose. No one leaves until she's caught."

"Our mistake," I apologize with a respectful bow. "We'll wait inside."

Dammit. I turn and walk back toward the stalls, scanning the frantic market. If all the exits are covered, we need a new plan. We need a new way to get—

Wait.

Though I'm almost back in the market, the girl isn't by my side. I turn to find her frozen before the guards, the slightest tremble visible in her awkwardly placed hands.

For gods' sakes!

I open my mouth to hiss her name, but I don't even know it. I've risked everything for a stranger. And now she's going to get us killed.

I try to distract the guards, but one is already reaching for the girl's hood. There's no time. I grab my metal rod and flick. "Duck!"

The girl drops to the ground. I whip my staff and smack it against the guard's skull. A sickening crack rings through the air as he collapses into the dirt. Before the other can unsheathe his sword, I thrust my staff into his sternum.

"Ugh!"

With a swift kick to the jaw, he falls back, lying unconscious in the red dirt.

"Skies!" The girl curses like a noble. I retract my staff. *Skies* is right. Now I've attacked the guards.

Now we're really going to die.

Tzain's imminent fury flashes in my mind as we take off, sprinting as fast as we can through the merchant quarter.

Don't screw this up. Get in. Get out. Where in that plan did it make sense to help a fugitive?

As we tear through the streets lined with pastel-colored buildings, two troops of royal guards fight to take us down. Their shouts grow loud. Their footsteps pound even louder. With swords drawn, they close in, only a few paces behind.

"Do you know where we are?" I ask.

"A little," she pants, eyes wide with panic. "Enough to get us to the slums, but—"

"Head there!"

She pushes forward, sprinting a step ahead of me to take the lead. I follow her as we run through the stone streets, blowing by confused merchants in our dash. Adrenaline rushes through my veins. Heat buzzes beneath my skin. We're not going to make it. There's no way we'll escape.

Relax, I hear Mama Agba in my head. I force myself to take a deep breath. *Be resourceful. Use the surroundings to your advantage.*

I scan the compact streets of the merchant quarter in desperation. As we round the corner, I spy a towering stack of wooden barrels. *That'll do.*

I expand my staff and take a giant swing at the tower's base. When the first barrel comes crashing to the ground, I know the rest are soon to follow.

The guards' screams fill the air as the barrels take them down. The diversion gives us enough time to sprint into the slums and stop to catch our breaths.

"What now?" the girl gasps.

"You don't know the way out?"

She shakes her head, sweat dripping down her face. "I've never been to this part of town."

The slums looked like a labyrinth from afar, but from within, the shacks and shanties cluster like a web. The narrow paths and dirt streets tangle before our eyes. There's no exit in sight.

"This way." I point to the street opposite the merchant quarter. "If that way leads toward the city center, this has to lead out."

We kick up clouds of dirt running as fast as we can. But a troop of guards cuts us off—we have no choice but to dash the other way.

"Skies," the girl gasps as we race through an alley, riling up a group of homeless kosidán. For a moment, I'm amazed she's made it this far. I doubt evading her soldiers was part of her noble education.

We round another corner, just paces ahead of the guards. I push myself to run faster when the girl yanks me back.

"What are you—"

She presses her hand to my mouth and pushes me against a shanty's wall. It's only then that I notice the narrow space we've squeezed between.

Please work. For the second time in over a decade, I lift up a prayer, calling to any god who might still be there. *Please*, I beg. *Please, please hide us.*

My heart threatens to break free of my rib cage, pounding so hard I'm convinced the sound will give us away. But when the troop nears, they rumble by like rhinomes chasing prey.

I look up to the sky, blinking as the clouds pass overhead. Bright rays of light shine in between their gaps. It's almost like the gods have risen from the dead, resurrected from the graveyard formed after the carnage of the Raid. Whatever's up there is blessing me.

I just hope that blessing doesn't run out.

We shimmy out of the crawl space and tear down another path, accidentally slamming into a pair of curious divîners. One drops his bottle of rum, and the sharp scent wafts into my nose, so strong my nostrils burn. With its odor, another lesson from Mama Agba's hut resurfaces.

I scoop the bottle off the ground and scan the streets for my missing ingredient. *There.* It's only a few meters from the girl's head.

"Grab the torch!"

"What?"

"The torch!" I shriek. "The one right in front of you!"

It takes her a second to wrestle the metal torch from its hold, but when she does, we take off running. As we pass the last of the slums, I rip a piece of cloth from my cloak and stuff it into the bottle.

"What is this for?" she asks.

"Let's hope you don't find out."

We break free of the slums, and the wooden gate of Lagos's entrance comes into view. The key to our escape.

Barred by a royal blockade.

My stomach sinks as we skid to a halt before the endless line of armed guards. The soldiers ride menacing black panthenaires, each giant beast baring its fangs. Their dark fur shines like a thin layer of oil under the sun, matte rainbows of color embedded throughout their black coats. Even as the panthenaires crouch, they still tower over us, primed and ready to pounce.

"You're surrounded!" The captain's amber eyes bore into me. "By the decree of King Saran, I order you to halt!"

Unlike his soldiers, the captain rides a vicious snow leopanaire nearly as big as my hut. Eight thick horns protrude from its back, sharp and glistening in black. The monster licks its long, serrated fangs as it snarls, eager to decorate its spotted white coat with our blood.

The captain has the same dark copper complexion as the girl, skin free of wrinkles and the scars of battle. When the girl sees him, her hands fly to her hood; her legs begin to shake.

Though the captain is young, the guards follow his lead without question. One by one, each soldier unsheathes his sword, pointing the blades our way.

"It's over," the girl breathes in dismay. Tears stream down her face as she kneels to the ground. She drops the torch in defeat and pulls out a scroll of wrinkled parchment.

I pretend to follow her lead and crouch, touching the cloth in the bottle to the torch's flame. The acrid stench of smoke fills my nose. As the captain closes in, I hurl the weapon at the line of panthenaires.

Come on, I will the glass bottle, trailing its arc with my eyes. As it flies, I worry nothing will happen.

Then the world erupts in flames.

The fire burns brilliantly, sweeping men and horned panthenaires into its blaze. The beasts howl in hysteria, bucking their riders in an attempt to get away.

The girl stares in horror, but I grab her arm and force her to move. We're only a few meters away from the gate now, only a few meters away from freedom.

"Close the gate!" the captain yells as I brush by. The girl crashes into him but manages to slip through his grasp when he stumbles.

The metal gears groan and churn and the wooden gate starts falling down. The checkpoint guards brandish their weapons, our last obstacles to freedom.

"We won't make it!" the girl wheezes.

"We don't have a choice!"

I sprint faster than I knew it was possible to run. The drunk guard from before unsheathes his sword, raising his arm to slash. His sluggish movement invites more laughter than fear. I smack his skull with a vengeance, taking an extra second to knee him in the groin when he drops.

Another guard manages to get in a swing of his sword, but it's easy to block with my staff. I spin the metal rod in my hands, knocking the sword from his grip. His eyes widen as I deliver a roundhouse kick to the face, slamming him against the wooden gate before I pass.

We did it! I want to scream as I run under the cover of the jackalberry trees. I turn to smile at the girl, but she's not there. My heart seizes as I watch her tumble to the ground, a finger's breadth before the gate. Clouds of dirt greet her fall.

"No!" I shriek. The gate's only moments away from shutting.

After all that, she's not going to make it.

After coming so close, she's going to die.

Run, I order myself. *Escape. You have Tzain. Baba. You've done all you can.*

But the despair in her eyes pulls me back, and I know my blessings have run out. Because despite every protest in my body, I dash through the gates, rolling through moments before they slam shut.

"You're done." The captain steps forward, bloody from the firebomb. "Drop your weapon. Now!"

It seems like every guard in Lagos is staring us down. They circle us in droves, blocking each path before we can attempt another escape.

I pull the girl to her feet and hold my staff high. *This ends here*. They will not take me. I will force them to kill me where I stand.

My heart slams against my chest as the guards close in. I take a moment to enjoy my last breaths, picturing Mama's soft eyes, her ebony skin.

I'm coming, I think to her spirit. She probably roams alâfia now, floating through the peace of the afterlife. I imagine myself beside her. *I'll be with you so—*

A thunderous roar rings through the air, freezing the guards in their steps. The cry grows louder and louder, deafening in its approach. I barely have enough time to pull the girl out of harm's way when Nailah's monstrous figure leaps over the gate.

Guards tumble back in fear as my lionaire lands on the dirt path, saliva dripping from her massive fangs. I'm convinced she's a hallucination until I hear Tzain shouting from atop Nailah's back.

"The hell you waiting for?" he yells. "*Get on!*"

Without wasting another second, I hop onto Nailah's back and pull the girl aboard. We take off, jumping from shack to shack before the shanties crumble under her weight. When Nailah gets enough height, she makes a final leap, flying toward the gate.

We've almost cleared it when a shock like lightning surges through my veins.

The shock travels through every pore in my skin, igniting my being, catching my breath. Time seems to freeze as I look down, locking eyes with the young captain.

An unknown force burns behind his amber gaze, a prison I can't escape. Something in his spirit seems to claw onto mine. But before I can spend another second locked in his eyes, Nailah flies over the gate, severing our connection.

She lands on the ground with a thud and takes off, thundering through the jackalberry trees.

"My gods," I breathe. Every part of my body screams with strain. I can't believe we actually made it.

I can't believe I'm still alive.

CHAPTER SIX

INAN

FAILURE.

Disappointment.

Disgrace.

Which insult shall Father brand me with today?

I run through the possibilities as I enter the gate and ascend the white marble steps of the palace. *Failure* would be fitting. I'm returning with no fugitive in hand. But Father might not waste his words.

He could lead with his fist.

This time, I cannot blame him. Not truly.

If I can't defend Lagos from a single thief, how in the world am I supposed to become Orïsha's next king?

Curse the skies. I pause for a moment, gripping the smooth alabaster railing. Today was to be my victory.

Then that silver-eyed wretch got in the way.

The divîner's face flashes behind my eyes for the tenth time since I watched her fly over Lagos's gate. The image of her obsidian skin and long white hair stains. Impossible to blink away.

"Captain."

I ignore the salute of the front guards as I enter the main hall. The title feels like a taunt. A proper captain would've sent an arrow through that fugitive's heart.

"Where's the prince?" A shrill voice echoes against the palace walls.

Dammit. This is the last thing I need.

Mother pushes toward the castle entrance, gele tilting as she fights through the guards blocking her path. "Where *is* he?" she cries. "Where is—Inan?"

Mother's face softens with relief. Tears spring to her eyes. She leans in close, pressing a hand against the cut on my cheek.

"There were reports of assassins."

I pull away from Mother and shake my head. Assassins would've had clearer targets. They'd be easier to track. The fugitive was just one runaway. One I couldn't catch.

But Mother does not care about the attackers' true identity. About my failure. Wasted time. She wrings her hands together, fighting back more tears.

"Inan, we must . . ." Her voice trails off. It's only then that she realizes everyone is staring. She straightens her gele and steps back. I can almost see the claws extending from her hands.

"A maggot attacked our city," she snaps at the assembled crowd. "Do you not have places to be? Go to the market, flush out the slums. Make sure this never happens again!"

Soldiers, nobles, and servants clear the hall at once, tripping over one another in their haste. When they're gone, Mother grabs my wrist and yanks me toward the throne room doors.

"No." I'm not prepared for Father's wrath. "I don't have any news—"

"And you never will again."

Mother throws open the large wooden doors and drags me across the tiled floors.

"Leave the room!" she barks. Like mice, the guards and fanners scatter.

The only soul brave enough to defy Mother is Kaea. She looks unusually handsome in the black chest plate of her new uniform.

Admiral? I stare at the decorated seal denoting her elevated rank. There's no mistaking it. She's moved up. *But what about Ebele?*

The harsh smell of spearmint stings my nose as we near the throne. I scan the tiles and sure enough, two distinct patches of fresh blood stain the cracks.

Skies.

Father's already in a mood.

"That includes you, *Admiral*," Mother hisses, folding her arms across her chest.

Kaea's face tightens; it always does when Mother addresses her with ice. Kaea glances at Father. He gives a reluctant nod.

"My apologies." Kaea bows to Mother, though there is no apology in her tone. Mother trails Kaea with a scowl until she exits the throne room doors.

"Look." Mother pulls me forward. "Look what the maggots did to your son. This is what happens when you send him to fight. This is what happens when he plays captain of the guard!"

"I had them cornered!" I yank my wrist out of Mother's hand. "Twice. It's not my fault my men broke position after the explosion."

"I am not saying it's your fault, my love." Mother tries to grab my cheek, but I slip away from her rose-scented hand. "Just that it's too dangerous for a prince."

"Mother, it's *because* I am a prince that I must do this," I press. "It's my responsibility to keep Orïsha safe. I can't protect my people if I hide inside the palace walls."

Mother waves me away, shooing my words as she turns back to Father. "He's the next king of Orïsha, for skies' sake. Gamble with some peasant's life!"

Father's expression remains blank. As if he's blocked Mother out. He stares out the window as she speaks, twisting the royal ruby that sits on his finger.

Beside him, his majacite blade stands tall in its golden stand, the snow leopanaire carved into its pommel gleaming with Father's reflection. The black sword is like an extension of Father, never more than an arm's length from his side.

"You said 'them,' " Father finally says. "Who was the fugitive with? When she left the palace, she was alone."

I swallow hard, forcing myself to meet Father's eyes as I step forward. "We don't know her identity at the moment. We only know she isn't native to Lagos." *But I know she has eyes like the moon. I know the faded scar that nicks her eyebrow.*

Once again the divîner's face floods my mind with such clarity it could be a painting hung on the palace wall. Her full lips part in a snarl; her muscles tense against her lean build.

Another prick of energy pulses under my skin. Sharp and burning, like liquor over an open wound. The searing throbs beneath my scalp. I shudder, forcing the vile sensation away.

"The royal physician is reviving the checkpoint guards," I continue. "When they come to, I will have her identity and origin. I can still track them down—"

"You will do no such thing," Mother says. "You could have died today! And then what? Leave Amari to take the throne?" She walks forward—fists clenched, headdress high. "You must stop this, Saran. Stop it this instant!"

I jerk my head back. She called Father by his name. . . .

Her voice echoes against the red walls of the throne room. A harsh reminder of her gall.

We both look at Father. I can't fathom what he'll do. I begin to think Mother's actually won for once when he speaks.

"Leave."

Mother's eyes widen. The confidence she wore so proudly drips off her face like sweat. "My king—"

"Now," he orders, even in his tone. "I require a private word with my son."

Mother grabs my wrist. We both know how Father's private words usually end. But she can't interfere.

Not unless she wants to face Father's wrath herself.

Mother bows, stiff as a sword. She catches my gaze as she turns to leave. New tears streak the powder caked onto her cheeks.

For a long while Mother's departing footsteps are the only sounds to fill the vast throne room. Then the door slams shut.

Father and I are alone.

"Do you know the fugitive's identity?"

I hesitate—a white lie could save me from a brutal beating. But Father sniffs out lies like hyenaires on the hunt.

A lie will only make it worse.

"No," I answer. "But we'll get a lead by sunset. When we do, I'll take my team—"

"Call off your men."

I tense. He won't even give me a chance.

Father doesn't think I can do it. He's going to take me off the guard.

"Father," I say slowly. "Please. I didn't anticipate the fugitive's resources before, but I'm prepared now. Grant me a chance to make this right."

Father rises from his throne. Slow and deliberate. Though his face is calm, I've seen firsthand the rage that can hide behind his empty gaze.

I drop my eyes to the floor as he approaches. I can already hear the coming shouts. *Duty before self.*

Orïsha before me.

I failed him today. Him, and my kingdom. I let a divîner wreak havoc on all of Lagos. Of course he's going to punish me.

I lower my head and hold my breath. I wonder how badly this will hurt. If Father doesn't ask me to remove my armor, he'll go for my face.

More bruises for the world to see.

He raises his hand and I shut my eyes. I brace for the blow. But instead of his fist against my cheek, I feel his palm grip my shoulder.

"I know you can do this, Inan. But it can only be you."

I blink in confusion. Father's never looked at me this way before.

"It's not just any fugitive," he says through his teeth. "It's Amari."

CHAPTER SEVEN

ZÉLIE

WE'RE HALFWAY TO ILORIN before Tzain feels safe enough to pull on Nailah's reins. When we come to a stop, he doesn't move. I must've sparked a new level of rage.

As the crickets chirp in the towering trees, I slide off the saddle and hug Nailah's gigantic face, massaging the special spot between her horns and her ears. "Thank you," I whisper into her fur. "You're getting the biggest treat when we get home."

Nailah purrs and nuzzles her snout against my nose like I'm the cub she's been tasked to protect. It's enough to bring a smile to my face, but when Tzain drops to the ground and stalks toward me, I know even Nailah can't protect me from this.

"Tzain—"

"What's wrong with you?" he shouts with such fury that a family of blue-whisked bee-eaters flees from the trees overhead.

"I didn't have a choice!" I rush out. "They were going to kill her—"

"What in gods' names do you think they're going to do to you?" Tzain slams his fist into a tree with so much force the bark splits. "Why don't you ever *think*, Zél? Why don't you just do what you're supposed to do?"

"I did!" I reach into my bag and throw a velvet purse at Tzain. Silver pieces spill across the ground. "I got five hundred for the sailfish!"

"All the money in Orïsha won't save us now." Tzain palms his eyes, smearing tears on his cheeks. "They're going to kill us. They're going to kill *you,* Zél!"

"Please," the girl squeaks, drawing our attention. She possesses an uncanny ability to shrink; I forgot she was even here.

"I . . ." Her face blanches. Under her long hood, I can barely make out her stark amber eyes. "This is my fault. All of it."

"Thank you." I roll my eyes, ignoring Tzain's glare. Without her, Tzain would be nothing but smiles. Our family would finally be safe.

"What did you do?" I ask. "Why were the king's men chasing you?"

"Don't tell us." He shakes his head and jabs his finger toward Lagos. "Go back. Turn yourself in. It's the only chance we have to—"

She removes her cloak, silencing us both. Tzain can't look away from her regal face. I can't stop staring at the golden headdress fastened into her braid. It dips onto her forehead, all swooping chains and glittering leaves. In the center, a diamond-crusted seal shines. An adorned snow leopanaire, which only one family is allowed to wear.

"Oh my gods," I breathe.

The princess.

Amari.

I kidnapped Orïsha's princess.

"I can explain," Amari says quickly. Now I hear the royal affect that makes my teeth grind. "I know what you must be thinking, but my life was in danger."

"Your life," I whisper. "Your *life*?"

Red flashes behind my eyes. The princess cries out when I slam her against a tree. She chokes, eyes wide with fear as I wrap my hands around her neck and squeeze.

"What are you doing?" Tzain shouts.

"Showing the princess what it looks like when her life's *actually* in danger!"

Tzain yanks me back by the shoulders. "Have you lost your damn mind?"

"She lied to me," I shout back. "She told me they were going to kill her. She swore she needed my help!"

"I did not lie!" Amari wheezes. Her hand flies to her throat. "Father's executed members of the royal family just for *sympathizing* with divîners. He would not hesitate to do the same to me!"

She reaches into her dress and pulls out a scroll, gripping it so tightly her hand shakes.

"The king needs this." Amari coughs and gazes at the parchment with a weight I can't place. "This scroll can change everything. It can bring magic back."

We stare at Amari with blank faces. *She's lying.* Magic can't come back. Magic died eleven years ago.

"I thought it was impossible, too." Amari registers our doubt. "But I saw it with my own eyes. A divîner touched the scroll and became a maji. . . ." Her voice softens. "She summoned light with her hands."

A Lighter?

I step closer, studying the scroll. Tzain's disbelief sticks to me like the heat in the air, yet the more Amari speaks, the more I dare to dream. There was too much terror in her eyes. A genuine fear for her well-being. Why else would half the army chase down the princess if her escape didn't pose some greater risk?

"Where's the maji now?" I ask.

"Gone." Tears brim in Amari's eyes. "Father killed her. He murdered her just because of what she could do."

Amari wraps her arms around herself, squeezing her eyes shut to keep the tears inside. She seems to shrink. Drowning in her grief.

Tzain's exasperation softens, but her tears don't mean a thing to me. *She became a maji*, her voice echoes in my head. *She summoned light with her hands.*

"Give me that." I motion for the scroll, eager to inspect it. But the moment it touches my fingers, an unnatural shock travels through my body. I jump back in surprise, dropping the parchment to cling to the bark of a jackalberry tree.

"What's wrong?" Tzain asks.

I shake my head. I don't know what to say. The strange sensation buzzes beneath my skin, foreign yet familiar at the same exact time. It rumbles in my core, warming me from the inside out. It beats like a second heartbeat, vibrating like . . .

Like ashê?

The thought makes my heart clench, revealing a gaping hole inside me that I didn't even know still existed. When I was young, ashê was all I ever wanted. I prayed for the day I would feel its heat in my veins.

As the divine power of the gods, the presence of ashê in our blood is what separates divîners from maji. It's what we draw on to use our sacred gifts. Ashê is what maji need to do magic at all.

I stare at my hands for the shadows of death Mama could conjure in her sleep. When ashê awakens, our magic awakens as well. But is that what's happening now?

No.

I crush the spark inside of me before it can blossom into hope. If magic's back, that changes everything. If it's truly returned I don't even know what to think.

With magic come the gods, thrust into the center of my life after eleven years of silence. I barely picked up the shattered pieces of me after the Raid.

If they abandon me once more, I won't be able to do it again.

"Can you feel it?" Amari's voice drops to a whisper as she takes a step back. "Kaea said the scroll transforms divîners into maji. When Binta touched it, all these lights burst from her hands!"

I turn up my palm, searching for the lavender glow of Reaper magic. Before the Raid, when a divîner transformed, there was no guarantee what kind of maji that divîner would be. Often divîners inherited the magic of their parents, almost always deferring to the magic in their mother's bloodline. With a kosidán father, I was sure I would become a Reaper like Mama. I longed for the day I would feel the magic of the dead in my bones, but right now all I can feel is an unnerving tingle in my veins.

I pick up the parchment with care, wary it'll trigger something again. While I can make out a yellow painting of the sun on the weathered scroll, the rest of the symbols are unreadable, so ancient they look older than time itself.

"Don't tell me you believe this." Tzain lowers his voice. "Magic's gone, Zél. It's never coming back."

I know he's just trying to protect me. These are words he's had to tell me before, wiping my tears, stifling his own. Words I've always listened to, but this time . . .

"Others who touched the scroll." I turn to Amari. "They're maji now? Their gifts returned?"

"Yes." She nods, eagerly at first, but with time her enthusiasm fades. "Their magic came back . . . but Father's men got to them."

My blood chills as I stare at the scroll. Though Mama's corpse flashes into my mind, it's not her face I picture bloodied and beaten.

It's mine.

But she didn't have her magic, a small voice reminds me. *She didn't have a chance to fight.*

And like that, I'm six years old again, curled behind the fire in our Ibadan home. Tzain wraps his arms around me and points me toward the wall, forever trying to shield me from the world's pain.

Crimson splatters into the air as the guard beats Baba again and again. Mama screams for them to stop while two soldiers jerk the chain over her neck, so tight the majacite links draw blood from her skin.

She chokes as they drag her from the hut like an animal, kicking and thrashing.

Except this time, she would have magic.

This time, she could win.

I close my eyes and let myself imagine what could have been.

"*Gbọ́ ariwo ikú!*" Mama hisses through her teeth, given new life with my imagination. *"Pa ipò dà. Jáde nínú ẹ̀jẹ̀ ara!"*

The guards strangling her freeze, shaking violently as her incantation takes hold. They scream as she rips their spirits from their bodies, killing them with the wrath of a Reaper in full command of her gifts. Mama's magic feeds off her rage. With the dark shadows twisting around her, she looks like Oya, the Goddess of Life and Death herself.

With a guttural cry, Mama tears the chain from her neck and wraps the black links around the remaining guard's throat. With magic, she saves Baba's warrior spirit.

With magic, she's still alive.

"If what you say is true"—Tzain's anger cuts into my imagination—"you can't stay. They're killing people for this. If they catch it with Zél—"

His voice cracks and my heart rips into so many pieces I don't know if my chest will hold. I could screw everything up for the remainder of his days, yet Tzain would still die trying to keep me safe.

I need to protect him. It's his turn to be saved.

"We have to go." I roll the parchment and place it in my pack, moving so quickly I almost forget the silver-filled purse on the ground. "Real or not, we have to get back to Baba. Escape while we still can."

Tzain swallows his frustration and mounts Nailah. I crawl on behind him when the princess speaks, shy like a child.

"W-what about me?"

"What about you?" I ask. My hatred for her family flares. Now that we have the scroll, I long to leave Amari stranded in the forest, let her starve or become a hyenaire's prey.

"If you're taking that stupid scroll, she has to come." Tzain sighs. "Otherwise she'll lead the guards straight to us."

Amari's face blanches when I turn back to her.

As if I'm the one she has to fear.

"Just get on." I scoot forward on Nailah's saddle.

As much as I want to leave her behind, we're not done with each other yet.

CHAPTER EIGHT

INAN

"I don't understand."

A thousand thoughts race through my mind. I try to latch onto the facts: magic in Orïsha; an ancient scroll; treason by *Amari's* hand?

It's not possible. Even if I could believe the magic, I can't accept my sister's involvement. Amari can barely speak up at a banquet. She lets Mother dictate her clothes. Amari's never spent a day outside these walls, and now she's fled Lagos with the only thing that can bring our empire down?

I think back, recalling the moment the fugitive girl crashed into me. When we collided, something sharp and hot crackled through my bones. A strange and powerful attack. In my shock, I didn't peer under the fugitive's hood. But if I had, would I really have seen my sister's amber eyes peering back?

"No," I whisper to myself. It's outlandish. I have half a mind to commit Father to the royal physician. But it's impossible to deny the look in his eyes. Crazed. Calculating. In eighteen years I've seen many things in his gaze. But never fear. Never terror.

"Before you were born, the maji were drunk with power, always plotting to overthrow our line," Father explains. "Even with their insurgency, my father fought to be fair, but that fairness got him killed."

Along with your older brother, I think silently. *Your first wife, your firstborn son.* There isn't a noble in Orïsha who doesn't know of the slaughter Father endured at the maji's hands. A carnage that would one day be avenged by the Raid.

Out of instinct, I finger the tarnished pawn in my pocket, a stolen "gift" from Father. The sênet piece is the only survivor of Father's childhood set, a game of strategy he used to play with me when I was young.

Though the cool metal usually anchors me, today it's warm to the touch. It almost stings as it passes through my fingers, burning with Father's impending truth.

"When I rose to the throne, I knew magic was the root of all our pain. It's crushed empires before ours, and as long as it lives, it shall crush empires again."

I nod, remembering Father's rants from long before the Raid. The Britāunîs. The Pörltöganés. The Spãní Empire—all civilizations destroyed because those who had magic craved power, and those in charge didn't do enough to stop them.

"When I discovered the raw alloy Bratonians used to subdue magic, I thought that would be enough. With majacite, they created prisons, and weapons, and chains. Following their tactics, I did the same. But even that wasn't enough to tame those treacherous maggots. If our kingdom was ever going to survive, I knew I had to take magic away."

What? I jerk forward, unable to trust my own ears. Magic is beyond us. How could Father attack an enemy like that?

"Magic is a gift from the gods," he continues, "a spiritual connection between them and mankind. If the gods broke that connection with royals generations ago, I knew their connection to the maji could be severed, too."

My head spins with Father's words. If he doesn't need to see the physician, I will. The only time I dared to ask him about the Orïshan gods, his answer was swift: *gods are nothing without fools to believe in them.*

I took his words to heart, built my world upon his unwavering conviction. Yet here he stands, telling me they exist. That *he* waged war against them.

Skies. I stare at the blood staining the cracks in the floor. I've always known Father was a powerful man.

I just never realized how deep that power ran.

"After my coronation, I set out to find a way to sever the spiritual bond. It took me years, but eventually I discovered the source of the maji's spiritual connection, and I ordered my men to destroy it. Until today, I believed I had succeeded in wiping magic from the face of this earth. But now that damned scroll is threatening to bring magic back."

I let Father's words wash over me, parsing through it all until even the most inconceivable facts move like sênet pawns in my head: break the connection; break the magic.

Destroy the people after our throne.

"But if magic was gone . . ." My stomach twists into knots, but I need to know the answer. "Why go through with the Raid? Why . . . kill all those people?"

Father runs his thumb down the serrated edge of his majacite blade and walks to the paneled windows. The same place I stood as a child when the maji of Lagos went up in flames. Eleven years later, the charcoal smell of burning flesh is still a constant memory. As vivid as the heat in the air.

"For magic to disappear for good, every maji had to die. As long as they'd tasted that power, they would never stop fighting to bring it back."

Every maji . . .

That's why he let the children live. Divîners don't manifest their abilities until they're thirteen. Powerless children who had never wielded magic didn't pose a threat.

Father's answer is calm. So matter-of-fact, I cannot doubt that he did the right thing. But the memory of ash settles on my tongue. Bitter. Sharp. I have to wonder if Father's stomach churned that day.

I wonder if I'm strong enough to do the same.

"Magic is a blight," Father breaks into my thoughts. "A fatal, festering disease. If it takes hold of our kingdom the way it's taken others, no one will survive its attack."

"How do we stop it?"

"The scroll is the key," Father continues. "That much I know. Something about it has the power to bring magic back. If we don't destroy it, it shall destroy us."

"And Amari?" My voice lowers. "Will we have to . . . will I . . ." The thought is so wretched I can't speak.

Duty before self. That's what Father will say. It's what he shouted at me that fateful day.

But the thought of raising my blade against Amari after all these years makes my throat dry. I can't be the king Father wants me to be.

I can't kill my little sister.

"Your sister has committed treason." He speaks slowly. "But it is no fault of her own. I allowed her to get close to that maggot. I should've known her simple disposition would lead her astray."

"So Amari can live?"

Father nods. "If she's captured before anyone discovers what she's done. That's why you can't take your men—you and Admiral Kaea must go and recover the scroll alone."

Relief slams into my chest like a blow from Father's fist. I can't kill my little sister, but I can bring her back in.

A sharp knock raps against the door; Admiral Kaea pops her head through. Father waves his hand, welcoming her in.

Behind her, I catch a glimpse of Mother scowling. A new heaviness settles on my shoulders. *Skies.*

Mother doesn't even know where Amari is.

"We found a noble. He claims he saw the maggot who aided the fugitive," Kaea says. "She sold him a rare fish from Ilorin."

"Did you cross-reference the ledger?" I ask.

Kaea nods. "It shows only one divîner from Ilorin today. Zélie Adebola, age seventeen."

Zélie . . .

My mind fits the missing piece to her striking image. The name rolls off Kaea's tongue like silver. Too soft for a divîner who attacked my city.

"Let me go to Ilorin," I blurt out. My mind runs through the plan as I speak. I've seen a map of Ilorin before. The four quadrants of the floating village. A few hundred villagers, most lowly fishermen. We could take it with—"Ten men. That's all Admiral Kaea and I need. I'll find the scroll and bring Amari back. Just give me a chance."

Father twists his ring as he thinks. I can hear the rejection sitting on his tongue. "If those men discover anything—"

"I'll kill them," I interrupt. The lie slips from my mouth with ease. If I can redeem my former failures, no one else needs to die.

But Father cannot know that. He barely trusts me as it is. He requires swift, unflinching commitment.

As captain, I must give it to him.

"Very well," Father agrees. "Head out. Be quick."

Thank the skies. I adjust my helmet and bow as deeply as I can. I'm almost out the door when Father calls out.

"Inan."

Something twists in his tone. Something dark.

Dangerous.

"When you have what you need, burn that village to the ground."

CHAPTER NINE

ZÉLIE

ILORIN IS ENTIRELY too peaceful.

At least, it feels that way after today. Coconut boats pull against their anchors, sheets fall over the dome of ahéré entrances. The village sets with the sun, making way for a calm night's sleep.

Amari's eyes widen with wonder as we sail through the water and head toward Mama Agba's on Nailah's back. She takes in every inch of the floating village like a starving laborer placed before a majestic feast.

"I've never seen anything like this," she whispers. "It's mesmerizing."

I breathe in the fresh scent of the sea, closing my eyes as mist sprays my face. The taste of salt on my tongue makes me imagine what would happen if Amari wasn't here; a fresh loaf of sweet bread, a nice cut of spiced meat. For once, we'd go to sleep with full bellies. A celebratory meal in my name.

My frustration reignites at Amari's ignorant bliss. Princess that she is, she's probably never missed a meal in her entire pampered life.

"Give me your headdress," I snap when Nailah docks in the merchant quarter.

The wonder drops from Amari's face and she stiffens. "But Binta—"

She pauses, collecting herself. "I wouldn't have this if it weren't for my handmaiden. . . . It is the only thing of hers I have left."

"I don't care if the gods gave you that wretched thing. We can't have people finding out who you are."

"Don't worry," Tzain adds gently. "She'll throw it in her pack, not the sea."

I glare at his attempt to comfort her, but his words do the trick. Amari fiddles with the clasp and drops the glittering jewels into my pack. The shimmer they add to the shine of silver coins is absurd. This morning I didn't have a bronze piece to my name. Now I'm weighed down by the riches of royals.

I crouch on Nailah's back and pull myself onto the wooden walkway. I poke my head through Mama Agba's curtained door to find Baba sleeping soundly in the corner, curled up like a wildcat in front of a heated flame. His skin has its color back, his face isn't so skeletal and gaunt. Must be Mama Agba's care. She could nurse a corpse back to life.

When I enter, Mama Agba peeks her head out from behind a mannequin stitched into a brilliant purple kaftan. The fitted seams suggest that it's noble-bound, a sale that might cover her next tax.

"How'd it go?" she whispers, cutting the thread with her teeth. She adjusts the green and yellow gele wrapped around her head before tying up the kaftan's loose ends.

I open my mouth to respond, but Tzain steps in, tentatively followed by Amari. She looks around the ahéré with an innocence only luxury can breed, running her fingers over the woven reeds.

Tzain gives Mama Agba a grateful nod as he takes my pack, pausing to hand Amari the scroll. He lifts Baba's sleeping body with ease. Baba doesn't even stir.

"I'm going to get our things," he says. "Decide what we're doing about this scroll. If we go . . ." His voice trails off, and my stomach tightens with guilt. There's no *if* anymore. I've taken that choice away.

"Just be fast."

Tzain leaves, biting his emotions back. I watch as his hulking frame disappears, wishing I wasn't the source of his pain.

"Leave?" Mama Agba asks. "Why would you leave? And who is this?" Her eyes narrow as she looks Amari up and down. Even in a dingy cloak, Amari's perfect posture and lifted chin denote her regal nature.

"Oh, um . . ." Amari turns to me, her grip tightening on the scroll. "I—I am . . ."

"Her name's Amari," I sigh. "She's the princess of Orïsha."

Mama Agba releases a deep laugh. "It's an honor, Your Highness," she teases with an exaggerated bow.

But when neither Amari nor I smile, Mama's eyes go wide. She rises from her seat and opens Amari's cloak, revealing the dark blue gown beneath. Even in the dim light, the deep neckline shimmers with glittering jewels.

"Oh my gods . . ." She turns to me, hands clutching her chest. "Zélie, what in the gods' names have you done?"

I force Mama Agba to sit as I explain the events of the day. While she wavers between pride and anger over the details of our escape, it's the possibilities of the scroll that make her go still.

"Is it real?" I ask. "Is there any truth to this?"

Mama's silent for a long moment, staring at the scroll in Amari's hands. For once her dark eyes are unreadable, obscuring the answers I seek.

"Give it here."

The moment the parchment touches Mama Agba's palms, she wheezes for air. Her body trembles and quakes so violently she falls off her chair.

"Mama Agba!" I run to her side and grab her hands, holding her down until the tremors stop. With time, they fade and she's left on the ground, as still as one of her mannequins. "Mama, are you okay?"

Tears come to her eyes, spilling into the wrinkles of her dark skin. "It's been so long," she whispers. "I never thought I would feel the warmth of magic again."

My lips part in surprise and I back up, unable to believe my ears. It can't be. I didn't think any maji survived the Raid. . . .

"You're a maji?" Amari asks. "But your hair—"

Mama Agba removes her gele and runs her hand over her shaved head. "Eleven years ago I had a vision of myself visiting a Cancer. I asked her to get rid of my white hair, and she used the magic of disease to take it all away."

"You're a Seer?" I gasp.

"I used to be." Mama Agba nods. "I lost my hair the day of the Raid, hours before they would've taken me away."

Amazing. When I was a child, the few Seers who lived in Ibadan were revered. The magic they wielded over time helped every other maji clan in Ibadan survive. I smile, though in my heart I should've known. Mama Agba's always had a sage sense about her, the wisdom of a person who's seen beyond her years.

"Before the Raid," Mama Agba continues, "I felt the magic sucked out of the air. I tried to conjure a vision of what would come, but when I needed it most, I couldn't see." She winces, as if reliving the pain of that day all over again. I can only imagine what horrible images play inside her mind.

Mama shuffles over to her netted windows and pulls the sheets closed. She stares at her weathered hands, wrinkled from years as a seamstress. "*Orúnmila*," she whispers, invoking the God of Time. *"Bá mi sọ̀rọ̀. Bá mi sọ̀rọ̀."*

"What is she doing?" Amari steps back as if Mama Agba's words could cut her. But hearing true Yoruba for the first time in over a decade makes it too overwhelming for me to answer.

Since the Raid, all I've heard are the harsh stops and guttural sounds of Orïshan, the tongue we are forced to speak. It's been so long since I heard an incantation, too long since the language of my people didn't only exist in my memories.

"Orúnmila," I translate as Mama Agba chants. "Speak to me. Speak to me. She's calling on her god," I explain to Amari. "She's trying to do magic."

Though the answer comes with ease, even I can't believe what I'm seeing. Mama Agba chants with a blind faith, patient and trusting, just as those who follow the God of Time are meant to be.

As she calls on Orúnmila for guidance, a pang of longing stirs in my heart. No matter how much I've wanted to, I've never had enough faith to call on Oya like that.

"Is it safe?" Amari presses against the ahéré wall when veins bulge against Mama Agba's throat.

"It's part of the process." I nod. "The cost of using our ashê."

To cast magic we must use the language of the gods to harness and mold the ashê in our blood. For a practiced Seer, this incantation would be easy, but with so many years out of practice, this incantation is probably drawing on all the ashê Mama Agba has. Ashê builds like another muscle in our bodies; the more we use, the easier it is to harness and the stronger our magic becomes.

"Orúnmila, bá mi sọ̀rọ̀. Orúnmila, bá mi sọ̀rọ̀—"

Her breath turns more ragged with every word. The wrinkles across her face stretch tight with strain. Harnessing ashê takes a physical toll. If she tries to harness too much, she could kill herself.

"*Orúnmila—*" Mama Agba's voice grows stronger. A silver light begins to swell in her hands. "*Orúnmila, bá mi sọ̀rọ̀! Orúnmila, bá mi sọ̀rọ̀*—"

The cosmos explodes between Mama's hands with so much force that Amari and I are knocked to the ground. Amari screams, but my shout vanishes under the lump in my throat. The blues and purples of the night sky twinkle between Mama Agba's palms. My heart seizes at the beautiful sight. *It's back. . . .*

After all this time, magic is finally here.

It's like a floodgate opening in my heart, an endless wave of emotion rushing through my entire being. The gods are back. *Alive.* With us after all this time.

The twinkling stars between Mama Agba's palms swirl and dance with one another. An image slowly crystallizes, sharpening like a sculpture before our eyes. With time, I can make out three silhouettes on a mountainous hill. They climb with relentless fury, making their way through thick underbrush.

"Skies," Amari curses. She takes a tentative step forward. "Is that . . . me?"

I snort at her vanity, but the sight of my cropped dashiki makes me stop. She's right—it's us and Tzain, climbing through the jungle greenery. My hands reach for a rock while Tzain guides Nailah by the reins to a ledge. We ascend higher and higher up the mountain, climbing till we reach the—

The vision vanishes, snapping to empty air in the blink of an eye.

We're left staring at Mama Agba's empty hands, hands that have just changed my entire world.

Mama's fingers shake from the strain of her vision. More tears spill from her eyes.

"I feel," she chokes through her silent sobs. "I feel like I can breathe again."

I nod, though I don't know how to describe the tightness in my own heart. After the Raid I truly thought I'd never see magic again.

When Mama Agba's hands are steady, she grasps the scroll, desperation leaking through her touch. She scans the parchment; from the movement of her eyes, I can tell she's actually reading the symbols.

"It's a ritual," she says. "That much I can see. Something with an ancient origin, a way to connect with the gods."

"Can you do it?" Amari asks, amber eyes shining with a mixture of awe and fear. She stares at Mama Agba as if she were made of diamonds, yet flinches whenever she draws near.

"It's not I who was meant to do this, child." Mama places the scroll in my hands. "You saw the same vision as I."

"Y-you cannot be serious," Amari stammers. For once I agree with her.

"What's there to argue?" Mama asks. "You three were on the journey. You were traveling to bring magic back!"

"Is it not already here?" Amari asks. "What you just did—"

"A fraction of what I could do before. This scroll sparks the magic, but to bring it back to its full power, you must do more."

"There has to be someone better." I shake my head. "Someone with more experience. You can't be the only maji to escape the Raid. We can use your power to find someone for the scroll."

"Girls—"

"We can't!" I cut in. "*I* can't! Baba—"

"I'll take care of your father."

"But the guards!"

"Don't forget who taught you how to fight."

"We don't even know what it says," Amari interrupts. "We cannot even read it!"

Mama Agba's eyes grow distant like an idea's taken hold in her head.

She scurries over to a collection of her belongings, returning with a faded map. "Here." She gestures to a spot in the Funmilayo Jungle, a few days east of Ilorin's coast. "In my vision you were traveling here. It must be where Chândomblé is."

"Chândomblé?" Amari asks.

"A legendary temple," Mama Agba answers. "Rumored to be the home of the sacred sêntaros, the protectors of magic and spiritual order. Before the Raid, only the newly elected leaders of the ten maji clans made the pilgrimage, but if my vision showed you traveling there, it must be your time. You must go. Chândomblé may hold the answers you seek."

The more Mama Agba speaks, the more I lose feeling in my hands and feet. *Why don't you understand?* I want to scream.

I'm not strong enough.

I look at Amari; for a moment, I almost forget she's a princess. In the glow of Mama Agba's candles she looks small, unsure of what to do next.

Mama Agba places a wrinkled hand on my face and grabs Amari's wrist with the other. "I know you're scared, girls, but I also know that you can do this. Of all the days to trade in Lagos, you went today. Of all the people you could've approached in that market, you chose her. The gods are at work. They are blessing us with our gifts after all this time. You have to trust that they wouldn't gamble with the fate of the maji. Trust in yourselves."

I release a deep breath and stare at the woven floor. The gods that once seemed so far away are closer now than I ever imagined they could be. I just wanted to graduate today.

I only needed to sell a fish.

"Mama—"

"Help!"

A scream breaks through the calm of the night. In an instant we're all on our feet. I grab my rod as Mama runs to her window. When she rips open the curtains, my legs go weak.

Fire rages in the merchant quarter, every ahéré engulfed in the roaring blaze. Plumes of black smoke tower into the sky with villagers' yells, cries for help as our world goes up in flames.

A line of burning arrows cuts through the darkness; each explodes as it makes contact with the reeds and wooden beams of the ahéré.

Blastpowder . . .

A powerful mix only the king's guards could obtain.

You, the voice in my head whispers in disgust. *You brought them here.*

And now the guards won't just kill everyone I love.

They'll burn the whole village to the ground.

I'm out the door before another second passes, undeterred when Mama Agba shouts my name. I have to find my family. I have to make sure they're okay.

With each step on the crumbling walkway, my home blazes into a living hell. The stench of burning flesh stings my throat. The fire's only raged a few minutes, yet all of Ilorin fries in the flames.

"Help!"

I recognize the cries now. Little Bisi. Her screams cut through the darkness, desperate in their shrieks. My chest heaves as I sprint past Bisi's ahéré. Will she even make it out of the blaze alive?

As I race home, villagers desperate to escape the flames jump into the ocean, their screams piercing the night sky. Coughing, they cling onto charred driftwood, fighting to stay afloat.

A strange sensation rushes through me, surging through my veins, trapping the breath in my chest. With it, warmth buzzes under my skin. *A death . . .*

A spirit.

Magic. I put the pieces together. *My magic.*

A magic I still don't understand. A magic that's brought us to this hell.

But even as embers burn my skin, I picture Tiders summoning streams of water to fight the flames. Burners keeping the blaze at bay.

If more maji were here, their gifts could stop this horror.

If we were trained and armed with incantations, the fire wouldn't stand a chance.

A loud crack rings through the air. The wooden panels beneath my feet moan as I near the fishermen's sector. I run for as long as the walkway holds before launching myself into the air.

Smoke sears my throat as I land on the teetering deck that supports my home. I can't see through the blaze, but still I force myself to act.

"Baba!" I scream through my coughs, adding more cries to the chaos of the night. "Tzain!"

There's not an ahéré in our sector that isn't engulfed in flames, yet still I run forward, hoping mine won't share the same fate.

The walkway wobbles beneath my feet and my lungs scream for air. I tumble to the ground before my home, burned from the heat radiating off the flames.

"*Baba!*" I shriek in horror, searching for any life in the blaze. "*Tzain! Nailah!*"

I scream till my throat rips raw, but no one answers my call. I can't tell if they're trapped inside.

I can't see if they're even alive.

I crawl to my feet and extend my rod, thrusting open our ahéré door. I'm about to run in when a hand clamps my shoulder, pulling me back with so much force I topple over.

Tears blur my vision. It's difficult to make out the face of my assailant. But soon flickering flames illuminate copper skin. *Amari.*

"You can't go in there!" she screams between her coughs. "It's coming down!"

I shove Amari to the ground with half a mind to drown her in the sea. When she releases her grip, I crawl toward my ahéré.

"No!"

The reed walls we spent a full moon building collapse with a sharp crack. They burn through the walkway and into the sea, sinking to the bottom.

I wait for Tzain's head to bob up from the waves, for Nailah to let out a roar of pain. But I only see blackness.

In one sweep, my family's been wiped away.

"Zélie . . ."

Amari grips my shoulder again; my blood boils under her touch. I grab her arm and yank her forward, grief and rage fueling my strength.

I'll kill you, I decide. *If we die, you die, too.*

Let your father feel this pain.

Let the king know unbearable loss.

"Don't!" Amari screams as I drag her to the flames, but I can barely hear her over the blood pounding in my ears. When I look at her, I see her father's face. Everything inside me twists with hate. "Please—"

"Zélie, stop!"

I release Amari and whip toward the open sea. Nailah paddles in the ocean water with Tzain on her back. Trailing behind him, Baba and Mama Agba sit safely inside a coconut boat attached to Nailah's saddle. I'm so overwhelmed by the sight that it takes a moment to grasp that they're actually alive.

"Tzain—"

The entire foundation of the fishermen's sector slants. Before we can jump, it goes down, taking us with it. Ice-cold water engulfs our bodies in a rush, soothing the burns I've forgotten.

I allow myself to sink among the lumber and shattered homes. The darkness cleanses my pain, cooling the rage.

You can stay down here, a small thought whispers. *You don't have to continue this fight. . . .*

I hold on to the words for a moment, grasping my only chance for escape. But when my lungs wheeze, I force my legs to kick, bringing me back to the broken world I know.

No matter how much I crave peace, the gods have other plans.

CHAPTER TEN

ZÉLIE

We float to a small inlet across from the northern coast in silence, unable to speak after such horror. Though the crashing waves grow loud, the memory of Bisi's screams crashes even louder in my head.

Four deaths. Four people who couldn't escape the flames.

I brought the fire to Ilorin.

Their blood stains my hands.

I grip my shoulders to keep everything inside as Mama Agba dresses our injuries with cloth ripped from her skirt. Though we made it through the flames, small burns and blisters dot our skin. But that pain is welcome; almost deserved. The sears on my skin are nothing compared to the guilt that scalds my heart.

A sharp pressure clamps my stomach as the memory of a burnt corpse crystallizes behind my eyes. Charred skin peeling from every limb, the stench of burning flesh still coloring my every breath.

They're in a better place, I try to ease my guilt. If their spirits have ascended to the peace of alâfia, death would almost be a gift. But if they suffered too much before they died . . .

I close my eyes and try to swallow the thought. If the trauma of their deaths was too much, their spirits won't rise to the afterlife. They'll stay in apâdi, an eternal hell, reliving the worst of their pain.

When we land on the rocky stretch of sand, Tzain helps Amari while I tend to Baba. I promised I wouldn't mess this up. Now our entire village is in flames.

I stare at the jagged rocks, unable to meet my father's eyes. Baba should've sold me to the stocks. If he had, he'd finally have peace. Baba's silence only intensifies my misery, but when he bends down to meet my gaze, tears soften his eyes.

"You can't run from this, Zélie. Not now." He takes my hands. "This is the second time these monsters took our home. Let it be the last."

"Baba?" I can't believe his fury. Since the Raid, he hasn't whispered a single curse against the monarchy. I thought he'd given up all fight.

"As long as we don't have magic, they will never treat us with respect. They need to know we can hit them back. If they burn our homes, we burn theirs, too."

Tzain's mouth falls open and he locks eyes with me. We haven't seen this man for eleven years. We didn't know he was still alive.

"Baba—"

"Take Nailah," he orders. "The guards are close. We don't have much time."

He points across the shore to the northern coast, where five figures in royal armor herd the survivors together. The flickering light of the flames illuminates the seal on one soldier's helmet. *The captain* . . . the same one who chased me and Amari.

He burned my home to the ground.

"Come with us," Tzain argues. "We can't leave you behind."

"I can't. I'll only slow you down."

"But Baba—"

"No," he cuts Tzain off, rising to place a hand on his shoulder. "Mama Agba told me about her vision. It's you three who will lead the fight. You need to get to Chândomblé and figure out how to bring magic back."

My throat tightens. I clutch Baba's hand. "They already found us once. If they're after us, they'll come after you, too."

"We'll be long gone by then," Mama Agba assures me. "Who better to evade the guards than a Seer?"

Tzain looks back and forth between Mama Agba and Baba, his jaw clenching as he fights to keep his face even. I don't know if he can leave Baba behind. Tzain doesn't know his place without keeping others safe.

"How'll we find you?" I whisper.

"Bring magic back for good," Mama Agba says. "As long as I have my visions, I'll always know where to go."

"You have to leave," Baba presses, forceful as a new round of screams rings out. One guard grabs an elderly woman by her hair and holds a sword to her throat.

"Baba, no!"

I try to pull him forward, but he overpowers me, kneeling down to wrap his arms around my shaking frame. He holds me tighter than he has in years. "Your mother . . ." His voice cracks. A small sob escapes my throat. "She loved you fiercely. She would be so proud right now."

I cling to Baba so hard that my nails dig into his skin. He squeezes me back before rising to embrace Tzain. Though Tzain towers over Baba in height and might, Baba matches the ferocity of his hug. They hold each other for a long moment, as if they never have to let go.

"I'm proud of you, son. No matter what. I'll always be proud."

Tzain hurriedly wipes his tears away. He's not one to show his emotions. He saves his pain for the isolation of night.

"I love you," Baba whispers to us both.

"We love you, too," I croak.

He gestures at Tzain to mount Nailah. Amari follows, silent tears leaking onto her cheeks. Despite my grief, a prickle of anger flares. Why is she crying? Once again, her family is the reason mine is being torn apart.

Mama Agba kisses my forehead and wraps her arms around me tight. "Be careful, but be strong."

I sniffle and nod, though I feel everything but strength. I'm scared. Weak.

I'm going to let them down.

"Take care of your sister," Baba reminds Tzain as I mount the saddle. "And Nailah, be good. Protect them."

Nailah licks Baba's face and nuzzles his head, a sign of a promise she'll always keep. My chest seizes when she walks forward, traveling away from my heart and my home. When I turn back, Baba's face shines with a rare smile.

I pray we'll live to see that smile again.

CHAPTER ELEVEN

INAN

"Count to ten," I whisper to myself. "Count. To. Ten."

Because when I finish counting, this horror shall end.

The blood of the innocent will not stain my hands.

"One . . . two . . ." I grip Father's sênet pawn with a shaking hand, so tight the metal stings. The numbers rise, but nothing changes.

Like Ilorin, all my plans have gone up in flames.

My throat tightens when the village falls in a fiery blaze, taking the homes of hundreds with it. My soldiers drag the corpses through the sand, bodies charred beyond recognition. The shrieks of the living and the injured fill my ears. My tongue tastes nothing but ash. So much waste. Death.

This was not my plan.

Amari should be in one hand, the divîner thief chained in the other. Kaea should've retrieved the scroll. Only the divîner's hut need have burned.

If I had succeeded in returning the scroll, Father would've understood. He would've thanked me for my discretion, praised my shrewd judgment in sparing Ilorin. Our fish trade would be protected. The only threat to the monarchy would be crushed.

But I've failed. Again. After begging Father for another chance. The scroll is still missing. My sister at risk. An entire village wiped away. Yet I have nothing to show for it.

The people of Orïsha are not safe—

"Baba!"

I grab my blade as a small child hurls his body to the ground. His cries cut through the night. It's only then I discover the sand-covered corpse at his feet.

"Baba!" He grasps at the body, willing it to wake. The blood of his father stains the skin of his small brown hands.

"Abeni!" A woman trudges through the wet sand. She gasps at the sight of the approaching guards. "Abeni, no, you must be quiet. B-baba wants you to be quiet!"

I turn away and squeeze my eyes shut, forcing my bile down. *Duty before self.* I hear Father's voice. The safety of Orïsha before my conscience. But these villagers *are* Orïsha. They're the very people I'm sworn to protect.

"This is a mess." Admiral Kaea stomps to my side, knuckles bloody from beating the soldier who lit the fire too soon and started the blaze. I fight the urge to walk over and beat him myself as he lies moaning in the wet sand. "Get up and bind their wrists!" Kaea barks at the guard before lowering her voice again. "We don't know if the fugitives are dead or alive. We don't even know if they came back here."

"We'll have to round up the survivors." I release a frustrated breath. "Hope that one of them . . ."

My voice trails off as a vile sensation crawls up my skin. Like in the market, the heat prickles my scalp. It pulses as a thin wisp of air floats toward me. A strange turquoise cloud cutting through the black smoke.

"Do you see that?" I ask Kaea.

I point, stepping back as the smoke slithers near. The strange cloud carries the scent of the sea, overwhelming the bite of ash in the air.

"See what?" Kaea asks, but I don't have a chance to respond. The turquoise cloud passes through my fingers. A foreign image of the divîner ignites in my head. . . .

The sound around me fades out, turning murky and muddled. The cold sea washes over me as the moonlight and fire fade from above. I see the girl who haunts my thoughts, sinking among the corpses and driftwood, falling into the blackness of the sea. She doesn't fight the current that pulls her down. She relinquishes control. Sinking into death.

As my vision fades, I return to the screaming villagers and shifting sand. Something stings under my skin, the same bite that started when I last saw the divîner's face.

Suddenly all the pieces come together. The thrashing. The vision.

I should've known all along.

Magic . . .

My stomach twists in knots. I rake my nails over my tingling arm. I have to get this virus out of me. I need to rip the treacherous sensation from my skin—

Inan, focus.

I squeeze Father's sênet pawn so hard my knuckles crack. I swore to him I was prepared. But how in the skies could I have prepared for this?

"Count to ten," I whisper again, gathering all the pieces like pawns. By the time I hiss "five," a terrifying realization hits: the divîner girl has the scroll.

The spark I felt when she brushed against me. The electric energy that surged through my veins. And when our eyes locked . . .

Skies.

She must've infected me.

Nausea churns inside my stomach. Before I can stop myself, this morning's roasted swordfish fights its way up. I double over as vomit burns my throat and hits the sand with a splash.

"Inan!" Kaea wrinkles her nose as I cough, a hint of concern eclipsed by her disgust. She probably thinks me weak. But better that than her discovering the truth.

I clench my fist, almost positive I can feel the magic attacking my blood. If maji can infect us now, they'll defeat us before we have a chance to take them out.

"She was here." I wipe my mouth on the back of my hand. "The divîner with the scroll. We need to locate her before she hurts anyone else."

"What?" Kaea's thin brows crease. "How do you know?"

I open my mouth to explain when the sickening sting erupts under my scalp again. I turn. The prickle grows—it's strongest when I face the southern forest.

Though the air stinks of charred flesh and black smoke, I catch the fleeting scent of the sea again. *It's her.* It has to be. Hiding among the trees . . .

"Inan," Kaea snaps. "What do you mean? How do you know she was here?"

Magic.

My grip tightens around the tarnished pawn. My palm itches at the touch. The word feels dirtier than *maggot*. If I can hardly stomach the idea, how will Kaea react?

"A villager," I lie. "He told me they went south."

"Where is the villager now?"

I point blindly at a corpse, but my finger lands on the scorched body of a child. Another turquoise cloud shoots toward me. All rosemary and ash.

Before I can run away, the cloud passes through my hand with sickening heat. The world fades out in a wall of flames. Screams bleed into my ears.

"Help—"

"Inan!"

I snap back to reality. A cold tide rushes over my boots.

The beach. I squeeze the pawn. *You're still on the beach.*

"What happened?" Kaea asks. "You were moaning. . . ."

I whip around, looking for the girl. She has to be behind this. She's using her wretched magic to fill my head with sounds.

"Inan—"

"We should interrogate them." I ignore the concern in Kaea's eyes. "If one of the villagers knew where they were headed, another might have information, too."

Kaea hesitates and purses her lips. She probably wants to pry. But her duty as admiral comes first. It always will.

We walk over to the surviving villagers. I focus on the tide to ignore their shrieks, but the screaming only grows louder as we draw near.

Seven . . . , I count in my head. *Eight . . . nine . . .*

I am the son of Orïsha's greatest ruler.

I am their future king.

"Silence!"

My voice booms into the night with a power that doesn't feel like my own. Even Kaea gives me a surprised glance as the cries quiet into nothingness.

"We're looking for Zélie Adebola. She has stolen something valuable from the crown. We were told she's heading south, and now we need to know why."

I scan the dark faces of those who refuse to meet my eyes, searching for any sign of the truth. Their fear soaks into the air like humidity. It seeps into my own skin.

"—gods, please—"

"—if he kills me—"

"—in the gods' names did she steal—"

My heart slams against my chest as their voices attack in flickers, broken thoughts that threaten to overwhelm me. More turquoise clouds rise into the air. Like wasps, they dart toward me. I start to fall back into the blackness of my mind—

"Answer him!"

Thank the skies. Kaea's bark pulls me back.

I blink and grip the pommel of my sword. The smooth metal grounds me in reality. With time, their fear fades. But the unnerving sensation remains. . . .

"I said, *answer* him!" Kaea growls. "Do not make me repeat myself."

The villagers keep their gazes to the ground.

In their silence, Kaea lunges.

Screams erupt as she grabs an elderly woman by her gray hair. Kaea drags the moaning woman through the sand.

"Admiral—" My voice chokes when Kaea unsheathes her sword. She places the blade against the woman's wrinkled neck. A single drop of blood falls onto the ground.

"You want to stay silent?" Kaea hisses. "Stay silent and you die!"

"We don't know anything!" a young girl cries out. Everyone on the beach freezes.

The girl's hands are trembling. She shoves them into the sand.

"We can tell you about her brother and father. We can tell you of her skill with a staff. But not a soul in Ilorin knows where she's gone or why."

I give Kaea a stern look; she drops the woman like a rag doll. I trudge through the wet sand until I reach the girl.

Her shaking intensifies as I approach, but I can't tell if it's her fear or the cold of the night tides licking her knees. All she wears is a soaked nightgown, ripped and frayed around her being.

"What's your name?"

Standing this close to her, I see how her oak-brown skin stands out against the darker chestnut and mahogany hues of the villagers. Perhaps there's some nobility in her blood. A father who played in the mud.

When she doesn't answer, I bend down, keeping my voice low. "The faster you answer, the faster we leave."

"Yemi," she chokes out. Her hands grip the sand as she speaks. "I'll tell you everything you want to know, but only if you leave us alone."

I nod. A simple concession. Duty or not, I don't want to see more bodies.

I can't bear to hear more screams.

I reach down and untie the rope binding her wrists. She flinches at my touch. "Give us the information we need and I promise your people will be safe."

"Safe?"

Yemi meets my eyes with a hatred that impales me like a sword. Though her mouth never opens, her voice rings in my skull.

"Safe ended a long time ago."

CHAPTER TWELVE

ZÉLIE

MY EYES ACHE from hours of silent tears by the time we halt Nailah to rest. It takes all of five seconds for her and Tzain to pass out on the moss-covered ground, escaping our fractured reality for the safety of sleep.

Amari inspects the ground, shivering in the forest cold. She eventually lays her cloak down and sleeps on top of it, too regal to grace the earth with her bare head. I stare at her, remembering how close I dragged her to the flames.

The memory feels distant now, like someone else held all that hate.

Now only cool anger simmers, anger I shouldn't bother feeling. I'd bet five hundred silver pieces she won't last another day.

I wrap myself in my cloak and nestle into Nailah, relishing the sensation of the soft fur against my skin. Through the shadowed leaves, the star-filled sky reignites the magic of Mama Agba's vision in my mind.

"It's back," I whisper to myself. With the insanity of the day, that fact is still hardest to believe. We can reclaim our magic.

We can thrive again.

"Oya . . ."

I whisper the name of the Goddess of Life and Death, my sister deity who has granted me magic's gift. As a child, I called to her so often you'd think she slept in my cot, but now that I search for the words of a prayer, I don't know what to say.

"*Bá mi sọ̀rọ̀*," I attempt, but it lacks all the conviction and power Mama Agba's chant had. She believed in her connection to Orúnmila so much she could conjure a premonition. Right now, I just want to believe that someone is up there.

"*Ràn mí lọ́wọ́*," I pray instead. *Help me.* Those words feel so much realer, so much more like my own. "Mama Agba says you've chosen me. Baba agrees, but I . . . I'm scared. This is too important. I don't want to screw it up."

Saying it out loud makes the fear tangible, a new weight hanging in the air. I couldn't even protect Baba. How am I supposed to save the maji?

But as the fear breathes, I get the smallest sense of comfort. The idea that Oya could be here, right by my side. Gods only know there's no way I can get through this without her.

"Just help me," I repeat once more. "*Ràn mí lọ́wọ́.* Please. And keep Baba safe. No matter what happens, just let him and Mama Agba be okay."

Not knowing what else to say, I bow my head. Though stiff, I almost feel like I can see my prayers drifting to the sky. I hold on to the brief moment of contentment it grants me, forcing it above the pain, the fear, the grief. I hold it until it cradles me in its arms, rocking me to sleep.

WHEN I WAKE, something feels off. Unnatural. Not quite right.

I rise, expecting to find Nailah's sleeping mass, but she's nowhere to be seen. The forest is gone, no trees, no moss. Instead, I sit in a field of towering reeds whistling with the burst of wind in the air.

"What is this?" I whisper, confused by the fresh sensation and light. I look down at my hands and jerk my head back. No scars or burns stain my skin. It's as clear as the day I was born.

I rise in the endless field of reeds stretching far and wide. Even when I'm on my feet, the stems and leaves grow far above my head.

In the distance the plants are obscured, blurring into white at the horizon. It's as if I wander in an unfinished painting, trapped inside its canvased reeds. I'm not asleep, yet I'm not awake.

I float in a magical world between.

Dirt shifts under my feet as I move through the heavenly plants. Minutes seem to stretch into hours, yet I don't mind the time in this haze. The air is cool and crisp, like the mountains of Ibadan where I grew up. *Maybe it's a sanctuary*, I think to myself. A gift of rest from the gods.

I'm ready to embrace the thought when I sense the presence of another. My heart skips a beat as I turn. All breath seems to cease when realization dawns.

I recognize the smolder in his amber eyes first, a look I could never forget after today. But now that he's standing still, without a sword or surrounded by flames, I take in the curve of his muscles, the bright hue of his copper skin, the strange white streak in his hair. When he's this still, the features he shares with Amari are stark, impossible to miss. *He's not just the captain. . . .*

He's the prince.

He stares at me for a long moment, as if I'm a corpse risen from the dead. But then he clenches his fists. "Release me from this prison at once!"

"Release you?" I arch my brow in confusion. "I didn't do this!"

"You expect me to believe that? When I've seen your wretched face in my head all day?" He reaches for his sword, but there's nothing there.

For the first time, I notice we both wear simple white clothes, vulnerable without our weapons.

"My face?" I ask slowly.

"Don't feign ignorance," the prince snaps. "I felt what you did to me in Lagos. And those—those *voices*. End these attacks at once. End them or you'll pay!"

His rage stirs with a lethal heat, but the threat is lost as I ponder his words. He thinks I brought him here.

He thinks this meeting is by my hand.

Impossible. Though I was too young for Mama to teach me the magic of death, I saw it unfold. It came in cold spirits and sharp arrows and twisting shadows, but never in dreams. I didn't even touch the scroll until after we escaped Lagos, after our eyes locked and electric energy tickled my skin. If magic brought us here, it can't be my own. It has to be—

"You."

I breathe in amazement. *How is this possible?* The royal family lost magic generations ago. A maji hasn't touched the throne in years.

"Me what?"

My eyes return to the streak of white in his hair, running from his temple to the nape of his neck.

"You did this. *You* brought me here."

Every muscle in the prince's body goes rigid; the anger in his eyes transforms to terror. A cold breeze whips between us. The reeds dance in our silence.

"Liar," he decides. "You're just trying to get into my head."

"No, little prince. It's you who's gotten into mine."

Mama's old stories prickle through my memories, tales of the ten clans and the different magic each could wield. As a child, all I wanted to learn about were the Reapers like Mama, but she insisted I know just as much about every other clan. She always warned me about the Connectors, maji who wielded power over mind, spirit, and dreams. *Those are the ones you must watch out for, little Zél. They use magic to break into your head.*

The memory chills my blood, but the prince is so distraught it's difficult to fear his abilities. With the way he stares at his shaking hands, he looks like he would sooner take his own life than use magic to go after mine.

But how is this even happening? Divîners are selected by the gods at birth. The prince wasn't born a divîner and kosidán can't develop magic. How has he suddenly become a maji now?

I look at our surroundings, inspecting the work of his Connector abilities. The magical reeds twist in the wind, ignorant of the impossibilities blowing all around us.

The power required for a feat like this is inconceivable. Even a well-seasoned Connector would need an incantation to pull it off. How could he harness the ashê in his blood to create this when he didn't even realize he was a maji? What in the gods' names is going on?

My eyes go back to the jagged white streak running through the prince's hair, the only true marker of a maji. Our hair is always as stark and white as the snow that covers the mountaintops of Ibadan, a marker so dominant, even the blackest dye couldn't hide maji hair for more than a few hours.

Though I've never seen a streak like his among maji or divîners, I can't deny its existence. It mirrors the whiteness of my hair all the same.

But what does it mean? I look to the skies. What game are the gods playing? What if the prince isn't the only one? If the royals are regaining their magic—

No.

I can't let fear make me spiral out of control.

If royals were getting their magic back, we would already know.

I suck in a deep breath, slowing my mind before it can wander further. Amari had the scroll in Lagos. She crashed into her brother when we ran past. Though I don't understand why, it must've happened then. Inan awakened his powers the same way I awakened mine—by touching that damn scroll.

And the king has touched the scroll, I remind myself. Amari, probably the admiral, too. They didn't awaken any abilities. This magic only resides in him.

"Does your father know?"

The prince's eyes flash, giving me the answer I need.

"Of course not." I smirk. "If the king knew, you'd already be dead."

Color drains from his face. It's so perfect I almost laugh. How many divîners have fallen by his hands—been slaughtered, abused, used? How many lives has he taken to destroy the same magic now running through his veins?

"I'll make you a deal." I walk toward the prince. "Leave me alone and I'll keep your little secret. No one has to know you're a dirty little ma—"

The prince lunges.

One moment his grip is around my throat, and the next—

MY EYES FLY OPEN. I'm greeted by the familiar sound of crickets and dancing leaves. Tzain's snores ring steady and true as Nailah adjusts her body against my side.

I jolt forward and grab my staff to fight an enemy that isn't here.

Though I scan the trees, it takes me a few moments to convince myself the prince won't appear.

I breathe the damp air in and out, trying to calm my nerves. I lie back down and close my eyes, but sleep doesn't return easily. I'm not sure it ever will. Now I know the prince's secret.

Now he won't stop until I'm dead.

CHAPTER THIRTEEN

ZÉLIE

When I wake the next morning, I'm more exhausted than when I went to sleep.

It leaves me feeling robbed, like a thief made off with my dreams. Slumber usually brings an escape, a break from the misery I face when I wake. But when every one of my dreams ended with the prince's hands wrapped around my throat, the nightmares hurt just as much as reality.

"Dammit," I mutter. They're just dreams. What do I have to fear? Even if his magic is powerful, gods know he's far too terrified to use it.

Tzain grunts across the small clearing as he does crunch after crunch with unwavering concentration, training as if this was his regular morning practice. Except there won't be another practice for him this year. Because of me, he may never play agbön again.

Guilt adds to my exhaustion, dragging me back to the ground. I could apologize for the rest of my days and it still wouldn't be enough. But before I can sink further into my guilt, a flurry of movement catches my eye. Amari stirs underneath a large brown cloak, waking from her royal slumber. The sight puts a bitter taste in my mouth, reigniting the image of Inan.

Knowing her family, I'm surprised she didn't slit our throats in our sleep.

I search her dark hair for a streak to match her brother's, muscles relaxing when I find none. Gods only know how much worse this would be if she could trap me inside her head, too. I'm still glaring at Amari when I recognize the cloak she's using as a blanket. I rise and crouch by Tzain's side.

"What do you think you're doing?"

He ignores me and keeps exercising. The bags under his eyes warn me to leave him alone, but I'm too angry to stop now.

"Your cloak," I hiss. "Why'd you give it to her?"

Tzain fits in two more crunches before muttering, "She was shivering."

"And?"

"And?" he shoots back. "We have no idea how long this trip will take. The last thing we need is her getting sick."

"You know she's used to that, right? People who look like you making sure she gets her way?"

"Zél, she was cold and I wasn't using my cloak. That's all there is to it."

I turn back toward Amari and try to let it go. But in her eyes, I see her brother's. I feel his hands around my throat.

"I want to trust her—"

"No, you don't."

"Well, even if I did, I can't. Her father ordered the Raid. Her brother burned down our village. What makes you think she's any different?"

"Zél . . ." Tzain's voice trails off as Amari approaches, always delicate and demure. I have no way of knowing if she's heard us or not. Either way, I can't pretend I care.

"I think this is yours." She hands him the cloak. "Thank you."

"Don't worry about it." Tzain takes the cloak and folds it into his pack. "It'll be warmer as we get into the jungle, but let me know if you need it again."

Amari smiles for the first time since we've met, and I bristle when Tzain smiles back. It should take more than a pretty face for him to forget she's the daughter of a monster.

"Is that all?" I ask.

"Um, well, actually . . ." Her voice grows quiet. "I was wondering . . . what are we planning to do for, um—"

A deep groan escapes Amari's stomach. Color rises to her cheeks and she grips her slim belly, failing to cage in another roar.

"Excuse me," she apologizes. "All I ate yesterday was a loaf of bread."

"A whole loaf?" I salivate at the thought. It's been moons since I've had a good slice. Though I can't imagine the stale bricks we trade for in the market could hold a candle to a fresh loaf from the royal kitchen.

I itch to remind Amari of her good fortune, but my own stomach twists and turns with emptiness. Yesterday passed without one meal. If I don't eat soon, my stomach too will growl.

Tzain reaches into the pockets of his black pants and pulls out Mama Agba's weathered map. We follow his finger as it trails down the coast from Ilorin, stopping just outside a dot marking the settlement of Sokoto.

"We're about an hour out," he says. "It's the best place to stop before we head east to Chândomblé. There'll be merchants and food, but we'll need something to trade."

"What happened to the coin from the sailfish?"

Tzain dumps out my pack. I groan as a few silver pieces and Amari's headdress fall to the ground. "Most of it was lost in the fire," Tzain sighs.

"What can we trade?" Amari asks.

Tzain stares at the finery of her dress. Even with dirt stains and a few burn marks, its long, elegant cut and lined silk scream of noble origin.

Amari follows Tzain's eyes and her brows knit. "You cannot be serious."

"It'll trade for good coin," I jump in. "And we're going to the jungle, for gods' sakes. You'll never make it through in that."

Amari scans my draped pants and cropped dashiki, gripping the fabric of her dress tighter. I'm amazed she thinks she has a choice when I could hold her down and cut it off with ease.

"But what will I wear?"

"Your cloak." I point to the dingy brown cloth. "We'll trade the dress for some food and get new clothes on the way."

Amari steps back and looks at the ground.

"You were willing to evade your father's guards to save the scroll, but you won't take off your stupid dress?"

"I didn't risk everything because of the scroll." Amari's voice cracks. For a moment her eyes glimmer with the threat of tears. "My father killed my best friend—"

"Your best friend or your slave?"

"Zél," Tzain warns.

"What?" I turn to him. "Do *your* best friends press your clothes and make your food without pay?"

Amari's ears redden. "Binta *was* paid."

"A mighty wage, I'm sure."

"I am trying to help you." Amari clenches the skirt of her dress. "I've given up *everything* to help you people—"

" 'You people'?" I fume.

"We can save the divîners—"

"You want to save the divîners, but you won't even sell your damn dress?"

"Fine!" Amari throws her hands in the air. "Skies, I'll do it. I never said no."

"Oh, thank you, gracious princess, *savior* of the maji!"

"Cut it out." Tzain nudges me as Amari walks behind Nailah to change. Her delicate fingers move to the buttons on her back, but she hesitates, glancing over her shoulder. I roll my eyes as Tzain and I look the other way.

Princess.

"You need to lay off," Tzain mutters as we face the natal mahogany lining the vibrant forests of Sokoto. A small family of blue-butt baboonems swings from the branches, shaking the glossy leaves free when they pass.

"If she can't handle being around a divîner not enslaved by her father, she's free to return to her little palace."

"She hasn't done anything wrong."

"She hasn't done anything *right*, either." I nudge Tzain back. Why is he so insistent on defending her? It's as if he really thinks she deserves better. Like somehow *she's* the victim.

"I'm the last person to give a noble a chance, but Zél, look at her. She just lost her closest friend, and instead of grieving she's risking her life to help maji and divîners."

"I'm supposed to feel bad because her father killed the one maji servant she liked? Where's her outrage been all these years? Where was she after the Raid?"

"She was six." Tzain keeps his tone flat. "A child, just like you."

"Except she got to kiss her mother that night. We didn't."

I turn to mount Nailah, positive I've given Amari enough time. But when I glance over, her bare back is still exposed.

"Oh my gods . . ."

My heart lurches as I take in the gruesome scar carved along Amari's spine. The mark ripples across her skin, so ghastly it makes my own skin tingle with pain.

"What?"

Tzain turns just before Amari whips around, sucking in his breath at the mark. Even the scars lining Baba's back don't look half as hideous as hers.

"How dare you!" Amari scrambles to cover herself with the cloak.

"I wasn't trying to peek," I say quickly. "I promise, but—gods, Amari. What happened?"

"Nothing. A-an accident when my brother and I were young."

Tzain's jaw drops. "Your brother did that to you?"

"No! Not on purpose. It wasn't . . . he didn't—" Amari pauses, trembling with an emotion I can't place. "You wanted my dress, you have it. Let us trade and be on with it!"

She holds her cloak close and mounts Nailah, keeping her face hidden. With nothing more we can say, Tzain and I have no choice but to follow suit.

He mumbles an apology before urging Nailah ahead. I try to apologize as well, but the words stall when I look at her cloaked back.

Gods.

I don't want to imagine what other scars hide along her skin.

THE WEATHER WARMS as we reach the forest clearing that marks the settlement of Sokoto. Kosidán children run along the bank of the crystal clear lake, squealing with delight when one young girl falls in. Travelers set up camp between the trees and muddy patches; merchant carts and wagons line up their wares along the rocky shore. One cart's aroma of spiced antelopentai meat envelops me, making my stomach rumble.

I was always told that before the Raid, Sokoto was home to the best Healers. People traveled from all over Orïsha, hoping to be cured by the magic of their touch. As I survey the travelers, I try to imagine what that might look like. If Baba were still with us, he might've liked this. A moment of refuge after losing our home.

"So peaceful," Amari breathes, clutching her cloak as we slide off Nailah.

"You've never been here before?" Tzain asks.

She shakes her head. "I barely left the palace."

Though crisp air fills my lungs as we walk, the sight reawakens the memory of burning flesh. In the lake I see the calm waves of the floating market back home, the coconut boat I should be in as I fight with Kana for a hand of plantain. But like Ilorin, the market's gone, all burnt at the bottom of the sea. The memories sit among the charred lumber.

Another piece of me taken by the monarchy.

"You two trade the dress," Tzain says. "I'll take Nailah to get a drink. See if you can find a few canteens."

I chafe at the prospect of trading with Amari, but I know she won't leave my side until she gets new clothes. We part ways with Tzain, traveling through the campsites toward the row of merchant carts.

"You can relax." I arch my eyebrow. Amari flinches whenever someone so much as looks her way. "They don't know who you are, and no one cares about your cloak."

"I know that." Amari speaks quickly, but her stance softens. "I've just never been around people like this."

"How terrifying. Orïshans who exist to do more than serve you."

Amari inhales sharply but swallows any retort. I almost feel bad. Where's the fun if she doesn't fight back?

"Skies, look at that!" Amari slows as we pass a couple setting up their tent. The man uses vines to bind dozens of long, thin branches into a cone while his partner creates a protective layer by piling on moss. "Can people really sleep in those?"

Part of me itches to ignore her, but she stares at the simple tent as if it's made of gold. "We used to build those all the time when I was young. Do it right and it'll even keep out snow."

"You get snow in Ilorin?" Again her eyes sparkle, like snow is an ancient legend about the gods. How strange that she was born to rule a kingdom she's never even seen.

"In Ibadan," I answer. "We lived there before the Raid."

At the mention of the Raid, Amari goes quiet. The curiosity vanishes from her eyes. She grips her cloak tighter and keeps her focus on the ground.

"Is that what happened to your mother?"

I stiffen; how can she be bold enough to ask this when she can't even ask for food?

"I apologize if that is too forward . . . it's just that your father mentioned her yesterday."

I picture Mama's face. Her dark skin seemed to glow in the absence of sun. *She loved you fiercely.* Baba's words echo in my mind. *She would be so proud right now.*

"She was a maji," I finally answer. "A powerful one, at that. Your father's lucky she didn't have her magic during the Raid."

My mind returns to the fantasy of Mama wielding her magic, a lethal force instead of a helpless victim. She would've avenged the fallen maji, marching on Lagos with an army of the dead. She'd be the one to wrap a black shadow around Saran's neck.

"I know this won't change anything, but I'm sorry," Amari whispers so quietly I can barely hear her. "The pain of losing a person you love, it's . . ." She squeezes her eyes shut. "I know you hate my father. I understand why you hate me, too."

As grief breaks through Amari's face, the very hatred she speaks of cools inside me. I still don't understand how her handmaiden could've been anything more than another servant to her, but there's no denying her sorrow.

No. I shake my head as guilt swells in the space between us. Grieving or not, she doesn't get my pity. And she's not the only one who gets to pry.

"So has your brother always been a heartless killer?"

Amari turns to me, brows raised in surprise.

"Don't think you can ask about my mother and hide the truth about that awful scar."

Amari steadies her vision on the merchant carts, but even so, I see the past playing out behind her eyes. "It wasn't his fault," she finally answers. "Our father forced us to spar."

"With actual swords?" I jerk my head back. Mama Agba made us train for years before we were allowed to pick up a staff.

"Father's first family was coddled." Her voice grows distant. "Weak. He said they died because of it. He wouldn't allow the same thing to happen to us."

She speaks as if this is normal, like all loving fathers spill their children's blood. I always pictured the palace as a safe haven, but my gods, is this what her life has been like?

"Tzain would never do that." I purse my lips. "He'd never hurt me."

"Inan didn't have a choice." Her face hardens. "He has a good heart. He's just been led astray."

I shake my head. Where does her loyalty come from? All this time I thought those of noble blood were safe. I never imagined what cruelty the monarchy could inflict on their own.

"Good hearts don't leave scars like that. They don't burn villages down."

They don't wrap their hands around my throat and try to bury me in the ground.

When Amari doesn't reply, I know that's the last we'll talk about her brother. Fine. If she won't tell the truth about Inan, neither will I.

I swallow his secret into silence, instead focusing on the roasted antelopentai meat as we near the merchant carts and wagons. We're about to approach an elderly trader with a robust supply when Amari tugs on my pack.

"I never thanked you for saving my life. Back in Lagos." She shifts her gaze to the ground. "But you did try to kill me twice . . . so perhaps it all cancels out?"

It takes me a second to realize she's joking. I'm surprised when I grin. For the second time today, she smiles and I get a glimpse of why it was so hard for Tzain to look away.

"Ah, two lovely ladies," an elderly kosidán says, beckoning us closer. He steps forward, his gray hairs glinting under the sun.

"Please." The merchant's smile widens, carving wrinkles into his leathery skin. "Come in. I promise you'll find something you like."

We walk around to the front steps of his wagon, pulled by two cheetanaires so large we stand eye to eye. I run my hands along their spotted fur, stopping to finger the grooves in the thick horn protruding from one's forehead. The ryder purrs and licks my hand with its serrated tongue before I step inside the extensive space of wares.

The musk of old fabrics hits me as we pass through the crowded wagon. On one end, Amari fingers through old clothes while I stop and inspect a pair of suede mongix-hide canteens.

"What are you in the market for?" the merchant asks, holding an array of sparkling necklaces. He leans in, magnifying the deep-set eyes that mark those from Orïsha's northern border. "These pearls come from the bays of Jimeta, but these glittering beauties come from the mines of Calabrar. Sure to turn any fella's head, though I'm sure you have no problem in that department."

"We need traveling supplies." I smile. "Canteens and some hunting gear, maybe flint."

"How much do you have?"

"What can we get for this?"

I hand him Amari's dress and he unfolds it, holding it up to the light outside. He runs his fingers along the seams like a man who knows his cloth, taking extra time to inspect the burns around the hem. "It's well made, no denying that. Rich fabric, excellent cut. I could do without the burns, but nothing a new hem can't fix. . . ."

"So?" I press.

"Eighty silver pieces."

"We won't take any less than—"

"I'm not in the business of haggling, dear. My prices are fair and so are my offers. Eighty is final."

I grit my teeth, but I know there's no talking him up. A merchant who's traded all over Orïsha can't be swindled like an insulated noble.

"What can we get with eighty?" Amari asks, holding up a pair of yellow draped pants and a black, sleeveless dashiki.

"With those clothes . . . these canteens . . . a skinning knife . . . a few pieces of flint . . ." The merchant begins filling up a woven basket, gathering supplies to get us on our way.

"Is it enough?" Amari whispers.

"For now." I nod. "If he throws in that bow—"

"You can't afford it," the merchant cuts in.

"But what if this does not end at Chân—at the temple?" Amari lowers her voice. "Won't we need more money? More food? Supplies?"

"I don't know." I shrug. "We'll figure it out."

I turn to leave, but Amari frowns and reaches into the depths of my pack.

"How much for this?" She pulls out her jeweled headdress.

The merchant's eyes bulge out of his head as he stares at the priceless adornment.

"My gods," he breathes. "Where on earth did you find that?"

"It doesn't matter," Amari says. "How much?"

He turns the headdress over in his hands, and his mouth falls open when he sees the diamond-studded snow leopanaire. He lifts his gaze to Amari, slow and deliberate. He looks to me, but I keep my face even.

"I cannot take this." He pushes the headdress away.

"Why?" Amari shoves it into his hands. "You'll take the dress off my back but not the crown off my head?"

"I can't." The merchant shakes his head, but now that gold sits in his hands, his conviction wavers. "Even if I wanted to, there's nothing I can trade. It's worth more than everything I have."

"Then how much can you give?" I ask.

He pauses, fear dancing with greed. He looks back at Amari once more, before staring at the headdress shining in his hands. He removes a ring of keys from his pocket and pushes aside a crate to reveal an iron safe. After unlocking and opening it, he inspects the glowing pile of coins inside.

"Three hundred gold pieces."

I lurch forward. That kind of coin could last our family a lifetime. Maybe two! I turn to celebrate with Amari when the look on her face brings me back. . . .

I wouldn't have this if it weren't for my handmaiden. It is the only thing of hers I have left.

There was so much pain in her eyes. Pain I recognized. Pain I wore when I was young, the first time my family couldn't pay a royal tax.

For months Tzain and Baba worked the sunfish harvest from dawn to dusk; at night they took extra work from the guards. They did everything possible to keep me out of it, but eventually their efforts fell short. That day I entered the floating market, Mama's gold amulet in hand. It was the only thing of hers that we could recover, torn to the ground when the guards dragged her away.

After Mama died, I grasped that amulet like it was the last remaining piece of her soul. I still rub my neck sometimes, plagued by its absence.

"You don't have to do this." It stings to say those words in the face of so much gold, but ripping myself from Mama's amulet felt like ripping away her heart; a pain so harsh I couldn't even wish it on Amari.

Her eyes soften and she smiles. "You mocked me for not wanting to take off my dress before, but you were right. I was fixated on what I've already lost, but after everything my father's done, my sacrifices will never be enough." Amari nods to the merchant, making her final decision. "I couldn't save Binta. But with the gold from this sale . . ."

We could save the divîners.

I stare at Amari as the merchant takes the headdress and piles the gold into velvet bags. "Take the bow." He beams. "Take whatever you like!"

Gazing around the wagon, my eyes land on a sturdy leather pack decorated with circles and lines. I lean in to inspect its firm texture but stop when I realize the design is composed entirely of dotted crosses. I run my hands over the disguised clan mark, the secret symbol of Oya, my sister deity. If the guards ever recognized the truth hidden in the bag's design, they could seize the merchant's entire cart. They might even cut off his hands.

"Be careful!" the merchant shouts.

I snatch my hand back before I realize he's talking to Amari.

She turns an empty hilt over in her hands. "What is this? No blade?"

"Point it away from yourself and give it a flick."

Like with my staff, a flick of the hilt extends a long blade with a lethal curved point. It glides through the air with a deadly grace, surprisingly nimble in Amari's small hands.

"I'll take this."

"If you don't know how to use it—" the merchant warns.

"Why do you assume I don't?"

I arch my eyebrow at Amari and think back to her mention of a training accident. I assumed the scar came from her brother's sword, but was she holding a sword, too? Despite her escape from Lagos, I can't imagine the princess locked in battle.

The merchant packs up our collection of coins and goods and sends us on our way, giving us everything we need to travel to Chândomblé. We walk back to meet Tzain in silence, but between the scar, the headdress, and the sword, I don't know what to think. Where's the spoiled princess I wanted to choke to death? And can she actually wield a sword?

As we pass a papaya tree, I pause, shaking the trunk until a yellow fruit falls. I give Amari a few moments to move forward before whipping the ripe papaya at her head.

For a heartbeat, Amari appears oblivious—*how will I explain this?* But as the fruit whistles near, she drops her basket and whips around, new blade extended, speed unmatched.

I gape as the ripe papaya falls to the ground, sliced in two clean halves. Amari smiles and picks up a piece, taking a triumphant bite.

"If you wish to hit me, you will have to try a little harder than that."

CHAPTER FOURTEEN

INAN

Kill her.

Kill magic.

My plan is all I have.

Without it, the world slips through my fingers. My maji curse threatens to break from my skin.

I'll make you a deal, the girl whispers in my mind, lips twisting as she speaks. *No one has to know you're a dirty little—*

"Dammit."

I grit my teeth. It doesn't block out the rest of her vile speech. With the memory of her voice, my infection simmers to the surface, prickling hot under my skin. As it rises, the broken voices grow. Louder. Sharper.

Like forcing a brick down my throat, I fight the magic back.

One . . . two . . .

I count as I struggle. The air around me begins to chill. Sweat gathers on my forehead. By the time my magic's pushed down, my breath escapes in rough spurts. But the threat is quelled. For a brief instant I'm safe. Alon—

"Inan."

I flinch and check that my helmet is still secure. My thumb runs over the latch for the fiftieth time today. I swear I can feel this new white streak growing.

Right into Kaea's view.

She rides forward, summoning me to follow in her stead. She must not realize I've been riding behind her all day, avoiding her line of vision. Mere hours ago she almost saw it, catching me off guard as I stared at my reflection in a stream. If she'd left a little earlier . . . if I'd stayed out a little later—

Focus, Inan!

What am I doing? What-ifs get me nowhere.

Kill the girl. Kill magic. That's all I need to do.

I squeeze my thighs around my snow leopanaire, Lula, and urge her after Kaea, careful to avoid the horns protruding from her back. If I hit one too hard, my ryder will buck me from my saddle.

"Now." I snap Lula's reins when she growls. "Don't be such a lazy bastard."

Lula flashes her serrated fangs but quickens her pace. She weaves in and out of the marula oak trees, dipping under the baboonems skittering along the fruit-covered branches.

I stroke her spotted fur in gratitude when we catch up to Kaea. She lets out another low growl but rubs her face against my hand.

"Tell me," Kaea says when I'm close. "What did the villager tell you?"

Again? Skies, she's relentless.

"It doesn't add up. I need to hear it once more." Kaea reaches behind her panthenaire to release her red-breasted firehawk from its cage. The bird perches on the ryder's saddle as Kaea fastens a note to its leg. Likely a message for Father. *Following the scroll's trail south. Also, I suspect Inan is a maj—*

"He claimed he was a mapmaker," I lie. "The thief and Amari visited him after they escaped Lagos."

Kaea raises her forearm, and the firehawk spreads its wide wings before taking to the sky.

"How did he know they were going south?"

"He saw them charting their path."

Kaea looks away, but not before I catch the doubt glimmering in her eyes. "You shouldn't have interrogated anyone without me."

"And the village shouldn't have burned!" I snap. "I fail to see the point in obsessing over what should or shouldn't have happened."

Relax, Inan. It's not Kaea I'm mad at.

But her lips are already pinched. I've pushed her too far.

"Sorry," I sigh. "I didn't mean that."

"Inan, if you can't handle this—"

"I'm fine."

"Are you?" She trains her eyes on me. "Because if you think I've forgotten about your little episode, you're sadly mistaken."

Curse the skies.

Kaea was there the first time magic attacked me on the shores of Ilorin. The night it filled my head with sounds.

My gut clenches as I push the evil further down.

"I won't have the prince die on my watch. If that happens again, you're headed back to the palace."

My heart seizes so hard an ache ripples through my chest. She can't send me home like this.

Not until the girl dies.

I'll make you a deal. Her voice crawls back into my mind. It's so vivid it's like she's whispering in my ear. *Leave me alone and I'll keep your little secret. No one has to know you're a dirty little—*

"No!" I shout. "It wasn't an episode. On the beach. I—I—" I take a deep breath. *Relax.* "I thought I saw Amari's corpse." *That's it.* "I was ashamed at how much it rattled me."

"Oh, Inan . . ." Kaea's hardness fades. She reaches over and grabs my hand. "Forgive me. I can't imagine how horrific that must have been."

I nod and squeeze her hand back. Too tightly. *Let go.* But my heart-beat quickens in my chest. A turquoise cloud seems to radiate from my chest, billowing like pipe smoke. The smell of rosemary and ash returns. The shrieks of the burning girl surface again. . . .

The heat of the flames licks my face. Sweltering smoke fills my lungs. With each second the fire crawls closer to my body, eliminating any chance of escape.

"Help!"

I drop to the ground. My lungs reject the rancid air. My feet get caught in the blaze—

"HELP!"

I jerk on Lula's reins. She lets out a menacing growl as we come to an abrupt stop.

"What is it?" Kaea whips her head around.

I dig my hands into Lula's fur to mask their tremble. I'm running out of time. The magic's getting stronger.

Like a parasite feeding on my blood.

"Amari," I choke out. My throat burns as if it's still full of smoke. "I'm worried. She's never left the palace before. She could get hurt."

"I know," Kaea soothes me. I wonder if she speaks the same way to Father when his temper flares. "But she's not completely helpless. There's a reason the king spent so many years making sure you could both wield a sword."

I force a nod, pretending to listen as Kaea continues to talk. Again, I shove my curse down, ignoring the way it makes the air around me thin. But even as my magic subsides, my heart still pounds.

The power burns inside me. Taunting. Tainting.

Kill her, I remind myself.

I'll kill the girl. I'll kill this curse.

If I can't—

I force a deep breath.

If I can't, I'm already dead.

CHAPTER FIFTEEN

AMARI

I USED TO DREAM of climbing.

Late at night, when everyone in the palace had gone to sleep. Binta and I would run through the painted halls by torchlight, skidding over the tiled floors in our trek to Father's war room. Hand in hand, we drew the torch over the handwoven map of Orïsha, a map that seemed as large as life itself to our young eyes. I thought Binta and I would see the world together.

I thought if we left the palace, we could be happy.

Now as I cling to the side of the third mountain we've climbed today, I question why I ever dreamed of ascending anything higher than the palace stairwell. Sweat clings to my skin, soaking through the rough cloth of my black dashiki. An endless swarm of mosquitoes buzz and sting at my back, feasting because I can't bear to let go of the mountain long enough to swat them away.

Another full day of travel has passed, along with, thankfully, one night of restful sleep. Though the weather warmed once we left Sokoto and made our way farther into the jungle, I felt Tzain lay his cloak over me again just as I began to fall asleep. With our new supplies, eating comes easy. Even foxer meat and coconut milk start to taste like seasoned hen and tea from the palace kitchen. I thought things were finally improving, but now my chest is so tight I can barely breathe.

This late into the day we've ascended thousands of meters, giving us startling views of the jungle beneath. Greens of all hues cover the land, creating endless canopies beneath our feet. A rushing river curves through the tropical brush, marking the only water in sight. It grows smaller and smaller as we climb, shrinking until it's only a thin blue line.

"How can anything exist up here?" I ask in between pants. I take a deep breath and give the rock above my head a firm pull. Earlier in our journey, I wouldn't test my handholds. My scraped knees are a reminder not to repeat that mistake.

When the rock holds firm, I hoist myself farther up the mountain, wedging my bare feet into a crack. The urge to cry wells up inside me, but I force it down. I've already hidden my tears twice. It would be humiliating to weep again.

"She's right," Tzain calls from behind me, searching for an area wide enough for Nailah to clamber up. Their lionaire is skittish after almost slipping off the last mountain. Now she climbs only after Tzain proves it's safe.

"Just keep going," Zélie calls from above. "It's here. It *has* to be here."

"Did you actually *see* it?" Tzain asks.

I think back to the moment in Mama Agba's hut, the moment the future exploded before our eyes. It all looked so magical back then. Stealing the scroll actually felt like a good idea.

"We saw ourselves climbing . . . ," I start.

"But did you see this legendary temple?" Tzain presses. "Just because Mama Agba saw us climbing doesn't mean Chândomblé's actually real."

"Stop talking and keep climbing!" Zélie shouts. "Trust me. I know it's real."

It's the same reasoning she's been shouting all day, the stubbornness that's carried us from cliff to cliff. Reality and logic don't matter to her. She needs this so badly, failure isn't even in the realm of possibilities.

I look down to reply to Tzain, but the sight of jungle trees thousands of meters below makes my muscles seize. I press my body against the mountain and clench the rocks tightly.

"Hey," Tzain calls. "Don't look down. You're doing great."

"You're lying."

He almost smiles. "Just keep climbing."

My beating pulse fills my ears as I look back up. The next ledge is in sight. Though my legs shake, I push myself farther up. *Sweet skies, if Binta could see me now.*

Her beautiful face bleeds into my mind in all its former glory. For the first time since I watched her die, I picture her alive, smiling and by my side. There was one night in the war room when she undid her bonnet. Her ivory hair fell in silky sheets around her head.

And what shall you wear when we cross the Olasimbo Range? she teased when I told her my plans for our escape to the Adetunji Sea. *Even if you were on the run, the queen herself would drop dead before she allowed you to wear trousers.* She put her hand on her head and pretended to shriek, mimicking Mother's pitch. I laughed so hard that night I nearly wet myself.

Despite the circumstances, a smile comes to my face. Binta could impersonate everybody in the palace. Yet my smile falls as I think of our lost dreams and abandoned plans. I thought we could escape through the tunnels beneath the palace. Once we got out, we would never go back. It all felt so certain in that moment, but did Binta always know it was a dream she'd never see?

The question haunts me as I reach the next ledge and pull myself over. The mountain flattens out for a brief stretch, wide enough for me to lie down in the wild grass.

As I drop to my knees, Zélie collapses in a garden of native bromeliads, crushing the vibrant red and purple petals under her feet. I bend down and breathe in their sweet scent. Binta would've loved these.

"Can we stay here?" I ask as the clove fragrance calms me. I can't imagine climbing any higher. The promise of Chândomblé can only take us so far.

I lift my head as Nailah claws her way onto the ledge. Tzain follows after, dripping with sweat. He peels off his sleeveless dashiki and I lower my eyes—the last time I saw a boy's bare body my nannies were giving Inan and me baths.

A warm flush rises to my cheeks as I realize how far from the palace I've truly come. Though it's not illegal for royals and kosidán to consort the way it is for maji and kosidán, Mother would have Tzain jailed for what he's just done.

I scoot away, eager to put more space between Tzain's bare skin and my blushing face. But as I move, my fingers knock against something smooth and hollow.

I turn and find myself face-to-face with a cracked skull.

"Skies!" I shout, and crawl backward, hairs rising on the nape of my neck. Zélie jumps to her feet and expands her staff, ready to fight at a moment's notice.

"What is it?" she asks.

I point to the fractured skull, lying on top of a pile of crushed bones. A gaping hole above its eye socket signals its violent death.

"Could it be another climber?" I ask. "Someone who did not make it through?"

"No," Zélie answers with a strange confidence. "It's not that." She tilts her head and bends down for a closer look. A chill passes through the air. Zélie reaches down, stretching her hand out toward the cracked bone. Her fingers barely graze the skull when—

I gasp as the sweltering jungle heat around us snaps to a freezing cold. The chill bites through my skin, cutting straight to the bone. But the icy rush only lasts an instant. As quick as it comes, it vanishes, leaving us bewildered on the mountainside.

"*Ugh!*" Zélie wheezes like she's been brought back to life. She grips the bromeliads so tightly the flowers rip straight off their stems.

"What in gods' names was that?" Tzain asks.

Zélie shakes her head, eyes growing wider and wider by the second. "I felt *him.* It was his spirit . . . his life!"

"Magic," I realize. No matter how many times I see it, the displays never fail to conflict me. Even as Father's childhood warnings of magic resurface, my heart fills with awe.

"Come on!" Zélie dashes forward, scurrying up the next incline. "That was stronger than anything I've ever felt. The temple has to be near!"

I scramble after her, casting aside my fear in my desire to reach the last ledge. When I pull myself up over the final cliff, I can't believe my eyes. Chândomblé.

It's actually here.

Moss-covered bricks are piled in mountains of rubble, coating every inch of the plateau. The destruction is all that remains of the temples and shrines that once covered this land. Unlike the jungle and mountains below, no crickets chirp, no birds squawk, no mosquitoes sing. The only signs that life ever existed are the shattered skulls littered around our feet.

Zélie pauses before a skull, brows knitting though nothing happens.

"What is it?" I ask.

"Its spirit . . ." She bends down. "It's *rising.*"

"Rising where?" I step back, stumbling over a piece of rubble.

Another chill fills me with unspoken dread, but I can't decipher if it's real or just in my head.

"I don't know." Zélie rubs her neck. "Something about the temple is amplifying my ashê. I can actually feel my magic."

Before I can ask another question, Zélie bends down and touches another skull.

My hand flies to my chest; this time it's not an icy cold that flashes around her, but an image, tinted in gold. Magnificent temples and towers rise, stunning structures adorned with elegant waterfalls. Dark men, women, and children in fine suede robes roam, beautiful lines and symbols dotting their skin in elegant swirls of white.

Though the flash lasts only an instant, the image of the lush grounds stains my memory as I look at the broken rubble before me. Chândomblé used to be radiant.

Now it's only air.

"What do you think happened here?" I ask Zélie, though I fear I already know. Father destroyed the beauty of magic in my life. Why wouldn't he have done the same throughout the world?

I wait for Zélie to answer, but she doesn't respond. Her face hardens with each passing second—she's seeing more, something I can't.

A soft lavender light begins to glow from her fingers, surfacing as she explores her powers for the first time. Watching her, my curiosity builds. What else can she see? Though the thought of magic still makes my pulse race, part of me wishes I could experience its rush just once. The rainbow that burst from Binta's hand begins to fill my mind until I hear Tzain call.

"Check this out."

We follow Tzain's voice until we're facing the only standing structure on the mountain. The temple towers into the sky, built against the ledge of the last rock's incline. Unlike the stone bricks, this structure's crafted from blackened metal, streaked with yellows and pinks that suggest it once shone gold. Vines and moss grow up the sides, obscuring endless rows of ancient runes carved into the temple's frieze.

Zélie moves toward the doorless entrance, but Nailah lets out a small growl. "Okay, Nailah." Zélie gives her nose a kiss. "Stay here, alright?"

Nailah grunts and collapses behind a pile of broken stone. With Nailah settled, we walk through the opening and greet a magical aura so thick even I can feel its weight in the room. Tzain scoots closer to Zélie as I run my hand against the air; the oscillations of magical energy slip through my fingers like grains of falling sand.

Rays of light peek through the cracked oculus above, illuminating the patterned dome ceiling. The designs feed into rows of pillars, decorated with colored glass and shimmering crystals.

Why didn't they destroy this? I wonder as I run my fingers along the carvings. The temple is strangely untouched, a lone tree in a scorched forest.

"See any doors?" Tzain calls from the other side of the room.

"Nothing," Zélie calls back. The only visible fixture is a large statue pressed against the back wall, collecting dust and overgrown vines. We walk over, and Tzain runs his hands over the weathered stone. The statue appears to be that of an elderly woman, cloaked in rich robes. A golden crown sits in her sculpted white coils, the only untarnished metal in sight.

"Is it a goddess?" I ask, inspecting the sculpture up close. In all my years, I've never seen a rendering of a single deity. No one would dare place one in the palace. I always assumed the first time I saw a god or goddess, it would be depicted like the royal portraits hanging in the main hall. But despite its tarnish, this statue holds a regal air even the most stunning painting couldn't achieve.

"What's this?" Tzain points to an object in the woman's hand.

"It looks like a horn." Zélie reaches up to inspect it. "It's strange. . . ." She runs her hand across its rusted metal. "I can almost hear it in my head."

"What's it saying?" I ask.

"It's a horn, Amari. It's not *saying* anything."

My cheeks flush. "Well, if it's a sculpture, it shouldn't be making sounds at all!"

"Just be quiet." Zélie hushes me and places both hands on the metal. "I think it's trying to tell me something."

I hold my breath as her brows pinch. After a few long moments, her hands begin to glow with a glittering, silver light. The horn seems to feed on her ashê, glowing brighter as she strains.

"Be careful," Tzain warns.

"I am." Zélie nods, though she begins to shake. "It's close. It just needs one more push—"

A slow creak rumbles under our feet. I yelp at the sound. We whip around in surprise as a large tile slides away from the floor. The opening reveals a staircase spiraling down into a room so dark it masks everything in blackness.

"Is it safe?" I whisper. The darkness makes my heartbeat spike. I lean down to get a better look, but there isn't a source of light in sight.

"There's no other door." Zélie shrugs. "What choice do we have?"

Tzain runs outside, returning with a charred femur bone wrapped in a torn bit of his cloak. Zélie and I recoil, but he brushes past us and lights the cloth with our flint, creating a makeshift torch.

"Follow me," he says, his commanding voice diminishing my fear.

We begin our descent with Tzain leading the way. Though the torch's bubble of light illuminates our steps, it touches nothing more. I keep a hand on the jagged wall, counting my breaths until we finally reach the next floor. The moment my foot leaves the last step, the opening above us slams shut with a deafening crack.

"Skies!"

My shriek rings through the darkness. I fling myself into Zélie. "What do we do now?" I tremble. "How do we get out of here?"

Tzain turns to run back up the stairs but stops when we hear a hissing in the air. Within seconds, his torch blows out, leaving us in total blackness.

"Tzain!" Zélie shouts.

The hiss grows louder until a warm gust of air hits me like rain. When I inhale, it instantly slows my muscles then begins to cloud my mind.

"Poison," Tzain manages to croak before I hear the thud of his body hitting the ground. I don't even have a chance to feel afraid before the darkness takes hold.

CHAPTER SIXTEEN

INAN

A HUSH CUTS THROUGH the air when my legion descends into Sokoto. It doesn't take long to figure out why.

We're the only guards in sight.

"Where're the patrols?" I whisper to Kaea. The silence is deafening. It's like these people have never laid eyes on the Orïshan seal. Skies only know what Father would do if he witnessed their complete lack of respect.

We dismount our ryders by a lake so clear it reflects the surrounding trees like a mirror. Lula gnashes her teeth at a group of children. They scamper away as she takes a drink.

"We don't post guards at traveling settlements. It would be a waste when the residents change every few days." Kaea unlatches her helmet and the wind runs through her hair. My scalp itches to feel the same, but I have to keep my white streak hidden.

Find her. I inhale the clean, brisk air, trying to forget about my streak, if only for a moment. Unlike the heat and smog of Lagos, the small settlement is fresh. Revitalizing. The cool breath dulls the burn in my chest as I try to keep my curse down, but my pulse races as I scan the surrounding divîners. I've been so focused on ending the girl.

I didn't stop to think of how she could end me.

I grip the hilt of my sword as my eyes flick from divîner to divîner. I have yet to see the extent of the girl's magic. How would I defend against her attack?

And what if she fights with her words? A prick of terror hits; the magic inside me spikes. All she'd have to do was point to my helmet, identify the curse hidden beneath. Kaea would see my white streak. My secret would be out for the world to see—

Focus, Inan. I close my eyes, holding the warm sênet pawn tight. I can't keep spiraling. I have to fulfill my duty. Orïsha is still under attack.

As the numbers force order into my head, I reach for the curved handle of my throwing knife. Magic or not, the right throw will disarm her. A sharp blade will still cut through her chest.

But for all my plotting and maneuvering, it's obvious the girl isn't here. Though there's no shortage of glaring divîners, her silver gaze is not among them.

I release the throwing knife as something I can't place deflates in my chest. It sinks like disappointment.

It breathes like relief.

"Take these posters," Kaea instructs the soldiers. She hands each of the ten men a roll of parchment inked with the girl's smug face. "Find out if anyone has seen her or a bull-horned lionaire—you usually don't find them so close to our coast." Kaea turns to me, lips pursed in determination. "We'll search the merchants. If they really came south, this would be the first place to gather supplies."

I nod and try to relax, but being this close to Kaea makes it impossible. Every little movement catches her eye; each sound practically makes her ears twitch.

As I walk behind her, the strain of pushing my powers down grows with every step. The iron of my armor begins to drag like lead. Though we walk slowly, I can't keep a steady pace. With time, I begin to fall behind. I hunch over, resting my hands on my knees. *I just need to catch my brea—*

"What're you doing?"

I snap up, ignoring how my curse spikes at the edge in Kaea's voice. "Th-the tents." I gesture at the natural shelters before me. "I was inspecting them." Unlike the metal poles and leathery hippone hides we use to build our tents, these are made with branches and coated in moss. In fact, there's a strange efficiency to their structure. Techniques the army could adapt.

"It's hardly the time for rudimentary architecture." Kaea narrows her eyes. "Focus on the task at hand."

She turns on her heel, walking even faster now that I've wasted her time. I rush to follow, but as we near the carts and wagons, a stout woman catches my eye. Unlike the other campers, she isn't glaring. She isn't looking at us at all. Her attention is directed toward the bundle of blankets she cradles to her chest.

Like a suppressed sneeze, my curse jumps to the surface. The mother's emotions hit like a smack to the face: sparks of rage, dull flashes of fear. But above all else, a protectiveness burns, snarling like a snow leopanaire guarding its only cub. I don't understand why until the bundle pressed against her chest begins to cry.

A child . . .

My eyes travel down the woman's chestnut skin to the jagged rock clasped in her hand. Her terror surges through my bones, but her resolve burns even stronger.

"Inan!"

I snap back to attention—I have to whenever Kaea calls my name. But as I reach the merchant wagons I glance back at the woman, shoving my curse down despite the way it makes my stomach burn. What does she have to fear? And what business would I have with her child?

"Wait." I stop Kaea as we pass a merchant wagon pulled by one-horned cheetanaires. The spotted creatures gaze at me with orange eyes. Sharp fangs peek from behind their black-lined lips.

"What?"

A turquoise cloud hangs around the doorway, bigger than the ones that have been appearing. "This one has a wide selection." I try to keep my voice light as we approach.

And the sea-salt scent of the girl's soul.

Though I fight my magic, her smell surrounds me when I pass through the cloud. The divîner appears in my mind fully formed, dark skin almost luminescent in the Sokoto sun.

The image lasts only a moment, but even a flicker makes my insides churn. The magic feeds like a parasite in my blood. I straighten my helmet as we walk through the wagon's door.

"Welcome, welcome!"

The wide smile of the elderly merchant drips from his dark face like wet paint. He stands, clenching the sides of the wagon for support.

Kaea shoves the scroll in his face. "Have you seen this girl?"

The merchant squints and cleans his spectacles against his shirt. Slowly. *Buying time.* He takes the sheet. "I can't say I have."

Droplets of sweat form on his brow. I glance at Kaea; she notices, too.

Doesn't take magic to tell this fool's lying.

I walk around the small wagon, searching, knocking over goods to get a rise. I spot a tear-shaped bottle of black dye and slip it into my pocket.

For a while the merchant stays still. Too still for someone with nothing to hide. He tenses when I near a crate, so I kick down with my foot. Wooden splinters fly. An iron safe is revealed.

"Don't—"

Kaea pushes the merchant against the wall and searches him, tossing a ring of keys my way. I test each in the lock of the hidden safe. *How dare he lie to me.*

When the right key fits, I slam open the vault, expecting to find an incriminating clue. But then I spot the jewels of Amari's headdress. My breath catches in my throat.

The sight takes me back, bringing me to the days when we were kids. The day she first wore this. The moment I hurt her . . .

I wrap myself in the curtains of the palace infirmary. It's a fight to stifle my cries. As I cower, the physicians tending to Amari's wounds expose her back. My stomach twists when I see the sword's slash. Red and raw, the cut rips across her spine. More and more blood leaks by the second.

"I'm sorry," I cry into the curtains, wincing every time the doctor's needles make her scream. "I'm sorry." I ache to shout, "I promise, I'll never hurt you again!"

But no words leave my mouth.

She lies on the bed. Screaming.

Praying for the agony to end.

After hours, Amari lies numb. So drained, she can't even speak. As she moans, her handmaiden Binta slips into her bed, whispering something that somehow draws a smile from Amari's lips.

I listen and watch intently. Binta comforts Amari in a way none of us can. She sings her to sleep with her melodic voice, and when Amari slumbers, Binta takes Mother's old dented tiara and places it on Amari's head. . . .

Not a day passed when Amari didn't wear that tiara. The only fight with Mother she ever won. It would take a gorillion to rip it off her head.

For this to be here, my sister would have to be dead.

I shove Kaea aside and thrust my blade against the merchant's neck.

"Inan—"

I silence Kaea with my hand. This isn't the time for rank or discretion. "Where did you get this?"

"Th-the girl gave it to me!" the merchant croaks. "Yesterday!"

I grab the parchment. "Her?"

"No." The merchant shakes his head. "She was there, but it was another girl. She had copper skin. Bright eyes—eyes like yours!"

Amari.

That means she's still alive.

"What did they buy?" Kaea interrupts.

"A sword . . . some canteens. It seemed like they were going on a trip, like they were heading into the jungle."

Kaea's eyes widen. She rips the parchment out of my hands. "It has to be the temple. Chândomblé."

"How close is it?"

"A full day's ride, but—"

"Let's depart." I grab the headdress and make for the door. "If we ride fast, we can catch them."

"Wait," Kaea calls. "What shall we do with him?"

"Please," the merchant trembles. "I didn't know it was stolen! I pay my taxes on time. I'm loyal to the king!"

I hesitate, staring at the pitiful man.

I know what I'm supposed to say.

I know what Father would do.

"Inan?" Kaea asks. She puts her hand on her blade. I need to give the order. I can't show weakness. *Duty before self.*

"Please!" the merchant begs, latching onto my hesitation. "You can take my cart. You can take everything I have—"

"He's seen too much—" Kaea cuts in.

"Just hold on," I hiss, pulse pounding in my ears. The burnt corpses of Ilorin flash into my mind. The seared flesh. The crying child.

Do it, I push myself. *One kingdom is worth more than one life.*

But too much blood has already been spilled. So much of it by my hands—

Before I can say anything, the merchant sprints for the exit. One hand makes it to the door. Crimson explodes in the air.

Blood splatters across my chest.

The merchant tumbles to the ground, collapsing with a dense thud.

Kaea's throwing knife sticks out of the back of his neck.

After a shuddered breath, the merchant bleeds in silence. Kaea eyes me as she bends down, extracting her knife as if pulling the perfect rose from a garden.

"You mustn't tolerate those who get in your way, Inan." Kaea steps over the corpse, wiping her blade clean. "Especially those who know too much."

CHAPTER SEVENTEEN

AMARI

A HAZE LIFTS from my mind as I blink into consciousness. My vision blurs the past and the present. For a moment, the silver of Binta's eyes shines.

But when the hallucination passes, the flicker of candle flames dances along jagged stone walls. A rodent scurries by my feet and I jolt back. It's only then that I realize I'm bound, tied to Tzain and Zélie with unyielding ropes.

"Guys?" Zélie stirs at my back, sleep dripping from her voice. She twists and turns, but no matter how much she writhes, the ropes do not give.

"Wha'appened?" Tzain's words slur together. He pulls, but even his considerable might doesn't loosen the ropes' hold. For a while his grunts are the only sounds in the cavern. But in time another sound grows louder; we freeze as footsteps near.

"Your sword," Zélie hisses. "Can you reach it?"

My fingers brush against Zélie's as I reach backward for my hilt, but I grasp only air.

"It's gone," I whisper back. "Everything is!"

We scan the dimly lit cave, searching for the brass of my hilt, the gleam of Zélie's staff. Someone's taken all our things. We don't even have the—

"Scroll?" a deep voice booms.

I tense as a middle-aged man appears in the candlelight, dressed in a sleeveless suede robe. White swirls and patterns dot every inch of his dark skin.

Zélie sucks in a quick breath.

"A sêntaro . . ."

"A *what?*" I whisper.

"Who's there?" Tzain growls, straining against the ropes to see. He bares his teeth in defiance.

The mysterious man doesn't even blink.

He leans against a staff carved from stone, gripping the face sculpted into its handle. An undeniable fury burns behind his golden eyes. I begin to think he won't move at all when suddenly he lurches forward; Zélie jumps as the man grasps a lock of her hair.

"Straight," he mutters with a hint of disappointment. "Why?"

"Get your hands off her!" Tzain yells.

Though Tzain poses no threat, the man steps back, releasing Zélie's hair. He pulls the scroll from the band of his robe, and his golden eyes narrow.

"This was taken from my people years ago." His accent hums thick and heavy, different than the Orïshan dialects I've heard. I stare at the unraveled scroll in his hand, recognizing a few symbols on the parchment inked onto his skin. "They stole it from us." His voice takes a violent turn. "I will not let you do the same."

"You are mistaken," I blurt out. "We are not here to steal!"

"Exactly what they said before." He wrinkles his nose at me. "You stink of their blood."

I draw back, shrinking into Tzain's shoulders. The man looks at me with a hatred I cannot deflect.

"She's not lying," Zélie rushes out, voice powered with conviction. "We're different. The gods sent us. A Seer guided us here!"

Mama Agba . . . I think back to her parting words. *We're meant to do this*, I want to cry out. But how can I argue that when right now all I wish was that I had never laid eyes on this scroll?

The sêntaro's nostrils flare. He raises his arms and the air thrums with the threat of magic. *He's going to kill us. . . .* My heart thrashes against my chest. This is where our journey ends.

Father's old warnings ring in my head: *Against magic, we don't stand a chance.* Against magic, we are defenseless.

Against magic, we die—

"I saw what this used to be," Zélie chokes out. "I saw the towers and temples, the sêntaros who looked like you."

The man brings his arms down slowly, and I know Zélie's caught his attention. She swallows hard. I pray to the skies she finds the right words.

"I know they came to your home, destroyed everything you loved. They did the same thing to me. To thousands of people who look like me." Her voice cracks and I close my eyes. Behind me, Tzain goes rigid. My throat dries with the realization of who Zélie's talking about. I was right.

Father destroyed this place.

I think back to all the rubble, the cracked skulls, the hard look in Zélie's gaze. The peaceful village of Ilorin up in flames. The tears streaming down Tzain's face.

The cascade of light that escaped Binta's palm fills my mind, more beautiful than the sun's own rays. Where would I be now if Father had allowed Binta to live? What would all of Orïsha look like if he had just given these maji a chance?

Shame beats down on me, making me want to crawl into myself as the man raises his arms again.

I squeeze my eyes shut in preparation for pain—

The ropes vanish into thin air; our belongings reappear by our sides.

I'm still stunned by the magic when the mysterious man walks away, leaning on his staff. As we rise, he utters a simple command.

"Follow me."

CHAPTER EIGHTEEN

ZÉLIE

WATER DRIPS DOWN the carved walls as we travel deep into the heart of the mountain, accompanied by the rhythmic thud of our guide's staff. Golden candles line the jagged stone, illuminating the darkness with their soft blaze. As my feet pass over the cool rock, I stare at the man, still unable to believe a sêntaro stands before my very eyes. Before the Raid, only the leaders of the ten maji clans ever got to meet them in this life. Mama Agba'll fall out of her seat when I tell her about this.

I nudge Amari aside to step closer to the sêntaro, inspecting the marks inked onto the man's neck. They ripple along his skin with every step, dancing with the shadows of the flame.

"They are called sênbaría," the man answers, somehow sensing my gaze. "The language of the gods, as old as time itself."

So that's what it looks like. I lean forward to study the symbols that would one day become the spoken language of Yoruba, giving us the tongue to cast our magic.

"They're beautiful," I respond.

The man nods. "The things Sky Mother creates always are."

Amari opens her mouth but shuts it quickly, as if thinking better of it. Something bristles inside me as she walks, gaping at things that only the most powerful maji in history have a right to see.

She clears her throat and appears to dig deep, finding her voice once again. "Pardon me," she asks. "But do you have a name?"

The sêntaro turns around and wrinkles his nose. "Everyone has a name, child."

"Oh, I did not mean—"

"Lekan," he cuts her off. "Olamilekan."

The syllables tickle the furthest corners of my brain. "*Olamilekan*," I repeat. "My wealth . . . is increased?"

Lekan turns to me with a gaze so steady I'm convinced he sees into my soul. "You remember our tongue?"

"Bits and pieces." I nod. "My mother taught it to me when I was young."

"Your mother was a Reaper?"

My mouth falls open in surprise. You can't identify a maji's powers on sight alone.

"How did you know?" I ask.

"I can sense it," Lekan answers. "Reaper blood runs thick through your veins."

"Can you sense magic in people who aren't maji or divîners?" The question spills out of me, Inan coming to mind. "Is it possible for kosidán to have magic in their blood?"

"As sêntaros, we do not make that distinction. Everything is possible when it comes to the gods. All that matters is Sky Mother's will."

He turns, leaving me with more questions than answers. What part of Sky Mother's will involves Inan's hands wrapped around my throat?

I try to push thoughts of him away as we move. It feels like we've traveled a full kilometer through the tunnels before Lekan leads us into a dark and wide dome hollowed out in the mountain. He raises his hands with the same gravitas as before, making the air buzz with spiritual energy.

"*Ìmọ́lè àwọn òrìshà*," he chants, the Yoruba incantation flowing from his lips like water. *"Tàn sí mi ní kíá báàyí. Tan ìmọ́lè sí ìpàsẹ̀ awọn ọmọ rẹ!"*

All at once the flames lining the walls go out, just like Tzain's makeshift torch. But in an instant, they reignite with new life, blanketing every inch of stone with light.

"Oh . . ."

"My . . ."

"Gods . . ."

We marvel as we enter the dome decorated with a mural so magnificent I can hardly speak. Each meter of stone is covered in vibrant paints illustrating the ten gods, the maji clans, everything in between. It's so much more than the crude pictures of the gods that used to exist before the Raid, the occasional hidden painting, the rare woven tapestry only brought out under the cover of darkness. Those were flickering rays of light. This mural is like staring at the face of the sun.

"What is this?" Amari breathes, spinning to take in the sights all at once.

Lekan motions us over and I pull Amari along, steadying her when she stumbles. He presses his hands into the stone before answering, "The origin of the gods."

His golden eyes spark and bright energy escapes his palm, feeding into the wall. As the light travels along the paint, the art glows and the figures slowly come to life.

"Skies," Amari curses, gripping my wrist. Magic and light bloom as each painting's soul animates before our eyes.

"In the beginning, our Sky Mother created the heavens and the earth, bringing life to the vast darkness." Bright lights swirl from the palms of the elderly woman I recognize as the statue on the first floor. Her purple robes glide like silk around her regal form as the new worlds spring to life. "On earth, Sky Mother created humans, her children of blood and bone. In the heavens she gave birth to the gods and goddesses. Each would come to embody a different fragment of her soul."

Though I've heard Mama tell this story before, it's never felt as real as it does now. It transcends the realm of fables and myths into actual history. We all stare with wide eyes and open mouths as humans and gods spring from Sky Mother at once. While the humans fall to the brown earth, the newborn deities float into the clouds above.

"Sky Mother loved all her children, each created in her image. To connect us all, she shared her gifts with the gods, and the first maji were born. Each deity took a part of her soul, a magic they were meant to gift to the humans below. Yemọja took the tears from Sky Mother's eyes and became the Goddess of the Sea."

A stunning dark-skinned goddess with vibrant blue eyes drops a single tear onto the world. As it lands, it explodes, creating oceans, lakes, streams.

"Yemọja brought water to her human siblings, teaching those who worshipped her how to control its life. Her pupils studied their sister deity with unrelenting discipline, gaining mastery over the sea."

Birth of the Tiders, I remember suddenly. Above us, the painted members of the Omi Clan twist the waters to their will, making them dance with masterful ease.

Lekan narrates the origin of god after god, explaining each deity and their maji clan as we pass. We learn of Sàngó, who took the fire from Sky Mother's heart to create Burners; Ayao, who took the air from Sky Mother's breath to make Winders. We study nine gods and goddesses until there's only one left.

I wait for Lekan to start speaking, but he turns to me, expectation heavy in his gaze.

"Me?" I step forward, palms sweating as I take his place. This is the part of the story I know best, the tale Mama told me so often even Tzain could recite it. But when I was a child, it was only a myth, a fantasy adults could weave for our young eyes. For the first time the tale feels real, stitched into the very fabric of my life.

"Unlike her sisters and brothers, Oya chose to wait until the end," I speak loudly. "She didn't take from Sky Mother like her siblings. Instead, she asked Sky Mother to give."

I watch as my sister deity moves with the grace of a hurricane, depicted in all her might and brilliance. The obsidian beauty kneels before her mother, red robes flowing like the wind. The sight takes my breath away. Her stance holds a power, a storm brewing beneath her black skin.

"For Oya's patience and wisdom, Sky Mother rewarded her with mastery over life," I continue. "But when Oya shared this gift with her worshippers, the ability transformed to power over death."

My heartbeat quickens as the Reapers of the Ikú Clan display their lethal abilities, the maji I was born to become. Even as paintings, their shadows and spirits soar, commanding armies of the dead, destroying life in storms of ash.

The magical displays take me back to my days in Ibadan, watching the newly elected elders demonstrate their prowess for our Reaper clan. When Mama was elected, the black shadows of death that swirled around her were magnificent. Terrifying, yet stunning as they danced by her side.

In that moment I knew that as long as I lived, I would never see anything as beautiful as that. I only hoped one day I would join her. I wanted her to watch me and feel even half as proud.

"I'm sorry." My throat closes up. Lekan seems to understand at once. With a nod, he steps forward, continuing the tale.

"Oya was the first to realize that not all her children could handle such great power. She became selective, like her mother, sharing her ability with only those who showed patience and wisdom. Her siblings followed suit, and soon the maji population dwindled. In this new era, all maji were graced with coiled white hair, an homage to Sky Mother's image."

I tuck back my straight locks, my cheeks growing hot. Even if I pass for wise, there can't be a god above who thinks I'm patient. . . .

Lekan's gaze turns to the last set of drawings on the heavenly mural, where men and women inked with white symbols kneel and worship.

"To protect the gods' will on this earth, Sky Mother created my people, the sêntaros. Led by the mamaláwo, we act as spiritual guardians, tasked with connecting Sky Mother's spirit to the maji below."

He pauses as the painting of a woman rises above the sêntaros with an ivory dagger in one hand and a glowing stone in the other. Though she's dressed in leather robes like her brothers and sisters, an ornate diadem rests on the mamaláwo's head.

"What is she holding?" I ask.

"The bone dagger," Lekan answers, removing it from his robes. "A sacred relic carved from the skeleton of the first sêntaro." The dagger seems to bathe in a light blue glow, emitting an energy that chills like ice. The same sênbaría inked onto Lekan's arms shine bright against its handle. "Whoever wields it draws strength from the life force of all those who have wielded it before."

"In her right hand the mamaláwo holds the sunstone, a living fragment of Sky Mother's soul. By holding Sky Mother's spirit, the stone tethers her to this world, keeping magic alive. Every century, our mamaláwo carried the stone, the dagger, and the scroll to a sacred temple to perform the binding ritual. By drawing her blood with the dagger and using the power imbued into the stone, the mamaláwo sealed the spiritual connection of the gods into the sêntaros' blood. As long as our bloodline survived, magic did, too."

As the mamaláwo in the mural chants, her words dance across the wall in painted symbols. The ivory dagger drips with her blood. The glow of the sunstone encompasses the entire mural in its light.

"Then that's what happened?" Tzain stares at the mural with dead eyes, rigid in his stance. "She didn't perform the ritual? That's why magic died?"

Though he says *magic*, I hear *Mama* in his voice. This is what left her defenseless.

This is how the king took her away.

The spark vanishes from Lekan's eyes and the paintings lose their animated life. In an instant, the magic of the mural dies, no more than ordinary, dry paint.

"The massacre of the maji—'the Raid,' as your people call it—was not a chance event. Before I went away on pilgrimage, your king entered Chândomblé's temples claiming false worship. In truth, Saran was searching for a weapon against the gods." Lekan turns so we can't see his face, only the symbols inked onto his arms. They seem to shrink as he slumps in the candlelight, withering with his heartache. "He learned of the ritual, of how magic in Orïsha was anchored to the sêntaros' blood. By the time I returned, Saran had slaughtered my people, severing Sky Mother's connection and ripping magic from our world."

Amari clasps her hand to her mouth, silent tears streaking her rosy cheeks. I can't fathom how one man could be so cruel. I don't know what I'd do if that man was my father.

Lekan turns back to us, and in that moment I realize I'll never understand his loneliness, his pain. After the Raid, I still had Tzain and Baba. All he had were skeletons; corpses and silent gods.

"Saran coordinated his massacres, one right after the other. As my people bled on this floor and magic disappeared, he instructed his guards to kill yours."

I close my eyes, willing away the images of fire and blood the Raid calls forth.

Baba's cries as a guard broke his arm.

Mama clawing at the black majacite chain around her neck.

My screams as they dragged her away.

"Why didn't they do something?" Tzain shouts. "Why didn't they stop him?"

I put a hand on his shoulder, squeezing to ease his rage. I know my brother. I know his yells mask the pain.

"My people are tasked with protecting human life. We are not allowed to take it away."

We stand for a long moment with only Amari's sniffles to break the silence. Staring at the painted walls, I begin to realize how far others will go to keep us down.

"But magic's back now, right?" Amari asks, wiping her eyes. Tzain hands her a ripped swatch of his cloak, but his kindness only seems to cause more tears. "The scroll worked for Zélie and Mama Agba," Amari continues. "It transformed my friend, too. If we can bring the scroll to all the divîners in Orïsha, won't that be enough?"

"Saran broke the old connection between the maji and the gods above when he slaughtered the sêntaros. The scroll brings back magic because it has the ability to spark a new connection with the gods, but to make that connection permanent and bring magic back for good, we need to perform the sacred ritual." Lekan pulls out the scroll with reverence. "I spent years searching for the three holy artifacts, almost all of it in vain. I managed to recover the bone dagger, but at times I worried Saran had managed to destroy the others."

"I don't think they can be destroyed," Amari says. "My father ordered his admiral to get rid of the scroll and the sunstone, but he failed."

"Your father's admiral failed because the artifacts cannot be destroyed by human hands. They were given life through magic. Only magic can bring about their death."

"So we can do it?" I press. "We can still bring magic back?"

For the first time, Lekan smiles, hope shining behind his golden eyes. "The centennial solstice is upon us, the tenth centenary of Sky Mother's gifts to mankind. It gives us one last chance to right our wrongs. One last chance to keep magic alive."

"How?" Tzain asks. "What do we have to do?"

Lekan unrolls the scroll, interpreting its symbols and pictures. "On the centennial solstice, a sacred island appears off the northern coast of the Orinion Sea. It is home to the temple of our gods. We must take the scroll, the sunstone, and the bone dagger there and recite the ancient incantation on this scroll. If we complete the ritual, we can create new blood anchors and restore the connection, securing magic for another hundred years."

"And every divîner will become a maji?" Amari asks.

"If you can complete the ritual before the solstice, every divîner who has reached the age of thirteen will transform."

The centennial solstice, I repeat in my head, calculating how much time we have left. Mama Agba's summer graduation always falls on the crescent moon, after the annual tigerfish harvest. If the solstice is upon us . . .

"Wait," Tzain exclaims. "That's less than one moon away!"

"What?" My heart seizes. "What happens if we miss it?"

"Miss it and Orïsha will never see magic again."

My stomach drops like I've been pushed off the mountain. *One moon? One moon or never again?*

"But magic's already coming back." Tzain shakes his head. "It came with the scroll. If we can get it to all the divîners—"

"That will not work," Lekan interrupts. "The scroll does not connect you to Sky Mother. It only ignites your connection to your sister deity. Without the ritual, the magic will not last beyond the solstice. Reestablishing the maji's connection to Sky Mother is the only way."

Tzain pulls out his map, and Lekan charts a course to where the sacred temple will appear. I pray the location is within reach, but Tzain's eyes bulge in alarm.

"Wait," Amari says as she raises her hands. "We have the scroll and the bone dagger, but where is the sunstone?" She eyes his robes expectantly, but no glowing stone comes forth.

"I have been tracking the stone from Warri since it first washed ashore. I was following a lead on it in Ibeji when my spirit called me back here. I have to assume it was so I could meet you."

"So you don't have it?" I ask.

Lekan shakes his head, and Tzain nearly explodes. "Then how are we supposed to do this? Travel alone will take a full moon!"

The answer becomes as stark as the paintings on the wall. The divîners will never become maji. Saran will always be in control.

"Can't you help us?" Amari asks.

"I can aid you." Lekan nods. "But I have limits. Only a woman can become our mamaláwo. I cannot perform the ritual."

"But you have to do it," Amari presses. "You are the only sêntaro left!"

"It does not work like that." Lekan shakes his head. "Sêntaros are not like maji. Your connection to the gods is cemented in your blood. That connection to Sky Mother is what's needed to complete the ritual."

"Then who can do it?"

Lekan looks at me, heavy in his gaze. "A maji. One tethered to the gods."

It takes a moment for Lekan's words to hit; when they do I nearly laugh.

"If Sky Mother brought the scroll to you through a descendant of Saran's blood, her will is clear."

Her will is wrong, I almost shoot back. I can't save the maji. I can barely save myself.

"Lekan, no." My gut clenches the way it did when Amari first grabbed me in the market. "I'm not strong enough. I've never even performed an incantation. You said the scroll only connected me to Oya. I'm not connected to Sky Mother, either!"

"I can amend that."

"Then amend yourself. Amend Tzain!" I push my brother forward. Even Amari would be a better candidate than me.

But Lekan grabs my hand and leads me forward, continuing through the dome. Before I can object, he cuts me off.

"The gods don't make mistakes."

BEADS OF SWEAT GATHER on my forehead as we climb another set of stone steps. We pass stair after stair, ascending toward the top of the mountain. With each step my mind twists and tumbles, reminding me of all the ways this can fail.

Maybe if we already had the sunstone . . .

If the royal guard wasn't breathing down our backs . . .

If Lekan would just get someone else to do the stupid ritual . . .

My chest tightens, suffocating under the threat of failure. Baba's crooked smile returns to my mind, the hope in his eyes. *As long as we don't have magic, they will never treat us with respect.*

We *need* this ritual. It's our only hope. Without it, we'll never get power.

The monarchy will always treat us like maggots.

"We are here."

At last, we reach the top of the stairs and emerge outside into the fading daylight. Lekan leads us to a glittering stone steeple that rises out of the mountaintop, far above the same temple we first entered. Though a few cracked tiles mark the entrance, the site is largely untouched. Towering pillars support the structure, bending into rows of elegant arches.

"Wow," I breathe out, running my fingers along the carved sênbaría marking each column. The symbols glow in the waning sunlight seeping in through the archways.

"Here." Lekan gestures to the only fixture in the steeple, an obsidian tub steaming with clear blue water. The liquid begins to bubble as he nears, though no flames dance in sight.

"What is this?"

"Your awakening. When I am done, your spirit will be re-tethered to Sky Mother's."

"You can do that?" Amari asks.

Lekan nods, the ghost of a smile tickling his lips. "It was my duty with my people. I trained for it all my life." He clasps his hands together, gaze soft and unfocused. Then suddenly he shifts, eyeing Tzain and Amari.

"You must leave." He gestures to them. "I've already broken centuries of tradition by letting you come this far. I cannot allow you to observe our most sacred ritual."

"Like hell you can't." Tzain steps in front of me, muscles flexing in challenge. "I'm not leaving you alone with my sister."

"You should stay," Amari whispers. "I have no right to see this—"

"No." Tzain extends his hand in front of Amari, stopping her before she can scurry down the stone steps. "Stay. No us, no ritual."

Lekan purses his lips. "If you stay, you are bound to secrecy."

"We vow." Tzain waves his hand. "We won't say anything."

"Do not take this vow lightly," Lekan warns. "The dead won't."

Lekan shifts his glare to Amari; she all but melts. He only relents to grasp the rim of the obsidian tub. The water instantly boils under his touch.

My throat goes dry as I approach the tub and a new wave of steam hits my face. Oya, help me. I can't even sell a fish without causing the destruction of my entire village. How am I supposed to be the maji's only hope?

"If I agree to this, you must awaken others."

Lekan stifles a frustrated breath. "Sky Mother brought you here—"

"Please, Lekan. You have to. I can't be the only one."

Lekan clicks his tongue and ushers me toward the tub. "Fine," he concedes. "But I must awaken you first."

I take a tentative step into the tub, sliding in slowly until water covers all but my head. My clothes float around me as the heat soothes my every limb, kissing the strain of today's climb away.

"Let us begin."

Lekan takes my right hand and removes the bone dagger from the folds of his robe.

"To unlock divine power, we must sacrifice that which is most divine to us."

"You're using blood magic?" Tzain steps toward me, body stiff with fear.

"Yes," Lekan says, "but your sister will be safe. I will keep it under control."

My heartbeat quickens, remembering Mama's withered body after she used blood magic for the first time. The boundless power ripped her muscles apart. Even with the aid of Healers, it took her a full moon to regain her ability to walk.

It was a risk she took to save Tzain when he nearly drowned as a child, a sacrifice that allowed him to cling to life. But in sacrificing herself, she nearly died.

"You'll be safe," Lekan assures me, seeming to read my thoughts. "This isn't like when maji use blood magic. Sêntaros have the ability to guide it."

I nod, though a dull spike of fear still pricks at my throat.

"Forgive me," Lekan says. "This may hurt."

I inhale a sharp breath as he slashes through the palm of my hand, gritting my teeth against the sting as blood begins to seep out. The pain turns into shock when my blood glows with a white light.

When it drips into the water, I feel something leave me, something deeper than a simple cut. The red droplets turn the clear blue liquid white; it boils even harder as more blood falls.

"Now relax." Lekan's booming voice drops to a soft timbre. My eyes flutter closed. "Clear your head, take deep breaths. Release yourself from your worldly tethers."

I bite back a retort. There are too many tethers to count. The flames of Ilorin lick my mind, the echoes of Bisi's screams ring in my ears. The prince's hands wrap around my throat. Squeezing. Tighter.

But as my body soaks in the heated water, the strains start to fade. Baba's safety . . . Inan's fury . . . One by one each burden sinks. They leave me in waves until even Mama's death seems to evaporate in the steam.

"Good," Lekan soothes. "Your spirit is being cleansed. Remember, whatever you feel, I will be here."

He places one hand on my forehead and another on my sternum before he chants. *"Ọmọ Mama, Arábìnrin Ọ̀yà. Sí ẹ̀bùn iyebíye rẹ̀. Tú idán mímọ́ rẹ sílẹ̀."*

A strange power whirls around my skin. The water boils with a new intensity and my breath hitches as its heat takes hold.

"Ọmọ Mama—"

Daughter of Sky Mother, I repeat in my head.

"Arábìnrin Ọ̀yà—"

Sister of Oya.

"Sí ẹ̀bùn iyebíye rẹ̀—"

Bare your precious gift.

"Tú idán mímọ́ rẹ sílẹ̀."

Release your holy magic.

The air above us tingles with electric energy, stronger than anything I've felt before. It surpasses the buzz of Inan's imprinting, eclipses the surge of touching the parchment for the first time. The tips of my fingers grow warm, igniting with white light. As Lekan chants, the power travels through my veins, making them glow beneath my skin.

"Ọmọ Mama, Arábìnrin Ọ̀yà—"

The louder his incantation rings, the more my body reacts. The magic overwhelms every cell in my being, pulsing as Lekan submerges my head beneath the water. My skull presses against the floor of the tub, and a new kind of air catches in my throat. I finally understand Mama Agba's words.

It's like breathing for the first time.

"Ọmọ Mama—"

Veins bulge against my skin as the magic grows, a swell about to burst. Behind my eyes, sheets of red dance around me, crashing like waves, spinning like hurricanes.

As I lose myself in their beautiful chaos, a glimpse of Oya emerges. Fire and wind dance around her like spirits, spinning like the red silks of her skirt.

"Arábìnrin Ọ̀yà—"

Her dance transfixes me, igniting everything that I never realized was trapped inside of me. It scorches through my body like a flame, yet chills my skin like ice, flowing in uncharted waves.

"*Sí ẹ̀bùn iyebíye rẹ̀!*" Lekan shouts above the water. "*Tú idán mímọ́ rẹ sílẹ̀!*"

In one final surge, the tsunami breaks free and magic flows through every inch of my being. It inks itself into each cell, staining my blood, filling my mind. In its power I glimpse the beginning and end at once, the unbreakable connections tethering all of our lives.

The red of Oya's wrath whirls around me.

The silver of Sky Mother's eyes shines. . . .

"ZÉLIE!"

I blink open my eyes to find Tzain shaking me by the shoulders.

"You okay?" he asks, leaning over the edge of the tub.

I nod, but I can't bring myself to speak. There are no words. Only the prickling sensation left behind.

"Can you stand?" Amari asks.

I try to push myself up out of the bath, but as soon as I do, the entire world spins.

"Be still," Lekan instructs. "Your body needs rest. Blood magic drains your life force."

Rest, I repeat. Rest with time we don't have. If Lekan's lead on the location of the sunstone is right, we need to head to Ibeji to find it. I can't complete the ritual without the stone, and we're already running out of time. The solstice is only three quarter moons away.

"You must spare one night," Lekan presses, somehow sensing my urgency. "Awakening magic is like adding a new sense. Your body needs time to adjust to the strain."

I nod and close my eyes, slumping against the cold stone. *Tomorrow you'll start. Head to Ibeji, find the stone. Go to the sacred island. Perform the ritual.*

I repeat the plan again and again, letting its repetition lull me to sleep. *Ibeji. Stone. Island. Ritual.*

With time my mind fades into a soft blackness, seconds away from sleep. I'm almost out when Lekan seizes my shoulders and drags me to my feet.

"Someone is coming," Lekan shouts. "Quick! We must go!"

CHAPTER NINETEEN

INAN

—*Drag us halfway across the world*—

—*why can't they just tell us what she stole*—

—*if that bastard thinks I'm willing to die on this cliff*—

"Inan, slow down!" Kaea calls from below. It takes a moment to realize she's not just another voice in my head.

The closer I get to Chândomblé, the louder they become.

Curse the skies. The guards' complaints buzz like honeybees sparring inside my skull. Though I want to block them out, I can't afford to push my curse down; even the slightest efforts cause my legs to slip from the cliff.

The bite of magic twists everything inside me, a virus destroying me from the inside out. But I have no choice. I cannot climb and weaken myself.

I have to let the darkness in.

It stings worse than the burn that sears in my chest when I fight my powers down. Each time a foreign thought hits me, my skin crawls. Every flash of another's emotion makes my lips curl.

Magic slithers inside me. Venomous, like a thousand spiders crawling over my skin. It wants more of me. The curse wants to fight its way in—

With a lurch, my foothold crumbles.

Stones at my feet tumble like an avalanche.

I grunt as my body is slammed flat against the wall, my feet flailing for a new hold.

"Inan!" Kaea's shouts from the ledge below. More of a distraction than an aid. She waits with the ryders and other soldiers while I stake out a path.

Rope and flint slip from pockets of my belt as I swing. Amari's headdress slides as well.

No!

Though it's a risk, I release my left hand, catching the headdress before it evades my grasp. As my feet discover new footing, memories I can't fight swell to the surface.

"*Strike, Amari!*"

Father's command boomed against the stone walls of the palace cellar. Deep underground, where his commands were law. Amari's small hands shook, barely strong enough to lift the iron sword.

It wasn't like the wooden swords he forced us to spar with, dull blades that bruised but never cut. The iron was sharp. Jagged at its edge. With the right strike, we wouldn't just bruise.

We'd bleed.

"*I said, strike!*" Father's yells were like thunder. A command no one could defy. Yet Amari shook her head. She let her sword fall.

I flinched as it clattered against the ground. Harsh and piercing. Defiance ringing in every sound.

Pick it up! I wanted to scream.

At least if she struck, I could defend myself.

"*Strike, Amari.*"

Father's voice hit an octave so low it could crack stone.

Yet Amari clutched herself and turned away. Tears streamed down her face. All Father saw was weakness. After all this time, I think it might have been strength.

Father turned to me, face dark, flickering in the shadows of the torchlight.

"Your sister chooses herself. As king, you must choose Orïsha."

All the air vanished from the room. The walls closed in. Father's orders echoed in my head. His commands to fight against myself.

"Strike, Inan!" Rage flared in his eyes. *"You must fight now!"*

Amari screamed and covered her ears. Everything in me wanted to run to her side. Protect her. Save her. Promise we would never have to fight.

"Duty before self!" Father's voice went hoarse. *"Show me you can be king!"*

In that moment, everything stopped.

I lunged forward with my sword.

"Inan!"

Kaea's barks pull me back, breaking through the depths of my memories.

I press against the mountainside, one foot still dangling. With a grunt, I continue my climb, not stopping until I reach the next ledge. Sweat pours from my body as I rub my thumb over the ornate seal in Amari's headdress.

We never spoke of it. Not once. Even after all these years. Amari was too kind to bring it up. I, far too scared.

We carried on, an invisible chasm always between us. Amari never had to go back to that cellar. I never left.

Though my muscles shake, I pocket the headdress. There's no time to waste. I failed my sister once. I shall not repeat that mistake again.

As I rise, the maji's spirit pulses like never before. A surge she can't control. The sea-salt scent of her soul is so strong it overwhelms the clove smell of bromeliads under my nose. I pause when I notice the flattened stems at my feet.

Tracks . . .

She's been here.

She's close.

I'm close.

Kill her, my heart thrums as I claw at the mountain ledge. *Kill her. Kill magic.*

When the girl's finally in my grasp, this will all be worth it. I shall take my kingdom back.

Amari's headdress pokes my side as I continue to rise. I couldn't save her from Father then. But today, I shall save her from herself.

CHAPTER TWENTY

ZÉLIE

"FASTER!" LEKAN CALLS as we run through the temple halls. Tzain carries me over his shoulders, grip tight around my waist.

"Who is it?" Amari asks, though the quiver in her voice suggests she already knows. Her brother's scarred her once. Who's to say it won't happen again?

"My staff," I moan. It takes every ounce of energy to speak. But I need it to fight. I need it to keep us alive.

"You can barely stand." Tzain catches me before I slide from his back. "Shut up. And for gods' sakes, try to hold on!"

We come to a dead end in the hall, and Lekan presses his palm to the stone. The inked symbols dance across his skin and travel into the wall. When his right arm is wiped clean of sênbaría, the stone clicks, sliding open to a golden room. We step into the hidden wonder, filled floor to ceiling with shelves of thin, colored scrolls.

"Do we hide here?" Tzain asks.

Lekan disappears behind a large shelf before returning with an armful of black scrolls. "We're here to retrieve these incantations," he explains. "Her powers will need maturation if she is to perform the mamaláwo's role."

Before Tzain can object, Lekan shoves them into my leather pack with the ritual parchment.

"Alright," Lekan says. "Follow me!"

With Lekan's guidance, we twist around the corners of the temple with new speed, descending endless flights of stairs. Another wall slides open and we emerge on the side of the tarnished temple, greeting the jungle heat.

In the dying sunlight, my head throbs. The entire mountain screams with life. Though a buzz of spiritual energy hummed before, now the temple grounds overwhelm me with haunted shrieks and cries. The shadowlike spirits of the slaughtered sêntaros swirl around my body like magnets finding their way home.

Awakening magic is like adding a new sense. Lekan's words resurface. *Your body needs time to adjust.*

Only the adjustment doesn't come. Magic crushes every other sense, making it almost impossible to see. My vision blacks in and out as Tzain scurries through the rubble. Lekan is about to lead us into the jungle brush when it hits me.

"Nailah!"

"Wait," Tzain whispers after Lekan, skidding to a halt. "Our lionaire's out front."

"We cannot risk it—"

"No!" I cry out. Tzain presses his hand against my mouth to stifle the sound. Guards or not, I will not abandon Nailah. I won't leave my oldest friend behind.

Lekan releases a frustrated sigh, but we creep back to the temple. My vision fades in as he motions us close, pressing against the side of the temple to peer out front.

Across the graveyard of skulls and ruins, I see Inan reach down, aiding his admiral as their remaining soldiers urge their ryders over the final ledge. There's a crazed drive in his eyes, a desire to find us that runs deeper than before. I look for the prince who trembled in his dreamscape. Instead all I see are the hands that wrapped around my throat.

Ahead of Inan, three guards kick over crumbled stones and broken bones. They're close.

Too close for us to hide.

"Sùn, ẹ̀mí ọkàn, sùn. Sùn, ẹ̀mí ọkàn, sùn." Lekan weaves an incantation under his breath like a needle through thread, moving his staff in circles. The words summon a coil of white smoke that twists and swirls through the air.

Sleep, spirit, sleep, I translate. *Sleep, spirit, sleep* . . .

We watch as the coil slithers along the ground like a snake. It wraps itself around the leg of the closest guard, squeezing until it seeps into his skin. The guard lurches forward, stumbling down behind a pile of stones. His eyes flash white with Lekan's spirit before rolling into unconsciousness.

The white coil slithers out of his body and incapacitates the next soldier by the same means. As he goes down, Inan and the admiral pull the vicious snow leopanaire over the edge.

"Lekan," Amari hisses, beads of sweat forming on her brow. At this speed we won't make it.

They'll find us before we get out.

Lekan chants faster and faster, moving his staff as if stirring tubani in an iron pot. The spirit slithers toward the final guard, seconds away from Nailah. Her yellow eyes glint with a predator's malice. *No, Nailah. Please—*

"*Agh!*" The guard's ear-shattering cry rings through the air. Flocks of birds soar into the sky. Blood spurts from his thigh as Nailah releases her giant fangs.

Inan whips around, death raging in his eyes. They land on me and narrow; a predator who's finally caught his prey.

"Nailah!"

My lionaire bounds across the destroyed ruins, reaching us in mere beats. Tzain hoists my body into the saddle before everyone else scrambles on.

Tzain snaps her reins as Inan and the admiral draw their swords. Before they can reach us, Nailah takes off, zipping across the mountainside. Broken stones tumble under her paws as she flees, clattering off the narrow ledge.

"There!" Lekan points to the jungle's thick underbrush. "There is a bridge a few kilometers ahead. If we get across and cut it, they will not be able to follow!"

Tzain snaps Nailah's reins and she tears through the jungle at breakneck speed, dodging vines and massive trees. Peering through the underbrush, I spot the bridge in the distance, but a menacing roar reminds me that Inan is right on our tail. I sneak a glance behind me. Thick branches snap against his snow leopanaire's massive frame as she rips through the underbrush. She bares her ghastly teeth as she nears, hungry like her master.

"Amari!" Inan yells.

Amari tenses and squeezes me tight. "Go faster!"

Nailah already sprints faster than I've ever seen her go, but somehow she finds the strength to push. Her bounds lengthen our life, creating needed distance between us and our pursuers.

We break through the underbrush and skid to a halt before the rickety bridge. Withered vines string together the rotted wood; with a gust of wind the entire structure quakes.

"One by one," Lekan orders. "It will not hold us all. Tzain, guide Zélie—"

"No." I slide to the ground, almost collapsing when I hit the dirt. My legs feel like water, but I compel myself to be strong. "Nailah first—she'll take the longest."

"Zél—"

"Go!" I scream. "We're running out of time!"

Tzain grits his teeth and grabs Nailah by the reins. He guides her across the creaking bridge, cringing as the wood moans with every step. The second they make it across, I push Amari forward, but she doesn't let go of my arm.

"You are weak," she chokes out. "You will not make it alone."

She pulls me onto the bridge, and my stomach flips when I make the mistake of looking down. Beneath the panels of decaying wood, sharp rocks shoot toward the sky, threatening to impale anyone unlucky enough to fall.

I shut my eyes and grip the jungle vines. They're already splintered and frayed. Terror grips my chest so tightly I can't even breathe.

"Look at me!" Amari commands, forcing my eyes open. Though her own body quakes, fierce determination flares in her amber gaze. My vision blacks out and she grabs my hand, forcing me forward plank by moaning plank. We're halfway across when Inan bursts through the thick underbrush, the admiral following moments later.

It's too late. We won't make it—

"Àgbájọ ọwọ́ àwọn òrìṣà!" Lekan slams his staff into the ground. *"Yá mi ní agbára à rẹ!"*

His body explodes with a powerful white glow that surrounds the ryders' bodies. He drops his staff and raises his arms. With them, the beasts rise into the sky.

Inan and his admiral cry out as they slide off the backs of their leopanaires, their eyes wide with horror. Lekan throws back his arms, sending each ryder flying off the cliff.

Oh my gods . . .

Their massive bodies writhe and twist. They claw at the sky. But their roars meet a sharp end as they're pierced by rocks.

A terrified rage takes hold of the admiral. With a guttural scream, she jumps to her feet and races toward Lekan with her sword.

"You maggot—"

She lunges forward only to be trapped in place by Lekan's magic. Inan rushes to her aid, but he too is caught in the white light—another fly in Lekan's web.

"Run!" Lekan shouts, veins bulging against his skin. Amari pulls me forward as fast as she can, though the bridge weakens with our every step.

"Go," I order her. "It can't hold us both!"

"You cannot—"

"I'll make it." I force my eyes open. "Just run. If you don't, we'll both fall!"

Amari's eyes glisten, but there's not a moment to waste. She bounds across the bridge and leaps onto the ledge, crashing onto the other side.

Though my legs shake, I push forward, dragging myself along the vine. *Come on.* Lekan's life is on the line.

A terrifying creak escapes the bridge, but I keep moving. I'm almost to the other side. I'm going to make it—

The vines snap.

My stomach flies into my throat as the bridge collapses under my feet. My arms flail, desperate to grab on to anything. I latch onto a plank as the bridge smacks against the stone cliff.

"Zélie!"

Tzain's voice is hoarse as he peeks over the ledge. My body quivers as I cling to the stone panel. Even now I hear it splintering. I know it won't hold.

"Climb!"

Through my blackening, tear-filled vision, I see how the broken bridge has formed a ladder. Three planks are all I need to reach Tzain's outstretched hands.

Three planks between life and death.

Climb! I order myself, but my body doesn't move. *Climb!* I scream again. *Move! Go now!*

With a trembling hand, I grip the plank above and pull myself up.

One.

I grab the next plank and pull again, heart in my throat when another vine snaps.

Two.

Just one plank to go. *You can do it. You didn't come this far to die.* I reach for the final panel.

"No!"

The plank snaps beneath my grip.

Time passes in an instant and an eternity. Wind whips at my back with fury, twisting me toward my grave. I close my eyes to greet death.

"Ugh!"

A thundering force crushes my body, knocking the air from my chest. White light wraps around my skin—*Lekan's magic.*

Like the hand of a god, the strength of his spirit lifts me, propelling me into Tzain's arms. I turn to face him just as the admiral breaks from his hold.

"Lekan—"

The admiral's sword plunges through Lekan's heart.

His eyes bulge and his mouth falls open. His staff drops from his hand.

Lekan's blood splatters as it hits the ground.

"No!" I scream.

The admiral yanks out her sword. Lekan collapses, ripped from our world in an instant. As his spirit leaves his body, it surges into mine. For a moment, I see the world through his eyes.

—running through the temple grounds with the sêntaro children, a glee like

no other alight in his golden gaze—his body steadies as the mamaláwo inks every part of his skin, painting the beautiful symbols in white—his soul rips, again and again, traveling through the massacred ruins of his people—his spirit soars like never before as he performs his first and only awakening—

As the vision ends, one whisper endures, a word teetering through the blackness of my mind.

"*Live*," his spirit breathes. "*Whatever you do, survive.*"

CHAPTER TWENTY-ONE

INAN

BEFORE TODAY, magic didn't have a face.

Not beyond beggars' tales and the hushed undertones of servants' stories. It died eleven years ago. It only lived in the fear in Father's eyes.

Magic didn't breathe. It didn't strike or attack.

Magic didn't kill my ryders and trap me inside its grasp.

I peer over the ledge of the cliff; Lula's body slumps, impaled on a jagged rock. Her eyes hang open in an empty stare. Blood stains her spotted coat. As a child I watched Lula rip through a savage gorillion twice her size.

In the face of magic, she couldn't even fight.

"One . . . ," I whisper to myself, leaning away from the ghastly sight. "Two . . . three . . . four . . . five . . ."

I will the numbers to slow my pulse, but my heart only beats harder in my chest. There are no moves. No counterattacks.

In the face of magic we become ants.

I watch a line of the six-legged creatures until I feel something sticky under the metal heel of my boot. I scoot back and follow the crimson droplets to the maji's corpse; blood still leaks from his chest.

I study him, really seeing the maji for the first time. Alive, he looked three times his actual size, a beast shrouded in white. The symbols that covered his dark skin glowed as he threw our ryders through the air. With his death, the symbols have vanished. Without them, he looks strangely human. Strangely empty.

But even dead, his corpse wraps a chill around my throat. He held my life in his hands.

He had every chance to throw it away.

My thumb grazes over Father's tarnished pawn, my skin prickling as I back away from his body. *I understand now, Father.*

With magic we die.

But without it . . .

My gaze drifts back to the dead man, to the hands gifted by the heavens, stronger than the earth. Orïsha cannot survive that kind of power. But if I used it to get the job done . . .

A bitter tang crawls onto my tongue as the new strategy takes hold. Their magic is a weapon; mine could be one, too. If there are maji who can fling me from a cliff with a wave of their hand, magic is my only chance of getting the scroll back.

But the very thought makes my throat close up. If Father were here . . .

I look down at the pawn. I can almost hear his voice in my head.

Duty before self.

No matter the cost or collateral.

Even if it's a betrayal of everything I know, my duty to protect Orïsha comes first. I release my hold on the pawn.

For the first time, I let go.

It starts slowly. Broken. Crawling limb by limb. The pressure in my chest is released. The magic I force down starts to stir underneath my skin. At the pulsing sensation, my stomach lurches, churning through every ounce of my disgust. But our enemies will use this magic against us.

If I'm to fulfill my duty and save my kingdom, I must do the same.

I sink into the warm thrum pulsing from within. Slowly, a cloud of the maji's consciousness appears. Wispy and blue like the others, twisting above his head. As I touch it with my hand, the dead man's essence hits first: a tinged scent. Rustic. Like burnt timber and coal.

My lips curl as I sink into his lingering psyche, reaching for it instead of running away. A single memory begins to flicker into my mind. A quiet day when his temple teemed with life. He ran across the manicured grass, hand in hand with a young boy.

The more I release the hold on my magic, the bigger the flicker grows. A whiff of clean mountain air fills my nose. A distant song rings through my ears. Each detail becomes rich and robust. As if the memory stored in his consciousness is my own.

With time, new knowledge begins to settle. A soul. A name. Something simple . . .

Lekan—

Metal heels clank against the stone cliff.

Skies! With a start, I force my magic down.

The smell of timber and coal vanishes in an instant. A sharp pain in my stomach reappears in its stead.

I pinch the bridge of my nose as my head reels from the whiplash. Moments later Kaea emerges from the thick underbrush.

Sweat-soaked hair sticks to her brown skin, now splattered with Lekan's blood. As she nears, I reach up to make sure my helmet is still covering my head. That was far too close. . . .

"There's no way across," she sighs, sitting down beside me. "I scouted a full kilometer. With the bridge destroyed, we can't travel between this mountain and the next."

Figures. In the brief flicker I got of Lekan, I guessed as much. He was intelligent. He pursued the only path that would allow them to escape.

"I told him not to do this." Kaea removes her black breastplate. "I knew this wouldn't work." She shuts her eyes. "He will blame me for their resurgence. He'll never look at me the same way again."

I know the look she speaks of; like she's the sun, and he the sky. It's the gaze Father reserves for her. The one he shares when he thinks they're alone.

I lean away and pick at my boot, unsure of what to say. Kaea never breaks down in front of me. Before today, I thought she never broke at all.

In her despair, I see my own. My concession, my defeat. But that is not my place. I must be a stronger king.

"Stop moping," I snap. We haven't lost the war yet.

Magic has a new face.

That simply means I must attack with a new blade.

"There's a guard post east of Sokoto," I say. *Find the maji. Find the scroll.* "We can send word of the collapsed bridge with your firehawk. If they dispatch a legion of stock laborers, we can build another one."

"Brilliant." Kaea buries her face in her hands. "Let's make it easier for the maggots to return and kill us when their powers are restored."

"We'll find them before that happens." *I'll kill her.*

I'll save us.

"With what leads?" Kaea asks. "Getting the men and supplies alone will take days. Building it—"

"Three days," I cut her off. *How dare she question my reasoning?* Admiral or not, Kaea cannot defy an order from me.

"If they work through the night, they can get it done," I continue. "I've seen stockers construct palaces with less."

"What use will a bridge be, Inan? Even if we build it, there'll be no trace of that maggot by the time it's done."

I pause and look across the cliff. The sea-salt scent of the girl's soul is almost gone, fading in the jungle's underbrush. Kaea's right. A bridge shall only take us so far. By nightfall, I won't be able to sense the divîner at all.

Unless . . .

I turn back to the temple, recalling the way it made voices surge in my head. If it could do that, perhaps it can allow my magic to sense more.

"Chândomblé." I shift the sênet pieces around in my mind. "They came here for answers. Maybe I can find some, too."

Yes, that's it. If I discover what's amplifying my curse, I can use it to pick up the girl's trail. Just this once.

"Inan—"

"It'll work," I interrupt. "Summon the stockers and lead the construction while I search. There will be traces of the girl there. I'll uncover the clues to where they're headed."

I pocket Father's pawn; in its absence, the air hits cold against my skin. This fight is not over yet. The war has only begun.

"Send a message and gather a team. I want those laborers on this ledge by dawn."

"Inan, as captain—"

"I'm not addressing you as your captain," I cut her off. "I'm commanding you as your prince."

Kaea stiffens.

Something between us breaks, but I force my gaze to stay even. Father wouldn't tolerate her fragility.

Neither can I.

"Fine." She presses her lips into a tight line. "Your desire is my command."

As she stalks away, I see the maji's face in my mind. Her wretched voice. The silver eyes.

I stare across the void to where her sea-salt soul has disappeared among the jungle trees.

"Keep running," I whisper.

I'm coming for you.

CHAPTER TWENTY-TWO

AMARI

Back home at the palace, every window in my quarters only allowed me to look in. Father had the new wing constructed right after I was born, insistent that every window could only face the courtyard. The most I could see of the outside world was the leopard orchids of the royal garden in full bloom. *The palace is all you need to be concerned with*, Father would say when I begged him for a different view. *Orïsha's future is decided within these walls. As princess, yours will be, too.*

I tried to hold on to his words, allow palace life to satiate me the way it did Mother. I made an effort to socialize with the other oloyes and their daughters. I attempted to find entertainment in palace gossip. But at night, I used to sneak into Inan's quarters and climb out to the balcony overlooking our capital. I would imagine what lay beyond the wooden walls of Lagos, the beautiful world I longed to see.

One day, I would whisper to Binta.

One day, indeed. She would smile back.

As I dreamed, I never imagined the hell of the jungle, all the mosquitoes and sweat and jagged stones. But after four days in the desert, I'm convinced there's no limit to the hells Orïsha can hold. The desert provides no foxer meat to eat, no water or coconut milk to drink. All it gifts us with is sand.

Endless mountains of sand.

Despite the scarf wrapped so tightly around my face I can barely breathe, grains settle in my mouth, my nose, my ears. Their persistence is matched only by the scorching sun, a final touch to this bleak wasteland. The longer we travel through it, the more my fingers itch to grab Nailah's reins and yank her the other way. But even if we turned around now, where in skies' name would I go?

My own brother hunts me. Father probably desires my head. I can hardly fathom all the lies Mother's spinning in my absence. Perhaps if Binta was still at the palace, I would risk crawling back with my tail between my legs. But even she's gone.

This sand is all I have left.

Sadness swells inside me as I close my eyes and picture her face. Just a brief thought of her is almost enough to take me away from the hell of this desert. If she were here, she'd be smiling, laughing at the grains of sand that got stuck between her teeth. She'd find beauty in all of this. Binta found the beauty in everything.

Before I can stop myself, my thoughts of Binta take me further, bringing me back to our days in the palace. One morning, when we were young, I snuck her into Mother's quarters, eager to show her my favorite jewels. As I climbed onto the vanity, I rambled on and on about the villages Inan was going to see on his military visits.

"*It's not fair,*" I whined. "*He'll go all the way to Ikoyi. He's going to* see *the actual sea.*"

"*You'll get your chance.*" Binta stayed back, hands clamped to her side. No matter how many times I motioned for her to join me, she insisted she couldn't.

"One day." I draped Mother's prized emerald necklace over my head, captivated by the way it glimmered in the mirror's light. "*What about you?*" I asked. *"When we leave, what village do you want to see?"*

"Anything." Binta's eyes lost focus. *"Everything."* She bit her bottom lip as a smile came to her face. *"I think I'd love it all. No one in my family has ever traveled past Lagos's walls."*

"Why not?" I wrinkled my nose and rose to my feet, reaching for the case that held Mother's antique headdress. It sat just above my reach. I leaned forward.

"Amari, don't!"

Before Binta's words could stop me, I lost my balance. With a jolt, I knocked the case over. It took all of two seconds before everything else came tumbling to the floor.

"Amari!"

I'll never know how Mother arrived so quickly. Her voice echoed under the arched entrance of her room as she took in the mess I had made.

When I couldn't speak, it was Binta who stepped forward. *"My deepest apologies, Your Highness. I was told to polish your jewelry. Princess Amari was only coming to my aid. If you must punish someone, it should be me."*

"You lazy brat." Mother snatched up Binta's wrist. *"Amari is a princess. She is not here to do your chores!"*

"Mother, that's not—"

"Quiet," Mother snapped, snarling as she dragged Binta away. *"It's clear we've been too lenient with you. You'll benefit from the teachings of a whip."*

"No, Mother! Wait—"

Nailah stumbles, pulling me from the depths of my guilt. Binta's young face fades out of my mind as Tzain struggles to keep us from collapsing down a mountain of sand. I grip the leather stirrups as Zélie leans down and rubs Nailah's fur.

"I'm sorry, girl," Zélie soothes. "I promise, we'll be there soon."

"Are you sure?" My voice comes out dry, as brittle as the sand surrounding us. But I can't tell if the lump in my throat is from the lack of water or the memory of Binta.

"We're close." Tzain turns back, squinting to keep out the sun. Even with his eyes nearly shut, his deep brown gaze holds me, making my cheeks flush. "If we don't get there today, we'll hit Ibeji tomorrow."

"But what if the sunstone isn't in Ibeji?" Zélie asks. "What if Lekan's lead was wrong? We only have thirteen days until the solstice. If it's not here, we're damned."

He can't be wrong. . . .

The thought makes my empty stomach lurch. All the determination I felt in Chândomblé crumbles. *Skies.* All of this would be so much easier if Lekan were still alive. With his guidance and magic, Inan pursuing us wouldn't be a threat. We'd have a chance to find the sunstone. We might already be on our way to the sacred island to perform the ritual.

But with Lekan gone, we're no closer to saving the maji. If anything, we're just running out of time. Marching toward our deaths.

"Lekan wouldn't lead us astray. It's here." Tzain pauses, craning his neck. "And unless that's a mirage, so are we."

Zélie and I peer past Tzain's broad shoulders. Heat bounces off the sand in waves, blurring the horizon, but in time a cracked clay wall crystallizes into view. To my surprise, we're only three of many travelers making their way into the desert city from all directions. Unlike us, several of the migrating parties travel in caravans crafted from reinforced timber and embellished with gold, vehicles so adorned they have to belong to nobles.

A pulse of excitement travels through me as I narrow my eyes to get a closer look. When I was a child, I once overheard Father warn his generals about the dangers of the desert, a land overpowered with Grounders. He claimed their magic could transform every single grain of sand into a lethal weapon. Later that night I told Binta what I learned as she combed through the tangles of my hair.

That's not true, she corrected me. *The Grounders in the desert are peaceful. They use their magic to create settlements from the sand.*

In that moment I pictured what a sand city could look like, unrestrained by the laws and materials governing our architecture. If Grounders really did rule the desert, their magnificent cities have crumbled, disappearing alongside them.

But after four days in the ghastly desert, the meager settlement of Ibeji shimmers. The first sign of hope in this wretched wasteland. *Thank the skies.*

Perhaps we shall survive after all.

Shanty tents and clay ahérés greet us when we make our way past the wall. Like the slum dwellings of Lagos, the sand huts are stout and square, soaking in the rays of the sun. The largest of the ahérés looms in the distance, bearing a seal I know all too well. The carved snow leopanaire flickers in the sun, its sharp fangs bared to bite.

"A guard post," I croak, tensing in Nailah's saddle. Though the royal seal is etched into the clay wall, it waves in my mind like the velvet banners in Father's throne room. After the Raid, he abolished the old seal, a gallant bull-horned lionaire that always used to make me feel safe. Instead, he proclaimed that our power would be represented by the snow leopanaires: ryders who were ruthless. Pure.

"Amari," Zélie hisses, snapping me out of my thoughts. She dismounts Nailah and wraps her scarf tighter around her face, urging me to do the same.

"Let's split up." Tzain slides off Nailah's back and hands us his canteen. "We shouldn't be spotted together. You guys get water. I'll find a place to stay."

Zélie nods and walks off, but once again Tzain holds my gaze.

"You okay?"

I force a nod, though I cannot bring myself to speak. One glimpse of the royal seal and it's like my throat has been filled with sand.

"Just stay close to Zélie."

Because you are weak, I imagine him spitting, though his dark eyes are kind. *Because despite the sword you carry, you cannot protect yourself.*

He gives my arm a gentle squeeze before taking Nailah by the reins and walking her in the opposite direction. I stare after his broad figure, fighting my desire to follow until Zélie hisses my name.

This will be fine. I put a smile in my eyes, though Zélie doesn't even look my way. I thought things were starting to ease between us after Sokoto, but whatever goodwill I earned was crushed the minute my brother showed up at the temple. For the past four days Zélie has barely spoken to me, as if I'm the one who killed Lekan. The only times she does seem to look at me, I catch her staring at my back.

I stay close as we continue down the empty streets, searching for food in vain. My throat screams for a cold cup of water, a fresh loaf of bread, a nice cut of meat. But unlike the merchant quarter of Lagos, there are no colorful storefronts, no displays of succulent delights. The town appears almost as starved as its surrounding desert.

"Gods," Zélie curses under her breath, pausing as her shivers worsen. Although the sun beats down with a fury, her teeth chatter as if she's in an ice bath. Since her awakening, she shakes more and more, recoiling whenever she senses that the spirits of the dead are near.

"Are there that many?" I whisper.

She pants when one shiver stops. "It's like walking through a burial ground."

"With heat like this, we probably are."

"I don't know." Zélie looks around, yanking her scarf close. "Every time one hits, I taste blood."

A chill rocks through me, though sweat leaks from every pore. If Zélie can taste blood, I don't want to know why.

"Perhaps—" I pause, stalling in the sand as a pack of men flood into the street. Though they're obscured by capes and masks, their dust-covered clothes bear Orïsha's royal seal.

Guards.

I grab on to Zélie as she reaches for her staff. Each soldier reeks of liquor; some stumble with every step. My legs quake as if made of water.

Then, quick as they came, they disperse, disappearing among the clay ahérés.

"Get yourself together." Zélie shoves me off her. I fight not to tumble into the sand. There is no sympathy in her gaze; unlike Tzain, her silver eyes rage.

"I just—" The words are weak, though I will them to be strong. "I apologize. I was caught off guard."

"If you're going to act like a little princess, turn yourself in to the guards. I'm not here to protect you. I'm here to fight."

"That's not fair." I wrap my arms around myself. "I'm fighting, too."

"Well, seeing as your father created this mess, if I were you, I'd fight a little harder."

With that Zélie turns, kicking up sand as she storms off. My face burns as I follow, careful to keep my distance this time.

We continue toward Ibeji's central square, a collection of tangled streets and square huts crafted from red clay. As we near, we see more nobles gathering, conspicuous with their bright silk kaftans and their trailing attendants. Although I don't recognize anyone, I adjust my scarf, worried that even the smallest slip will give my identity away. But what are they doing here, so far from the capital? There're so many nobles, they're only outnumbered by the laborers in the stocks.

I pause for a moment, aghast at the number of them filling the narrow path. Before today, I caught only glimpses of the laborers brought in to staff the palace—always pleasant, clean, groomed to Mother's satisfaction. Like Binta, I thought they lived simple lives, safe within the palace walls. I never considered where they came from, where else they might have ended up.

"Skies . . ." It's almost too hard to bear the sight. Mostly divîners, the laborers outnumber the villagers by hordes, dressed in nothing but tattered rags. Their dark skin blisters under the scorching sun, marred by the dirt and sand seemingly burned into their beings. Each is hardly more than a walking skeleton.

"What's going on?" I whisper, tallying the number of children in chains. Almost all of them are young—even the oldest still appears younger than me. I search for the resources they must be mining, the freshly laid roads, the new fortress erected in this desert village. But no sign of their efforts appear. "What are they doing here?"

Zélie locks eyes with a dark girl who has long white hair like hers. The laborer wears a tattered white dress; her eyes are sunken, devoid of almost all life.

"They're in the stocks," Zélie mutters. "They go where they're told."

"Surely it isn't always this bad?"

"In Lagos, I saw people who looked even worse."

She moves toward the guard post at the central square while my insides twist. Though no food fills my stomach, it churns with the truth. All those years sitting silent at the table.

Sipping tea while people died.

I reach forward to fill my canteen at the well, avoiding the guard's leering eyes. Zélie reaches to do the same—

The guard's sword slashes down with a fury.

We jump back, hearts pounding. His sword cuts into the wooden rim where Zélie's hand rested just seconds before. She grips the staff in her waistband, hand trembling with rage.

My eyes follow the sword up to the glaring soldier who wields it. The sun has darkened his mahogany skin, but his gaze shines bright.

"I know you maggots can't read," he spits at Zélie, "but for skies' sake, learn how to count."

He smacks his blade against a weathered sign. As sand falls from the grooves in the wood, its faded message clears: ONE CUP = ONE GOLD PIECE.

"Are you serious?" Zélie seethes.

"We can afford it," I whisper, reaching into her pack.

"But they can't!" She points to the laborers. The handful carrying buckets drink water so polluted it might as well be sand. But this isn't time for rebellion. How can Zélie not see that?

"Our deepest apologies." I step forward, calling forth my most deferential tone. I almost sound believable. Mother would be proud.

I place three gold coins in the guard's hand and take Zélie's canteen, forcing her to step back as I fill it.

"Here."

I press the canteen into her hand, but Zélie clicks her tongue in disgust. She grabs the canteen and walks back to the laborers, approaching the dark girl in white.

"Drink," Zélie urges. "Quick. Before your stocker sees."

The young laborer doesn't spare a second. She drinks the water hungrily, no doubt savoring her first drink in days. When she finishes a hearty swig, she passes the canteen down to the divîner shackled in front of her. With reluctance, I hand the two remaining canteens over to the other laborers.

"You're too kind," the girl whispers to Zélie, licking the last droplets off her lips.

"I'm sorry I can't do more."

"You've done more than enough."

"Why are there so many of you?" I ask, trying to ignore my dry throat.

"The stockers send us here for the arena." The girl nods toward a spot just barely visible beyond the clay wall. At first nothing sticks out against the red dunes and waves of sand, but soon the amphitheater fights its way through.

Skies . . .

I've never seen a structure so vast. A collection of weathered arches and pillars, the arena spreads wide across the desert, covering much of its arid land.

"You're building it?" I scrunch my nose. Father would never approve of the stockers building an edifice like this out here. The desert is too arid; there are only so many people this land can hold.

The girl shakes her head. "We compete in it. The stockers say if we win, they'll pay off all our debts."

"Compete?" Zélie wrinkles her brow. "For what? Your freedom?"

"And riches," the laborer in front of the girl pipes up, water dripping down his chin. "Enough gold to fill a sea."

"That's not why they have us compete," the girl cuts in. "The nobles are already rich. They don't need gold. They're after Babalúayé's relic."

"Babalúayé?" I ask.

"The God of Health and Disease," Zélie reminds me. "Every god has a legendary relic. Babalúayé's is the *ohun èṣọ́ aiyé*, the jewel of life."

"Is it actually real?" I ask.

"Just a myth," Zélie answers. "A story maji tell divîners before they go to sleep."

"It's not a myth," the girl says. "I've seen it myself. It's more of a stone than a jewel, but it's real. It grants eternal life."

Zélie tilts her head and leans forward.

"This stone." She lowers her voice. "What does it look like?"

CHAPTER TWENTY-THREE

ZÉLIE

THE ARENA BUZZES with the drunken chatter of nobles as the sun dips below the horizon. Though night falls, the amphitheater glows with light; lanterns hang against the pillared walls. We push past the hordes of guards and nobles filling the stone-carved stands. I grip Tzain for support, stumbling as we make our way through the weathered sand steps.

"Where'd all these people come from?" Tzain mutters. He forces his way through two kosidán wrapped in dirt-covered kaftans. Though Ibeji can't boast more than a few hundred residents, thousands of spectators fill the stands, a surprising number of them merchants and nobles. Everyone stares at the deep basin of the arena floor, united in their excitement for the games.

"You're shivering," Tzain says when we sit. Goosebumps travel up and down my skin.

"There are hundreds of spirits," I whisper. "So many died here."

"Makes sense if laborers built this place. They probably died by the dozens."

I nod and sip from my canteen, hoping to wash the taste of blood from my mouth. No matter what I eat or drink, the copper tang won't go away. There are too many souls around me trapped in the hell of apâdi.

I was always taught that when Orïshans died, the blessed spirits rose to alâfia: peace. A release from the pain of our earth, a state of being that exists only in the gods' love. One of our sacred duties as Reapers was to guide the lost spirits to alâfia, and in exchange, they would lend us their strength.

But spirits weighed down by sin or trauma can't rise to alâfia; they can't rise from this earth. Bound to their pain, they stay in apâdi, reliving the worst moments of their human memories again and again.

As a child, I suspected that apâdi was a myth, a convenient warning to keep children from misbehaving. But as an awakened Reaper, I can *feel* the spirits' torture, their unyielding agony, their never-ending pain. I scan the arena, unable to believe all the spirits trapped in the hell of apâdi within these walls. I've never heard of anything like this. What in the gods' names happened here?

"Should we be looking around?" Amari whispers. "Search the arena for clues?"

"Let's wait for the competition to start," Tzain says. "It'll be easier when everyone's distracted."

As we wait, I look past the ornate silks of the nobles to inspect the arena's deep metal floor. It's a curious sight among the sand bricks filling the cracked arches and steps. I search for a sign of bloodshed in the iron: the strike of a sword, the cut of giant claws from wild ryders. But the metal is untouched and untarnished. *What kind of competition is this—*

A bell rings through the air.

My eyes snap up as it incites cheers of excitement. Everyone rises to their feet, forcing Amari and me to stand on the steps just to see. The cheers grow louder when a masked man shrouded in black ascends a metal staircase, rising to a platform high above the arena floor. There's a strange aura about him, something commanding, something golden. . . .

The announcer removes his mask to reveal a smiling, light brown face tanned by the sun. He brings a metal cone to his lips.

"Are you ready?"

The crowd roars with a ferocity that makes my eardrums ring. A deep rumble thunders in the distance, growing louder and louder until—

Metal gates fly open on the sides of the arena floor, and an endless wave of water rushes in. *This has to be a mirage.* Yet liter after liter flows in. The water covers the metal ground, crashing with the expanse of a sea.

"How is this possible?" I hiss under my breath, remembering the laborers, no more than skin and bone. So many dying for water and they waste it on this?

"I can't hear you," the announcer jeers. "Are you ready for the battle of a *lifetime?*"

As the drunken crowd screams, metal gates open on the arena's sides. One by one, ten wooden vessels float in, sailing through the waves of the makeshift sea. Each ship spans almost a dozen meters, masts high, sails unfurled. They float as their crews take position, manning the rows of wooden rudders and cannon lines.

On every ship, an elaborately dressed captain stands at the helm. But when I look at the crews, my heart stops.

The laborer in white sits among dozens of rowers with tears in her dark eyes, the girl who told us of the stone. Her chest heaves up and down. She grips a paddle for life.

"Tonight ten captains from all over Orïsha battle for wealth greater than a king's. The captain and crew who win will bathe in a sea of glory, an ocean of endless gold!" The announcer raises his hands and two guards roll in a large chest of glittering gold pieces. An echo of awe and greed ripples through the stands. "The rules are simple—to win, you must kill the captain and crew of every other boat. Over the past two moons, no one has survived an arena fight. Will tonight finally be the night we crown a victor?"

The crowd's cheers erupt again. The captains join in, eyes glittering at the announcer's words. Unlike their helpless crews, they aren't afraid.

They only want to win.

"If a captain wins tonight, a special prize awaits, a recent find greater than any prize we've offered before. I have no doubt rumors of its greatness are why many of you have come tonight." The announcer saunters across his platform, building suspense. Dread gathers inside me as he raises the metal cone to his lips again.

"The captain who wins will walk away with more than just gold. He will receive the jewel of life, lost to time until this very moment. Babalúayé's legendary relic. The gift of immortality!"

The announcer takes the glowing stone from his cloak. Words catch in my throat. More brilliant than the painting Lekan brought to life, the sunstone dazzles. The size of a coconut, the stone shines with oranges, yellows, and reds pulsing beneath its smooth crystal exterior. The very thing we need to complete the ritual.

The last thing we need to bring magic back.

"The stone grants immortality?" Amari cocks her head. "Lekan didn't mention that."

"No," I reply, "but it looks like it could."

"Who do you think will wi—"

Before Amari can finish, deafening blasts explode through the air.

The arena quakes as the first ship fires.

Two cannonballs shoot from the metal muzzles, merciless in their aim. They crash into the next boat's rowers, obliterating lives on impact.

"Ah!" Vicious pain rips through my body, even though nothing strikes me. The thick taste of blood coats my tongue, stronger than it's ever been.

"Zél!" Tzain shouts. At least, I think he shouts. It's impossible to hear him over the screams. As the ship sinks, the crowd's cheers blur with the shrieks of the dead overwhelming my mind.

"I feel it," I say, gritting my teeth to avoid a mangled cry. "Each one, each death."

A prison I can't escape.

The blast of cannonballs shakes the walls. Shattered wood flies through the air as another ship goes down. Blood and corpses rain into the water, while injured survivors fight not to drown.

Each new death hits me as hard as Lekan's spirit did at Chândomblé, flowing through my mind and body. My head surges with broken disparate memories. My body harbors all their pain. I black in and out of the agony, waiting for the horror to end. I get a flash of the girl in white, only now she's drowned in red.

I don't know how long it lasts—ten minutes, ten days.

When the bloodshed is finally over, I'm too weak to think, to breathe. Little remains of the ten ships or their captains, each blown apart at another's hand.

"Looks like another night without a victor!" The announcer's voice booms over the cries of the spectators. He brandishes the stone, making sure it catches the light.

It glimmers above the crimson sea, shining above the corpses floating among the shards of wood. The sight makes the crowd scream louder than they have all night. They want more blood.

They want another fight.

"We'll just have to see if tomorrow's captains can win this magnificent prize!"

I lean into Tzain and shut my eyes. At this rate, we'll die before we ever touch that stone.

CHAPTER TWENTY-FOUR

INAN

THE DISTANT SHOUTS of stockers ring over the faint clinks of construction. Kaea's disgruntled barks reign over them. Though reluctant, she appears to be taking the assembly lead. After three days under her rule, the bridge is almost complete.

But as our path to the other side of the mountain grows, I'm no closer to finding any clues. No matter how far I get, the temple is an enigma, an endless mystery I can't crack. Even loosening my hold on my magic isn't enough to track down the girl. I'm running out of time.

If I'm to have any chance at finding the girl, I have to let all my magic in.

The realization haunts me, challenging everything I believe. But the alternative is far worse. Duty before self. Orïsha first.

Taking a deep breath, I release every last restraint bit by bit. The ache in my chest decreases. With time, the sting of magic rises to my skin.

I hope the scent of the sea will hit me first, but like every day thus far, only the scent of timber and coal fills the narrow halls.

When I turn a new corner, the scent becomes overwhelming; a turquoise cloud hangs in the air. I pass my hand through it, allowing Lekan's lingering consciousness to break in.

"Lekan, stop!"

Shrieks of laughter ring when I turn another corner. I press against the cool stone as the sêntaro's memories overtake me. Phantom children pass, each squealing and painted and naked. Their joy bounces and echoes, sharp against the rock walls.

They're not real, I remind myself, heart pounding against my chest. But even as I try to hold on to the lie, the mischievous glint in a child's eyes champions the truth.

Torch in hand, I move on, rushing through the temple's narrow halls. For a moment a whiff of sea salt hangs in the air, shrouded in the scent of coal. I turn the corner and another turquoise cloud appears. I race to it, teeth clenching as the new flash of Lekan's consciousness takes hold. His timber scent becomes overwhelming. The air shifts. A soft voice sounds.

"But do you have a name?"

My body goes rigid. Amari's timid form materializes before my eyes. My sister stares at me in apprehension, fear clouding her amber gaze. An acidic scent wafts into my nostrils. My nose wrinkles at the burn. *"Everyone has a name, child."*

"Oh, I did not mean—"

"*Lekan*," his voice booms in my head. *"Olamilekan."*

I almost laugh when I see Amari; she looks ridiculous in commoner clothes. But even after all this, she's the same girl I've always known: a web of emotions spinning behind a wall of silence.

My own memory breaks in—the brief look we shared across the broken bridge. I thought I'd be her savior; instead I was the cause of her pain.

"My wealth . . . is increased?"

Lekan's memory of the maji girl emerges. She flickers to life in the burn of the torchlight.

"*You remember our tongue?"*

"Bits and pieces." She nods. *"My mother taught it to me when I was young."*

Finally. After all these days, the scent of the sea hits me like a gust of wind. Yet for the first time since our paths collided, the girl's image doesn't make me reach for my sword. Through Lekan's gaze she is soft yet striking. Her dark skin seems to glow in the torchlight, highlighting the ghosts behind her silver eyes.

She is the one. Lekan's thoughts ring in my mind. *Whatever happens, she must survive.*

"The one for what?" I wonder out loud. Only silence answers.

The images of the girl and Amari fade away, leaving me staring after where they used to be. Her scent disappears. Though I try to reach for the flash again, nothing happens. I'm forced to move on.

As my footsteps echo through the temple's nooks and crannies, I feel the change in my body. Suppressing my curse has become a constant drain. A draw on every breath. Though the buzz of magic in my head still makes my stomach clench, my body revels in its new freedom. It's as if I've spent years drowning underwater.

For a moment, I get to suck in air.

With deep breaths, I press on through the temple, traversing the halls with a new vigor. I chase after the ghosts of Lekan, searching for answers, hoping to find the girl again. When I turn another corner, the scent of his soul overwhelms me. I enter the domed room. Remnants of Lekan's consciousness pulse stronger than they have all week. A turquoise cloud seems to encompass the entire space. Before I can brace myself, the room flashes in white.

Though I stand in the shadows, Lekan's consciousness bathes the jagged walls in light. My jaw drops as I study the stunning mural of the gods. Each portrait floods with brilliant color.

"What is this?" I breathe, in awe of the magnificent sight. The paintings are so expressive they appear to come to life.

I lift my torch to the gods and goddesses, to the maji who dance at their feet. It's imposing. Invading. It unravels everything I've been taught to think.

Growing up, Father led me to believe that those who clung to the myth of the gods were weak. They relied on beings they could never see, dedicating their lives to faceless entities.

I chose to place my faith in the throne. In Father. Orïsha. But now, staring at the gods, I can't even bring myself to speak.

I marvel at the oceans and forests that spring from their touch, at the world of Orïsha created by their hand. A strange joy seems to breathe within the layers of paint, filling Orïsha with a light I didn't know it could hold.

Seeing the mural forces me to see the truth, confirming everything Father told me in the throne room. The gods are real. Alive. Connecting the threads of the maji's lives. But if all that is true, why in the skies' name has one forged a connection with me?

I scan each portrait again, observing the different types of magic that seem to spring from the gods' hands. When I come to a god dressed in rich, cobalt robes, I pause. My cursed magic flares at the sight of him.

The god stands tall, imposing with chiseled muscles. A dark blue ipélè stretches across his broad chest like a shawl, vibrant against his dark brown skin. Turquoise smoke twists in his hands, just like the wispy clouds that appear with my curse. When I move my torchlight, a pulse of energy travels under my scalp. Lekan's voice booms in my head as another blue cloud appears.

"Orí took the peace from Sky Mother's head to become the God of Mind, Spirit, and Dreams. On earth, he shared this unique gift with his worshippers, allowing them to connect with all human beings."

"God of Mind, Spirit, and Dreams . . . ," I whisper to myself, putting all the pieces together. The voices. The flickers of others' emotions. The strange dreamscape I found myself trapped in. This is it.

The god of my origin.

Anger thrashes inside me with the realization. *What right do you have?* A few days ago I didn't even know this god existed, yet he took it upon himself to poison me?

"Why?" I shout, voice echoing inside the dome. I almost expect the god to shout back, yet only silence answers me.

"You'll regret this," I mutter to myself, not knowing if that makes me insane or if somewhere, despite all the noise of the world, he can hear me. The bastard should rue this day. The magic he's cursed me with will be magic's undoing.

My insides twist and I whip around, stomach clenching as I call on my curse even more. There's no fighting it. To find the answers I need, there's only one place I can go.

I slide to the ground and close my eyes, letting the world fade as magic slithers through my veins. If I'm going to kill this curse, I need it all.

I need to dream.

CHAPTER TWENTY-FIVE

ZÉLIE

"Is it clear?"

Amari peeks through the stone halls leading away from the arena floor. Crumbling arches curve over our heads, cracked stones under our feet. After footsteps pass, Amari nods and we dash. We weave in and out of the weathered pillars, rushing to make it through before we're seen.

Hours after the last man died and the spectators had left their seats, the guards drained the arena's red sea. I thought the horrors of the games would end there, but now the cracks of canes echo through the empty stands. Guards command a new batch of laborers to clean up the blood and gore that weren't washed away when they drained the stadium. I can't fathom their torture. Cleaning up tonight's mess only to become tomorrow's carnage.

I'll come back, I decide. *I'll save them.* After I perform the ritual and bring magic back, after Baba is safe and sound. I'll rally a group of Grounders to sink this monstrosity into the sand. That announcer will pay for every wasted divîner life. Every noble will answer for their crimes.

I let thoughts of vengeance soothe me as we press against a jagged wall. I close my eyes, concentrating as hard as I can. The sunstone stirs the ashê in my blood. When I open my eyes, its glow is faint, like a firefly fading into the night. But with time it grows until the sunstone's aura heats the bottom of my feet.

"Below us," I whisper. We move through empty halls and descend the stairs. The closer we get to the arena's rot-stained floor, the more men we have to dodge. By the time we reach the bottom, we're practically a finger's breadth from the crooked guards and broken laborers. Their canes crack over our footsteps. We slip beneath a stone archway.

"It's here," I hiss, pointing to a large iron door. Bright light shines through the slits, filling the archway with the heat of the sunstone. I run my fingers over the metal door's handle, a rusted turnwheel caught by a giant padlock.

I whip out the dagger Tzain had given me and jam it into the lock's narrow keyhole. Though I try to push forward, I'm blocked by an intricate pattern of teeth.

"Can you pick it?" he whispers.

"I'm trying." It's more complex than the typical lock. To get through, I need something sharper, something with a hook.

I grab a thin rusted nail on the ground and press it into the wall, curving its point. When it's bent, I close my eyes and concentrate on the delicate touch of the lock's teeth. *Be patient.* Mama Agba's old lesson echoes through my mind. *Let feeling become your eyes.*

My heartbeat spikes as I listen for the sound of any footsteps approaching, but when I push my knife, the teeth yield. One more shimmy to the left and . . .

A small click sounds. The padlock breaks free, and I'm so relieved I almost cry. I grab the wheel and pull to the left, but the metal won't give.

"It's stuck!"

Amari keeps watch as Tzain yanks at the rusted wheel with all his might. The metal groans and screeches loud enough to drown out the shouts of the guards, but the wheel doesn't budge.

"Be careful!" I hiss.

"I'm trying!"

"Try harder—"

The wheel rips off with a strained crank. We stare at the broken metal in Tzain's hand. What in gods' names are we supposed to do now?

Tzain rams his body into the door. Though it shudders with the impact, it refuses to give.

"You'll alert the guards!" Amari whispers.

"We need the stone!" Tzain whispers back. "How else are we going to get it?"

I cringe with each thrust of Tzain's body, but he's right. The stone is so close the heat of its glow warms me like a freshly lit fire.

A string of curses runs through my mind. *Gods, if only we had another maji's help.* A Welder would be able to warp the metal door. A Burner could melt the handle right off.

Half a moon, I remind myself. *Half a moon to do this right.*

If we're going to recover the sunstone in time for the solstice, we need to get it tonight.

The door budges a millimeter and I gasp. We're close. I can feel it. A few more knocks and it'll fly open. A few more pushes and the stone is ours.

"Hey!"

A guard's voice booms through the air. We freeze in response. Footsteps pound against the stone floors, thundering toward us with frightening speed.

"Over here!" Amari gestures to a section just past the sunstone's door, lined with cannonballs and crates of blastpowder. As we crouch behind the crates, a young divîner dashes into the room, white hair glowing in the dim light. In seconds he's cornered by the announcer and another guard. They skid to a halt when they see the half-open door to the sunstone.

"You maggot." The announcer's lips peel back in a snarl. "Who're you working with? Who did this?"

Before the young boy can speak, the crack of the announcer's cane cuts him down. He collapses to the stone floor. As he screams, another guard joins in the beating.

I flinch behind the crate, tears stinging my eyes. The boy's back is already ripped raw from former beatings, but neither monster lets up. He'll die under their blows.

He'll die because of me.

"Zélie, no!"

Tzain's hiss stalls me for a second, but it's not enough to stop me. I burst free from our hiding spot, fighting my nausea when I see the child.

Angry tears cut through his skin. Blood streams down his back. He clings to life by a thread, one that frays before my eyes.

"Who the hell are you?" the announcer seethes, withdrawing a dagger. My skin prickles as he nears me with its black majacite blade. Three more guards run to his side.

"Thank gods!" I force a laugh, searching for the words to fix this. "I've been looking all over for you!"

The announcer narrows his eyes in disbelief. His grip tightens on his cane. "Looking for me?" he repeats. "In this cellar? By the stone?"

The boy moans, and I flinch as a guard kicks him in the head. His body lies motionless in a pool of his own blood. It looks like a killing blow. *But why can't I feel his spirit?* Where's his last memory? His final pain? If he went straight to alâfia I might not feel it, but how can anyone pass in peace after a death like this?

I force my gaze back on the snarling announcer. There's nothing I can do now. The boy's dead. And unless I think of something quick, I'm dead, too.

"I knew I'd find you here." I swallow hard. Only one excuse will do. "I want to enter your games. Let me compete tomorrow night."

"YOU CANNOT BE SERIOUS!" Amari exclaims when we finally enter the safety of the sands. "You saw that bloodbath. You *felt* it. Now you want to be in it?"

"I want the stone," I yell back. "I want to stay alive!" Despite my fire, the image of the beaten boy crawls back into my head.

Better that. Better whipped to death than blown apart on a ship. But no matter how hard I try to convince myself, I know the words aren't true. There's no dignity in a death like that, whipped to his last breath for something he didn't even do. And I couldn't even help his spirit pass on. I couldn't be the Reaper he needed if I wanted to.

"The arena's crawling with guards," I mumble. "If we couldn't grab it tonight, there's no way we can steal it tomorrow."

"There's gotta be something," Tzain jumps in. Grains of sand stick to his blood-covered feet. "He won't keep the sunstone here tonight after all this. If we figure out where he stores the stone next—"

"We have thirteen days before the solstice. Thirteen days to cross Orïsha and sail to the sacred island. We don't have time to search. We need to get the stone and go!"

"The sunstone won't be of any use to us when our corpses line the arena floor," Amari says. "How will we survive? The competition leaves everyone dead!"

"We won't be playing like everyone else."

I reach into my pack and pull out one of Lekan's black scrolls. The white ink glistens on its label, translating into *Reanimation of the Dead*. The incantation was a common practice for Reapers, often the first technique new maji mastered. The magic grants its caster the aid of a spirit trapped in the hell of apâdi in exchange for helping that spirit pass on to the afterlife.

Of all the incantations in Lekan's scrolls, this was the only one I already knew. Every moon, Mama would lead a group of Reapers to the isolated mountaintops of Ibadan and use this incantation to cleanse our village of trapped souls.

"I've been studying this scroll," I rush out. "It has an incantation my mother casted often. If I can master it, I'll be able to transform dead spirits in the arena into actual soldiers."

"Are you deranged?" Amari cries. "You could barely breathe in the stands with all those spirits. It took you hours to regain your strength and walk out. If you could not handle it up there, what makes you think you can cast magic below?"

"The dead overwhelmed me because I didn't know what to do. I wasn't in control. If I learn this incantation and harness them, we could have a hidden army. There are thousands of angry spirits in that arena!"

Amari turns to Tzain. "Tell her this is deranged. Please."

Tzain crosses his arms and shifts his stance, weighing the risk as he looks between Amari and me.

"See if you can figure it out. After that, we'll decide."

THE CLEAR NIGHT BRINGS a freeze to the desert almost as harsh as its beating sun. Though the chilling wind blows sand off the dunes surrounding Ibeji, sweat pours down my skin. For hours, I try to perform the incantation, but each attempt is worse than the last. After a while I have to send Tzain and Amari back to the hut we rented. At least now I can fail alone.

I hold Lekan's scroll up to the moonlight, trying to make sense of the Yoruba translation scribbled under the sênbaría. Since the awakening, my memory of the old tongue is precise, as clear as it was when I was young. But no matter how many times I recite the words, my ashê doesn't flow. No magic occurs. And the more my frustration builds, the more I remember I shouldn't have to do this by myself.

"Come on." I grit my teeth. *"Oya, bá mi sọ̀rọ̀!"*

If I'm risking everything to do the work of the gods, why aren't they here when I need them the most?

I release a shuddering breath and sink to my knees, running my hand through the new waves in my hair. Had I been a maji before the Raid, our clan scholar would've taught me incantations when I was young. She would've known exactly what to do to coax my ashê out now.

"Oya, please." I look back at the scroll, trying to discover what I've missed. The incantation is supposed to create an animation, a spirit of the dead reincarnated into the physical materials around me. If all goes well, an animation should form out of the dunes. But it's been hours and I haven't even managed to move one grain of sand.

As I run my hands over the script, the new scar across my palm makes me pause. I hold it up to the moonlight, inspecting where Lekan sliced me with the bone dagger. The memory of my blood glowing with white light still fills my mind. The surge of ashê was exhilarating, a blinding rush only blood magic can bring.

If I used that now . . .

My heartbeat quickens with the thought. The incantation would flow with ease. I'd have no problem getting a legion of animations to rise from the ground.

But before the thought can tempt me further, Mama's raspy voice comes to mind. Her sunken skin. Her shallow breaths. The trio of Healers who toiled endlessly at her side.

Promise me, she whispered, squeezing my hand after she used blood magic to bring Tzain back to life. *Swear it now. No matter what, you can never do it. If you do, you won't survive.*

I promised her. Swore it on the ashê that would one day run through my veins. I can't break my vow because I'm not strong enough to perform an incantation.

But if this doesn't work, what choice will I have? This shouldn't be so hard. Just hours ago ashê vibrated in my blood. Now I can't feel a damn thing.

Wait a minute.

I stare at my hands, recalling the young divîner who bled to death before my eyes. It wasn't just his spirit I couldn't feel. I haven't sensed the pull of the dead in hours.

I turn to the scroll again, searching for a hidden meaning behind its words. It's like my magic bled dry in the arena. I haven't felt anything since—

Minoli.

The girl in white. Those large, empty eyes.

So much happened at once, I didn't realize the girl's spirit had passed on her name.

In death, the other spirits of the arena passed on their pain. Their hate. In their memories I felt the sting of the guards' whips. I tasted the salt of fallen tears on my tongue. But Minoli brought me to the dirt fields of Minna, where she and her sharp-nosed siblings worked the land for autumn's corn crop. Though the sun shone brutal and the work was hard, each moment passed with a smile, with song.

"Ìwọ ni ìgbọ́kànlé mi òrìshà, ìwọ ni mó gbọ́jú lé."

I sing the words aloud, my voice carrying in the wind. As I repeat the lyrics a soulful voice sings in my head.

It's there that Minoli spent her final moments, forgoing the brutal arena for the peaceful farm in her mind. It's there she chose to live.

There she chose to die.

"*Minoli*," I whisper the incantation into the depths of my mind. *"Ẹ̀mí àwọn tí ó ti sùn, mo ké pè yín ní òní. Ẹ padà jáde nínú ẹ̀yà mímọ̀ yín. Súre fún mi pẹ̀lú ẹ̀bùn iyebíye rẹ."*

All of a sudden sand swirls before me. I flinch backward as the mist-like vortex rises and twirls in waves before settling back to the ground.

"Minoli?" I breathe the question aloud, though deep down I know the answer. When I close my eyes, the scent of earth fills my nose. Smooth corn seeds slip through my fingers. Her memory shines: vivid, vibrant, alive. If it resides in me with such force, I have to believe she does, too.

I repeat the incantation with conviction, stretching my hands out toward the sand. *"Minoli, I call on you today. Come forth in this new element, bless me with your precious li—"*

White sênbaría leap from the parchment and rush up my skin. The symbols dance along my arms, infusing my body with new power. It hits my lungs like the first breath of air after diving underwater. As sand swirls around me with the force of a storm, a grainy figure emerges from the whirlwind, animated with the rough carvings of life.

"Oh my gods." I hold my breath as Minoli's spirit reaches forward with a hand of sand. Her grainy fingers brush against my cheek before the whole world fades to black.

CHAPTER TWENTY-SIX

INAN

CRISP AIR FILLS my lungs. I've returned. The dreamscape lives. Just seconds ago I sat beneath Orí's image—now I stand in the field of dancing reeds.

"It worked," I breathe in disbelief as I run my fingers along the sagging green stems. The horizon still blurs into white, surrounding me like clouds in the sky. But something's different. Last time, the field stretched as far as I could see. Now wilted reeds form a tight circle around me.

I finger another stem, surprised at the coarse grooves that radiate from its center. My mind runs through escape routes and attack plans, yet my body feels strangely at home. It's more than the relief of not suppressing my magic, the sensation of breathing once again. The air of the dreamscape holds an unnatural peace, as if more than anywhere else in Orïsha, it's here that I belon—

Focus, Inan. I reach for my sênet pawn, but I can't hold on to it here. I shake my head instead, as if I could shake out the traitorous thoughts. This isn't a home. A peace. It's only the heart of my curse. If I accomplish what I need to do, this place won't even exist.

Kill her. Kill magic. My duty writhes in my mind until it takes hold of my core. I don't have a choice.

I must follow my plan.

I imagine the face of the girl. In a sudden breeze, the reeds part. She materializes like a condensing cloud, her body forming as blue smoke travels from her feet to her arms.

I hold my breath, counting down the seconds. When the blue haze lifts, my muscles tense; her obsidian form blows to life.

She stands with her back to me, hair different than it was before. White locks that once fell in smooth sheets now cascade down her back in flowing waves.

She turns. Softly. Almost ethereal in her grace. But when her silver eyes meet mine, the rebel I know emerges.

"I see you dyed your hair." She points at the color hiding my white streak and smirks. "You might want to add another coat. Some of your maggot's still peeking through."

Dammit. It's only been three hours since I last dyed it. Out of instinct, I touch the streak. The girl's smile widens.

"I'm actually glad you called me here, little prince. There's something I'm dying to know. You were raised by the same bastard, but Amari can't kill a fly. So tell me, how'd you become such a monster?"

The peace of the dreamscape evaporates in an instant. "You fool," I hiss through my teeth. "How dare you slander your king!"

"Did you enjoy your visit to the temple, little prince? How'd you feel when you saw everything he destroyed? Were you proud? Inspired? Excited to do the same?"

Lekan's memories of the sêntaros flash through my mind. The mischief in the running child's eyes. The ruins and rubble of the temple made it clear those lives were taken.

The smallest part of me prayed it wasn't by Father's hands.

Guilt hits me like the sword that went through Lekan's chest. But I can't forget what's at stake. *Duty before self.*

Those people died so Orïsha could live.

"Could it be?" Zélie steps forward, taunting. "Is that remorse I see? Is the little prince hiding a little shriveled-up heart?"

"You're so ignorant." I shake my head. "Too blinded to understand. My father was once on your side. He supported the maji!"

The girl snorts. I resent the way it crawls under my skin.

"Your people took his family!" I shout. "*Your* people caused the Raid!"

She steps back like I've punched her in the gut.

"It's my fault *your* father's men broke into my home and took my mother away?"

A memory of a dark-skinned woman fills her head with such clarity it leaks into mine. Like the girl, the woman has full lips, high cheekbones, a slight upturn in her eyes. The only difference is her gaze. Not silver. Dark as the night.

The memory steels something inside of her.

Something black.

Twisted with hate.

"I can't wait," the girl breathes, barely above a whisper. "I can't wait till he finds out what you are. Let's see how bold you feel when your father turns on his own son."

A violent chill runs down my spine. *She's wrong.*

Father was willing to forgive Amari for treason. When I take magic away, he will forgive me for this.

"That'll never happen." I try to sound strong. "I'm his son. Magic won't change that."

"You're right," she says with a smirk. "I'm sure he'll let you live."

She turns and retreats into the reeds. My conviction withers with her taunts. Father's blank stare invades my mind. With it, the air around me thins.

Duty before self. I hear his voice. Flat. Unwavering. Orïsha must always come first.

Even if it means killing me—

The girl gasps. I tense, whipping around to scan the blowing reeds.

"What is it?" I ask. *Have I summoned Father's spirit here?*

But nothing appears. No human, at least. As the girl steps into the white horizon binding the dreamscape, reeds bloom under her feet.

They grow nearly up to my head, a rich green that reaches for the sun. She takes another tentative step toward the horizon, and the surge of reeds expands.

"What in the skies?" Like a wave crashing over sand, the reeds spread throughout the horizon, pushing back the white boundary of the dreamscape. A warmth buzzes in my core. *My magic* . . .

Somehow she's wielding it.

"Don't move!" I order.

But the girl takes off, running into the white space. The dreamscape yields to her whims, wild and alive under her reign. As she sprints, the reeds growing under her feet change to soft dirt, white ferns, towering trees. They grow high into the sky, obscuring the sun with their jagged leaves.

"Stop!" I yell, sprinting through the new world that grows in her wake. The rush of magic makes me faint, sliding down my chest and thrumming in my head.

Despite my yells, she keeps running, a fire in her step as the soft dirt under her feet transforms to a hard rock. She doesn't skid to a stop until she's face-to-face with a staggering cliff.

"My gods," she breathes at the sight of the grand waterfall created through her touch. It foams in an endless wall of white, pouring into a lake so blue it shimmers like Mother's sapphires.

I stare at her in bewilderment, head still pulsing with the thrum of flowing magic. Over the edge of the cliff, emerald-green foliage fills the crevices along the jagged stone. Beyond the lake's outer rim, a small bank of trees blurs into white.

"How in skies' name did you do that?" I ask. There's a beauty to this new world I cannot deny. It makes my entire body buzz as if I've consumed a whole bottle of rum.

But the girl pays me no mind. Instead, she shimmies out of her draped pants. With a shout, she leaps from the cliff and hits the water with a splash.

I lean over the ledge as she resurfaces, soaking wet. For the first time since I've known her, she smiles. True joy lights her eyes. The image brings me back, faster than I can stop it. The memory of Amari's laughter feeds into my ears. Mother's cries follow. . . .

"Amari!" Mother shrieks, grabbing on to the wall when she almost slips.

Amari giggles as she dashes away, soaking the tiled floor with the remnants of her bathwater. Though an army of nurses and nannies chase her down, they're no match for the determined toddler. Now that Amari's made a decision to escape, they've lost.

She won't stop till she gets what she wants.

I jump over a fallen nanny and take off, laughing so hard I can barely breathe. One moment my shirt slips off my head. The next, my pants fly through the air. House servants laugh as we run by, stifling their giggles at Mother's glare.

By the time we reach the royal pool we're two naked menaces, jumping in just in time to drench Mother's finest gown. . . .

I can't remember the last time Amari giggled so hard water came out her nose. After I hurt her, she was never the same with me. Laughter was reserved for the likes of Binta.

Watching the girl swim brings it all back, but the longer I gaze, the less I think of my sister. The girl slides out of her top and my breath falters. The water shimmers around her dark skin.

Look away. I turn my head, attempting to study the grooves in the cliff instead. *Women are distractions*, Father would say. *Your focus is on the throne.*

Just being near the girl feels like a sin, threatening the unbreakable law designed to keep maji and kosidán apart. But despite the rule, my eyes pull me back. She makes it impossible not to stare.

A trick, I decide. *Another way to get inside your head.* But when she resurfaces, I'm at a loss for words.

If it's a trick, it's working.

"Really?" I force out. I try to ignore the curves of her body under the rippling water.

She looks up and narrows her eyes, as if remembering I exist. "Forgive me, little prince. This is the most water I've seen since you burned down my home."

The crying villagers of Ilorin creep back into my mind. I squash the guilt like a bug. *Lies.* It's her fault.

She helped Amari steal the scroll.

"You're mad." I cross my arms. *Look away.* I keep staring.

"If your water cost a gold piece per cup, you'd be doing the same exact thing."

A gold piece a cup? I ruminate as she dives below the surface. Even for the monarchy, coin like that is a stretch. No one could sustain those prices. Not even in—

Ibeji.

My eyes widen. I've heard of the crooked guards who run that desert settlement. They're crooked enough to overcharge, especially when water is scarce. It takes everything to keep a smile off my face. I've got her. And she doesn't even know it.

I close my eyes to leave the dreamscape, but the memory of Amari's smile makes me pause.

"My sister," I call above the roaring water. "Is she alright?"

The girl stares at me for a long moment. I don't expect an answer, but something indecipherable burns in her eyes.

"She's scared," she finally responds. "And she shouldn't be the only one. You're a maggot now, little prince." Her eyes darken. "You should be scared, too."

THICK AIR INVADES my lungs.

Dense and heavy and hot.

I open my eyes to find Orí's painted image above my head. *I'm back.*

"Finally." Despite myself, I smile. This will all be over soon. When I catch her and that scroll, the threat of magic will die for good.

Sweat drips down my back as my mind runs through the next steps. How close is the bridge to completion? How fast can we ride to Ibeji?

I spring to my feet and grab my torch. *I must find Kaea.* It's only when I whip around that I realize she's already here.

Sword outstretched. Pointed right at my heart.

"Kaea?"

Her hazel eyes are wide. The slightest tremble in her hand rocks her blade. She shifts, steadying its aim on my chest. "What was that?"

"What was what?"

"Don't." She speaks through her teeth. "You were *muttering*. Y-your head . . . it was surrounded by light!"

The girl's words echo through my ears.

You're a maggot now, little prince. You should be scared, too.

"Kaea, put the sword down."

She hesitates. Her eyes go to my hair. *The streak . . .*

It must be showing again.

"It's not what you think."

"I know what I saw!" Sweat drips from her forehead, pooling on her upper lip. She steps closer with her blade. I'm forced to back into the wall.

"Kaea, it's me. Inan. I would never hurt you."

"How long?" she breathes. "How long have you been a *maji*?" She hisses the word like it's a curse. Like I'm the spitting image of Lekan. Not the boy she's known since birth. The soldier she's trained for years.

"The girl infected me. It's not permanent."

"You're lying." Her lips peel back in disgust. "Are you . . . are you working with her?"

"No! I was looking for clues!" I step forward. "I know where she is—"

"Stay back!" Kaea screams. I freeze, hands in the air. There's no recognition in her eyes.

Only unbridled fear.

"I'm on your side," I whisper. "I have been this entire time. In Ilorin, I felt her going south. In Sokoto, I sensed she'd been to that merchant." I swallow hard, pulse rising when Kaea takes another step forward. "I'm not your enemy, Kaea. I'm the only way to track her down!"

Kaea stares at me. The tremble of her blade grows.

"It's me," I plead. "*Inan.* The crown prince of Orïsha. Heir to Saran's throne."

At the mention of Father, Kaea falters. Her sword finally drops to the ground. *Thank the skies.* My legs wobble as I collapse against the wall.

Kaea holds her head in her hands for a few minutes before looking at me. "This is why you've been acting so strange all week?"

I nod, heart still slamming against my chest. "I wanted to tell you, but I had a feeling you would react like this."

"I'm sorry." She leans against the wall. "But after what that maggot did to me, I had to make sure. If you were one of them . . ." Her eyes return to the streak in my hair. "I had to ensure you were on our side."

"Always." I grip Father's pawn. "I've never wavered. I want magic to die. I need to keep Orïsha safe."

Kaea studies me, keeping the slightest guard up. "Where is the maggot now?"

"Ibeji," I rush out. "I'm sure of it."

"Very well." Kaea straightens up and sheathes her sword. "I came because the bridge is finished. If they're in Ibeji, I'll take a team and leave tonight."

"*You'll* take a team?"

"You must return to the palace at once," Kaea says. "When the king finds out about this—"

I can't wait, the girl's voice returns. *I can't wait till he finds out what you are. Let's see how bold you feel when your father turns on his own son.*

"No!" I say. "You need me. You can't track them without my abilities."

"Your abilities? You're a *liability*, Inan. At any moment you could turn against us or endanger yourself. And what if someone finds out? Think of how it will look for the king!"

"You can't." I reach for her. "He won't understand!"

Kaea eyes the hallway, face ashen. She starts to back away.

"Inan, my duty—"

"Your duty is to *me*. I command you to stop!"

Kaea takes off in a sprint, tearing through the dimly lit halls. I race after her and lunge forward, tackling her to the floor.

"Kaea, please, just—*ugh!*"

She drives her elbow into my sternum. Air catches in my throat. She breaks free of my hold, scrambling to her feet to scale the stairs.

"Help!" Her screams are frantic now, echoing through the temple halls.

"Kaea, stop!" No one can know about this. No one can know what I am.

"He's one of them!" she shrieks. "He has been all along—"

"Kaea!"

"Stop him! Inan is a maj—"

Kaea freezes as if she's run into an invisible wall.

Her voice shrinks into silence. Her every muscle shakes.

Turquoise energy swirls from my palm to Kaea's skull, paralyzing her just like Lekan's magic did. Kaea's mind struggles to break free of my mental hold, fighting against a force I didn't even know I could control.

No . . .

I stare at my quaking hands. I can't tell whose fear surges through my veins.

I'm really one of them.

I'm the very monster I hunt.

Kaea's breath turns ragged as she writhes. My magic continues to swell out of control. A strangled scream escapes Kaea's mouth.

"Let go!"

"I don't know how!" I shout back, fear wrapping around my throat. The temple amplifies my abilities. The more I try to push my magic down, the harder it fights to get out.

Kaea's cries of agony grow. Her eyes turn red. Blood trickles from her ears, trailing down her neck.

My thoughts run a million meters a second. All the pawns in my mind crumble to dust. There's no way to fix this.

If she feared me before, she abhors me now.

"Please!" I beg. I have to keep her contained. She has to listen to me. I am her future king—

"Ugh!"

A shuddered gasp escapes Kaea's lips. Her eyes roll back.

The turquoise light binding her evaporates into nothingness.

Her body hits the ground.

"Kaea!" I run to her side and press my hand to her neck, but her pulse beats weakly under my fingers. After a moment, it's nearly gone.

"No!" I shout, as if my cries could bind her to life. Blood leaks from her eyes, down her nose. It trails from her mouth.

"I'm sorry," I choke through my tears. I try to wipe the blood from her face, but I only smear it over her skin. My own chest tightens, filling with the echo of her blood.

"I'm sorry." My vision blurs. "I'm sorry. I'm so sorry."

"Maggot," Kaea exhales.

Then there's nothing. Her body stiffens.

The light fades from her hazel eyes.

I don't know how long I sit holding Kaea's corpse. Blood drips onto the turquoise crystals lining her black hair. A mark of my curse. As they glint, the smell of iron and wine fills my nose. Fragments of Kaea's consciousness take hold.

I see the first day she met Father, the way she held him when the maji murdered his family. A kiss they shared in the secrecy of the throne room while Ebele bled out at their feet.

The man who kisses Kaea is a stranger. A king I've never met. For him, Kaea is more than his sun. She's all that's left of his heart.

And I took her away.

With a start, I drop Kaea's body, backing away from the bloodied mess. I push my magic so far down the ache in my chest is debilitating, sharp like the sword I might as well have put in Kaea's back.

Father can never know.

This monstrosity never occurred.

Maybe Father could've overlooked me being a maji, but he will never forgive this.

After all this time, magic's stolen his love once again.

I take one step back. Then another. I step again and again, until I'm fleeing the horrible mistake. There's only one way out of this mess.

And she's waiting in Ibeji.

CHAPTER TWENTY-SEVEN

AMARI

THOUGH THE GAMES have yet to start, the arena howls with excitement. Drunken cheers ring through the stone halls, each spectator hungry for blood. *Our blood.* I swallow hard and press my fists to my side to hide my trembling hands.

Be brave, Amari. Be brave.

Binta's voice rings through my head with such clarity, it makes my eyes sting. When she was alive, the sound of her voice fortified something inside of me, but tonight her words are drowned out by the arena's calls for carnage.

"They'll love this." The announcer grins as he leads the three of us underground. "Women never compete as captains. 'Cause of you, we got to charge double."

Zélie snorts, but it lacks her usual bite. "Glad our blood is worth a little extra."

"Novelty's always worth extra." The announcer flashes her a disgusting smile. "Remember that in case you ever go into *business.* A maggot like you could turn a fair amount of coin."

Zélie grabs Tzain's arm before he can react and fixes the announcer with a murderous glare. Her fingers slide along her metal staff.

Do it, I almost whisper.

If she beats the announcer senseless, perhaps we'll have another shot at stealing the sunstone. Anything would be better than the fate that awaits us if we board that boat.

"Enough talk." Zélie takes a deep breath and unhands her staff.

My heart sinks as we continue forward. *To our deaths we go.*

When we enter the rusted cellar housing the ship, our designated crew barely looks up. The laborers appear small against the vast hull of the wooden vessel, weakened from years of hard work. Though most of them are divîners, the oldest appears to have only a year or two on Tzain. A guard unshackles their chains, a moment of false freedom before the slaughter.

"Command them as you wish." The announcer waves as if the laborers are cattle. "You have thirty minutes to strategize. Then the games begin."

With that he turns, retreating from the dark cellar. As soon as he's gone, Tzain and Zélie pull loaves of bread and canteens from our packs and distribute them throughout the crowd. I expect the laborers to devour the meager feast, but they stare at the stale bread like it's the first time they've ever seen food.

"Eat," Tzain coaxes. "But not too fast. Go slow or you'll get sick."

One young divîner moves to take a bite of bread, but a gaunt woman holds him back.

"Skies," I mutter. The child can't be much older than ten.

"What is this?" an older kosidán asks. "Your idea of a last meal?"

"No one's going to die," Tzain assures them. "Follow my lead and you'll leave with your lives and the gold."

If Tzain feels even half the terror I do, he does not show it. He stands tall, commanding respect, confidence laced through his voice and gait. Watching him, it's almost possible to believe we'll be alright. *Almost.*

"You can't fool us with bread." A woman with a grisly scar running across her eye speaks up. "Even if we win, you'll kill us and keep the gold."

"We're after the stone." Tzain shakes his head. "Not the gold. Work with us and I promise you can keep every piece."

I study the crowd, hating the smallest part of me that wants them to revolt. Without a crew, we couldn't enter the arena. Zélie and Tzain would have no choice but to stay off the ship.

Be brave, Amari. I close my eyes and force a deep breath. Underground, the memory of Binta's voice is louder, stronger inside my head.

"You don't have a choice." All eyes turn to me and my cheeks flush. *Be brave.* I can do this. This is no different from elocution at the palace. "It's not fair and it's not right, but it's happening. Whether you want to work with us or not, you have to get on that boat."

I lock eyes with Tzain and he nudges me forward. I clear my throat as I walk, forcing myself to sound strong. "Every other captain competing tonight just wants to win. They don't care who gets killed or hurt. *We* want you to live. But that's only going to happen if you trust us."

The crew looks around the cellar before turning to the strongest among them—a divîner almost as tall as Tzain. A tapestry of scars ripples across his back as he walks over and meets Tzain's eye.

The air seems to hold its breath as we wait for his decision. My legs nearly collapse when he holds out his hand.

"What do you need us to do?"

CHAPTER TWENTY-EIGHT

AMARI

"CHALLENGERS IN POSITION!"

The announcer's voice booms below the arena. My heart lurches against my chest. Thirty minutes have passed in a blur as Tzain discussed strategies and delegated commands. He leads like a seasoned general, wise from years of war. The laborers hang on Tzain's every word, a spark alight in their eyes.

"Alright." Tzain nods. "Let's do this."

With more nourishment and renewed hope, the laborers move with purpose. But as everyone shuffles onto the deck of the ship, my feet grow heavy like lead. The roar of rushing water approaches, bringing back all the bodies that drowned in its wrath. I can already feel the water pulling down my limbs.

This is it. . . .

In moments, the games shall begin.

Half the laborers settle into their rowing stations, ready to grant us speed. The rest take position around the cannons in the efficient formation Tzain conceived: two laborers maneuver the muzzle for aim, two load the blastpowder into the breech. Soon, everyone is on the boat.

Everyone except me.

With the water rising, I force my leaden feet to move and I board the ship. I walk across the deck to get in position behind a cannon, but Tzain blocks my path.

"You don't have to do this."

Terror rings so loudly in my ears it takes a moment to process Tzain's words. *You don't have to do this.*

You don't have to die.

"There are only three people who know about the ritual. If we're all on the boat . . ." He clears his throat, swallowing the fatal thought. "I didn't come all this way for nothing. No matter what, one of us *has* to survive."

Alright. The words slip to the edge of my lips, desperate to escape. "But Zélie," I choke out instead. "If anyone stays behind, it should be her."

"If we stood a chance in hell without her on this ship, I would be persuading my sister instead."

"But—" I stop as the water of the arena surges, splashing onto the boat. In minutes the chamber will be covered, trapping me inside this burial chamber. If I'm going to run, it has to be now. In a moment it'll be too late.

"Amari, just go," Tzain presses. "Please. We'll fight better if we don't have to worry about you getting hurt."

We. I almost find the heart to laugh. Behind us Zélie grips the railing, eyes closed and lips quick as she practices the incantation. Despite her obvious fear, she still fights. No one allows her to run away.

If you're going to act like a little princess, turn yourself in to the guards. I'm not here to protect you. I'm here to fight.

"My brother is after me," I whisper to Tzain. "My father, too. Staying off this boat does not keep me or the secret of the scroll alive. It only buys me time." As the water splashes my feet, I step forward, joining a team at the cannons. "I can do this," I lie.

I can fight.

Be brave, Amari.

This time I hold on to Binta's words, wrapping them around my body like a suit of armor. I can be brave.

For Binta, I must be everything.

Tzain holds my gaze for a moment, then nods. He leaves to take his place. With a groan, the boat surges forward with the water, taking us to battle. We sail through the final tunnel. The screams of the crowd grow wild, frenzied for our blood. For the first time I wonder if Father knows of this "entertainment." If he knew, would he care?

I grip the railing of the ship as hard as I can, a futile attempt to quell my nerves. Before I can brace myself, we enter the arena, exposed, out for the world to see.

The smell of brine and vinegar hits like a wave as I blink in the astounding sight. Nobles line the first few rows above the arena, vibrant silks waving as they pound their fists against the railings.

Turning away, my heart constricts as I lock eyes with a young, wide-eyed divîner on another boat. His blank face says it all.

For one of us to live, the other must die.

Zélie laces her fingers and cracks her knuckles, walking to the bow of the ship. She mouths the incantation, steeling herself against the distractions before we begin.

The crowd roars with each new boat that enters the games, but as I survey the opponents, a terrible realization strikes. Last night there were ten boats.

Today there are thirty.

CHAPTER TWENTY-NINE

ZÉLIE

No . . .

I count again and again, waiting for someone to announce that there's been a mistake. We can't outlast twenty-nine other boats. Our plan could barely outlast ten.

"Tzain," I shriek as I run to him, betraying all my fear. "I can't do it! I can't take them all down."

Amari follows, shaking so much she nearly trips on the deck. The crew trails her, bombarding Tzain with endless questions. His eyes go wild as we swarm him, trying to focus on any one thing. But then his jaw sets. He closes his eyes.

"Quiet!"

His voice booms over the madness, silencing our cries. We watch as he surveys the arena while the announcer riles up the crowd.

"Abi, take the boat on the left. Dele, the one on the right. Form an alliance with the crews. Tell them we'll last longer if we target the boats farther away."

"But what if—"

"Go!" Tzain shouts over their objections, sending the brother and sister running. "Rowers," he continues, "new plan. Only half of you guys stay at the paddles. Keep us moving. We won't get much speed, but we're dead if we stay still." Half the laborers scramble to resume their positions at the wooden oars. Tzain turns back to us, the agbön champion alive in his eyes. "The rest of you join the cannon assembly line and aim for the boats in front. I want steady cannon fire. But be measured—the blastpowder will only last us so long."

"And the secret weapon?" Baako, the strongest of the crew, asks.

The brief calm I felt under Tzain's leadership evaporates. My chest squeezes so tight a sharp pain runs up my side. *The weapon isn't ready*, I want to shout. *If you put your faith in her, you'll die.*

I can picture it now: Tzain screaming above the water, me holding my breath as I try to push my magic out. I'm not the maji Mama was. What if I can't be the Reaper they need?

"It's under control," Tzain assures him. "Just make sure we stay alive long enough to use it."

"Who's ready . . . for the *battle of a lifetime*?"

The crowd roars in response to the announcer's goading. Their screams drown out even his amplified voice. I grip Tzain's arm as the crew splits. My throat is so dry it's hard to speak. "What's my plan?"

"Same as the old. We just need you to take out more."

"Tzain, I can't—"

"Look at me." He puts both hands on my shoulders. "Mama was the most powerful Reaper I've ever seen. You're her daughter. I know you can do this."

My chest tightens, but I can't tell if it's fear or something else.

"Just try." He squeezes my shoulders. "Even one animation will help."

"Ten . . . nine . . . eight . . . seven . . ."

"Stay alive!" he yells before positioning himself by the armory.

"Six . . . five . . . four . . . three . . ."

The cheers rise to deafening levels as I run to the ship's railing.

"Two . . ."

There's no chance to back out now. We either get the stone—

"One!"

—or we die trying.

The horn sounds and I jump overboard, crashing into the warm sea with rushing speed. As I hit, our ship shakes.

The first cannons fire.

Vibrations shudder through the water, rippling through my core. Spirits of the dead chill the space around me; fresh kills from today's games.

Alright, I think to myself, remembering Minoli's animation. Goosebumps prick my skin as the spirits near, my tongue curls at the taste of blood though I keep my mouth closed. The souls are desperate for my touch, for a way to return to life. This is it.

If I'm truly a Reaper, I have to show it now.

"Ẹ̀mí àwọn tí ó ti sùn, mo ké pè yín ní òní—"

I wait for the animations to swirl out of the water before me, but only a few bubbles escape my hands. I try again, drawing from the energy of the dead, but no matter how hard I concentrate, no animations come forth.

Dammit. The air in my throat thins, going faster as my pulse quickens. I can't do this. I can't save us—

A blast thunders from above.

I spin as the ship beside ours sinks. Corpses and shattered wood rain down. The water around me reddens. A bloodied body plunges past me to the bottom.

My gods . . .

Terror grips my chest.

One cannonball to the right and that could've been Tzain.

Come on, I coach myself as the air in my lungs shrivels further. There's no time to fail. I need my magic now.

Oya, please. The prayer feels strange, like a language half-learned and entirely forgotten. But after my awakening, our connection should be stronger than ever. If I call, she has to answer.

Help me. Guide me. Lend me your strength. Let me protect my brother and free the spirits trapped in this place.

I close my eyes, gathering the electric energy of the dead into my bones. I've studied the scroll. I can do this.

I can be a Reaper now.

"Ẹ̀mí àwọn tí ó ti sùn—"

A lavender light glows in my hands. Sharp heat courses through my veins. The incantation pushes my spiritual pathways open, allowing ashê to flow through. The first spirit surges through my body, ready for my command. Unlike Minoli, my only knowledge of this animation is his death; my stomach aches from the cannonball that ripped through his gut.

When I finish the incantation, the first animation floats before me, a swirl of vengeance and bubbles and blood. The animation takes the shape of a human, forming its body out of the water around us. Though its expression is clouded by the bubbles, I sense the militant resolve of its spirit. My own soldier. The first in an army of the dead.

For the briefest moment, triumph overpowers the exhaustion running through my muscles. I've done it. I'm a Reaper. A true sister of Oya.

A pang of sadness flashes through me. If only Mama could see me now.

But I can still honor her spirit.

I will make every fallen Reaper proud.

"Ẹ̀mí àwọn tí ó ti sùn—"

With the dwindling ashê in me, I chant, casting one more animation to life. I point to a ship, then give my command.

"Bring it down!"

To my surprise, the animations tear through the water with the speed of arrows. They shoot forward at my target, moments away from a strike.

The water rumbles when they hit, blowing straight through the vessel's hull. Planks of wood fly like spears, twisting as water rushes in.

I did it. . . .

I don't know whether to search for Oya in the sky or within my own hands. Spirits of the dead answered my call. They bent to *my* will!

The water swallows the ship whole, capsizing the vessel. But before my excitement can settle, falling divîners crash into the water.

I spin, taking in the collateral damage. The fallen crew thrashes for the top, kicking toward the edge of the arena. Terror hits when I see one girl plunge through the water with limp limbs. My chest seizes as her unconscious body begins to sink like lead.

"Save her!"

I push the command out, but my connection to the animations withers like the final breath left in my chest. I can already feel the spirit soldiers fading, leaving the hell of this arena for the peace of the afterlife.

As I kick upward, the animations dive like horn-tailed manta rays, surrounding the girl before she can hit the bottom of the arena. Ashê buzzes in my veins as they pull her up to a floating piece of dirftwood, granting her a chance to live.

"*Ugh!*" I cough when I break through the surface. Something leaves me as the animations disappear. I send silent thanks to their spirits as I wheeze for air.

"Did you see that?" the announcer booms. The arena erupts, not knowing what took the boat down.

"Zélie!" Tzain shouts from above, a crazed smile on his face despite the nightmare around us. His grin holds a glow I haven't seen in over a decade, a light he would have whenever he watched Mama's magic at work.

"That!" He points. "Keep doing that!"

Pride swells in my chest, heating me from within. I take a deep breath before diving back down.

Then I begin to chant.

CHAPTER THIRTY

AMARI

CHAOS.

Before this moment, I never truly understood the word. Chaos meant Mother's screams before a luncheon. It meant the scramble of oloyes to their gold-lined chairs.

Now chaos surrounds me, pulsing through every breath and heartbeat. It sings as blood splatters through the air, screams as boats explode into oblivion.

I scramble to the back of the boat and cover my head as a boom rings. Our vessel shakes as another cannon strikes its hull. Only seventeen ships float, yet somehow, we are still in this fight.

Before me, everyone moves with unmatched precision, fighting despite the mayhem. Tendons bulge against the rowers' necks as they drive the ship forward; sweat pours down the crew's faces as they load more blastpowder into the breeches of the cannons.

Go, I yell at myself. *Do something. Anything!*

But no matter how hard I try, I cannot help. I cannot even *breathe*.

My insides lurch as a cannonball rips through the deck of another boat. Injured cries hit my ears like shattered glass. The stench of blood stains the air, bringing Zélie's old words to mind. The day we came to Ibeji, she tasted death.

Today I taste it for myself.

"Incoming!" Tzain yells, pointing through the smoke. Another vessel approaches, its rowers panting with spears at the ready. *Skies . . .*

They're going to board us.

They'll bring the battle here!

"Amari, take the rowers!" Tzain yells. "Help me lead this fight!"

Ever the fearless captain, he takes off, disappearing before he can see the paralysis in my feet. My lungs gasp for air; why can't I remember how to breathe?

You trained for this. I grip my sword as the boat nears. *You* bled *for this.*

But when the enemy crew jumps aboard, years of forced lessons freeze in my fingertips. Though I try to flick my blade open, my hands only tremble. *Strike, Amari.* Father's voice rumbles into my ears, cutting deep into the scar on my back. *Raise your sword, Amari. Attack, Amari. Fight, Amari.*

"I can't . . ."

After all these years, I still can't. Nothing has changed. I cannot move. I cannot fight.

I can only stand still.

Why am I here? What in the skies was I thinking? I could've left that scroll and returned to my quarters. I could still be grieving Binta's death in my room. But I made that choice, one fateful decision that once seemed so right. I thought I could avenge my dear friend.

Instead, I will only die.

I press against the side of the ship, hiding away as the crew fights through the invaders. Their blood spills at my feet. Their anguish rings, filling my ears.

The chaos envelops me, so overwhelming I can hardly see. It takes a moment too long to realize that one of the blades is coming for me.

Strike, Amari.

Yet my limbs do not move. The blade whistles toward my neck—

Tzain cries out as his fist collides with the man's jaw.

The attacker collapses, but not before his sword slashes through Tzain's arm.

"Tzain!"

"Stay back," he yells, grabbing his bleeding bicep.

"I'm sorry!"

"Just get out of the way!"

Hot tears of shame well in my eyes as he runs off. I retreat into the back corner of the ship. I shouldn't have boarded. I shouldn't be here. I should never have left the palace—

A thunderous crash rings through my ears. Our vessel jolts with a violent force, knocking me to the ground. I grip the railing of the ship as the boat shudders. This is it.

We've been hit.

Before I can scramble to my feet, another cannonball blows through our deck. Shards of wood and smoke fly through the air. With a lurch, the bow of the boat tips up. Smoke fills my lungs as I slide across the bloodstained deck.

I grab onto the base of the mast and squeeze for dear life. Liters of water rush across the carnage on the ship.

With another lurch, our boat begins to sink.

CHAPTER THIRTY-ONE

ZÉLIE

"Zélie!"

I break back to the surface and whip my head up. Tzain grips the rail of the ship, teeth clenched with strain. Blood covers his clothes and his face, but I can't tell whether it's his.

Only nine other vessels float through the arena. Nine vessels left in this bloodbath. But the stern of our boat groans under the surface.

Our ship's going down.

I take a deep breath and plunge back into the water. Immediately, bile rises in my throat. Clouds of red and debris make it all but impossible to see.

I struggle to keep my eyes open as I kick as hard as I can. Each stroke down is a stroke through water thick and heavy with blood.

"*Ẹ̀mí àwọn tí ó ti sùn—*"

Though I chant, the last of my ashê dwindles from my fingers. I'm not strong enough. My magic's run dry. But if I can't do it, Tzain and Amari might die. Our ship will go down, our chance at the sunstone will disappear. We won't be able to bring magic back.

I stare at the scar on my palm. Mama's face flashes behind my eyes.

I'm sorry, I think to her spirit.

I don't have a choice.

I bite into my hand. The copper tang of blood fills my mouth as my teeth break through the skin. The blood spreads into the water, glowing with a white light that wraps around my form. My eyes bulge as the light travels within me, vibrating in my blood, radiating through my core.

Ashê tears through my veins, searing my skin from the inside out.

"Ẹ̀mí àwọn tí ó ti sùn—"

Waves of red flash behind my eyes.

Oya dances for me again.

Water twists around me, writhing with new and violent life. The blood magic takes over, enacting my will. With a rush, a new army of animations swirls before my eyes.

Their watery skin bubbles with blood and white light, coming alive with the force of a storm. Ten more animations awaken to join the army, water swirling as their bodies take form. They draw the blood and the debris into their skin, creating new armor for my army of the dead. They look to me when the last animation comes forth.

"Save the boat!"

My spirit soldiers shoot through the water like dual-finned sharks, fiercer than any ship or cannon in sight. Though my insides burn, the thrill of my magic overwhelms the chaos of our fight.

Pleasure swells through me as they follow my silent directive and disappear into the holes left by the cannonballs. A second later all the water inside begins to rush out.

Yes!

In an instant our ship gains buoyancy, bobbing back up to the surface. When all the water is out, the animations join with the wood, patching the holes with the watery remains of their bodies.

It worked!

But my wonder doesn't last long.

Though the animations have disappeared, the surge of the blood magic remains.

My skin sears as it tears through me, burning as if the blood magic is ripping my organs apart. The violence shreds through my muscles. My hands go numb.

"Help!"

I try to scream, but bubbles rush through my throat. Horror sinks into my bones. Mama was right.

This blood magic will destroy me.

I swim for the surface, but each kick is harder than the last. My arms lose feeling, then my feet.

Like vengeful spirits, the blood magic overwhelms me, clinging to my mouth, my chest, my skin. Though I fight for the surface, I can't move. Once so close, our ship now falls farther and farther away.

"Tzain!"

The crimson sea muffles the sound of my screams.

The little air I have in my lungs disappears.

Water rushes in.

CHAPTER THIRTY-TWO

AMARI

I GRIP THE EDGE of the boat, heartbeat racing as its sinking slows to a rough halt.

"She did it!" Tzain pounds a fist against the ship's railing. "Zél, you did it!"

But when Zélie doesn't resurface, Tzain's triumph disappears. He yells her name over and over again, shouting himself hoarse.

I lean over the edge of the ship and scan the waters, frantically searching for a shock of white hair against the red. There's only one vessel left, but Zélie is nowhere in sight.

"Tzain, wait!"

He jumps overboard, leaving the boat without its captain. The final ship turns in the water, altering its course.

"And just like that, our final competitors are out of blastpowder!" the announcer's voice sings. "But only one captain can make it to the end. To win, only one captain can live!"

"Tzain!" I scream over the edge of the ship, heart quaking as the final boat nears. I can't do this on my own. We *need* him to take down the last ship.

The enemy's rowers paddle as fast as they can, while those who manned their cannons arm themselves with blades. Our own crew abandons their posts, scrambling for the spears and swords attached to the ship. Though I shake, they do not hesitate. They are ready, eager, prepared to bring this hell to an end.

Relief rocks my core when Tzain breaks above the surface, one arm wrapped tightly around Zélie's unconscious body. I untack a rope from the side and throw it over the edge; Tzain secures it under Zélie's arms and yells at us to pull her up.

Three laborers join me as I yank, raising Zélie onto the deck. The enemy is moments away now. If she can summon her animations again, we can all live through this.

"Wake up!" I shake Zélie, but she doesn't stir. Her skin burns to the touch. Blood drips from a corner of her lip.

Skies, this won't work. We have to bring Tzain back up. I claw at the knots binding Zélie's torso, but before the final knot is undone, the enemy ship smashes into ours.

With a wild roar, our competitors jump aboard.

I scramble to my feet and wave my sword like a child trying to keep a lionaire away with a flame. There is no technique in my thrust, no sign of the years spent in pain.

Strike, Amari, Father's voice thunders in my head, bringing me back to the tears spilled when he commanded me to fight Inan. I dropped my sword. I refused.

Then my brother's blade ripped through my back.

My stomach lurches as our crew dives into the fight, the chance at victory spurring them on. They overpower the other crew with ease, blowing past their swords to land lethal strikes. Crazed men run toward us, but by the grace of the gods, our crew cuts them down. One man dies just steps from me, blood pooling in his mouth as a knife protrudes from his neck.

Let it end, I plead. *Just let me make it out!*

But as I pray, the captain breaks through, sword plunging forward. I brace myself for the attack, but then I realize he's not coming at me. His sword aims down, angled to the side.

He's targeting Zélie.

Time freezes as the captain nears, his glinting blade drawing closer and closer by the second. Everything around me goes quiet.

Then blood splatters into the air.

For a moment, I am too shocked to realize what I have done. But when the captain falls, my blade goes with him. Pierced straight through his gut.

The arena falls quiet. Smoke begins to clear.

I cannot breathe when the announcer speaks.

"It appears we have a winner. . . ."

CHAPTER THIRTY-THREE

ZÉLIE

538.

That's how many times my body was ripped apart.

How many spirits perished for sport. How many innocent souls shriek in my ears.

Corpses float among the wood in the never-ending sea of blood. Their presence stains the air, invading my lungs with every breath.

Gods, help us. I close my eyes, trying to drown the tragedy out. Through it all, the cheers never stop. The praise never ends. As we stand on the platform, the crowd rejoices as if there's a reason to celebrate this bloodbath.

Beside me, Tzain holds me close; he hasn't really let go since he carried me from the ship. He keeps his expression vacant, but I can sense his remorse.

Though the competitor in him has prevailed, we're still covered in the blood of those who have fallen. We may have triumphed, but this is no victory.

To my right, Amari stands still, hands clenched around her bladeless hilt. She hasn't said one word since we got off that ship, but the laborers told me she was the one who protected me and killed the other captain. For the first time, looking at her doesn't remind me of Saran or Inan. I see the girl who stole the scroll.

I see the seeds of a warrior.

The announcer forces a grin as Dele and Baako roll the shimmering chest of gold away. Gold he probably intended to keep, gold traded for every death.

The crowd roars as our crew is awarded their prize, but not one laborer smiles at the bounty. Wealth and freedom from the stocks are nothing when this horror will haunt them every night.

"Get on with it." I grit my teeth, stepping away from Tzain's protection. "You've already had your show. Give up the sunstone."

The announcer narrows his eyes, his brown skin crinkling with hard lines.

"The show's never over," he hisses away from the metal cone. "Especially when it involves a maggot."

The announcer's words make my lips twitch. Though my body feels hollow, I can't help but plot. How many animations would it take to drag him into the carnage, drown him at the bottom of his own red sea?

The announcer must sense my silent threat, because the smirk falls from his lips. He steps back and raises his cone, turning back to the crowd.

"And now . . ." His voice booms through the arena. He sells the performance with his words, though his face barely hides his dismay. "I present . . . the stone of immortality!"

Even from a distance, the sunstone's warmth seeps into my shivering bones. Oranges and yellows pulse behind its crystal exterior like molten lava. Like a moth, I'm drawn to its holy light.

The last piece, I think, remembering Lekan's words. With the scroll, the stone, and the dagger, we finally have everything we need. We can head to the sacred temple and perform the ritual. We can bring magic *back*.

"You've got this." Tzain places a hand on my shoulder and squeezes. "Whatever happens, I'm right by your side."

"Me too," Amari says softly, regaining her voice. Though dried blood coats her face, her eyes are reassuring.

I nod at her and step forward, reaching for the golden stone. For the first time the crowd around me falls silent, their curiosity heavy in the air.

I brace myself for what might come from holding a living fragment of Sky Mother's soul. But once my fingers touch the polished surface, I know nothing could have prepared me for this.

Like the awakening, touching the stone fills me with a force more powerful than anything I've ever known. The sunstone's energy warms my blood, electrifying the ashê surging through each vein.

The crowd gasps in amazement as the stone's light shines between the gaps in my fingers. Even the announcer backs up; as far as he knows, the stone was only a part of his hoax.

The surge continues to fill me, bubbling up like steam. I close my eyes and Sky Mother appears, more glorious than anything I've ever imagined.

Her silver eyes shine bright against her ebony skin, framed by the crystals dangling from her headdress. Tight white coils fall around her face like rain, twisting with the power radiating from her being.

Her spirit swells through me like lightning breaking through a thunder cloud. It's more than the feeling of breathing.

It's the very essence of life.

"Ẹ̀mí àwọn tí ó ti sùn—" I whisper the first few words of the incantation under my breath, relishing a rush like no other. With the sunstone's power, I could call hundreds of animations from the dead. I could command an unstoppable army.

We could rip through the arena, take down the announcer, punish every spectator who cheered on the slaughter for sport. But that's not what Sky Mother wants. It's not what these spirits need.

One by one, the shrieking dead race through me, not to become animations, but to escape. It's just like the cleanse Mama led every full moon. A final purge to help the spirits pass on to alâfia.

As the souls escape their trauma for the peace of the afterlife, the image of Sky Mother in my mind begins to fade. A goddess with skin like the night takes her place, clothed in waves of red, beautiful with her dark brown eyes.

My gods.

Oya shines in my mind like a torch against the dark. Unlike the chaos I glimpsed when I used blood magic, this vision holds an ethereal grace. She stands still, but it's like the entire world shifts in her presence. A triumphant smile spreads across her lips—

"Ugh!" My eyes fly open. The sunstone glows so brightly in my hands, I have to look away. Though the initial rush of its touch has passed, I can feel its power humming in my bones. It's like Sky Mother's spirit has spread through my body, stitching every wound left by the blood magic's destruction.

With time, the blinding light fades and Oya's stunning image disappears from my head. I stumble backward, clutching the stone as I fall into Tzain's arms.

"What just happened?" Tzain whispers, eyes wide with amazement. "The air . . . It felt like the whole arena was shaking."

I press the sunstone to my chest, trying to hold on to the images that danced in my mind. The light that glinted off the crystals in Sky Mother's headdress; the way Oya's skin shimmered, dark and enchanting like the queen of the night.

This is how Mama must've felt. . . . The realization makes my heart swell. This is why she loved her magic.

This is how it feels to be *alive*.

"The Immortal!" a man from the crowd shouts, and I blink, reorienting myself to the arena. The cry travels throughout the stands until everyone joins in. They chant the false title, rabid in their praise.

"Are you alright?" Amari asks.

"More than alright," I reply with a smile.

We have the stone, the scroll, the dagger.

And now we actually have a chance.

CHAPTER THIRTY-FOUR

AMARI

IT TAKES HOURS for the celebrations to die down, though I don't understand how anyone can feel like celebrating. Such a tremendous waste of life. One stolen by my own hand.

Tzain tries to guard us from the masses, but even he can't overpower the force of the spectators as we pour out of the arena. They parade us through the streets of Ibeji, creating titles to commemorate the occasion. Zélie becomes "the Immortal," while Tzain reigns as "the Commander." When I pass, the spectators shout the most ridiculous name of all. I cringe as it rings once more: "The Lionaire!"

I want to yell of their mistake; replace "lionaire" with a more fitting title like "coward" or "impostor." There is no ferocity behind my eyes, no vicious beast hidden inside. The name is nothing more than a lie, but fueled by liquor, not one of the spectators cares. They just need something to shout. Something to praise.

When we near our rented ahéré, Tzain finally breaks us free. With his guidance, we make it into our clay hut and take turns out back washing the blood away.

As the cold water runs over me, I scrub as hard as I can, desperate to wipe every remnant of that hell from my flesh. When the water turns red, I think of the captain I killed. *Skies* . . .

There was so much blood.

It seeped through the navy kaftan pasted to his skin, leaked through my leather soles, stained the hem of my pants. In his last moments, the captain reached for his pocket with a shaking hand. I don't know what he wanted to grab. Before he could retrieve it, his hand fell limp.

I close my eyes and dig my nails into my palms, letting out a deep, shuddering breath. I don't know what disturbs me more: that I killed him, or that I could do it again.

Strike, Amari. A thin whisper of Father's voice plays in my ears.

I wipe him from my mind as I wash the last of the arena blood from my skin.

Back in the ahéré, the sunstone glows inside Zélie's pack, lighting the scroll and the bone dagger in reds and sunflower yellows. A day ago I hardly believed we held two of the sacred artifacts, yet here all three sit. With twelve days left until the centennial solstice, we can make it to the sacred island with time to spare. Zélie can perform the ritual. Magic will actually return.

I smile to myself, picturing the glittering lights that escaped Binta's hand. Not cut short by Father's blade, but everlasting. A beauty I could witness every day.

If we succeed, Binta's death will mean something. One way or another, Binta's light will spread throughout Orïsha. The hole she left in my heart might one day heal.

"Can't believe it?" Tzain whispers from the doorframe.

"Something like that." I give him a small smile. "I'm just grateful it's all over."

"I heard they're out of business. Without the coin from the pot, they can't afford to bribe the stockers for more laborers."

"Thank the skies." I think of all the young divîners who perished. Although Zélie helped their spirits pass, their deaths still weigh on my shoulders. "Baako told me he and the other laborers will use the gold to cover more divîners' debts. If they're lucky, they'll be able to save hundreds of people from the stocks."

Tzain nods, looking at Zélie as she sleeps in the corner of the hut. Freshly bathed, she's almost hidden against Nailah's soft fur, recovering after her blinding display with the sunstone. Watching her, I don't feel the prickle of discomfort that usually surfaces in her presence. When the crew told her that I was the one who ended the fight, she gave me a look that almost resembled a smile.

"Do you think your father knew about this?"

I snap my head up. Tzain averts his gaze and his face hardens.

"I don't know," I say quietly. "But if he knew, I'm not sure he would bother to stop it."

An uncomfortable silence falls between us, stealing our brief moment of relief. Tzain reaches for a roll of bandages, but winces. The pain in his arm must be too great.

"Allow me." I step forward, avoiding the reddening bandages around his bicep. His only battle wound, sustained because I got in his way.

"Thanks," Tzain mutters when I hand him the roll. My stomach tightens with the guilt that eats away at my core.

"Don't thank me. If I'd stayed off that boat, you wouldn't have this wound at all."

"I also wouldn't have Zél."

He meets my eyes with an expression so kind it catches me off guard. I thought for sure he'd resent me, but if anything, he's grateful.

"Amari, I've been thinking. . . ." He picks at the roll of bandages, unraveling it only to wrap it up again. "When we pass through Gombe, you should go to the guard post. Tell them you've been kidnapped, blame everything on us."

"Because of what happened on the boat?" I try to keep my tone even, but a slight shrillness breaks in. Where's this coming from? Just a moment ago he was thanking me for being here.

"No!" Tzain closes the space between us, placing a tentative hand on my shoulder. For someone so large, there's a surprising tenderness to his touch. "You were amazing. I don't want to think about what would've happened if you weren't there. But the look on your face afterward . . . If you stay, I can't promise you won't have to kill again."

I stare at the ground, counting the cracks in the clay. He's offering me another escape.

He's trying to keep the blood off my hands.

I think back to that moment on the boat, back when I regretted everything and wished I had never stolen the scroll. This is the out I prayed for. I craved it with all my heart.

It could work. . . .

Though a flash of shame hits me, I imagine what would happen if I turned myself in. With the right story, enough tears, the perfect lies, I could convince them all. If I showed up disheveled enough, Father might believe I'd been kidnapped by the evil maji. Yet even as I play with the possibility, I already know my response.

"I'm staying." I swallow the part of me that wants to give in, tucking it deep down inside. "I can do this. I proved that tonight."

"Just because you can fight doesn't mean you're meant to—"

"Tzain, do *not* tell me what I am meant to do!"

His words stab like a needle, locking me back inside the palace walls.

Amari, sit up straight!

Do not eat that.

That's more than enough dessert for you—

No.

No more. I have lived that life before and lost my dearest friend because of it. Now that I've escaped, I shall never return. With my escape, I must do more.

"I am a princess, not a prop. Do not treat me any differently. My father is responsible for this pain. *I* will be the one to fix it."

Tzain jerks back and raises his hands in surrender. "Alright."

I tilt my head. "That's it?"

"Amari, I want you here. I just needed to know it was your choice. When you took that scroll, there's no way you could know everything would turn out like this."

"Oh . . ." I fight back a smile. *I want you here.* His words make my ears burn. Tzain actually wants me to stay.

"Well, thank you," I say quietly, sitting back. "I want to be here, too. Despite how loudly you snore."

Tzain smiles, and it softens up every hard line in his face. "You're not so quiet yourself, Princess. The way you snore, I should've called you the Lionaire this whole time."

"Ha." I narrow my eyes and grab our canteens, praying my face isn't flushed. "I'll remember that the next time you need help grabbing a roll of bandages."

Tzain grins as I leave the hut, a lopsided smile that lifts my very steps. The brisk night air greets me like an old friend, thick with the scent of ogogoro and palm wine from the celebration.

A hooded woman spots me and breaks out into a wide smile. "The Lionaire!"

Her call incites the cheers of those around her. It makes my cheeks flush, but this time the name doesn't sound so wrong. With a shy wave, I skirt the crowd, fading into the shadows.

Perhaps I made a mistake.

Maybe a lionaire lives in me after all.

CHAPTER THIRTY-FIVE

INAN

THE DESERT AIR is lifeless.

It cuts with each inhale.

Without Kaea's steady instruction, every breath blurs together, marred by the magic that took her away.

I never realized how riding alongside Kaea passed the time. Traveling alone, minutes merge into hours. Days blend into nights. The food supply dwindles first. Water follows close behind.

I grab the canteen hooked to the saddle of my stolen panthenaire and squeeze the last droplets out. If Orí is really watching me from above, he must be laughing now.

Maji attack.

Kaea killed.

Pursuing the scroll.

—I

The message I sent home with the soldiers should arrive soon.

Knowing Father, he'll dispatch guards the moment he receives it, order them to return with the culprit's head or not at all. Little does he know the monster he hunts is me.

Guilt rips at my insides like the magic I fight back. Father'll never understand the extent to which I'm already punishing myself.

Skies.

My head rings as I push my magic down. Deep into my bones, further than I ever knew it could go. Now it's not just an ache in my chest or a winded breath that I fight, it's a constant tremor shaking my hands. The burning hatred in Kaea's eyes. The venom in her final word.

Maggot.

I hear it again and again. A hell I can't escape. With that one foul word, Kaea might as well have declared me unfit to be king.

The slur disparages everything I've ever worked for. The duty I fight to fulfill. The destiny Kaea herself forced upon me.

Dammit. I close my eyes against the memories of her that day. It was Kaea who found me after I hurt Amari, tucked in the darkest corner of my room, clutching the bloodied blade.

When I threw the sword to the floor, Kaea placed it back into my hands.

You're strong, Inan. She smiled. *Do not let that strength scare you. You will need it all your life. You'll need it to be king.*

"Strength," I scoff. It's that very strength I need now. I only used magic to protect my kingdom. Kaea of all people should've understood that.

Sand whips at my face as I pass the clay walls of Ibeji. I force thoughts of Kaea away. She's dead. I can't change that.

The threat of magic still lives.

Kill her. In the dead of night, I'd expected the desert settlement to be asleep, but the streets of Ibeji swell with the remnants of some celebration. Low-ranking nobles and villagers pull generous swigs from their cups, each drunker than the last. At times they cry out mythic names, cheering for "the Lionaire," "the Commander," or "the Immortal." None pay any mind to the disheveled soldier who rides in their midst, or waste a glance at the dried blood coating my skin. No one realizes that I am their prince.

I pull on my panthenaire's reins, stopping before a villager who looks sober enough to remember his own name. I reach to pull out the wrinkled poster.

Then I catch the scent of the sea.

Though I've pushed every part of my curse down, it hits. Distinct, like an ocean breeze. It strikes me like the first drop of water in days. Suddenly it all comes together.

She's here.

I yank on the reins and urge the panthenaire toward the scent.

Kill her. Kill magic.

Get my life back.

I slide to a stop in an alleyway lined with sand ahérés. The smell of the sea is overpowering now. She's here. Hiding. Behind one of these doors.

My throat tightens as I dismount the panthenaire and unsheathe my sword. Its blade catches the moonlight.

I kick down the first door.

"What're you doing?" a woman cries. Even with the haze slowing my thoughts, I can see it's not her.

Not the girl.

Not what I need.

I breathe deep and search again, letting the sea-salt scent guide my way. It's this door. *This* ahéré. The only thing standing in my way.

I kick down the clay door and run forward, teeth bared in a growl. I raise my sword to fight—

No one is here.

Folded sheets and old clothes line the walls. All stained with blood.

But the hut is empty, filled only with shed lionaire fur and the unmistakable scent of the girl.

"Hey!" a man shouts from outside. I don't turn to look.

She was here. In this city. In this hut.

And now she's gone.

"You can't just—" A hand grips my shoulder.

In an instant, my own hands are around the man's throat.

He lets out a yelp as I point my blade at his heart.

"Where is she?"

"I don't know who you're talking about," he cries.

I draw my blade across his chest. A thin line of blood appears. His tears almost look silver in the moonlight.

Maggot, the girl whispers with Kaea's voice. *You'll never be king. You can't even catch me.*

I tighten my grip on the man's neck.

"Where is she?"

CHAPTER THIRTY-SIX

ZÉLIE

After the six days traveling through the hell of the desert, the lush forests of the Gombe River Valley are a welcome sight. The hilly land breathes with life, filled with trees so wide one trunk could fit an entire ahéré. We weave in and out of the towering giants, moonlight spilling through their leaves as we travel toward a winding river. Its quiet roar hits my ears like a song, soft like the crash of ocean waves.

"This is so soothing," Amari purrs.

"I know. It's almost like being back home."

I close my eyes and take in the trickling sound, letting it fill me with the calm that came in the early mornings spent drawing the fishing net with Baba. That far out at sea, it was like we lived in our own world. It was the only time I truly felt safe. Not even the guards could touch us.

My muscles relax as I settle into the memory. I haven't felt this still in weeks. With the sacred artifacts scattered and Inan's sword at our backs, every second felt stolen, borrowed at best. We didn't have what we needed for the ritual, and the chances of us getting the artifacts were far smaller than the chances of getting killed. But now, we have it all: the scroll, the sunstone, and the bone dagger are safe in our grasp. For once, I feel more than at ease. With six days until the centennial solstice, I finally feel that we can win.

"Do you think they'll tell stories about this?" Amari asks. "About us?"

"They better." Tzain snorts. "With all the dung we've had to wade through for this magic, we better get a whole festival."

"Where would the story even start?" Amari chews on her bottom lip. "What would they call it? 'The Magic Summoners'? 'The Restorers of Magic and the Sacred Artifacts'?"

"That doesn't have a ring to it." I scrunch my nose and recline on Nailah's furry back. "A title like that will never withstand the test of time."

"What about something simpler?" Tzain offers. " 'The Princess and the Fisherman'?"

"That sounds like a love story."

I roll my eyes. I can hear the smile in Amari's voice. I have no doubt that if I sat up, I would catch Tzain smiling as well.

"It does sound like a love story," I tease. "But that's not accurate. If you want a love story so bad, why not call it 'The Princess and the Agbön Player'?"

Amari whips her head around, a flush rising to her cheeks. "I didn't mean—I—I wasn't trying to say—" Her mouth clamps shut before she can choke out anything else.

Tzain shoots me a glare, but it lacks true malice. As we approach the Gombe River, I can't decide whether it's endearing or annoying how the smallest taunt makes them both clam up.

"Gods, it's a beast!" I slide down Nailah's tail and find my footing over the large, smooth stones lining the muddy bank. The water stretches wide, curving a path through the heart of the forest and the trunks of massive trees. I kneel down in the mud and bring the water to my lips, remembering the way my throat burned for it in the desert. The ice-cold water feels so good in this humid air that I'm tempted to thrust my entire face in.

"Zél, not yet," Tzain says. "There'll be water up ahead. We still have a ways to go."

"I know, but just take a sip. Nailah could use the rest."

I rub Nailah's horn and nuzzle my face against her neck, grinning when she nuzzles me back. Even she hated the desert. Since we've left, she's had an extra spring in her step.

"For Nailah," Tzain concedes. "Not for you."

He jumps down and crouches by the river, careful as he fills up his canteen. A smile spreads across my lips. The opportunity is too great to resist.

"Oh my gods!" I point. "What's that?"

"What—"

I ram into his body. Tzain yells as he topples over, hitting the river with a splash. Amari gasps when Tzain reemerges, soaked, teeth chattering with cold. He locks eyes with me, a wicked grin breaking through.

"You're dead."

"You have to catch me first!"

Before I can take off, Tzain lunges forward, grabbing me by the leg. I shriek as he pulls me under. The water is so cold it hits my skin like Mama Agba's wooden needles.

"Gods!" I sputter for air.

"Was it worth it?" Tzain laughs.

"That's the first time I've tricked you in ages, so I'm going to have to say yes."

Amari jumps down from Nailah, giggling as she shakes her head. "You two are ridiculous."

Tzain's grin turns mischievous. "We're a team, Amari. Shouldn't you be ridiculous, too?"

"Absolutely not." Amari backs away, but she doesn't stand a chance. Tzain rises from the water like an Orïshan river python. Amari only gains a few meters before he hunts her down. I smile as she squeals with laughter, spouting every excuse she can think of when Tzain throws her over his back.

"I can't swim."

"It's not that deep." He laughs.

"I'm a princess."

"Don't princesses bathe?"

"I have the scroll!" She takes it out of her waistband, reminding Tzain of his own strategy. To keep all of the artifacts from being in one place, he carries the bone dagger, Amari holds the scroll, and I guard the sunstone.

"Good point." Tzain snatches the scroll out of her hand and places it on Nailah's saddle. "And now, Your Majesty, your royal bath awaits."

"Tzain, no!"

Amari's shriek is so loud that birds fly out of the trees in alarm. Tzain and I burst into laughter as she crashes into the water, flailing around although she can stand.

"It's not funny." Amari shivers, grinning in spite of herself. "You're going to pay for that."

Tzain bows. "Do your best."

A new kind of smile rises to my face, one that warms me even as I sit on the bank of the freezing river. It's been far too long since I've seen my brother play. Amari fights in earnest to dunk him under the water, though she can't be more than half his weight soaking wet. Tzain entertains her, crying out in pretend pain, pretending she might win—

Suddenly, the river vanishes.

The trees.

Nailah.

Tzain.

The world spins around me as a familiar force carries me away.

When the spinning stops, reeds tickle my feet. Brisk air fills my lungs.

By the time I realize I'm in the prince's dreamscape, I'm thrust back into the real world.

I wheeze, clutching my chest as the cold of the river hits my feet again. The flash of the dreamscape only lasted a moment, but it was powerful, stronger than it's ever felt. A chill strikes my core as the realization settles in. Inan isn't just in my dreams.

He's close.

"We have to go."

Tzain and Amari are laughing too loudly to hear me. He's lifted her once again, threatening to throw her back in.

"Stop." I kick water at them. "We have to *go*. We're not safe here!"

"What are you talking about?" Amari giggles.

"It's Inan," I rush out. "He's clo—"

My voice chokes in my throat. A distant noise pounds near.

Our heads whip toward the sound, thumping and constant.

At first I can't decipher it, but as it approaches I recognize the steady patter of paws. When they round the riverbend, I finally see what I feared most: Inan speeds toward us.

Rabid on his panthenaire.

Shock slows my steps as we scramble out of the river. The water that once held our joy weighs us down, current strong now that Amari and Tzain fight to get out. *We're idiots.* How could we be so foolish? The very second we let ourselves relax is the second Inan finally catches us.

But how did Inan get over the broken bridge at Chândomblé? How did he know where to go? Even if he somehow tracked us to Ibeji, we left that hell six nights ago.

I race over to Nailah and mount first, gripping her reins tight. Tzain and Amari quickly scramble up behind me. But before I snap the leather, I turn around—*what have I missed?*

Where are the guards he traveled with before? The admiral who killed Lekan? After surviving a sêntaro's attack, surely Inan wouldn't strike without backup.

But despite all reasonable logic, no other guards shoot forth. The little prince is vulnerable. Alone.

And I can take him in a fight.

"What're you doing?" Tzain screams as I release Nailah's reins, drawing her to a halt before we even start.

"I got this."

"Zélie, no!"

But I don't turn back.

I throw my pack to the ground and jump off Nailah's back, landing in a crouch. Inan halts his own ryder and dismounts, sword brandished and ready for blood. With a growl, the panthenaire lopes off, but Inan hardly seems to notice. Crimson stains haunt his uniform, a desperation burns in his amber eyes. And yet, he looks thinner. Fatigue rises from his skin like heat. Something crazed shifts in his gaze.

Suppressing his powers has left him weak.

"Wait!" Amari's voice quivers.

Though Tzain tries to hold her back, she slides off Nailah's saddle. Her nimble feet hit the ground without making a sound, tentative as they walk past me.

Color drains from Amari's face, and I see the fear that's plagued her all her life. The girl who grabbed me all those weeks ago in the market. The princess with the scar traveling down her back.

But as she moves, something different sets into her stance, something steady like on the arena ship. It allows her to approach her brother, concern eclipsing the terror in her eyes.

"What happened?"

Inan redirects his sword from my chest to Amari's. Tzain jumps down to fight, but I grab his arm. "Let her try."

"Out of my way." Inan's voice is commanding, but a tremble shakes his hand.

Amari pauses for a second, illuminated by the moonlight reflecting off Inan's blade.

"Father's not here," she finally says. "You won't hurt me."

"You don't know that."

"Maybe you don't." Amari swallows hard. "But I do."

Inan is silent for a long moment. Still. Too still. The clouds shift and moonlight shines, lighting the space between them. Amari takes a step forward. Then another, bigger this time. When she places a hand on Inan's cheek, tears fill his amber eyes.

"You don't understand," he croaks, still clenching his sword. "It destroyed her. It'll destroy *all* of us."

Her? Whether or not Amari knows who Inan's talking about, she doesn't seem to care. She guides his sword to the ground as if soothing a wild animal.

For the first time I notice how different she and her brother truly look, the contrast in her round face, the angles of Inan's square jawline. Though they share the same amber gaze and copper complexion, that seems to be where their similarities end.

"Those are Father's words, Inan. His decisions. Not yours. We are our own people. We make our *own* choices."

"But he's right." Inan's voice cracks. "If we don't stop magic, Orïsha will fall."

His eyes return to me, and I tighten my grip on my staff. *Try it*, I want to bark. I'm done running away.

Amari redirects Inan's line of vision, her delicate hands cupping the back of his head.

"Father is not the future of Orïsha, brother. We are. We stand on the right side of this. You can stand there, too."

Inan stares at Amari, and for a moment I don't know who he is. The ruthless captain; the little prince; the scared and broken maji? There's a longing in his eyes, a desire to give up the fight. But when he lifts his chin, the killer I know comes back.

"Amari—" I cry out.

Inan pushes her aside and lunges forward, sword raised to my chest. I jump in front of Tzain with my staff brandished. Amari tried.

Now it's my turn.

The air rings as Inan's sword hits the metal of my staff. I expect a chance to counterattack, but now that the true Inan's awakened, he won't let up. Though fatigued, his blows are fierce, fueled by a hatred of me, a hatred of what I know. Yet as I defend against each strike, my own rage builds. The monster who burned my village, the man responsible for Lekan's death. The root of all our problems.

And I can wipe him away.

"I see you took my advice," I yell, somersaulting to dodge the strike of his blade. "I can barely see your streak. How many coats this time, little prince?"

I swipe my staff at his skull, striking to kill, not maim. I'm tired of fighting.

I'm tired of him getting in our way.

He ducks to avoid my staff, but he's quick to thrust his sword at my gut. I spin out of harm's way and strike. Once again, our weapons collide with a piercing clink.

"You won't win," I hiss, arms shaking under the force. "Killing me won't change what you are."

"Doesn't matter." Inan jumps back, freeing himself for another blow. "If you die, magic dies, too."

He runs forward and raises his sword with a cry.

CHAPTER THIRTY-SEVEN

AMARI

DESPITE ALL THE YEARS spent fighting my brother, watching him now is like watching a stranger spar. Though slower than usual, Inan's strikes are merciless, fueled by a burning rage I cannot comprehend. As he and Zélie trade blow for blow, their battle flows to the constant clinks of his sword and her staff. When their fight pushes them farther into the forest, Tzain and I run after them.

"Are you alright?" Tzain asks.

I long to say yes, but watching Inan, my heart fractures. After all this time, he's so close to doing the right thing.

"They're going to kill each other," I whisper, flinching at their hate-fueled blows.

"No." Tzain shakes his head. "Zél's going to kill him."

I pause and study Zélie's movements, powerful and precise, the fighter she's always been. But she's not trying to knock him down—she fights to take my brother out.

"We have to stop this!" I run forward, ignoring Tzain's pleas to stay back. The battle pushes our siblings down a hill, deep into the forested valley. I sprint to reach them, though the closer I get, the more I don't know what to do. Should I extend my blade or stay defenseless and throw myself in harm's way? They charge at each other with such a vengeance,

I don't know if either plan would stop them. I don't even know if either would make them hesitate.

But as I run, a new dilemma distracts me; the pressure of unseen eyes. It's a weight I would know anywhere, honed from a lifetime of carrying it inside the palace walls.

As the sensation grows, I stumble to a stop, searching for its source. *Did Inan summon other soldiers?* It isn't like him to fight alone. If the army's approaching, we could be more vulnerable than I thought.

But the seal of Orïsha doesn't appear. Instead, leaves tussle above us. Before I can extend my blade, a whipping sound cracks through the air—

Nailah crashes to the ground with a yelp, thick bolas wrapped around her legs and snout. I pivot as a net shoots over her massive frame, capturing her with the ease of a practiced poacher. Caged roars shrink into frightened whimpers as Nailah fights in vain to get free. Her whimpers shrivel into silence. She's helpless as five soldiers emerge from the forest and drag her away.

"Nailah!" Tzain jumps into action, skinning knife brandished. He bounds forward with impressive speed, blade poised to cut—

"Ugh!"

Tzain tumbles to the ground like a boulder with bolas binding his wrists and ankles. The hunting knife skids against the forest floor as a net is launched, trapping him like a jungle cat.

"No!"

I run after him and extend my own blade, heart slamming against my chest. I dodge a whipping bola with ease, but when the five figures who took Nailah reappear, I don't know where to turn. They blend in and out of the shadows, masked and clad in black. In brief flashes I catch their beady eyes. *Not soldiers . . .*

But if not more of Inan's guards, who are these fighters? Why do they attack us? What are they after?

I slash at the first figure who approaches and duck to avoid another's strike. Each attack wastes precious time, time Tzain and Nailah do not have.

"Tzain!" I call after him as more masked figures emerge from the darkness and drag him away. He fights against the net with all his might, but a swift blow to the head leaves his body limp.

"Tzain!" I slash my sword at a lunging assailant, striking a moment too late. The masked man grabs my weapon and disarms me. Another covers my face with a soaked cloth.

Its acidic smell burns to a vicious sting, raging as my vision darkens.

CHAPTER THIRTY-EIGHT

ZÉLIE

AMARI'S SCREAMS REVERBERATE through the trees.

Inan and I freeze mid-attack. We whip our heads to see Amari struggling with a masked man several meters away.

Though she thrashes, a black glove closes over her mouth. Her eyes glaze before rolling back.

"Amari!" Inan takes off after her, and I move to follow. But the forest is empty. I can't find Nailah.

I don't see Tzain.

"Tzain?" I brace myself against a tree and survey the silhouetted trees filling the valley. A cloud of dirt plumes in the distance, a netted body, heavy and strong. A limp hand presses against the cords. *No . . .*

"Tzain!"

I sprint.

Faster than I knew I could run.

It's like I'm six years old again, reaching after the chain, clawing after Mama.

I push the memories down as I go, screaming Tzain's name into the night. This can't happen. Not to me. Not to Tzain.

Not again.

"Tzain!"

My screams rip my throat raw, my feet quake as I pound against the dirt. I pass Inan in pursuit of Amari. I can save him—

"No!"

Tight cords wrap around my ankles, pulling me to the ground. The breath rushes from my chest as a net ensnares my body.

"Agh!" I scream again, twisting and kicking as I'm pulled through the forest. They've taken Tzain. They've taken Amari.

And now they're going to take me.

Rocks and twigs tear at my skin, knocking my staff from my hand. I try to unearth Tzain's dagger, but it too escapes my grasp. Dirt flies into my eyes, burning as I blink the debris away. It's useless. I've lost—

The cord pulling my net snaps.

My body rolls to a halt as the two masked figures dragging me pitch forward with a start. In a flash, Inan lunges, striking while they're still on the ground.

One masked man runs, seeming to disappear under the gaping tree roots. The other moves too slowly; Inan rams the hilt of his sword against the man's temple and his knees buckle.

When the man crumples to the ground, Inan turns on me. He readjusts his grip on his sword.

A fire rages behind his eyes.

My fingers tremble as I rip at the cords with my bare hands, struggling to free myself. As Inan approaches, the seal of Orïsha catches the moonlight, carrying every pain endured under its leopanaire's watch. The guards' boots. The blood in the dirt. The black chain around Mama's neck.

The way they kicked Tzain down.

The way they threw me to the ground.

Each new memory constricts everything inside me, crushing my ribs. My breath catches as Inan crouches down and pins my arms under his knees.

This is how it ends—

Inan's blade flashes from above.

—exactly how it began.

CHAPTER THIRTY-NINE

INAN

I'M SO CLOSE.

This one thought consumes me as I stalk toward the girl. Trapped in the net, she's defenseless. No staff. No magic.

With this one kill, I'll fulfill my duty. Protect all of Orïsha from her madness. Every sin committed in this hunt disappears. The only living being who knows of my curse goes with them.

"Huh!" I pin down her arms with my knees, pressing harder when she fights. I raise my sword and push down on her sternum with one hand, angling to drive the blade through her heart.

But the moment my hand touches her chest, my magic roars through my skin. A force that can't be stopped. Stronger than any magic I've felt.

"Ugh!" I wheeze. The world disappears in a burning blue cloud. Though I fight, I can't get out.

My curse holds me down.

Red skies.

Shrill screams.

Running blood.

In one moment, the girl's whole world flashes before my eyes. Her heartbreak rips through my own chest.

Rawer than I knew pain could be.

Cold rock hits my bare feet as she climbs the snow-capped mountains of Ibadan. The warm smell of jollof rice wraps around me. My heart stops when the guards kick down the wooden door of their home. Orïsha's guards.

My guards.

The very sight of them suffocates me. Like a gorillion squeezing my throat.

A thousand instances flash before me, a thousand crimes bearing the seal of Orïsha.

The snow leopanaire shines as the guard's ironclad fist collides with her father's jaw.

It gleams when the blood-covered chain wraps around her mother's neck.

I see it all. The world Father created.

The pain she's forced to live in.

"Mama!"

Zélie screams. A cry so mangled it doesn't even sound human.

Tzain covers her in the corner of their hut, a desperate attempt to hide her from the world's pain.

It all speeds past. A blur, yet an endless stretch of time.

Thrashing as she runs after her mother.

Freezing when she gets to the tree—

Skies.

The horror sears into my brain. Maji bound by majacite chains. Ornaments of death.

Hanging for the whole world to see.

It's a wound that reverberates through my core. A decree to any divîner who lived through that night.

In Father's Orïsha, this was the only end maji could meet.

It takes everything in me to fight Zélie's memories back. Her sorrow drags me down like a vengeful current.

With a lurch, I snap back to reality.

My sword hangs above her chest.

Curse the skies.

My hand shakes. The moment to kill still hangs between us. Yet I can't bring myself to move.

Not when all I see is the scared and broken girl.

It's like seeing her for the first time: the human behind the maji. Fear embedded in the pain. Tragedy caused in Father's name.

Father . . .

The truth sears, a bitter liquor burning down my throat.

Zélie's memories don't hold the villains Father always warned of. Only families he tore apart.

Duty before self. His creed rings through my ears.

My father.

Her king.

The harbinger of all this suffering.

With a cry, I strike down. Zélie flinches at my speed.

The cords binding her fall into the dirt.

Her eyes snap open and she scrambles back, waiting for my attack. But it doesn't come.

I can't be another person bearing the seal of Orïsha who causes her pain.

Zélie's mouth falls open. Questions and confusion hang on the curve of her lips. But then her head snaps to the masked figure in the dirt. Her eyes go wide with the realization.

"Tzain!"

She rushes to her feet, nearly tripping in the process. Her brother's name echoes through the darkness.

When nothing answers her, she falls to the earth. Against my will, I sink with her.

I finally know the truth.

Yet I don't know what in skies' name I'm supposed to do.

CHAPTER FORTY

ZÉLIE

I DON'T KNOW how long I lie in the dirt.

Ten minutes.

Ten days.

A cold like I've never known settles into my bones.

The chill of being alone.

I don't understand. Who were those masked fighters? What were they after? They moved so fast, there was no way we could've avoided them.

Unless you kept running . . .

The truth puts a bitter tang on my tongue. Even the fastest mask would be nothing compared to Nailah's speed. If we had just ridden off on Nailah, the men couldn't have ambushed us. Amari and my brother would be safe. But I ignored Tzain's warning and he paid the price.

Tzain's always paying my price.

When I ran after the guards who took Mama, he weathered their beatings to drag me back. When I saved Amari from Lagos, he gave up his home, his team, his past. And when I decide to fight Inan, it's not me who gets taken. It's him. Always Tzain paying for my mistakes.

Get up, a voice rings through my head, harsher than it's ever been. *Go after Tzain and Amari. Get them back now.*

Whoever these masked men are, they've made a fatal mistake. One I will ensure is their last.

Though my body feels like lead, I drag myself to my feet and go over to where Inan and the masked figure lie.

Inan leans against a trunk, face pinched, still clutching his chest. When he sees me, he wraps his hand around the hilt of his sword, but still he doesn't attack.

Whatever fire he summoned to fight me is extinguished; in its ashes, dark circles have formed under his eyes. He seems smaller than he did before. His bones pull against his blanched skin.

He's fighting it. . . . The realization sets in as the air around me chills. He's pushing down his magic.

He's making himself weak again.

But why? I stare at him, confusion gathering by the second. Why did he cut me from that net? Why isn't he raising his sword against me again?

The "why" doesn't matter, the harsh voice rings inside my head. Regardless of his reasons, I'm still alive.

If I waste any more time, my brother could end up dead.

I turn away from Inan and press my foot to the masked boy's chest. Part of me itches to unmask him, but this will be easier if I can't see his face. He seemed like a giant when he dragged me through the forest. Now his limp body looks frail. Perfectly weak.

"Where'd you take them?" I ask.

The boy stirs but stays silent. *Wrong choice.*

Worst choice.

I reach for my dropped staff and thrust down, smashing the bones in his hand. Inan's head snaps up as the boy lets out a violent howl that echoes into the night.

"Answer me!" I yell. "Where'd you take them?"

"I don't—*agh!*" His screams grow louder, but they're not loud enough. I want to hear him cry. I want to see him bleed.

I let my staff fall and pull my dagger from my waistband. *Tzain's dagger . . .*

The memory of him placing it in my hands before I walked into Lagos breaks through my grief.

Just in case, he said that day.

Just in case I endangered him.

"Tell me!" My eyes sting. "Where's the girl? Where's my brother? Where's your *camp*?"

The first strike is intentional, a cut in the arm to get him to talk. But when the blood flows, something snaps, something feral I can't contain.

The second strike is quick, the third passes too fast to follow. The darkest part of my rage breaks free as I slash him again and again, drowning out all my pain.

"Where are they?" I thrust my knife into his hand as the corners of my vision blur. Mama vanishes into the darkness. Tzain's netted body follows after her. "Answer me!" I shriek, pulling the blade up once more. "Where'd they take him? *Where's my brother?*"

"Hey!"

A voice calls from above, but I can barely hear it. They took magic. They took Mama. They won't take Tzain, too.

"I'll kill you." I move the dagger over the masked boy's heart and pull back. "I'll kill y—"

"Zélie, don't!"

CHAPTER FORTY-ONE

INAN

I REACH OUT, seizing both her wrists just in time.

She stiffens as I drag her onto her feet.

The moment our skin touches, my magic thrums, threatening to engulf me in Zélie's memories once more. I clench my teeth and force the beast back down. Skies only know what'll happen if I lose myself in her head again.

"Let go," she seethes. Her voice. It still carries all the rage and ferocity of before. Completely ignorant of the fact that now I've seen her memories.

Now I see her.

Unable to stop myself, I drink Zélie in, every curve, every line. The crescent-shaped birthmark along the slope of her neck. The specks of white swimming in the silver pools of her eyes.

"Let *go*," Zélie repeats, more violently than before. She drives her knee toward my groin; I jump back just in time.

"Wait." I try to reason with her, but without the masked man, her rage has found a new outlet. Her fingers tighten around her crude dagger. She rears back to attack.

"Hey—" *Zél.* The word pops into my mind. A rough voice. Her brother's voice.

Tzain calls her Zél.

"Zél, stop!"

It feels foreign on my lips, but Zélie halts, stunned at the sound of her nickname. Her brows knit with pain. Just like the way they knit when the guards dragged her mother away.

"Calm down." I loosen my grip. A small show of faith. "You have to stop. You'll kill our only lead."

She stares at me. The tears hanging off her dark lashes fall onto her cheek. Another surge of painful memories simmers to the surface. I have to brace myself to keep them at bay.

" 'Our'?" Zélie asks.

The word sounds even stranger coming out of her mouth. We are not supposed to have anything. We are not even supposed to be a "we."

Kill her. Kill magic.

It was all so simple before. It's what Father would have wanted.

It's what he's already done.

But the maji hanging from the tree still scar my mind.

Just one of Orïsha's endless crimes.

Looking at Zélie, I finally have the answer to the question I was too afraid to ask. I cannot be like Father.

I will not be that type of king.

I let go of her wrists, but inside I let go of so much more. Father's tactics. His Orïsha. Everything I now realize I don't want to be.

My duty has always been to my kingdom, but it must be for a better Orïsha. A new Orïsha.

A land in which a prince and a maji could coexist. A land where even Zélie and I could be a "we."

If I am to truly fulfill my duty to my kingdom, that is the Orïsha I must lead.

"Our," I repeat, forcing confidence into my voice. "We need each other. They took Amari, too."

Her eyes search me. Hoping. Fighting that hope at the same time. "You held Amari at sword point ten minutes ago. You're just after the scroll."

"Do you *see* the scroll?"

Zélie looks around for where she tossed her pack before our fight, but even when she spots it her face falls. They took her brother. Her ryder, her ally. And the scroll we both need is gone.

"Whether I'm after my sister or that scroll, those men have both. For now our interests are aligned."

"I don't need you." Zélie narrows her eyes. "I'll find them by myself." But fear drips from her skin like sweat.

Her fear of being alone.

"Without me, you'd be knocked out in a net. Your only clue to their camp would be dead. You really think you can take these fighters on without my help?"

I wait for her to concede. She only glares.

"I'll take your rare bout of silence as a no."

She stares at the dagger in her hand. "If you give me a reason to kill you—"

"It's amusing that you think you could."

We face off as if we're still fighting, an invisible staff pressing against an unseen sword. But when she can oppose me no longer, Zélie walks back to the boy bleeding in the dirt.

"Okay, little prince. What do we do now?"

My blood simmers at her pet name, but I force myself to brush it aside. A new Orïsha has to begin somewhere.

"Hold him up."

"Why?"

"For skies' sake, just do it."

She cocks an eyebrow in defiance but drags the poor bastard up. His eyelids flutter slightly and he moans. An uncomfortable heat prickles the air between us as I step closer.

I take inventory of the masked figure. *Both hands broken. More wounds than I can count.* He hangs like a rag doll in her hands. We'll be lucky if he doesn't bleed out.

"Listen here." I grab his chin, forcing him to look into my eyes. "If you want to live, I suggest you start talking. Where's our family?"

CHAPTER FORTY-TWO

AMARI

THE STABBING ACHE comes first, pulsing through my head with an intensity that stirs me awake. The burns follow soon after, stinging from the endless cuts and scratches peppering my skin.

I blink my eyes open, but the darkness remains; they've tied a tweed bag over my face. The rough fabric sticks to my nose as I breathe in too deeply, a futile attempt to keep myself from hyperventilating.

What is the meaning of this?

I pull forward, but my arms hold me back, wrists bound against a column. *Wait, not a column.* I shift to explore the rough surface. *A tree . . .*

That means we're still in the forest.

"*Tzain?*" I try to call out, but my mouth is gagged. The fried pork rinds from dinner churn in my stomach. Whoever these people are, they've taken every precaution to protect themselves.

I strain to hear another clue—running water, the shift of other captives. But no other sounds come forth. I'm forced to mine my memories for more.

Though I can't see, I close my eyes, reliving the surprise attack: Tzain and Nailah disappearing in woven nets, the acidic stench that turned everything black. So many masked figures, quick and silent, blending with the shadows. These strange fighters are the culprits.

They took all of us down.

But why? What is it these people want? If their aim was to rob us, they already succeeded. If they desired our deaths, I wouldn't be breathing now. This has to be something different, an attack shrouded in a greater aim. With enough time, I can decipher it. Plot a way to escape—

"She's awake."

I tense, keeping still as a female voice speaks. Something rustles as footsteps near. The faint smell of sage hits me when she gets closer.

"Should we get Zu?"

This time I catch a drawl in her speech, an accent I've only heard from the nobles hailing from the east. I picture Father's map of Orïsha in my mind. Besides Ilorin, the only eastern village large enough to garner nobles in the palace is Warri.

"Zu can wait," a male voice answers her, his speech carrying the same eastern lilt. The heat rising off his body hits me in a wave when he nears.

"Kwame, don't!"

The bag is ripped off my head so hard my neck jerks forward. The pounding in my head surges with the flood of lantern light. My vision blurs as I fight against the pain to take everything in.

A divîner's face fills my gaze, dark brown eyes narrowed in suspicion. A thick beard highlights his defined jaw. As he gets closer, I catch a small silver ring pierced through his right ear. Despite his menacing expression, the boy can't be much older than Tzain.

Behind him, another divîner stands, beautiful with her dark skin and catlike eyes. Long white locs travel down her back, tangling over her arms when she crosses them. A large canvas tent surrounds us, built around the trunks of two mammoth trees.

"Kwame, our masks."

"We don't need them," he replies, breath warm against my face. "For once, she's the one in danger. Not us."

Another body sits behind him, bound to a large tree root, head hidden behind a tweed bag. *Tzain.* I exhale as I recognize his shape, but the relief doesn't last. A stain bleeds through the top of Tzain's bag, thick and dark. Cuts and bruises mar his skin; transporting him here must have been rough.

"You want to speak to him?" Kwame asks. "Tell me where you got this scroll."

The blood freezes in my veins when he waves the parchment in front of my face. *Skies. What else did he take?*

"Itching for your blade?" Kwame seems to read my mind, pulling the bone dagger from his waist. "Couldn't leave your boyfriend with a weapon like this."

Kwame cuts the gag binding my mouth, unflinching even when he nicks my cheek in the process.

"You have one chance," he says through gritted teeth. "Don't bother lying."

"I took it from the royal palace," I rush out. "We're on a mission to bring magic back. I've been tasked by the gods."

"I'm going to get Zu—" the girl behind him starts.

"Folake, wait." Kwame's tone is sharp. "Without Jailin, we need to go to her with answers."

He turns back to me, narrowing his eyes once more.

"A kosidán and a noble are on a mission to bring magic back, yet not one maji is with you?"

"We have a—"

I stop myself, sifting through all the information he revealed with his simple question. It brings me back to the luncheons in the palace, times when I had to search for the truth behind all the smiles and lies. He thinks we're alone. That means Zélie and Inan must have gotten away. Or they were never taken. *It's quite possible they're still safe. . . .*

I cannot decide whether this should give me hope. Together, Zélie and Inan could find us. But at the rate they were fighting, one of them might already be dead.

"Run out of lies?" Kwame asks. "Good. Tell the truth. How did you find us? How many of you are there? What's a noble like you doing with a scroll like this?"

A scroll like this?

I dig my nails in the dirt. *Of course.* Why didn't I notice right away? Kwame didn't bat an eye when said I wanted the scroll to bring magic back. And though he's a divîner, touching it for the first time doesn't make his magic react.

Because this isn't the first time he's held it. . . .

In fact, it might just be the thing he and his fellow masked vigilantes are after.

"Listen—"

"No," Kwame cuts me off, and moves to Tzain, ripping the bag from his head. Tzain is barely conscious, his head lolling to the side. Anxiety grips my chest as Kwame holds the bone dagger to Tzain's neck.

"Tell the truth."

"I am!" I shriek, pulling against my bonds.

"We need to get Zu." Folake backs up to the entrance of the tent, as if distance absolves her of this horror.

"We need the truth," Kwame yells back. "She's lying. I know you see it, too!"

"Don't hurt him," I beg.

"I gave you a chance." Kwame tightens his lips. "This is on you. I won't lose my family again—"

"What's going on?"

My eyes snap to the tent's entrance as a young girl enters, her fists clenched. Her green dashiki sits bright against her coconut-brown complexion. Her white hair settles around her head, big and fluffy like a cloud. She can't be more than thirteen, but Kwame and Folake stand to attention in her presence.

"Zu, I wanted to get you." Folake speaks quickly.

"I wanted answers first," Kwame finishes. "My scouts saw them by the river. They had the scroll."

Zu's dark brown eyes widen as she grabs the parchment from Kwame and scans its weathered ink. The way she runs her thumb over the symbols gives me all the confirmation I need.

"You've seen this scroll before."

The girl looks at me, taking in the cuts on my skin, the shallow gash on Tzain's forehead. She fights to keep her face blank, but the corners of her lips turn into a frown.

"You should've woken me."

"There wasn't time," Kwame says. "They started moving. We had to act or they'd be out of our range."

"They?" Zu asks. "There were more of them?"

"Two others," Folake answers. "They got away. And Jailin . . ."

"What about him?"

Folake exchanges a guilty look with Kwame. "He still hasn't returned. There's a chance he's been taken."

Zu's face falls. The scroll wrinkles in her grasp. "You didn't go after him?"

"There wasn't time—"

"You don't get to make that call!" Zu rasps. "We don't leave anybody behind. It's our job to keep everyone safe!"

Kwame's chin drops to his chest. He shifts and crosses his arms.

"The scroll was in play, Zu. If more guards are coming, we need it. I weighed the risk."

"We're not guards," I cut in. "We're not part of the army."

Zu glances at me before walking up to Kwame. "You've put us all in danger. I hope it was fun playing king."

Though her words are harsh, each is filled with sadness. With her thin brows pinched, she looks even younger than she really is.

"Gather the others in my tent," she instructs Kwame before pointing to Tzain. "Folly, clean and bandage his head. The last thing I need is him getting an infection."

"What about her?" Folake nods in my direction. "What do you want us to do?"

"Nothing." Zu turns her gaze on me, unreadable once more. "She's not going anywhere."

CHAPTER FORTY-THREE

INAN

SILENCE SURROUNDS US.

Thick and heavy, hanging in the air.

The only sounds between Zélie and me are our footsteps as we trudge up the tallest hill in the forest. It amazes me that with the soft soil and weighted nets, the masked figures didn't leave more tracks. Whenever I stumble on a path, it seems to disappear.

"This way." Zélie takes the lead, scouting the trees.

Following the advice of the masked boy we interrogated, I search the trunks for the painted symbol of his people: an *X* with two diverging crescents. According to him, following the discreet symbols is the only way to discover their camp.

"There's another one." Zélie points to the left, changing the direction of our path. She climbs with an unyielding resolve, but I struggle to keep up. Slung over my shoulder, the unconscious fighter weighs down my frame, making each inhale a battle. I almost forgot how much it hurts to breathe when I have to push my magic down.

Fighting Zélie, I was forced to let go. I needed my full strength to gain control. Now it takes everything in me to block my magic again. No matter how hard I fight, the risk of feeling Zélie's pain lingers. A constant and growing threat—

My feet slip on the soil. I grunt, digging my heel into the dirt to keep from sliding down the hill. The slip is all my curse needs.

Like a leopanaire escaping its cage, the magic breaks free.

I close my eyes as Zélie's essence rushes in like a crashing tidal wave. First cold and sharp, then soft and warm. The smell of the sea surrounds me, the clear night sky mirrored bright against its black waves. Trips to the floating market with Tzain. Hours passed on a coconut boat with Baba.

There are parts of it, parts of her, that light something inside me. But the light only lasts a moment.

Then I drown inside the darkness of her pain.

Skies. I push it all down, push every part of her and this virus away. When it's gone I feel lighter, though the strain of suppression causes sharp pains in my chest. Something about her essence calls to my curse, bringing it up at every chance. Her spirit seems to hover around me, crashing with the force of the turbulent sea.

"You're slowing me down," Zélie calls back, nearing the top of the hill.

"Do *you* want to carry him?" I ask. "I'm more than happy to watch him bleed on you instead."

"Maybe if you stopped suppressing your magic, you could handle the extra weight."

Perhaps if you closed your wretched mind, it wouldn't take so much energy to block you out.

But I bite my tongue; not every part of her mind is wretched. Laced in the memories of her family is a fierce love, something I've never felt. I think back to days sparring with Amari, to nights spent flinching from Father's wrath. If Zélie had my magic, what parts of me would she see?

The question haunts me as I grit my teeth to finish the final ascent. When I reach the top, I set our captive's body down and walk until the hill plateaus. Wind whips at my face, and I yearn to take my helmet off.

I glance at Zélie; she already knows my secret. For the first time since getting this miserable streak, I don't have to hide.

I unlatch my helmet and savor the way the cool breeze runs over my scalp as I approach the hill's steep edge. It's been so long since I could remove my helmet without fear.

Below us the forested hills of the Gombe River Valley spread beneath the shadows and moonlight. Mammoth trees fill the land, but from up here, one unique symbol makes itself clear. Unlike the random spread of trees throughout the forest, this grove is arranged, forming a giant circle. From our vantage point, their special *X* is just visible, painted onto some of the trees' leaves.

"He told the truth." Zélie sounds surprised.

"We didn't give him much of a choice."

"Still." She shrugs. "He easily could've lied."

Between the circular formation of trees, a secret wall has been erected, formed from mud, stones, and crisscrossed branches. Though rudimentary, the wall sits high, reaching several meters up the trees' trunks.

Two figures armed with swords stand in front of the wall, guarding what must be their gate. Like the boy we interrogated, the fighters wear masks and are completely clad in black.

"I still don't understand who they are," Zélie mutters under her breath. I echo her question. Besides their location, the only other thing we learned from the boy was that his people were after the scroll as well.

"Maybe if you hadn't beaten him half to death, we could've gotten more answers."

Zélie snarls. "If I didn't beat that boy, we wouldn't have found this place at all."

She stalks forward, starting her trek down the forested terrain.

"Where do you think you're going?"

"To get our siblings back."

"Wait." I grab her arm. "We can't just storm in."

"I can take two men."

"There are far more than two of them." I point to the areas around the gate. It takes Zélie a moment to see through the shadows. The hidden soldiers are so still they blend completely into the darkness. "There are at least thirty of them on this side alone. And that doesn't count the archers hidden in the trees."

I point to a foot dangling from the branches, the only sign of life in the thick leaves. "If their formation matches the feet on the ground, we should expect at least fifteen of them up there as well."

"So we'll attack at daybreak," Zélie decides. "When they can't hide."

"Sunlight isn't going to change how many of them there are to fight. We have to assume they're all as skilled as the men who took Amari and Tzain."

Zélie scrunches her nose at me; I hear it, too. Her brother's name sounds strange coming out of my mouth.

She turns; her white curls glow in the moonlight. Her hair was straight as a blade before, but now it bunches in tight spirals, twisting further in the wind.

Her curls remind me of one of her young memories, back when she was a child and her coils were even tighter. Her mother chuckled while trying to comb Zélie's hair into a bun, magically summoning dark shadows to hold Zélie in place as her daughter struggled.

"What's our move?" Zélie breaks through my thoughts. I return my focus to the wall, letting the facts of battle wash away all memories of Zélie's mother and her hair.

"Gombe is only a day's ride away. If I leave now, I can bring back guards by morning."

"Are you serious?" Zélie steps back. "You want to bring the guards into this?"

"We need a force if we're getting into that camp. What other choice do we have?"

"With the guards, you have a choice." Zélie jabs her finger in my chest. "I don't."

"That boy is a divîner." I point to the captive. "What if there are more behind that wall? They have the scroll now. We don't know what we'll have to face."

"Of course. The scroll. Always the scroll. How stupid am I to think this could be about rescuing my brother or your *sister*—"

"Zélie—"

"Come up with a new plan," she demands. "If there are divîners behind that wall and you summon the guards, we won't get our siblings back. They'll all die as soon as your soldiers arrive."

"That's not true—"

"Bring the guards into this, and I'll tell them your secret." She crosses her arms. "When they come for us, I'll make sure they kill you, too."

My insides twist and I step back. Kaea's blade strikes back into my mind. The fear in her grip. The hatred in her eyes.

A strange sadness settles in me as I reach into my pocket and wrap my hand around Father's pawn. I bite back all the words I want to shoot back. If only she was wrong.

"Then what do you propose we do without guards?" I push. "I don't see a way past that wall without a fighting force."

Zélie turns back to the camp and wraps her arms around herself. She shivers even though the humidity around us makes me perspire.

"I'll get us in," she finally says. "Once we break through, we go our separate ways."

Though she doesn't say it, I know she's thinking about the scroll. Once those walls come down, the fight for it will be fiercer than ever.

"What kind of plan do you have in mind?"

"That's not your concern."

"It is when I'm putting my life in your hands."

Her eyes flick to me. Sharp. Untrusting. But then she presses her hands into the ground. A hum ignites in the air.

"Ẹ̀mí àwọn tí ó ti sùn—"

Her words bend the earth to her will. It creaks and crumbles and cracks. An earthly figure rises beneath her touch. Brought to life by the magic of her hands.

"Skies," I curse at her power. When did she learn this trick? But she doesn't care what I know; she turns back to the camp.

"They're called animations," she says. "They follow my command."

"How many can you make?"

"At least eight, maybe more."

"That won't do." I shake my head.

"They're powerful."

"There're too many fighters down there. We need a stronger force—"

"Fine." Zélie turns on her heel. "If we're attacking tomorrow night, I'll figure out how to make more in the morning."

She starts to walk away, but pauses.

"And a piece of advice, little prince. Don't put your life in my hands unless you want that life to end."

CHAPTER FORTY-FOUR

ZÉLIE

BEADS OF SWEAT soak through my cropped dashiki and drip onto the mountain stone. My muscles shake with the strain of practicing a hundred incantations, but Inan doesn't let up. He rises from our latest skirmish, brushing hardened earth from his bare chest. Though a red welt swells on his cheek from my last animation, Inan squares his stance.

"Again."

"Dammit," I pant. "Just give me a break."

"There's no time for a break. If you can't do this, we need another plan."

"The plan is fine," I say through my teeth. "What else do you need to prove that? They'll be strong, we won't need that many—"

"There are over fifty fighters down there, Zélie. Armed, battle-ready men. If you think eight animations will be enough—"

"It's more than enough for you!" I point to the bruise forming on Inan's eye, to the blood staining the right sleeve of his kaftan. "You can barely fight one. What makes you think they can handle more?"

"Because there are *fifty* of them!" Inan shouts. "I'm not even at half my strength. I should hardly be your gauge."

"Then prove me wrong, little prince." I clench my fists, eager to draw more of his royal blood. "Show me how weak I am. Show me how strong you really are!"

"Zélie—"

"*Enough!*" I roar, pressing my palms into the ground. For the first time my spiritual pathways unlock without an incantation; my ashê drains and the animations flow. With a rumble, they come to life, rising from the earth at my silent command. Inan's eyes widen as ten animations charge across the hill.

But in the brief moment before the attack, his gaze narrows. A vein bulges against his throat. His muscles tense against his strong build. His magic surfaces like a warm breeze, heating the air around us.

He cuts through two animations; they crumble into dirt. He strikes like lightning against the others, dodging and attacking at the same time. *Dammit.* I bite the inside of my cheek and chew. He's faster than the average guard.

Deadlier than the typical prince.

"*Ẹ̀mí àwọn tí ó ti sùn*—" I chant again, giving three more animations new life. I hope the rush will slow Inan down, but after a few frenzied seconds, he stands alone. Sweat rolls down his forehead, dried soil crunches under his feet.

Twelve animations later and still, he stands.

"Satisfied?" Though he pants, he looks more alive than I've ever seen him. Sweat glistens off the curves of his muscles; for once he's more than skin and bone. His face flushes red with color as he stabs his sword into a crack in the ground. "If I can take down twelve at full strength, how do you think fifty fighters will fare?"

I press my palms into the cliff. I'll make an animation he can't defeat. The ground rumbles, but my ashê is too drained to breathe new spirit soldiers. Without resorting to blood magic, I can't do it. No matter how hard I strain, no animations spring forth.

Whether Inan sees my desperation on my face or senses it with his magic, I don't know. He pinches the bridge of his nose, all but stifling a low groan.

"Zélie—"

"No," I cut him off. My eyes drift toward my pack. The sunstone lies beneath the leather, silently tempting me.

If I used it, I could conjure more than enough animations to take down fifty fighters. But Inan doesn't know I have it. And if those masked figures are after the scroll, they'll want the sunstone, too. My frustration grows, though I know I'm right. I have a chance at retrieving the scroll and the bone dagger, but if the sunstone falls into the wrong maji's hands, they'll become too powerful for me to ever get it back.

But if I used blood magic . . .

I look down at my hand; the bite marks around my thumb have just begun to scar. A blood sacrifice would be more than enough, but after what happened in the arena in Ibeji, I never want to use blood magic again.

Inan stares at me with expectant eyes, solidifying my answer. I can't use either.

"I just need more time."

"We don't *have* time." Inan runs his hand through his hair; the white streak seems wider now than it did before. "You're not even close. If you can't do this, we need to summon the guards."

He takes a deep breath, and the warmth of his magic begins to fade. The color drains from his skin. His vigor dies as he pushes his magic away.

It's like the very life is being sucked out of him.

"Maybe the problem isn't me." My voice cracks and I close my eyes. I hate him for making me feel weak. I hate him for weakening himself. "If you would just use your magic, we wouldn't need guards."

"I can't."

"Can't or won't?"

"My magic doesn't have offensive capabilities."

"Are you sure?" I press, remembering Mama's stories, Lekan's pictures of the Connectors. "You've never stunned anyone? You've never cast a mental attack?"

A flicker passes across his face, something I can't read. He clenches the handle of his sword and looks away. The air grows colder as he pushes his magic even further down.

"For gods' sakes, Inan. Have some resolve. If your magic could help save Amari, why aren't you doing everything you can?" I step closer to him, trying to put gentleness in my tone. "I'll keep your stupid secret. If we use your magic to attack—"

"No!"

I jump back at the force of Inan's words.

"My answer is *no*." He swallows hard. "I can't. I'm never doing that again. I know you're wary of the guards, but I'm their prince. I promise you, I will keep them under control—"

I turn on my heel, walking back toward the ledge of the hill's incline. When Inan shouts my name, I grit my teeth, fighting the urge to smack him with my staff. I'll never save my brother. I'll never get back the dagger or the scroll. I shake my head, fighting the swirl of emotions that wants to explode.

"Zélie—"

"Tell me, little prince." I whip around. "What hurts more? The feeling you get when you use your magic or the pain of pushing it all down?"

Inan jerks back. "You can't possibly understand."

"Oh, I understand perfectly." I get in his face, close enough to see the stubble dotting his cheeks. "You would let your sister die and see all of Orïsha burn if it meant keeping your magic a secret."

"Keeping my magic a secret is *how* I keep Orïsha safe!" The air warms as his powers surge. "Magic is the root of all our problems. It's the root of Orïsha's pain!"

"Your *father* is the root of Orïsha's pain!" My voice shakes with anger. "He's a tyrant and a coward. That's all he'll ever be!"

"My father is your king." Inan closes in. "A king trying to protect his people. He took magic away so Orïsha would be safe."

"That monster took magic away so that he could slaughter thousands. He took magic away so the innocent couldn't defend themselves!"

Inan pauses. The air continues to warm as guilt creeps into his expression.

"He did what he thought was right." He speaks slowly. "But he wasn't wrong to take magic away. He was wrong for the oppression that followed."

I dig my hands into my hair, skin growing hot at Inan's ignorance. How can he *defend* his father? How can he not see what's truly going on?

"Our lack of power and our oppression are one and the same, Inan. Without power we're maggots. Without power the monarchy treats us like scum!"

"Power is not the answer. It will only intensify the fight. Maybe you can't trust my father, but if you could learn to trust me, to trust my guards—"

"*Trust* the guards?" I scream so loud there's no doubt every fighter hidden in this godsforsaken forest hears my voice quake. "The same guards who chained my mother by her neck? The guards who beat my father half to death? The guards who grope me whenever they have a chance, just waiting for the day they can take everything when I'm forced into the stocks?"

Inan's eyes grow wide, but he presses, "The guards I know are good. They keep Lagos safe—"

"My gods." I stalk away. I can't listen to this. I'm a fool for thinking we could ever work together.

"Hey," he yells. "I'm talking to you."

"I'm done talking, little prince. Clearly you'll never understand."

"I could say the same thing!" He runs after me with labored steps. "You don't need magic to fix things."

"Leave me alone—"

"If you could just see where I'm coming from—"

"Go—"

"You don't have to be afraid—"

"I am *always* afraid!"

I don't know what shocks me more—the power in my voice or the words themselves.

Afraid.

I am always afraid.

It's a truth I locked away years ago, a fact I fought hard to overcome. Because when it hits, I'm paralyzed.

I can't breathe.

I can't talk.

All at once, I crumple to the ground, clasping my palm over my mouth to stifle the sobs. It doesn't matter how strong I get, how much power my magic wields. They will always hate me in this world.

I will always be afraid.

"Zélie—"

"No," I breathe through my sobs. "Stop. You think you know what it's like, but you don't. You never will."

"Then help me." Inan kneels by my side, careful to keep his distance. "Please. I want to understand."

"You can't. They built this world for you, built it to love you. They never cursed at you in the streets, never broke down the doors of your home. They didn't drag your mother by her neck and hang her for the whole world to see."

Now that the truth is out, there's nothing I can do to stop. My chest billows as I sob. My fingers tremble at the terror.

Afraid.

The truth cuts like the sharpest knife I've ever known.

No matter what I do, I will always be afraid.

CHAPTER FORTY-FIVE

INAN

ZÉLIE'S PAIN FALLS through the air like rain.

It sinks into my skin.

My chest heaves with her sobs. My heart rips with her anguish.

And all the while I feel a terror unlike anything I've ever known. It crushes my soul.

It destroys all will to live.

This can't be her world. . . .

This can't be the life Father built. But the longer her pain grips me, the more I realize: this fear is always there.

"If your guards were here, everything would be just as broken, just as hopeless. There's no living under their tyranny. Our only salvation is power."

As soon as the words leave her mouth, Zélie's sobs quiet. It's like she's remembered a deeper truth. A way to escape the pain.

"Your people, your guards—they're nothing more than killers, rapists, and thieves. The only difference between them and criminals is the uniforms they wear."

She pulls herself to her feet and palms the tears from her eyes.

"Fool yourself all you want, little prince, but don't feign innocence with me. I won't let your father get away with what he's done. I won't let your ignorance silence my pain."

With that, she disappears. Her quiet footsteps fade into the silence.

In that moment I realize how wrong I've truly been.

It doesn't matter if I'm in her head.

I'll never understand all her pain.

CHAPTER FORTY-SIX

AMARI

THERE WAS A ROOM in the palace that Father disappeared into. Every day, always at half past noon.

He would rise from his throne and walk through the main hall, Admiral Ebele on one side, Commander Kaea on the other.

Before the Raid, I would trail behind them, curiosity driving my small legs. Every day I watched them disappear down those cold marble stairs until the day I decided to follow them instead.

My legs were so short I had to grip the alabaster railing, scooting from step to step. I imagined a room full of moín moín pies and lemon cakes, the shining toys that might lie in wait. But as I neared the bottom, I didn't smell the sweet tang of citrus and sugar. I didn't hear joy or laughter. The cold cellar only held shouts.

Only a young boy's screams.

A loud crack rang through the air—Kaea's fist against a servant's face. Kaea wore sharp rings on her fingers; when she smacked the servant, the rings cut into his skin.

I must have screamed when I saw the bloodied boy. I must have screamed, because they all turned to stare. I didn't know the servant's name. I just knew he was the one who made my bed.

Father picked me up and rested me against his hip, carrying me out without a passing glance. "*Prisons are no place for a princess*," he said that day.

Another crack rang as Kaea's fist made contact again.

As the sun sets and the long day passes into night, I think back to Father's words. I have to wonder what he would say if he could see me now. Perhaps he would string me up himself.

I ignore the strain in my shoulders and pull at my restraints, wriggling though the rope burns my wrists red and raw. After dragging the rope back and forth across a jagged piece of bark all day, the fibers are fraying, but I need to wear it down further to break free.

"Skies," I sigh as sweat gathers above my lips. For the tenth time, I search the tent for something sharper. Yet the only thing in here besides Tzain is dirt.

The one time I got a glimpse of the outside was when Folake entered to bring us water. Behind the tent flap, I caught Kwame glowering. The bone dagger still sat in his hand.

A shudder runs through me and I close my eyes, forcing a deep breath. I can't get the image of the dagger pressed against Tzain's neck out of my head. If it weren't for the faint whistle of his breathing, I wouldn't be sure he was still alive. Folake cleaned and bandaged his wound, but he has yet to do so much as stir.

I need to get him out of here before they come back. I need to find a way to save him, the dagger, and the scroll. A full night has already passed. We only have five days left until the centennial solstice.

The tent flap swings open and I pause my movements. Zu has finally returned. Today she sports a black kaftan, sweet with the green and yellow beads stitched into its hem. Instead of the militant child who entered last night, she looks more like the young girl she is.

"Who are you?" I ask. "What is it you want?"

She barely spares me a glance. Instead she kneels by Tzain's side.

"Please." My heartbeat quickens in my chest. "He's innocent. Don't hurt him."

Zu closes her eyes and lays her small hands over the bandages on Tzain's head. My breath hitches when a soft orange light radiates from her palm. Though weak at first, it glows, brighter and brighter, creating a warmth that fills the tent. The light from her hands grows until it encompasses all of Tzain's head.

Magic . . .

The same awe that struck when light escaped Binta's hands hits me now. Like Binta, Zu's magic is beautiful, so different from the horrors of what Father taught me to believe. But how is she doing this? How has her magic come so far so fast? She must've been a baby when the Raid occurred. Where did she learn the incantation she's whispering now?

"What're you doing to him?"

Zu doesn't answer, teeth clenched in a grimace. Beads of sweat form at her temple. The slightest quiver rocks her hand. A light fills Tzain's skin as his visible cuts shrink into nothingness. The black and purple bruises fade completely, restoring him to the handsome boy who's fought by my side.

"Thank the skies." My body relaxes as Tzain grunts, the first sound he's made since we were abducted. Though he remains unconscious, he stirs slightly against his rope.

"You're a Healer?" I ask.

Zu glances at me, though it's like she doesn't see me at all. She focuses on the scratches on my skin like she's searching for more things she can fix. It's as if her need to heal isn't only in her magic, it's in her heart.

"Please," I try once more. "We are not your enemy."

"Yet you have our scroll?"

Our? I focus on the word. It can't be a coincidence that she, Kwame, and Folake are all maji. There must be more outside this tent.

"We weren't alone. The girl Kwame couldn't apprehend was a maji, a powerful Reaper. We've been to Chândomblé. A sêntaro revealed the secrets of that scroll—"

"You're lying." Zu crosses her arms. "A kosidán like you would never meet a sêntaro. Who are you really? Where is the rest of the army?"

"I'm telling you the truth." My shoulders slump. "Just like I told Kwame. If neither of you will believe me, there's nothing I can do."

Zu sighs and removes the scroll from inside her kaftan. As she unravels it, her hard exterior drops. A wave of sadness settles in. "The last time I saw this, I was cowering under a fishing boat. I was forced to sit and watch as royal guards cut my sister down."

Skies . . .

Zu has the same eastern drawl in her voice. She must have been in Warri when Kaea recovered the scroll. Kaea thought that she killed all the new maji, but Zu, Kwame, and Folake must have found a way to survive.

"I'm so sorry," I whisper. "I cannot imagine what that must've been like."

Zu stays silent for a long moment. A weariness weighs her down that makes her seem so much older than her young years.

"I was a baby when the Raid happened. I don't even remember what my parents looked like. All I remember was feeling afraid." Zu bends down, yanking the wild grass at her feet until their roots rip from the ground. "I always wondered what it would be like to live with the memories of something so horrible. I don't have to imagine what that's like anymore."

Binta's face breaks into my mind; her bright smile, her dazzling lights. For a moment the memory shines in all its old glory.

Then it turns red, drowning in her blood.

"You're a noble." Zu rises and walks toward me, a new fire alight in her eyes. "I can practically smell it on you. I won't let your monarchy take us down."

"I'm on your side." I shake my head. "Release me, and I can prove that to you. The scroll can do more than give magic back to those who touch it. It has a ritual that will bring magic back throughout the land."

"I can see why Kwame has his guard up." Zu steps away. "He thinks you've been sent to infiltrate us. With such clever lies, I think he could be right."

"Zu, please—"

"Kwame." Her voice cracks. She clutches the neckline of her kaftan as he enters.

He runs his fingers over the blade of the bone dagger, threat evident on his face.

"Is it time?"

Zu's chin quivers as she nods. She squeezes her eyes shut.

"I'm sorry," she whispers. "But we have to protect ourselves."

"Go," Kwame instructs her. "You don't need to see this."

Zu rubs her tears and backs out of the tent, sparing me one last look. When she's gone, Kwame steps into my line of vision.

"I hope you're ready to tell the truth."

CHAPTER FORTY-SEVEN

INAN

"ZÉLIE?"

I shout her name, though I doubt she'll answer my call. After the way she ran away from me earlier, part of me wonders if I'll be able to find her at all.

The sun begins to set, disappearing behind hills on the horizon. Twisting shadows stretch around me as I lean against a tree to rest.

"Zélie, please," I call between pants, gripping the bark when an ache cuts through my core. Since our argument, my magic scalds with a vengeance. Just breathing causes sharp spasms throughout my chest. "Zélie, I'm sorry."

But as the apology echoes through the forest, the words feel hollow—I don't know what I'm sorry for. Not understanding or for being Father's son? Any apology seems insurmountable against everything he's already done.

"A new Orïsha," I mutter. Now that I say it aloud, it sounds even more ludicrous. How am I supposed to fix anything when I'm inextricably linked to the problem?

Skies.

Zélie's done more than mess with my head. Her very presence unravels everything I've been led to think, everything I know I need.

Night falls upon us, and we still don't have a plan. Without her animations, we'll lose everything to these masks. Our siblings, the scroll—

A stinging pain stabs my abdomen. I keel over, gripping the trunk for support. Like a wild leopanaire, my magic claws its way to the surface.

"Mama!"

I close my eyes. My mind echoes with Zélie's shrieks. Bitter cries no child should ever make. Trauma she never should've witnessed.

For magic to disappear for good, every maji had to die. As long as they'd tasted that power, they would never stop fighting to bring it back.

Father's face enters my mind. Voice steady. Eyes blank.

I believed him.

Despite the fear I felt, I admired his unwavering strength.

"Could you be any louder?"

My eyes snap open; for some reason, my magic calms in Zélie's presence.

"With you wailing like that, I'm surprised the fighters haven't taken you as well."

Zélie steps forward, further calming my magic. Her spirit settles over me like a cool ocean breeze as I slide to the ground.

"It's not my fault," I breathe through my teeth. "It hurts."

"It wouldn't hurt if you embraced it. Your magic attacks you because you fight it back."

Her face stays hard, but I'm surprised at the hint of pity in her tone. She moves out of the shadows and leans against a tree. Her silver eyes are red and swollen, signs of tears spilled long after our fight.

Suddenly, reliving the pain of her past doesn't feel like punishment enough. I suffer for moments. The poor girl's suffered her entire life.

"Does this mean you'll fight with me?" I ask.

Zélie crosses her arms. "I don't have a choice. Tzain and Amari are still trapped. I can't get them out on my own."

"But what about the animations?"

Zélie pulls a glowing orb from her pack; instantly, Kaea's old conversations play in my head. With the way oranges and reds pulse beneath the crystal exterior, this object can only be the sunstone.

"If they're after the scroll, they'll want this, too."

"You've had that the whole time?"

"I didn't want to risk losing it, but it'll help me make all the animations we need."

I nod; for once her plan is sound. This should be enough, but it's about so much more than that now.

Your people, your guards—they're nothing more than killers, rapists, and thieves. The only difference between them and criminals is the uniforms they wear.

Her words echo in my mind, no longer a staff pressed against my sword.

After everything that's happened, we can't go back. One of us must yield.

"You asked me what hurts more." I force the words out, though they want to stay in. "The sensation of using my magic or the pain of pushing it down. I don't know the answer." I grip the tarnished sênet pawn, focusing on the way it stings against my palm. "I hate it all."

The threat of tears pricks at my eyes. I clear my throat, desperate to keep them down. I can only imagine how fast Father's fist would fly if he could see me now.

"I hate my magic." I lower my voice. "I despise the way it poisons me. But more than anything, I hate the way it makes me hate myself." It takes more strength than I have to lift my head and meet Zélie's gaze. Looking at her stirs up every single shame.

Zélie's eyes water once more. I don't know what chord I've struck. Her sea-salt soul seems to shrink away. For the first time, I want it to stay.

"Your magic isn't poison." Her voice shakes. "You are. You push it down, you fight it back. You carry around that pathetic toy." She stomps over and rips the sênet pawn out of my hand, shoving it in my face. "This is majacite, you idiot. I'm surprised all your fingers haven't fallen off."

I stare at the tarnished pawn, the gold and brown rust hiding its original color. I always thought the piece was painted black, but could it really have been made of majacite the whole time?

I take it from her hands, holding it gently, feeling the way it pricks my skin. All this time I thought I was just squeezing too tight.

Of course . . .

I almost laugh at the irony. The realization brings me back to the moment I got it. The day Father "gifted" it to me.

Before the Raid, we played sênet every week. An hour where Father became more than a king. Every piece and move was a lesson, wisdom for the day I would lead.

But after the Raid, there was no time for games. No time for me. One day I made the mistake of carrying the game into the throne room and Father threw the pieces in my face.

Leave it, he barked when I bent down to pick them up. *Servants clean. Kings don't.*

This pawn was the only piece I managed to salvage.

Shame ripples through me as I stare at the tarnished metal.

The only gift he's ever given me, and at its core is hate.

"This belonged to my father," I speak quietly. A secret weapon taken from others who despised magic. Created to destroy others like me.

"You clutch it the way a child clutches a blanket." Zélie releases a heavy sigh. "You fight for a man who will always hate you just because of what you are."

Like her hair, her silver gaze glows in the moonlight, more piercing than any eyes that have ever seen through me. I stare.

I stare though I need to talk.

I drop the pawn in the dirt and kick it aside. I must draw a line in the sand. I've been a sheep. A sheep when my kingdom needed me to act like a king.

Duty before self.

The creed unravels before my eyes, taking Father's lies with it. Magic may be dangerous, but the sins of eradicating it have made the monarchy no better.

"I know you can't trust me, but give me this chance to prove myself. I'll get us into that camp. I'll bring your brother back."

Zélie bites her lip. "And when we find the scroll?"

I hesitate; Father's face flashes in my mind. *If we don't stop magic, all of Orïsha will burn.*

But the only fires I've seen have been by his hand. His and mine. I've given him a lifetime. I can't abide by any more of his lies.

"It's yours," I decide. "Whatever you and Amari are trying to do . . . I won't stand in your way."

I hold out my hand and she stares at it; I don't know if my words are enough. But after a long moment, she places her palm in mine. A strange warmth fills me at her touch.

To my surprise, her hands are calloused, perhaps toughened from using her staff. When we let go, we avoid each other's eyes, instead staring at the night sky.

"So we're doing this?" she asks.

I nod. "I'll show you what type of king I can be."

CHAPTER FORTY-EIGHT

ZÉLIE

OYA, PLEASE LET THIS WORK.

I lift up a silent prayer as my heart thumps against my chest. We move through the shadows, crouching at the periphery of the masks' camp. My plan seemed perfect before, but now that it's time, I can't stop thinking of all the ways it could fail. What if Tzain and Amari aren't inside? What if we have to face off against a maji? And what about Inan?

I glance at him, dread building at the sight. My plan starts with me handing the little prince the sunstone; either I've lost my mind, or I've already lost this fight.

Inan peers ahead, jaw tight as he takes a count of the guards surrounding the gate. Instead of his usual armor, he wears the black attire the captive fighter wore.

I still can't tell what to make of him, of all the things he made me feel. Watching his misguided hate brought me back, wrapping me in the darkest days after the Raid. I despised magic. I blamed Mama.

I cursed the gods for making us this way.

A lump forms in my throat as I try to forget that old pain. I can still feel the shadow of the lie inside, pushing me to hate my blood, rip out my white hair.

It almost ate me alive, the self-hatred spun from Saran's lies. But he already took Mama. I couldn't let him take the truth, too.

In the moons following the Raid, I held on to Mama's teachings, embedding them in my heart until they ran through me like blood. No matter what the world said, my magic was beautiful. Even without powers, the gods had blessed me with a gift.

But Inan's tears brought it all back, the lethal lie this world forces us to swallow. Saran did well.

Inan already hates himself more than I ever could.

"Alright," he whispers. "It's time."

It takes an unusual amount of effort to unclench my fingers and hand him my leather pack.

"Don't overextend yourself," he warns. "And remember, keep some animations behind to provide a defense."

"I know, I know." I roll my eyes. "Get on with it."

Though I don't want to feel anything, my stomach clenches as Inan emerges from the shadows and stalks toward the gate. The memory of his rough hand in my own comes back to me. A strange comfort filled me from his touch.

The two masked figures posted at the entrance point their weapons. The ones hidden in the shadows shift as well. From above, I hear a chorus of plucks: bowstrings with arrows being pulled taut.

Though I know Inan can sense it all, he walks with brash confidence. He doesn't stop until he's hundreds of meters ahead, halfway between me and the entrance.

"I've come to make a trade," he declares. "I have something you want."

He drops my pack to the ground and removes the sunstone. I should've prepared him for the rush. Even from afar, I hear a gasp.

A tremor runs from his hands to his head, his palms pulsing with a soft blue light. I wonder if Orí appears behind his eyes.

The show is exactly what the masks need. A few slither out of the shadows and begin to circle him, weapons raised and ready to strike.

"On your knees," a masked woman barks, cautiously leading the charge outside the gate. She points her ax and gives a nod, drawing more of their fighters out of hiding.

Gods. There are already more than we bargained for. *Forty . . . fifty . . . sixty?* How many more aim at him from the trees?

"Bring out the prisoners first."

"After you're restrained."

The wooden gate swings open. Inan surveys the female leader and takes a step back.

"I'm sorry." Inan turns. "I'm afraid I can't make that deal."

I bolt from the underbrush, sprinting as fast as my legs will take me. Inan hurls the sunstone like an agbön ball, thrusting with all his might. It sails through the air with impressive speed. I have to leap to catch it. I clutch it to my chest and somersault as I hit the ground.

"Ah!" I wheeze as the sunstone fills me, an intoxicating rush I'm beginning to crave. Heat explodes under my skin as its power surges, igniting all the ashê in my blood.

Behind my eyes a different glimpse of Oya plays, red silks luminescent against her black skin. Wind swirls her skirts and twists in her hair, making the beads dance around her face.

A white light radiates from her palm as she reaches out her hand. I can't feel my body, yet I feel myself reaching back. In one fleeting moment, our fingers brush—

The world rumbles to life.

"Get her!"

Someone cries beyond me, but I can't truly hear it. Magic roars from my blood, amplifying spirits far and wide. They call to me, rising like a tsunami wave. Their thrum overpowers the sounds of the living.

Like tides pulled by the moon, the souls crash into me.

"Ẹ̀mí àwọn tí ó ti sùn—"

I thrust my hand into the earth. A deep fracture ripples through it at my touch.

The ground beneath us groans as an army of the dead rises from the dirt.

They swirl out of the ground, a hurricane of twigs and rocks and soil. Their bodies harden with the silver glow of my magic. I unleash the storm.

"Attack!"

CHAPTER FORTY-NINE

AMARI

A SHARP CRACK rings through the air.

I reel as Kwame's fist crashes into Tzain's jaw.

Tzain's head lolls to the side, a mess of reds and blacks and bruises.

"Stop it!" I scream, tears spilling down my cheeks. Fresh blood drips into Tzain's eye, undoing all of Zu's healing.

Kwame pivots and grabs my chin. "Who else knows you're here? Where are the rest of your soldiers?" Despite everything, his voice is strained, almost heavy with desperation. It's like this is hurting him as much as it's hurting me.

"There *are* no soldiers. Go find the maji we're traveling with. She'll confirm that everything I've said is true!"

Kwame closes his eyes and breathes deeply. He stays so still, a shudder runs through me.

"When they came to Warri, they looked like you." He pulls the bone dagger from his waist. "They *sounded* like you."

"Kwame, please—"

He thrusts the dagger into Tzain's leg. I don't know who yells louder, me or him.

"If you're angry, hurt me!" I thrash against the tree, pulling uselessly at my restraints. If only he would cut me instead. Hit me. Punch *me*.

Like a battering ram to the heart, Binta forces herself into my mind. She, too, suffered. She suffered in my place.

Kwame stabs Tzain's thigh again and I cry out once more, my vision blurring with new tears. He withdraws the dagger with a shaking hand. His tremor intensifies as he moves the blade up to Tzain's chest.

"This is your last chance."

"We are *not* your enemy!" I rush out. "The guards in Warri killed the people we loved, too!"

"Lies." Kwame's voice chokes up. He steadies his hand and pulls back the blade. "Those guards *are* your people. They're the ones you love—"

The tent flaps open. Folake rushes in, almost flinging herself into Kwame.

"We're under attack."

Kwame's face falls. "Her guards?"

"I don't know. I think they have a maji!"

Kwame pushes the bone dagger into Folake's hand and runs out.

"Kwame—"

"Stay here!" he calls back.

Folake pivots and takes us in. My tears, the blood gushing from Tzain's leg. She covers her mouth, then drops the dagger in the dirt and flees from the tent.

"Tzain?" I ask. He clenches his teeth and presses against the tree root. The bloodstains spread on his pants leg. He blinks slowly, though his eyes are nearly swollen shut.

"You okay?"

The most painful tears yet prick at my eyes. Beaten. Stabbed. Yet still, he asks about me.

"We have to get out of here."

I pull against the ropes binding my wrists with a new fervor. There's a snapping sound as the bonds begin to fray. The rope rips at my skin, but my chest fills with a different kind of pain.

It's like all those days back at the palace, back when my bonds were golden chains. I should've fought them the way I fight now.

If I had only done more, Binta would still be safe.

I clench my teeth, digging my heels into the dirt. With a grunt, I brace my heel against the bark and leverage my whole body to pull free.

"Amari." Tzain's voice is weaker now. He's lost so much blood. Bark cuts into the soles of my feet, but I press even harder to pull at the ropes.

Strike, Amari.

Father's voice rings in my head, but it's not his strength I need.

Be brave, Amari. Binta soothes instead.

Be the Lionaire.

"Ugh!" I scream against the pain. It almost sounds like a roar. Folake's voice rings from outside. The tent flap opens—

The rope binding me snaps. I pitch forward, falling face-first in the dirt. Folake dives for the bone dagger. I scramble to my feet and lunge at her.

"Agh!" she grunts as I tackle her headfirst, knocking her to the ground. She grabs the bone dagger, but I jab her in the throat. While she chokes, I drive my elbow into her gut.

The bone dagger falls from her hand. I wrap my hand around its ivory blade. Its touch fills me with a chill, a strange and violent power.

Strike, Amari.

Father's face returns. Hard. Unforgiving.

This is what I warned you about. If we don't fight, these maggots will be our end.

But staring at Folake, I see the pain in Kwame's eyes. The fear that weighed down Zu's small shoulders. All the grief that lies in Father's wake, the lives he's already taken away.

I cannot be like Father.

The maji are not my enemy.

I drop the dagger and pull my fist back, twisting from my hips as my fist collides with her jaw. Her head snaps with a lurch. Her eyes roll before she blacks out.

I leap off her and grab the dagger, slicing through the ropes binding Tzain's wrists. The cords barely hit the ground before I start tying them around his thigh.

"Go." Tzain tries to urge me on, but his arms are weak. "There's not enough time."

"Hush."

His skin is clammy to the touch. When I tie the ropes tight, the blood flow slows. But he can hardly keep his eyes open. This might not be enough.

I peek outside the tent—unmasked figures run in every direction, creating the cover of chaos. Though the boundaries of the camp aren't visible, we can at least follow the surge of people.

"Alright." I break a branch off a tree and duck back into the tent, placing the makeshift cane in Tzain's right hand. I sling his other arm over my shoulder, locking my knees to stop myself from buckling under the weight.

"Amari, no." Tzain grimaces, breaths rapid and shallow.

"Be quiet," I snap. "I'm not leaving you behind."

With me for leverage and the cane for balance, Tzain takes his first labored step on his good leg. We make our way to the tent's entrance before taking our last moment of rest.

"We're not dying here," I say.

I won't allow it.

CHAPTER FIFTY

INAN

THE GROUND BEFORE ME is a maze.

A labyrinth of masks and earthly animations.

I sprint through the chaos, dodging blades, leaping over tree roots to make it through the gate.

More masked figures run out, confused, attempting to make sense of the insanity. Zélie's animations break through the ground like rising mountains. They swarm like an infestation, a plague no one can escape.

It's working. Despite myself, a smile comes as I sprint. It's a whole new world of battle. A game of sênet more chaotic than anything I could've imagined.

All around me fighters go down, screaming as Zélie's animations grab hold. Like cocoons, the earthly soldiers wrap themselves around the assailants, pinning the assailants to the ground.

For the first time, the sight of magic is thrilling. Not a curse, but a gift. A fighter lunges toward me and I don't even have to reach for my blade; an animation crashes into him, knocking him out of my way.

As I leap over the fallen fighter, the earthly animation looks up. Though it has no visible eyes, I can sense its gaze. A chill runs through me as I near the gate.

"Ugh!"

The cry is distant, yet it seems to echo in my head.

The smell of the sea wavers.

I turn; an arrow's pierced Zélie's arm.

"Zélie!"

Another arrow flies, this time striking her side. The impact knocks her to the ground. New animations rise to take the arrows head-on.

"Go!" she shouts from down the field, finding me in the frenzy. She keeps one hand gripped on the sunstone as the other stanches the wound in her side.

My feet drag like cement, but I can't ignore her instruction. The gate is only a few meters away. Our family and the scroll are still inside.

I push forward, making it through the gate and toward the camp. But before I can move on, a different sight gives me pause.

A divîner with a powerful frame races out the gate. Blood stains his hands and face. For some reason the sight makes me think of Tzain.

But most troubling of all is the smell of smoke and ash. It overpowers me as he runs past. I don't understand why until I whip my head around and see the divîner's hands begin to blaze.

A Burner . . .

The sight stops me in my tracks, reigniting a fear Father's pounded into me my whole life. The type of maji that incinerated Father's first family. The monsters who set him on his warpath.

An indomitable fire rages around the maji's hands, billowing in shocking red clouds. Its flames shine bright against the night, crackling so loud it practically roars. As it floods my ears, the sound twists into screams. The futile pleas Father's family must've made.

A new wave of arrows launches from the trees with the Burner's arrival, forcing Zélie back. It's too much to handle at once.

The sunstone slips from her grasp.

No!

The world shifts, time freezing as the forthcoming horror dawns. The Burner lunges for the orb. This must have been his plan all along.

Zélie stretches forward for the stone, pained face illuminated by the blaze in the Burner's hands. But her reach falls short.

The Burner's fingers barely graze the stone when his body erupts in flames.

The fire burns inside his chest, shooting from his throat, his hands, his feet.

Curse the skies.

It's unlike anything I've ever seen.

The blaze is all-consuming. The air incinerates to a scalding degree. The ground beneath the Burner's feet smolders red. Just his presence melts the dirt around him like metal in a blacksmith's forge.

My feet move before my mind catches up. I sprint through the mammoth trees and paralyzed masks in my way. I have no plan. No viable attack. But still, I run.

As I race to get there in time, the Burner holds his flaming hands in front of his face. Through the fire he almost looks confused, unsure of what to do.

But as his fists clench, darkness radiates from his stance. A new strength, a rediscovered truth. He has the power now.

And it's a power he's hungry to use.

"Zélie!" I scream.

He stalks toward her. A swarm of animations charge with a vengeance, but he breaks straight through them, unwavering as they splinter into burning rubble.

Zélie tries to rise from the ground and fight, but her wounds are too severe. As she falls back, the Burner raises his palm.

"No!"

I lunge, throwing myself between his hand and Zélie's body. A surge of terror and adrenaline races through me as I face the Burner's flames.

A comet of fire twists in his hand. Its heat bends the air.

My magic builds in my chest. Thrashing into my fingers. The image of my powers restraining Kaea's mind returns. I raise my hands to fight—

"Stop!"

The Burner freezes.

Confusion rocks me as he turns to the voice's source. A young girl makes her way across the camp, thin brows knit in concern.

The moonlight illuminates her face, glowing against the puff of white on top of her head. When she reaches us, she stares at the streak of white in my own hair.

"They're one of us."

The comet of fire in the Burner's hands goes out.

CHAPTER FIFTY-ONE

ZÉLIE

He tried to protect me.

In all the questions and confusion, this surprise rises above the rest. It surges when Inan retrieves the sunstone and places it in my hands. It swells when he lifts me in his arms and holds me tight against his chest.

Following the young girl with a crown of white hair, Inan carries me past the gate. As we pass, the fighters remove their masks and reveal their white locks. Almost every person behind the gate is a divîner, too.

What is this?

I try to make sense of everything through the haze of pain: the Burner, the countless divîners, the child who appears to lead them. But any notion of what this could all mean vanishes when we finally lay eyes on their camp.

In the center of the mammoth trees lies a convergence of several valleys. The dip creates a depression in the earth, forming a wide plain filled with bright tents, wagons, and carts. From afar the sweet scent of fried plantain and jollof rice hits me, somehow rising above the copper tang of my own blood. I catch murmurs of Yoruba in the crowd filled with the most divîners I've seen since I was a child.

We pass a group of divîners laying flowers around a tall lavender vase. *A shrine.* A tribute to Sky Mother.

"Who're all these people?" Inan asks the young girl they call Zu. "What is it you're doing?"

"Give me a moment. Please. I promise, I'll return your friends and answer your questions, but I need some time."

Zu whispers to a divîner beside her, a girl with a green patterned skirt and matching wrap tied around her white hair.

"They weren't in the tent," the divîner whispers back.

"Then find them." The girl's voice is strained. "They didn't make it past the gate, so they can't have gotten far. Tell them we have their friends. We know they were telling the truth."

I strain my neck to hear more, but an ache ripples through my core. When I writhe, Inan holds me closer. The sound of his beating heart pulses through my ears, steady and strong, like the crest of the tides. I find myself leaning into the sound. Again, my greatest confusion rises.

"That Burner would've killed you," I whisper. Just lying in the maji's presence seared my skin. It still itches, raw and red, a patch on my arm burnt and blistering.

As it prickles, it brings me back to the scorching breaths I thought would be my last. For the first time, magic wasn't my ally.

It was almost my end.

"What were you thinking?" I ask.

"You were in danger," he answers. "I wasn't."

He reaches down and grazes a cut on my chin. A strange flutter travels through me at his touch. Any possible response jumbles in my throat. I don't know what to say to that.

Inan still bathes in the glow of the sunstone's touch. With his magic still at the surface, his copper complexion is rich with health. In the lantern's light, his bones are elegantly pronounced instead of harsh and protruding against his skin.

"This'll do." Zu brings us into a tent where a few makeshift cots have been set up.

"Set her down here." Zu points to a cot, and Inan lays me down with care. As my head hits the rough cotton, I fight a wave of nausea.

"We need liquor and bandages for the wounds," Inan says.

Zu shakes her head. "I'll take care of it."

She presses her palms to the gash in my side, and I cringe. A searing stabs at my insides as she chants.

"Babalúayé, dúró tì mí bayi bayi. Fún mi ní agbára, kí nle fún àwọn tókù ní agbára—"

I force my head up; a bright orange light glows beneath Zu's hands. The pain of her touch transforms into a numbing warmth. The searing inside me cools to a dull ache.

The soft light from her hands kneads its way into my skin, spreading throughout every ripped muscle and torn ligament.

I let out a long breath as Zu's magic mends my wounds.

"Are you alright?"

I look up; I didn't even realize I was squeezing Inan's hand. My face heats as I let go and run my fingers over where the arrow pierced me. Wet blood still trickles down my skin, but the wound is completely healed.

Once again questions arise, louder now that they don't have to fight through the haze of my pain. In the past hour, I've seen more different types of magic than I've seen in the past decade.

"You need to start talking." I study Zu; the russet hue of her brown skin is strangely familiar, like the fishermen who sailed up to Ilorin every two moons to exchange their saltwater trout for our cooked tigerfish.

"What's going on? What is this place? Where are the bone dagger and scroll? And where are our siblings? You said you had my brother—"

I pause as the tent flap flies open; Amari stumbles in with a half-conscious Tzain slung around her arm. I jump to my feet to help her. My brother is so battered he can hardly stand.

"What have you done?" I yell.

Amari withdraws the bone dagger and points it at Zu's neck. "Heal him!"

The girl steps back, palms raised.

"Set him down." She takes a deep breath. "I'll answer all your questions now."

WE SIT IN RIGID SILENCE, digesting everything as Zulaikha heals Tzain's leg and head. Behind her, Kwame and Folake stand at attention, stances tense.

When Kwame shifts, my hand moves to my leather pack, searching for the heat of the sunstone under its skin. It's still hard to look at him without imposing the memory of flames around his face.

I lean against Nailah, relieved to be reunited after Zu ordered her people to release my ryder. I tuck my pack behind her paw to keep it and the stone out of sight. But when Zu's limbs begin to shake from the strain of her incantation, I find myself wanting to pull out the sunstone and lend it to her.

Watching Zu, it's like I'm five years old again, trailing after Mama with bandages and pots of heated water. Whenever the village Healer couldn't tend to the worst of Ibadan's sick alone, she and Mama would work together. Side by side they sat, the Healer using the magic of her touch while Mama kept the patient from taking his last breath. *The best Reapers don't only command death, little Zél. We also help others live.*

I stare at Zu's small hands, remembering the hands of my mother. Though young, Zu exhibits great skill over her magic. It all begins to make sense when we learn that she was the very first divîner to touch the scroll.

"I didn't realize what I had," she speaks, voice scratchy from the toll of her magic. Folake hands her a wooden cup of water. Zu nods in thanks before taking a sip. "We weren't ready when Saran's guards descended in Warri and attacked. We barely escaped after they took the scroll away."

Inan and Amari stare at each other, a silent conversation playing in their eyes. The guilt that's crept onto Inan's face all day spreads to Amari's.

"After Warri, I knew we needed a place where we could be safe. A place where the guards couldn't hunt us. It started as only a few tents, but when we sent coded messages to the divîners of Orïsha, the camp began to grow."

Inan lurches forward. "You built this settlement in under a moon?"

"It doesn't feel like it." Zu shrugs. "It's like the gods kept sending divîners this way. Before I knew what was happening, the camp built itself."

The ghost of a smile comes to Zu's face, but fades when she turns to Amari and Tzain. She swallows hard and looks down, running her hands up and down her arms.

"The things we did to you—" Zu stops herself. "The things I *allowed* them to do . . . I'm so sorry. I promise you, it made me sick. But when our scouts saw a noble with the scroll, we couldn't take the risk." She squeezes her eyes shut, a thin line of tears breaking through. "We couldn't let what happened in Warri happen here."

Zu's tears make my own eyes prickle. Kwame's face pinches with pain. I want to hate him for what he did to Tzain, but I can't. I'm no better. If anything, I'm worse. If Inan hadn't stopped me, I would've stabbed that masked divîner to death just to get answers. He'd be facedown in the dirt instead of lying on a cot, being treated as he awaits Zu's healing.

"I'm sorry," Kwame forces out, voice low and strained. "But I promised these people I would do anything to keep them safe."

My mind paints the flames around his face once more, but somehow they aren't as menacing. His magic made my blood run cold, but he fought for his people. *Our* people. Even the gods wouldn't fault him for that. How can I?

Zu palms the tears away from her cheeks. In that moment she appears so much younger than the world has allowed her to be. Before I can stop myself, I reach out and pull her into my arms.

"I'm so sorry," she cries into my shoulder.

"It's okay." I rub her back. "You were trying to protect your people. You did what you had to do."

I lock eyes with Amari and Tzain, and they nod in agreement. We can't blame her. Not when we would do the exact same thing.

"Here." Zulaikha pulls the scroll from the pocket of her black dashiki and presses it into my hands. "Whatever you need, everyone here is behind you. They listen to me because I was the first to touch the scroll, but if what Amari said is true, you've been chosen by the gods. Whatever your command, we'll all follow it."

Discomfort bristles beneath my skin at the thought. I can't lead these people. I can barely lead myself.

"Thank you, but you're doing good work here. Just keep these people safe. Our job is to get to Zaria and charter a ship. The solstice is only five days away."

"I have family in Zaria." Folake speaks up. "Traders we can trust. If I go with you, I can get you their ship."

"I'll go, too." Zulaikha grabs my hand, hope tangible in her tiny grasp. "There are enough people here for security, and I'm sure you guys could use a Healer."

"If you'll have me . . ." Kwame's voice trails off. He clears his throat and forces himself to meet Tzain's and Amari's eyes. "I would like to fight with you. Fire is always a good defense."

Tzain fixes Kwame with a cool glare, hand rubbing his wounded thigh. Though Zu stopped his bleeding, she wasn't strong enough to take away all the pain.

"Protect my sister, or the next time you close your eyes, you'll be the one with a dagger in the leg."

"I can accept that." Kwame extends a hand. Tzain reaches up and shakes it. A comfortable silence fills the tent as an apology travels between their grips.

"We have to celebrate!" A wide smile erupts on Zu's face, so bright and innocent it makes her look like the child she should get to be. Her joy is so infectious, even Tzain finds himself with a grin. "I've been wanting to do something fun, a way to bring everyone in the camp together. I know it isn't the typical time, but we should hold the Àjọyọ̀ tomorrow."

"Àjọyọ̀?" I lean forward, unable to believe my ears. When I was a child, celebrating Sky Mother and the birth of the gods was the best part of my year. Baba would always purchase Mama and me matching kaftans, silk and beaded, with long trains that flowed down our backs. In the last Àjọyọ̀ before the Raid, Mama saved up all year so she could buy gold-plated rings to braid throughout my hair.

"It would be perfect." Zu's voice speeds up as her excitement grows. "We could clear out tents and hold the opening procession. Find a place for the sacred stories. We could build a stage and let each maji touch the scroll. Everyone can watch their powers return!"

A prickle of hesitation runs through me, burning with the echo of Kwame's flames. Just a day ago, turning all these divîners into maji would've been a dream, but for the first time I pause. More magic means more potential, more wrong hands for the sunstone to fall into. *But if I keep a close eye on it . . . if all these divîners already follow Zu . . .*

"What do you think?" Zu asks.

I look between her and Kwame. He breaks into a smile.

"That sounds amazing," I decide. "It'll be an Àjọyọ̀ people will never forget."

"What about the ritual?" Amari asks.

"If we leave right after the celebration, we'll have enough time. We still have five days to get to Zaria, and using Folake's boat will cut our time in half."

Zu's face goes so bright, it's like its own source of light. She squeezes my hand, and I'm surprised at the warmth it fills me with. It's more than another ally. It's the start of our community.

"Then we'll do it!" Zu grabs Amari's hand, too, almost jumping up and down. "It's the least we can do. I can think of no better way to honor the four of you."

"Three," Tzain corrects us. His terseness cuts through my budding excitement. He nods at Inan. "He's not with us."

Tightness gathers in my chest as Inan and Tzain lock eyes. I knew this moment was coming. I just hoped we'd have more time.

Zu nods stiffly, sensing the tension. "We'll let you talk among yourselves. There's a lot we have to do if we're going to be ready for tomorrow."

She rises to her feet, and Kwame and Folake follow, leaving us with only silence. I'm forced to stare at the scroll in my hands. What now? Where do we—*are we even a "we"?*

"I know this will be hard to digest." Inan speaks first. "But things changed when you and Amari were taken. I'm aware that it's a lot to ask, but if your sister can learn to trust me—"

Tzain whips to me, his glower hitting like a staff to the gut. His face says it all: *Tell me this isn't true.*

"Tzain, if it weren't for him, I would've been taken, too—"

Because he wanted to kill me himself. When the fighters attacked, he still wanted to drive his sword through my heart.

I take a breath and start over, running my hands over my staff. I can't afford to mess this up. I need Tzain to listen to me.

"I didn't trust him, not at first. But Inan fought by my side. When I was in danger, he threw himself in harm's way." My voice seems to shrink. Unable to look at anyone, I stare at my hands. "He's seen things, felt things I could never explain to anyone else."

"How am I supposed to believe that?" Tzain crosses his arms.

"Because . . ." I look back at Inan. "He's a maji."

"What?" Amari's jaw drops and she whips toward Inan. Though I've seen her eye the streak in his hair before, now the realization dawns.

"How is that possible?"

"I don't know," Inan says. "It happened sometime in Lagos."

"Right before you burned our village to the ground?" Tzain yells.

Inan clenches his jaw tight. "I didn't know then—"

"But you knew when you cut Lekan down."

"He attacked us. My admiral feared for our lives—"

"And when you tried to kill my sister last night? Were you a maji then?" Tzain tries to rise but grimaces, hand flying to his thigh.

"Let me help," I start, but Tzain throws off my hand.

"Tell me you're not this stupid." A different kind of pain flashes behind his eyes. "You can't trust him, Zél. Maji or not, he isn't on our side."

"Tzain—"

"He tried to *kill* you!"

"Please." Inan speaks up. "I know you have no reason to trust me. But I don't want to fight anymore. We all desire the same thing."

"What's that?" Tzain scoffs.

"A better Orïsha. A kingdom where maji like your sister don't have to live in constant fear. I want to make it better." Inan locks his amber eyes with mine. "I want to fix it with you."

I force myself to look away, afraid of what my face will betray. I turn to Tzain, hoping something in Inan's words moved him. But he's clenching his fists so hard his forearms shake.

"Tzain—"

"Forget it." He rises with a wince and heads for the tent exit, fighting through the pain in his leg. "You're always screwing everything up. Why stop now?"

CHAPTER FIFTY-TWO

AMARI

"INAN, WAIT!"

I push through the divîners filling the grassy walkway between two long rows of tents. Their curious gazes add a weight to my step, but they're not enough to distract me from the questions filling my head. When Tzain left, Zélie ran after him, trying in vain to make him understand. But then my brother ran after her, leaving me all alone in that tent.

Inan stops when he hears my voice, though he doesn't turn around. His eyes follow Zélie, trailing her as she disappears into the crowd. When he turns to me, I don't know which question I should ask first.

It's as if I'm back inside the palace walls, so close to him, yet always worlds apart.

"You should have Zulaikha heal that." He grabs my wrists, inspecting the dark red bruises and dried blood where the ropes cut through my skin. Distracting myself from the pain was easy when I was carrying Tzain, but now the throbbing is constant, burning wherever the cool wind hits my exposed flesh.

"When she's rested." I pull my hands back, crossing my arms to hide them. "She's too drained after healing Tzain and she still needs to take care of Jailin. I don't want her to get hurt."

"She reminds me of you." Inan smiles, but it doesn't reach his eyes. "You used to get that crazed look on your face when you had an idea and you knew you would get your way."

I know the look he speaks of; he had one of his own. He'd get a smile so wide his nose would scrunch up and his eyes would nearly crinkle closed. It's that look that got me out of bed at night, to sneak into the royal stables or dive headfirst into a barrel of sugar in the kitchen. Back when things were simpler. Before Father and Orïsha wedged themselves between us.

"I've been meaning to give this to you." Inan reaches inside his pocket. I expect a death threat from Father. I can hardly breathe when I see the glint of my old headdress.

"How?" My voice cracks when he places it in my hand.

Though dented, rusted, and stained with blood, holding it warms my chest. It's like getting a little piece of Binta back.

"I've been carrying it since Sokoto. Thought you would want it back."

I clutch the headdress to my chest and stare at him, a wave of gratitude rushing through me. But the gratitude only makes our reality worse.

"Are you really a maji?" The question fights its way out as I study the white streak in Inan's hair. Headdress or not, I still don't understand: What are his powers? Why him and not me? If the gods ordain who receives their gifts, what made them choose Inan?

Inan nods, running his hands through the streak. "I don't know how or why. It happened when I touched the scroll in Lagos."

"Does Father know?"

"Am I still breathing?" Inan attempts to keep his voice light, but the pain breaks through. The image of the sword that cut Binta forces itself into my mind. It's far too easy to imagine Father plunging that sword into Inan's chest as well.

"How could you?"

Every other question vanishes as the only one that matters finally comes out. I feel every time I defended him to Zélie balloon inside me. I thought I knew my brother's true heart. Now I'm not sure I know him at all.

"I can understand being under Father's influence, but he's not here," I press. "How am I ever supposed to trust you when you've been fighting against yourself this entire time?"

Inan's shoulders slump. He scratches the back of his neck.

"You can't," he replies. "But I'll earn your trust. I promise."

In another life, those words would be enough, but Binta's death still scars my memories. I can't help but think of all the signs, every chance I had to release her from palace life. If I had only been more vigilant then, my friend would still be alive.

"These people." I clutch her headdress. "They mean the world to me. I love you, Inan, but I won't allow you to hurt the maji the way you've hurt me."

"I know." Inan nods. "But I swear on the throne, that is not my aim. Zélie's taught me how wrong I was about the maji. I know I've made mistakes."

His voice softens when he speaks Zélie's name, as if recalling a fond memory. More questions bubble inside me as he turns to search for her in the crowd, but for now I push them back down. I can't begin to fathom what she did to change my brother's mind, but the only thing that matters now is that this change is here for good.

"For your sake, I hope you don't make any more."

Inan eyes me, face difficult to read as he looks me up and down.

"Is that a threat?"

"It's a promise. If I suspect any treachery, it'll be my sword you'll have to face."

It wouldn't be the first time our swords clashed. It certainly won't be like the last.

"I'll prove myself to you, to all of you," Inan declares. "You're on the right side of this. My only desire is to stand there as well."

"Good." I lean forward to hug him, holding on to his promise.

But when his hands wrap around my back, all I can think of are how his fingers are resting just above my scars.

CHAPTER FIFTY-THREE

ZÉLIE

THE NEXT MORNING Zu is quick to bound into my tent.

"There's so much I have to show you." She shakes my arm. "Zélie, come *on*. It's almost midday!"

With enough prodding, I concede and sit up, working through the new coils in my hair to scratch my scalp.

"Be quick." Zu shoves a sleeveless red dashiki into my arms. "Everyone's waiting outside."

When she leaves, I offer Tzain a smile, but he keeps his back to me. Even though I can tell he's awake, he doesn't make a sound. The uncomfortable silence that burned between us last night returns, the frustrated sighs and empty words filling our tent. No matter how many times I apologized, Tzain wouldn't respond.

"Do you want to come?" I ask quietly. "A walk could be good for your leg."

Nothing. It's like I'm speaking to the air.

"Tzain . . ."

"I'm staying." He shifts and stretches his neck. "I don't feel like walking with *everyone*."

I remember Zu's words. I assumed she meant Kwame and Folake, but Inan's probably right outside. If Tzain's still this upset, seeing Inan will only make everything worse.

"Okay." I slip into the dashiki and tie my hair back with a blue-and-red-patterned scarf Zu lent me. "I'll be back soon. I'll try to bring you some food."

"Thanks."

I latch onto the response, repeating it in my head. If Tzain can manage a grumble of gratitude now, maybe things will turn out alright.

"Zél." He looks over his shoulder, meeting my eye. "Be careful. I don't want you alone with him."

I nod and leave the tent, the weight of Tzain's warning dragging me down. But as soon as I step into the camp, all the heaviness evaporates.

Sunlight fills the spacious valley; every acre of the lush greens explodes with life. Young divîners bustle through the maze of pop-up shacks, tents, and carts. Each person shines with white hair and vibrant patterns woven throughout their dashikis and spirited kaftans. It's like Sky Mother's promise laid before my eyes, come to life after all this time.

"Gods." I spin, taking it all in as Zu waves me over. I've never seen so many divîners in one spot, especially with so much . . . joy. The crowd laughs and smiles through the hills, white hair braided, dreaded, and flowing. An unfamiliar freedom breathes in their shoulders, in their gait, in their eyes.

"Look out!"

I throw my hands up, smiling as a group of young children run past. The oldest among the crowd look to be in their twenties, none older than twenty-five. Of all the divîners before us, they're the most bewildering to see; never in my life have I encountered so many grown divîners outside the prison cells or the stocks.

"Finally!" Zu hooks her arm in mine, sporting a smile almost too big for her face. She pulls me past the yellow-painted cart where Inan and Amari are waiting. Amari grins when she sees me, but her face falls when she doesn't find Tzain.

"He wanted to rest," I answer her unasked question. *And he didn't want to see your brother.*

Inan looks at me, handsome in a cobalt kaftan with fitted, patterned pants. He looks different without the harsh lines and jagged metal of his uniform. Softer. Warmer. His streak flashes bright in his hair, for once not hidden behind a helmet or black dye. Our eyes linger on each other, but it takes only a second for Zu to whip between us and pull us both along.

"We've made progress, but we still have a ways to go if we're going to be ready for tonight." She seems to speak a million meters a second, always discovering something new she has to say before finishing her last thought.

"This is where the old stories are going to be." Zu points to a makeshift stage occupying a grassy knoll between two tents. "There's a divîner from Jimeta who's telling them. You have to meet her, she's enchanting. We think she'll be a Tider. Oh, and this! This is where we'll have the divîners touch the scroll. I can't wait to watch that, it'll be incredible!"

Zulaikha moves through the crowd with the magnetism of a queen. Divîners stop and stare as she passes, pointing and whispering about us because she's holding my hand. Usually I hate when others stare, but today I find myself reveling in it. It's not like the guards or kosidán, who want me to disappear. The divîners' gazes hold a reverence, a new kind of respect.

"Here's the best part." Zu gestures to a large clearing being decorated with painted lanterns and colorful sheets. "This is where the opening procession will take place. Zélie, you must be in it!"

"Oh, you don't want that." I shake my head fervently, but I laugh when Zu grabs my wrist and jumps up and down. Her joy is contagious; even Inan can't help but smile.

"You would be so great!" Her eyes go wide. "We don't have a Reaper yet, and Oya's attire would fit you perfectly. It has this long red skirt and golden top—Inan! Don't you think she would look incredible?"

Inan's eyes widen and he stammers, looking between me and Zu as if one of us will release him from answering.

"Zu, it's fine." I wave her off. "I'm sure you can find someone else."

"Probably be for the best." Inan recovers his voice. His eyes drift to me for a moment, before looking away. "But yes, I think Zélie would look beautiful."

My face heats, growing warmer when Amari studies us. I turn away and focus my attention elsewhere, trying to ignore the way Inan's answer makes something inside me tingle. Once again the way he carried me into the camp forces itself back into my mind.

"Zu, what's that?" I point to a black cart with a long line of divîners.

"That's where Folake's painting the clan baajis." Zu's eyes light up. "You have to get one!"

"Baajis?" Amari's nose scrunches in confusion.

Zu gestures to the symbol painted on her neck. She grabs Inan and Amari by the hands and pulls, running ahead. "They're lovely. Come on, you have to see it now!"

Zu moves fast, leading them farther through the crowd. I consider a brisker pace, but there's something about walking through this camp that makes me want to slow down. Each time I pass a new divîner, my mind runs wild imagining all the different types of maji they could become. There could be future Winders on my left, or Seers on my right. With ten clans, there's even a chance a future Reaper is right in front of m—

A stranger bumps into me, clad in red and black. He grips my waist, steadying me before I tumble back.

"Apologies." He smiles. "My feet have a nasty habit of following my heart."

"It's fi . . ." My voice trails off. The stranger looks like no one I've ever seen, no descendant of Orïshan blood. His complexion is like sandstone, rich with copper undertones. Unlike the round eyes of Orïshans, his are angular and hooded, highlighting his stormy gray eyes.

"Roën." He smiles again. "It's a delight. I hope you can find the heart to forgive my clumsiness." His accent clips the *t*'s and rolls the *r*'s in his speech. He has to be a merchant, some trader from another land.

Finally.

I look the young man up and down. Tzain's told me about meeting the occasional foreigner while traveling Orïsha for his agbön matches, but I've never met one myself. Over the years I've heard descriptions of unique traders in crowded markets and travelers passing through Orïsha's busiest cities. I always hoped one would come to Ilorin, but they never make it all the way to our eastern coast.

Questions fill my mind, but then I realize his hand is still on the small of my back. My cheeks warm as I slide away from his touch. I shouldn't stare, but from the smirk on Roën's lips, I can almost guarantee he likes it.

"Till we meet again." He winks and struts off, holding my gaze. But before he can take another step, Inan reappears and grabs his arm.

The smile fades from Roën's eyes as he glances at Inan's grip. "I don't know your intention, brother. But that's a good way to lose a hand."

"So is pickpocketing." Inan sets his jaw. "Give it back."

The gray-eyed stranger glances at me; with a sheepish shrug he removes a compacted staff from the pocket of his draped pants. My eyes widen as I reach for my empty waistband.

"How the hell did you do that?" I swipe back the staff. Mama Agba's trained us to feel a thief's touch. I should've sensed his hand.

"First bump."

"Then why'd you linger?" I ask. "If you're that smooth, you could've gotten away."

"I couldn't resist." Roën grins like a foxer, revealing teeth that shine a little too bright. "From behind I saw only the beautiful staff. I didn't know it'd be on a beautiful girl."

I glare at him, but it only makes his smile wider. "As I said before, love"—he gives a little bow—"till we meet again."

With that he saunters off, walking over to Kwame in the distance. They grasp each other's fists in a familiar greeting, exchanging words I can't hear.

Kwame eyes me for a second before the two disappear into a tent. I can't help but wonder what Kwame would be doing meeting with a man like that.

"Thanks," I say to Inan as I run my fingers over the carved staff markings. It's the only thing I have left from Ilorin. The only tie to the life I once had. I think back to Mama Agba, wishing I could see her and Baba again.

"If I knew all it took to distract you was a charming smile, I would've tried that ages ago."

"It wasn't his smile." I lift my chin. "I've never seen someone from another land."

"Ah, was that all it was?" Inan grins, subtle yet completely disarming. In our time together I've seen everything from rage to pain play across his lips, but never anything close to an actual smile. It creates a dimple in his cheek, crinkling the skin around his amber eyes.

"What is it?" he asks.

"Nothing." I turn back to my staff. Between the kaftan and the smile, it's hard to believe I'm still looking at the little prince—

"Ugh!"

Inan's grin transforms to a wince. He clenches his teeth and grips his side.

"What's wrong?" I put my hand on his back. "Do you need me to get Zu?"

He shakes his head, exhaling a frustrated breath. "This isn't the type of thing she could heal."

I tilt my head until I realize the meaning behind his words. He looked so different in a cobalt kaftan I didn't even notice the air around him was cold.

"You're suppressing your magic." My heart falls in my chest. "You don't have to, Inan. No one here knows who you are."

"It's not that." Inan braces himself before standing up straight. "There are too many people. I have to control it. If I let it out, someone could get hurt."

Once again, I get a glimpse of the broken little prince who charged me with his blade; I knew he was scared, but was he really this afraid of himself?

"I can help you." I drop my hand. "At least a little. If you learned how to control it, it wouldn't hurt you like this."

Inan pulls at the collar of his kaftan, though it hangs loose around his neck. "You wouldn't mind?"

"It's fine." I grab his arm, leading him away from the crowds. "Come on. I know a place we can go."

The Gombe River trickles beside us, filling the air with its song. I thought the new surroundings might calm Inan, but now that we sit, I realize I need calming myself. The nerves that hit when Zu asked me to lead the maji return, stronger this time. I don't know how to help Inan. I'm still trying to figure Reaper magic out myself.

"Talk to me." I take a deep breath and feign the confidence I wish I had. "What does your magic feel like? When does it hit you the strongest?"

Inan swallows, fingers twitching around a phantom object. "I don't know. I don't understand anything about it at all."

"Here." I reach into my pocket and place a bronze piece into his palm. "Stop fidgeting, you're making me itch."

"What's this?"

"Something you can play with without poisoning yourself. Have at it and calm down."

Inan smiles again, this time fully, one that reaches and softens his eyes. He runs his thumb over the cheetanaire engraved in the coin's center, marking it as Orïshan. "I don't think I've ever held a bronze piece."

"Ugh," I choke in disgust. "Keep facts like that to yourself or I won't be able to stomach this."

"Forgive me." Inan tests the weight of the coin in his palm. "And thank you."

"Thank me by making this work. When was the last time you really let your magic flow?"

With the bronze piece passing between his fingers, Inan begins to think. "That temple."

"Chândomblé?"

He nods. "It amplified my abilities. When I was trying to find you,

I sat under a painting of Orí and . . . I don't know. It was the first time I felt like there was something I could control."

The dreamscape. I think back to the last time we were there, wondering what I must've said. Did I give something away?

"How does it work?" I ask. "There are times when it feels like you're reading a book inside my head."

"More like a puzzle than a book," Inan corrects me. "It's not always clear, but when your thoughts and emotions are intense, I feel them, too."

"You get that with everyone?"

He shakes his head. "Not to the same degree. Everyone else feels like being caught in the rain. You're the whole tsunami."

I freeze at the power of his words, trying to imagine what that would be like. The fear. The pain. The memories of Mama being ripped away.

"Sounds awful," I whisper.

"Not always." He stares at me like he can see straight into my heart, straight into everything I am. "There are times when it's amazing. Beautiful, even."

My heart swells in my chest. A coil of hair falls in front of my face, and Inan tucks it behind my ear. Goosebumps prickle down my neck when his fingers brush my skin.

I clear my throat and look away, ignoring the thumping inside my head. I don't know what's going on, but I know I can't allow myself to feel like this.

"Your magic is strong." I push the focus back. "Believe it or not, it comes naturally to you. You channel things instinctively that most maji would need a powerful incantation to do."

"How can I control it?" Inan asks. "What do I do?"

"Close your eyes," I instruct. "Repeat after me. I don't know Connector incantations, but I do know how to ask for help from the gods."

Inan closes his eyes and grips the bronze piece tight.

"It's simple—*Orí, bá mi sọ̀rọ̀.*"

"Ba me sorro?"

"*Bá mi sọ̀rọ̀.*" I correct his pronunciation with a smile. It's endearing how clumsy Yoruba sounds on his lips. "Repeat it. Picture Orí. Open yourself up and ask for his help. That's what being a maji is about. With the gods on your side, you're never truly alone."

Inan looks down. "They're really always there?"

"Always." I think back to all those years I turned my back on them. "Even in the darkest times the gods are always there. Whether we acknowledge them or not, they always have a plan."

Inan's hand closes over the bronze piece, face turning pensive.

"Alright." He nods. "I want to try."

"Orí, bá mi sọ̀rọ̀."

"*Orí, bá mi sọ̀rọ̀,*" he chants under his breath, fingers twisting around the bronze piece. At first nothing happens, but as he continues, the air begins to heat. A soft blue glow appears in his hands. The light creeps its way over to me.

I close my eyes as the world spins away, a hot rush, just like the other day. When the spinning ends, I'm back in the dreamscape.

But this time when the reeds tickle my feet, I don't have to feel afraid.

CHAPTER FIFTY-FOUR

INAN

THE AIR OF THE DREAMSCAPE hums like a melody. Soft.

Resonant.

As it sings, my eyes trail Zélie's bare skin through the lake.

Like a black-feathered swan, she glides above the shimmering waves, face at ease, an expression I've never seen. It's like for one single moment the whole world doesn't weigh on her shoulders.

She dives down for a few seconds and resurfaces, lifting her dark face to the rays above. With eyes shut, her lashes seem to never end. Her coils look like silver against her skin. When she turns to me, my breath catches. For a moment I forget how to breathe.

And to think.

I once thought she wore the face of a monster.

"You know it's creepy if you just watch."

A grin crawls onto my face. "Is that your clever way of getting me to join you?"

She smiles. A beautiful smile. With it, I glimpse the sun. When she turns, I long for that glimpse again, the warmth it spread through my bones. With that urge, I remove my shirt and jump in.

Zélie sputters and spits at the wave that hits when I crash through the rippling water. The current pulls me under with unexpected strength. I kick and push until I break back to the surface.

As I swim away from the waterfall's roar, Zélie studies the forest behind us—its end stretches farther than I can see. Far beyond the white border that sat on the lake's bank last time.

"I take it this is your first time in the water?" Zélie calls out.

"What gave it away?"

"Your face," Zélie answers. "You look stupid when you're surprised."

A smile spreads on my lips, one that's coming more and more often in her presence. "You rather enjoy insulting me, don't you?"

"It's almost as satisfying as beating you with my staff."

This time it's she who grins. It makes my own smile grow. She jumps up and floats on her back, passing between the drifting reeds and floating lilies.

"If I had your magic, I'd spend all my time here."

I nod, though I wonder what my dreamscape would look like without her in it. All I create are wilting reeds. With Zélie, the whole world flows.

"You seem at home in the water," I say. "I'm surprised you're not a Tider."

"Maybe in another life." She runs her hand through the lake, watching as it slips through her fingers. "I don't know why it is. I liked the lakes in Ibadan, but they were nothing compared to the ocean."

Like sparks igniting a fire, her memory engulfs me: her young eyes open wide; the awe of the never-ending waves.

"You lived in Ibadan?" I drift closer, breathing more of her in. Though I've never ventured to the northern village, Zélie's memories are so vivid it's as if I'm there now. I marvel at the stunning views from the mountaintop, inhale the crisp mountain air into my lungs.

Her memories of Ibadan hold a special warmth. The blanket of her mother's love.

"I lived there before the Raid." Zélie's voice falters as she relives the moments with me. "But afterward . . ." She shakes her head. "There were too many memories. We couldn't stay."

A pit of guilt opens in my chest, tainted with the smell of burning flesh. The fires I watched from the royal palace resurface, the innocent lives burned before my young eyes. A memory I've pushed down like my magic, a day I've longed to forget. But staring at Zélie now brings it all back: the pain. The tears. The death.

"We weren't supposed to stay in Ilorin." Zélie speaks more to herself than to me. "But then I saw the sea." She smiles to herself. "Baba told me we never had to leave."

In the dreamscape, Zélie's heartbreak hits me with unbearable force. Ilorin was her happiness. And I burned it to the ground.

"I'm sorry." The words fight their way out. I hate myself even more as they ring. They sound so inadequate. Weak in the face of her pain. "I know I can't fix it. I can't change what I've done, but . . . I can rebuild Ilorin. When this is over, it'll be the first thing I do."

Zélie releases a brittle laugh. Dry. Devoid of all joy.

"Keep saying naive things like that. You'll only prove Tzain right."

"What do you mean?" I ask. "What does he think?"

"That when this is over, one of us will be dead. He's scared it'll be me."

CHAPTER FIFTY-FIVE

ZÉLIE

I DON'T KNOW why I'm here.

I don't know why I baited Inan to jump in.

I don't know why something in me flutters each time he swims near.

This is temporary, I remind myself. *This isn't even real.* When this is over, Inan won't be wearing kaftans. He won't be welcoming me into the dreamscape.

I try to picture the feral warrior I know, the little prince who came at me with his sword. But instead, I see the blade that freed me from the masks' net. I see him standing up to Kwame's flames.

He has a good heart. Amari's words from so long ago play inside my head. I thought she was in denial. But did she see the parts of him I couldn't?

"Zélie, I would never hurt you." He shakes his head and grimaces. "Not after all I've seen."

When he lifts his eyes to mine, the truth leaks through. I can't believe I didn't realize it before. The guilt and pity he's been carrying . . . *Gods.*

He must've seen everything.

"I thought my father didn't have a choice. I was always taught that he did what he did to keep Orïsha safe. But after seeing your memories . . ." His voice trails off. "No child should have to live through that."

I turn back to the ripples in the lake, not knowing what to say. To feel. He's seen the worst parts of me. Parts I never thought I could share.

"My father was wrong." Inan speaks so quietly the waterfall nearly drowns him out. "Maybe I should have realized it earlier, but the only thing I can do now is try to make those wrongs right."

Don't believe him, I warn myself. *He's living in a fantasy, a dream.* But with each promise he makes, my heart swells, secretly hoping even one of them holds truth. When Inan looks up at me, I see a hint of the optimism that's always shining in Amari's eyes. Despite everything, he's determined to do this.

He really wants Orïsha to change.

If Sky Mother brought the scroll to you through a descendant of Saran's blood, her will is clear. Lekan's words echo through my head as I stare at Inan, entranced by his strong jaw, the stubble lining his chin. If one descendant of Saran's blood is supposed to help me, could the gods want Inan to rule and change the guard? Is that what we're doing here? Why they gifted him this magic?

Inan floats closer and my heartbeat spikes. I should swim away. But I stay still, cemented in place.

"I don't want anyone else to die," he whispers. "I can't take any more blood on my family's hands."

Pretty lies. That's all this is. But if they're just pretty lies, why can't I swim away?

My gods, is he even wearing clothes? My eyes comb over his broad chest, the curves of each muscle. But before I catch sight of anything under the water, I jerk my eyes up. What in Sky Mother's name am I doing?

I force myself to swim through the waterfall until my back rests against the cliff's edge. This is absurd. Why did I let him bring me here?

I hope the pounding water will keep Inan on the other side, but within moments, he swims through the cascading water to join me.

Go. I order my legs to kick, but I'm ensnared by the soft smile on his lips.

"Do you want me to leave?"

Yes.

That's what I need to say. But the closer he swims, the more something in me wants him to stay. He pauses before he's too close, forcing me to respond.

Do I want him to go?

Though my heart slams against my chest, I know the answer.

"No."

His smile fades and his gaze grows soft, a look I haven't seen on his face before. When others look at me this way, I want to claw their eyes out. Yet somehow, under Inan's gaze, I want more.

"Can I . . ." His voice trails off and his cheeks flush, unable to voice his desire. But he doesn't need words. Not when an undeniable part of me wants the same thing.

I nod and he raises a shaking hand, brushing it against my cheek. I close my eyes, taken away by the rush of his simple touch. It burns through my chest, rages down my spine. His hand slides past my cheek and into my hair, his fingers tickling my scalp.

Gods . . .

If a guard ever saw this, I'd be killed on the spot. Even as a prince, Inan could be thrown in jail.

But despite the rules of our world, Inan's other hand pulls me close, inviting me to let go. I close my eyes and lean in, closer to the little prince than I should ever be.

His lips graze mine—

"Zélie!"

WITH A LURCH, MY body jumps back into the real world.

My eyes snap open just as Tzain rips Inan away. He lifts him by the collar of his kaftan and throws him to the ground.

"Tzain, stop!" I scramble up, forcing my way between them.

"Stay away from my sister!"

"I should leave." Inan looks at me for a moment before backing away into the trees. He grips the bronze piece tight in his hands. "I'll be back at the camp."

"What's wrong with you?" I shout as soon as Inan is out of earshot.

"Wrong with *me*?" Tzain roars. "Gods, Zél, what the hell are you doing out here? I thought you could be hurt!"

"I was trying to help him. He doesn't know how to control his magic. It causes him pain—"

"For gods' sakes, he's the enemy. If he's in pain, that's better for us!"

"Tzain, I know it's hard to believe, but he wants to fix Orïsha. He's trying to make it safe for all the maji."

"Is he brainwashing you?" Tzain shakes his head. "Is this his magic? You're a lot of things, Zél, but I know you're not *this* naive."

"You don't get it." I look away. "You've never had to. You get to be the perfect kosidán everyone loves. Every day I have to be afraid."

Tzain steps back as if I've struck him. "You think I don't know what it's like to wake up every day and worry it's going to be your last?"

"Then give Inan a chance! Amari is only a princess. When magic comes back, she's not first in line. If I can convince the crown prince, we'll have the future king of Orïsha on our side!"

"If you could hear the dung you're spewing." Tzain pulls at his hair. "He doesn't *care* about you, Zél. He just wants to get in between your legs!"

My face burns. Hurt twists with shame. This isn't Tzain. This isn't the brother I love.

"He's the son of the man who murdered Mama, for gods' sakes. How desperate do you have to be?"

"You pine after Amari!" I scream. "How does that make you any better?"

"Because she's not a killer!" Tzain yells back. She didn't burn our *village* to the ground!"

The air around me hums. My heart pounds against my chest as Tzain's tirade continues. His words cut deep, sharper than any attack I've faced before.

"What would Baba say?"

"Leave Baba out of this—"

"Or Mama?"

"Shut up!" I shout back. The hum in the air rises to a fiery buzz. The darkest part of my rage simmers, though I try to fight it down.

"Gods, if she only knew she died so that you could be the prince's whore—"

Magic rushes out of me, hot and violent, raging without the direction of an incantation. Like a spear, a shadow twists from my arm, striking with the fury of the dead.

It all happens in a flash. Tzain shouts. I stumble back.

When it's over, he grabs his shoulder.

Blood leaks from under his grip.

I stare at my trembling hands, at the wispy shadows of death that twist around them. After a moment they fade.

But the damage remains.

"Tzain . . ." I shake my head; tears spill from my eyes. "I didn't mean to. I promise. I wasn't trying to!"

Tzain stares at me like he doesn't know who I am. Like I'm a betrayal to everything we have.

"Tzain—"

He blows by me, face hard. Unforgiving.

I choke back a sob as I fall to the ground.

CHAPTER FIFTY-SIX

ZÉLIE

I STAY ON THE OUTSKIRTS of the settlement until sunset falls. I don't have to face anyone in the trees. I don't have to face myself.

When I can sit in the dark no longer, I travel back to my tent, disappointing Zu, praying I don't run into Tzain. But as soon as Amari sees me, she rushes over with a silk kaftan.

"Where have you been?" She grabs my hand and pulls me into her tent, practically stripping me to pull the dress over my head. "It's almost time for the celebration and we haven't even done your hair!"

"Amari, please—"

"Don't bother fighting me." She slaps my hand away and forces me to sit still. "These people are looking to you, Zélie. You must look the part."

Tzain didn't tell her. . . .

It's the only explanation. Amari applies carmine to my lips and charcoal around my eyes like an older sister might, then makes me do the same to her. If she knew the truth, she would only be afraid.

"It's gotten so curly," she says, pinning one of my coils back.

"I think it's the magic. Mama's hair used to be like this."

"It suits you. I'm not even done and you look stunning."

My cheeks flush, and I gaze at the silk kaftan she's forced me into. Its purple pattern twists with vibrant yellows and deep blues; it shines bright against my dark skin. I finger the beaded neckline, wishing Amari would take it back to whoever lent it to her. I can't remember the last time I wore a dress; I feel naked without fabric covering my legs.

"You don't like it?" Amari asks.

"It doesn't matter," I sigh. "I don't care what I wear, I just want to get tonight over with."

"Did something happen?" Amari pries delicately. "This morning you couldn't wait. Now Zu tells me you don't want to share the scroll?"

I press my lips tight and grip the fabric of my kaftan. The way the smile dropped off Zu's face filled me with a different kind of shame. All these people looking to me to lead them, yet I can't even keep my own magic in check.

And not just my magic . . .

The memory of Kwame's inferno rages so hot, my skin prickles at the imagined heat. I convinced myself I had nothing to fear, but now fear is all I feel. What if Zu couldn't control him? What if she had never arrived? If Kwame hadn't stopped his flames, I wouldn't even be here.

"It's not the right time," I finally say. "The solstice is only four days away—"

"So why not give these divîners their powers back now?" Amari's hold on my hair tightens. "Please, Zélie, talk to me. I want to understand."

I hug my knees to my chest and close my eyes, almost smiling at Amari's words. I remember the days when the sight of magic made her flinch. Now it's her fighting for it as I cower.

I try to will away memories of Tzain's face, the coldest look I could ever get. I recognized the terror in his eyes. When Kwame touched the sunstone and ignited, I looked at him the same way.

"Is it because of Inan?" Amari presses when I stay silent. "Are you afraid of what he'll do?"

"Inan isn't the problem." At least not *this* problem.

Amari pauses, releasing my hair to kneel at my side. With her back straight and shoulders squared, she looks like the true princess she is, regal in a borrowed golden dress.

"What happened while Tzain and I were gone?"

Though my heart skips a beat, I keep my face blank. "I already told you—we teamed up to get you both back."

"Zélie, please, I need you to be honest. I love my brother, I do. But I have never seen this side of him."

"What side is that?"

"Going against my father. Fighting *for* the maji? Something happened to him, and I know it has to do with you."

She looks at me with knowing eyes, and my ears burn. I think about the dreamscape, the moment our lips almost touched.

"He learned." I shrug. "He saw what your father's done, what his guards are doing now. He wants to find a way to make things right."

Amari crosses her arms and arches her brow. "You must think I'm blind or stupid, and you know I'm not blind."

"I don't know what you're talking about—"

"Zélie, he *stares* at you. He smiles like—skies, I don't even know. I have never seen him smile the way he smiles with you." I look at the ground and she grabs my chin, forcing me to meet her eyes. "I want you to be happy, Zél. More than you realize. But I know my brother."

"What's that supposed to mean?"

Amari pauses, pinning another coil back. "Either he's about to betray us or something else is taking place."

I wrench my chin out of her grasp and turn toward the floor. Guilt seeps through every part of my body.

"You sound like Tzain."

"Tzain is worried, and he has every right to be. I can get through to him, but first I need to know if I should."

You shouldn't.

That's the obvious choice. But despite everything he has done, the memory of Inan carrying me into the camp stays strong. I close my eyes and breathe deeply.

I don't remember the last time I felt so safe in someone else's arms.

"When you told me Inan had a good heart, I thought you were a fool. Part of me feels like the fool now, but I've seen that heart for myself. He saved me from getting captured by Zu's fighters; he did everything he could to get you and Tzain back. And when the time came for him to grab the scroll and run, he stayed. He tried to save me."

I pause and search for the words she wants to hear, the ones I'm almost too afraid to speak aloud.

"He has a good heart. I think he's finally using it."

Amari's hands fidget. She presses them tight to her chest.

"Amari—"

She wraps her arms around me and squeezes. I stiffen in surprise. Not knowing what else to do, I slowly hug her back.

"I know this must seem ridiculous to you, I just . . ." She pulls away and wipes the tears threatening to fall from her eyes. "Inan has always been caught between wrong and right. I just want to believe he can be right."

I nod, thinking of the things I want from Inan. I hate how many times I've thought about him today, thought about his lips, his smile. Despite how much I push against it, the longing remains: a desperation to feel his touch again. . . .

More tears threaten to fall from Amari's eyes and I wipe them away with the sleeve of my kaftan.

"Stop," I order. "You'll ruin your makeup."

Amari snorts. "I think you did that for me."

"I told you not to trust me with the charcoal!"

"How can you wield a staff and not keep a steady hand?"

We dissolve into a fit of giggles, a sound so foreign it takes me by surprise. But our laughter dies as Tzain bounds into the tent. When he meets my eye, he stops.

At first, he regards me like a stranger, but something inside him thaws.

"What is it?" Amari asks.

Tzain's chin trembles. He drops his gaze to the ground. "She . . . Zél looks like Mama."

His words rip through my heart and warm it at the same time. Tzain never speaks of Mama like this. At times, I think he's truly forgotten her. But as our eyes meet, I realize he's just like me; he carries Mama like the air, a passing thought of her in every breath.

"Tzain—"

"The procession's starting." He turns to Amari. "You should finish up."

And with that he's gone, wringing my heart.

Amari slips her hand in mine. "I'll talk to him."

"Don't." I ignore the bitter taste on my tongue. "He'll just get mad at you, too." *And no matter what you say, it'll still be all my fault.*

I stand and tug the sleeves of my dress, smoothing out a crease that doesn't exist. After a lifetime of mistakes, there are so many things I regret. But this . . . this is the one thing I would give anything to take back.

With a heavy chest, I move for the exit, pretending my heart doesn't ache. But before I can leave, Amari grabs my hand again, forcing me to stay.

"You still haven't explained why you're not sharing the scroll." Amari stands, studying me. "There's a whole valley of divîners out there waiting to become maji. Why aren't we giving that to them?"

Amari's words hit me like Mama Agba's smacks. Like the sword Lekan took to the chest. They gave up everything to give me a chance like this, and yet all I can do is throw it away.

When I first thought about sharing the scroll tonight, I couldn't stop imagining all the beauty and joy the new magic would spread. For once it would feel like it did before the Raid. The maji would reign again.

But now each smiling divîner twists into all the pain that could lie in their wake: Grounders ripping the earth under our feet; Reapers losing control and unleashing waves of death. I can't risk their magic coming back. Not without rules. Leaders. Plans.

And if I can't do this now, how will I be able to complete the ritual?

"Amari, it's complicated. What if someone loses control? What if the wrong person touches the sunstone? We could awaken a Cancer and all die of a plague!"

"What are you talking about?" Amari grabs my shoulders. "Zélie, where is this coming from?"

"You don't understand. . . ." I shake my head. "You didn't see what Kwame could do. If Zu hadn't stopped him . . . if stockers had that kind of power or a man like your father—" My throat goes dry at the memory of the blaze. "Imagine all the people he'd incinerate if he could conjure flames!"

It all pours out of me at once, the fears, the shames that have plagued me all day. "And Tzain—" I start, but I can't even say the words. If I can't even trust myself to keep my magic in check, how can I expect untested maji to fare?

"For so long I thought we needed magic to survive, but now . . . now I don't know what to think. We have no plan, no way to make rules or establish control. If we just bring it back, innocent people could get hurt."

Amari stays silent for a long moment, letting my words simmer. Her eyes soften and she pulls me by the hand.

"Amari—"

"Just come."

She drags me outside the tent, and in an instant I'm blown away.

While we were inside, the settlement came alive. The valley bursts with youthful energy, glowing red with soft lantern lights. Savory meat pies and sweet plantain pass under our noses as vibrant music and thundering drums reverberate through our skin. Everyone dances to the joyous music, buzzing with the excitement of the procession.

In the festive craze I spot Inan, more handsome than anyone has a right to be in a dark blue agbada with matching pants. When he spots me, his mouth falls open. My chest flutters under his gaze. I look away, desperate not to feel anything else. He approaches, but before he can catch up, Amari pulls me through the crowd.

"Come on," she yells back at him. "We cannot miss it!"

We zip through the crowd while the celebrants thrust and shimmy by our sides. Though part of me wants to cry, I crane my neck to take in the crowd, craving their joy, their life.

The children of Orïsha dance like there's no tomorrow, each step praising the gods. Their mouths glorify the rapture of liberation, their hearts sing the Yoruba songs of freedom. My ears dance at the words of my language, words I once thought I'd never hear outside my head. They seem to light up the air with their delight.

It's like the whole world can breathe again.

"You look magnificent!" Zu smiles as she takes me in. "Every boy will be dying for a dance, though I think you may be spoken for."

I tilt my head and follow her finger to Inan; his eyes trail me like a lionaire on the hunt. I want to hold his gaze, to hold the rush that blossoms under my skin when he looks at me this way. But I force myself to turn around.

I can't hurt Tzain again.

"Mama! Òrìsà Mama! Òrìsà Mama, àwá un dúpẹ̀ pé egbọ́ igbe wá—"

The closer we get to the center, the louder the singing grows. It takes me back to the mountains of Ibadan, when Mama would use this song to sing me to sleep. Her voice flowed rich and soft, like velvet and silk. I breathe in the familiar sensation as a petite girl with a powerful voice leads the crowd.

"Mama, Mama, Mama—"

As the voices fill the night with their heavenly song, a young divîner with light brown skin and cropped white hair enters the circle. Dressed in rich blue robes, she looks like Lekan's painting of Yemọja, the goddess who took Sky Mother's tears, come to life. The divîner spins and twirls with the song, a jar of water resting on her head. When the chorus peaks, she throws the water in the air and opens her arms wide as it rains back down on her skin.

The crowd's cheers rise as the divîner twirls out of the circle and Folake shimmies in. The beads of her yellow kaftan catch the light, shimmering as they move along her skin. She teases everyone with her smile, no one more than Kwame. When the crowd can take no more, her hands erupt. The crowd cheers when sparks of golden light shoot from her hands, dancing with her through the camp.

"Mama, Mama, Mama—"

Divîner after divîner enters the ring, each dressed like Sky Mother's children. Though they can't do magic, their imitations fill the crowd with joy. At the end, a girl who mirrors my age steps forward. She's dressed in flowing red silks, and a beaded headdress glitters against her skin. *Oya . . .* My sister deity.

Though nothing like the brilliance of Oya in my visions, the divîner has a magical aura of her own. Like Folake, she has long white locs that spin as she dances, twirling around her like the red silks. In one hand she sports Oya's signature irukere, a short whip with the hair of a lionaire. As she spins it around the circle, the divîner's praises grow.

"You are a part of this, Zélie." Amari laces her fingers with mine. "Do not let anyone take this magic away."

CHAPTER FIFTY-SEVEN

AMARI

Though the procession ends, the music and dancing advance late into the night. I bite into another moín moín pie as I watch the festivities, savoring the melting of the steamed bean cake in my mouth. A divîner walks past with a platter of shuku shuku, and I almost cry when the sweet coconut hits my tongue.

"About time."

Tzain's breath tickles my ear, sending a pleasant tingle down my neck. For a rare moment he is alone, unbothered by the swarm of divîner girls who have tried to catch his eye all night.

"Pardon?" I ask, choking down the rest of the shuku shuku.

"I've been looking for you. You're a hard person to find."

I wipe the crumbs from my lips, desperate to hide the fact that I've eaten my way through half the festival. Though my dress started out a perfect fit, now the seams pull at my hips.

"Well, I suppose it's hard to find me when a gaggle of girls blocks your every path."

"My apologies, Princess." Tzain laughs. "But you should know it takes time to approach the prettiest girl here."

His smile softens, just like the night he threw me in the river and laughed when I tried to throw him back. It was a rare side of him;

after everything that happened since, I wasn't sure when I would see this side again.

"What is it?"

"Just thinking." I shrug and turn back to the sea of dancing divîners. "I've been worried about you. You're forgiving, but being tortured in that tent couldn't have been easy."

"Humph." Tzain grins. "I can think of a lot of better ways to spend a night with a girl locked in a tent."

My face turns so red I'm positive it clashes with the golden hues of my dress. "I guess the other night was my first time spending the night with a boy."

Tzain snorts. "Was it everything you ever dreamed?"

"I don't know . . ." I press my finger to my lips. "I always imagined less bondage."

To my surprise a laugh breaks free, louder than any he's had in my presence. The sound makes my chest swell. I haven't made anyone laugh this loud since Binta. Unspoken words swim inside me, but before I can respond, a giggle catches our attention.

I shift to find Zélie a few tents away, dancing at the edge of the crowd. She laughs as she sips on a bottle of palm wine, spinning a divîner child round and round. Though I smile at her joy, Tzain's face darkens into the sadness he showed in the tent. But all sadness fades when Tzain spots Inan. My brother stares at Zélie like she's the single red rose in a garden of white.

"Do you see that?" I grab Tzain's hand and pull him toward a circle of cheering divîners. A flutter erupts in my stomach when his hand wraps back over mine.

Tzain's broad shoulders part the crowd like a herder moving through a flock of sheep. Within moments we reach the vibrant dancer in the center of the circle, bursting with exuberance and life. Her beaded dress sparkles in the moonlight, accentuating every shake and roll of her hips. Each curve of her body circles to the beat, electrifying the crowd with every thrust.

Tzain nudges me forward and I grip his arm. "What in skies' name are you doing?"

"Get in," he laughs. "It's time I see your moves."

"You've had too much ogogoro," I laugh.

"What if I go?" Tzain asks. "If I do it, will you?"

"Absolutely not."

"Is that a promise?"

"Tzain, I said no—"

He jumps into the circle, startling the dancer, causing the whole crowd to step back. For a long moment he doesn't make a move, studying everyone with mock seriousness pasted on his face. But when the horns of the song ring, he practically explodes in dance. He shakes and pops like fire ants have been dropped in his pants.

I laugh so hard I cannot breathe, gripping the divîner next to me to stay upright. Each move he makes incites more cheers, causing the circle of onlookers to double in size.

As he shakes his shoulders and drops to the ground, the dancing girl joins back in, twirling around the space. My skin prickles as she moves, seduction dripping from each roll of her hips. She fixes Tzain with a flirtatious gaze that makes me grimace. How can I be surprised? With his kind smile, his strong, imposing frame—

Calloused hands wrap around my wrists. Large hands. *Tzain's hands.*

"Tzain, no!"

His mischief overpowers my fright. Before I know it, I stand in the center of the circle. I freeze, paralyzed as countless eyes land on me. I turn to escape, but Tzain holds me tight, spinning me for the world to see.

"Tzain!" I shriek, but my terror dissolves into a laughter I cannot stop. Excitement swirls through me as we move, my two left feet somehow catching the beat. For a moment the crowd disappears and I only see Tzain—his smile, his kind brown eyes.

I could live an eternity like this, spinning and laughing in the safety of his arms.

CHAPTER FIFTY-EIGHT

INAN

Zélie has never looked more beautiful than she does now.

Hand in hand with a young divîner boy, she shines in her soft purple dress, a twirling goddess among the crowd. The sea-salt scent of her soul rises above the vast aromas of festival foods. It hits me with full force.

An ocean tide pulling me in.

Watching her, it's almost easy to forget about the maji. The monarchy. Father. In this moment, all I can think about is Zél. Her smile lights the world like a full moon on a starless night.

When she can twirl no longer, she gives the child a hug. He squeals when she plants a kiss on his forehead. But as soon as he runs off, three young men step forward to take his place.

"Excuse me—"

"Hi, I'm Deka—"

"You look lovely tonight—"

I smile as they try to charm her. Each squawks over the other. While they chatter, I wrap my hand around Zélie's side and squeeze.

"May I have this dance?"

She whips around, outraged. Then she realizes it's me. As she smiles, I'm struck with her delight. Then longing. A hint of fear. Tzain flashes across her mind, and I pull her close. "I'll take you somewhere he can't see."

A warm rush flows from her body into mine. My grip tightens.

"I'll take that as a yes."

I grab her hand and lead her through the crowd, ignoring the glares of her pursuers. We make our way toward the forest at the edge of the camps. Away from the celebration and dance. The cool air is a welcome breeze. It carries the rich scent of campfires and bark and damp leaves.

"You're sure you don't see Tzain?"

"Positive."

"What about—whoa!"

Zélie stumbles to the ground. A girlish giggle escapes her mouth. As I stifle my own laughter to help her, a whiff of honey palm wine wafts into my nose.

"Skies, Zél, are you drunk?"

"I wish. Whoever brewed this clearly didn't know what they were doing." She takes my hand and leans against a tree for support. "I think all that twirling with Salim is catching up to me."

"I'll bring you water."

I make to leave, but Zélie grabs my arm.

"Stay." Her fingers slide to my hands. A rush travels through me at her touch.

"Are you sure?"

She nods and giggles again. Her melodic laughter draws me close.

"You asked me to dance." A playful glint flashes in her silver eyes. "I want to dance."

Like the eager boys circling Zélie before, I step forward. Close enough to catch the faintest hint of palm wine on her breath. When I slide my hand over her wrist, she closes her eyes and breathes in. Her fingers dig into the bark.

Her reaction fills every cell in my being with want, a visceral rush I've never experienced before. It takes everything in me not to kiss her; not to run my hands over her curves and press her against the tree.

When her eyes flutter open again, I bend so that my lips brush against her ear. "If we're actually going to dance, you have to move, little Zél."

She stiffens.

"Don't call me that."

"You can call me 'little prince' and I can't call you 'little Zél'?"

Her hands drop to her side. She turns her face away.

"Mama called me that."

Skies.

I release her. It's a fight not to bang my head against the tree. "Zél, I'm sorry. I didn't—"

"I know."

She stares at the ground. Her playfulness disappears, drowning in a sea of grief. But then a wave of terror swells inside her.

"Are you okay?"

She clings to me without warning, pressing her head into my chest. Her fear sinks into my skin. It wraps around my throat. It consumes her—raw and powerful—just like that day in the forest. Except now it's not only the monarchy that haunts her; it's the shadows of death thrashing from her own hands.

I wrap my arms around her and squeeze. What I wouldn't give to take her fear away. We stay like that for a long moment, disappearing into each other's arms.

"You smell like the sea."

She blinks up at me.

"Your spirit," I clarify. "It's always smelled like the sea."

She stares at me with an expression I can't discern. I don't spend too much time trying to decipher it. It's enough to be lost in her eyes. To exist only in her silver gaze.

I tuck a loose coil behind her ear. She presses her face back into my chest.

"I lost control today." Her voice cracks. "I hurt him. I hurt *Tzain*."

I open my mind a little further, just beyond the point of pure relief. Zélie's memory rushes in like a wave spilling onto shore.

I feel it all, Tzain's venomous words, the shadows that raged. The guilt, the hatred, the shame left in her magic's wake.

I squeeze Zélie tighter, a warm rush running through me when she squeezes back. "I lost control once, too."

"Did someone get hurt?"

"Someone died," I say quietly. "Someone I loved."

She pulls back and looks up, tears brimming in her eyes. "That's why you're so afraid of your magic?"

I nod. The guilt of Kaea's death twists a knife inside me. "I didn't want anyone else to get hurt."

Zélie leans back into my chest and releases a heavy breath. "I don't know what to do."

"About?"

"Magic."

My eyes go wide. Of all the things I imagined, I never thought I'd hear this doubt come from her mouth.

"This is what I want." Zélie waves a hand at the bliss of the festival. "This is everything I've been fighting for, but when I think of what happened . . ." Her voice trails off. Tzain's bleeding shoulder fills her mind. "These people are good. Their hearts are pure. But what will happen if I bring magic back and the wrong maji tries to take control?"

The fear is so familiar, it feels like my own. Yet somehow it's not nearly as strong as before. Even when I think back to Kwame in flames, the first image that comes to my mind is how they sputtered out when Zulaikha instructed him to stop.

Zélie opens her mouth to continue, but no words come out. I gaze at the fullness of her lips. I stare a bit too long when she bites them.

"It's so unfair," she sighs.

I look down at her. It's hard to believe we're both awake. How many times have I wanted to hold her like this? To have her hold me back?

"You just get to dance around in my mind while I have no idea what's going on in yours."

"You really want to know?"

"Of course I want to know! Do you realize how embarrassing it is to have no con—"

I push her against the bark of the tree. My mouth presses against her neck. She gasps as I run my hands up her back. A small moan escapes her lips.

"This," I whisper. My mouth brushes her skin with each word. "This is what I'm thinking. This is what's going through my head."

"Inan," she breathes, voice ragged. Her fingers dig into my back, pulling me closer. Everything in me wants her. Wants this. All the time.

With that desire, everything becomes clear. It all begins to make sense.

We don't need to fear magic.

We only need each other.

CHAPTER FIFTY-NINE

ZÉLIE

YOU CAN'T.

You can't.

You can't.

No matter how many times I repeat these words, my desire rages like a ryder out of control.

Tzain will kill us if he finds out. But even as this thought runs through my head, my nails dig into Inan's back. I pull him into me, pressing until I can feel the hard lines of his body. I want to feel more. I want to feel *him*.

"Come back to Lagos with me."

I force my eyes open, unsure whether I've heard him correctly. "What?"

"If freedom is what you want, come back to Lagos with me."

It's like diving into the cold lakes of Ibadan; a visceral shock that pulls me from our fantasy. A world where Inan is just a boy in a handsome kaftan; a maji, not a prince.

"You promised you wouldn't get in my way—"

"I shall keep my word," Inan cuts me off. "But Zélie, that's not what this is."

Walls start to form around my heart, walls I know he can feel. He pulls away, sliding his hands from my back to the sides of my face.

"When you bring magic back, the nobility will fight tooth and nail to stop you. The Raid will happen again and again. The war won't end until an entire generation of Orïshans is dead."

I look away, but deep down I know he's right. It's the reason the fear won't go away, the reason I can't allow myself to truly celebrate. Zu's built a paradise, but when magic returns, the dream will end. Magic doesn't give us peace.

It only gives us a fighting chance.

"How will me coming back to Lagos solve any of that?" I ask. "As we speak, your father calls for my head!"

"My father's scared." Inan shakes his head. "He's misguided, but his fear is justified. All the monarchy's ever seen is the destruction maji can bring. They've never experienced anything like this." He gestures to the camp, face alight with so much hope his smile practically glows in the darkness. "Zulaikha created this in one moon, and there are already more divîners in Lagos than anywhere else in Orïsha. Just imagine what we could accomplish with the resources of the monarchy behind us."

"Inan . . ." I start to resist, but he tucks a strand of my hair behind my ear and trails his thumb down my neck.

"If my father could see this . . . see *you* . . ."

With one touch, everything inside me shivers, pushing against my doubt. I lean into him, hungry for more.

"He'll see what you've shown me." Inan holds me close. "The maji of today are not the maji he fought. If we build a colony like this in Lagos, he'll understand he has nothing to fear."

"This settlement only survives because no one knows where we are. Your father would never allow maji to congregate anywhere besides chained in the stocks."

"He won't have a choice." Inan's grip tightens, a spark of defiance flaring for the first time. "When magic is back, he won't have the power to take it away. Whether or not he agrees with me at first, in time he'll come to understand what's best. We can unite as one kingdom for the very first time. Amari and I will lead the transition. We can do it if you're there by our side."

A flame of hope lights inside me, one I should put out. Inan's vision begins to crystallize in my mind, the structures Grounders could erect, the techniques Mama Agba could teach all of us. Baba would never have to worry about the taxes again. Tzain could spend the rest of his life playing ag—

Before I can finish the thought, guilt slams into me. The memory of the blood leaking from under my brother's hands extinguishes any excitement.

"It wouldn't work," I whisper. "Magic would still be too dangerous. Innocent people could get hurt."

"A few days ago I would've said the same thing." Inan pulls back. "But this morning you proved me wrong. With just one lesson, I realized that one day I could actually gain control. If we taught the maji how to do the same in designated colonies, they could reenter Orïsha after they're trained."

Inan's eyes light up and his words begin to rush together.

"Zélie, just imagine what Orïsha could become. Healers like Zu would eradicate sickness. A team of Grounders and Welders could eliminate the need for the stocks. Skies, think of what the army would fight like with your animations leading the charge."

He presses his forehead against mine, getting far too close for me to think clearly.

"It'll be a new Orïsha." He calms down. "Our Orïsha. No battles. No wars. Just peace."

Peace . . .

It's been so long since I've known that word. The peace I only get in the dreamscape. The comfort of being wrapped in Inan's arms.

For a moment, I let myself imagine an end to the maji's strife. Not with swords and revolution, but with peace.

With Inan.

"You're serious?"

"I'm more than serious. Zél, I need this. I want to keep every promise I made to you, but I can't do it alone. You can't do it with just magic. But together . . ." A delicious smile spreads across his lips, drawing me in. "We'd be unstoppable. A team Orïsha has never seen."

I look past him to the dancing divîners, catching sight of the young boy I danced with in the crowd. Salim spins himself in so many circles he tumbles into the grass.

Inan drops his hand from my cheek and interlaces his fingers with mine; his warmth spreads over me like a soft blanket as he pulls me into his arms. "I know we're meant to work together." He lowers his voice to a whisper. "I think . . . we're meant to be together."

His words make my head spin. His words or the alcohol. But through the haze I know he's right. This is the one thing that can keep everyone safe. The one decision that can end this endless fight.

"Okay."

Inan searches me with his eyes. Hope hums around him like the faint drumbeats in the air.

"Really?"

I nod. "We'll have to convince Tzain and Amari, but if you're serious—"

"Zél, I've never been more serious about anything in my life."

"My family will have to come to Lagos, too."

"I wouldn't have it any other way."

"And you still have to rebuild Ilorin—"

"It'll be the first thing the Grounders and Tiders do!"

Before I can make another objection, Inan wraps his arms around me and spins. His smile stretches so wide it's impossible for me not to smile back. I laugh as he sets me down, though it takes a moment for the world to stop turning.

"We probably shouldn't decide the fate of Orïsha while spinning around in some forest."

He mumbles in agreement, slowly sliding his hands up my sides and back up to my face. "We probably shouldn't do this, either."

"Inan—"

Before I can explain that we can't, that Tzain's ax is freshly sharpened and only a few tents away, Inan presses his lips to mine and everything fades. His kiss is tender yet forceful, gently pushing into me. And his lips . . . soft.

Softer than I knew lips could be.

They light every cell in my body, sending a warmth down my back. When he finally pulls away, my heart is beating so fast it feels like I've just finished a fight. Inan's slow to open his eyes as a delicious smile spreads across his face.

"Sorry . . ." He runs his thumb over my bottom lip. "Do you want to go back in?"

Yes.

I know what I should do. What I probably need to do. But now that I've had a taste, every restraint in me breaks.

Inan's eyes widen as I grab his head and force his lips back onto mine.

Restraint can wait for tomorrow.

Tonight I want him.

CHAPTER SIXTY

AMARI

I GIGGLE LIKE I haven't in years as Tzain spins me round and round. He bends to lift me again but stops, leaving me on the ground. The smile that stretched from ear to ear drops alongside his sweat. I follow his line of sight just in time to see Inan grab Zélie's face, embracing her with a kiss.

Skies!

A gasp slips from my lips. I sensed that something kindled between them; I just didn't know it would ignite so soon. But observing the way Inan kisses Zélie now, more questions brew. The tender way he holds her, the way his hands roam, *pulling* her into him—

My cheeks flush and I turn away; an embrace like this is far too intimate to watch. But Tzain does not share my discomfort. If anything, he stares more. Every muscle in his body tenses; his eyes grow hard, all joy banished.

"Tzain . . ."

He brushes past me, steeled to attack with a fury I've yet to witness.

"Tzain!"

He moves like he cannot see me, like he will not stop until his hands wrap around my brother's throat.

Then Zélie grabs Inan and pulls his lips to hers.

The sight halts Tzain midstep. He stumbles back, as if physically struck. Then all of a sudden he snaps, breaking in half like a twig between clenched fists.

He stalks past me into the divîner crowd, pushing through the festival into the campgrounds. I struggle to keep pace with his sprint as he rushes into his tent. He bypasses Nailah and Zélie's pack to grip the handle of his ax—

"Tzain, no!"

My screams fall on deaf ears as he shoves the ax into his pack. Along with his cloak, his food . . . the rest of his belongings?

"What are you doing?"

Tzain ignores me, forcing his cloak down as if it too kissed his sister. I reach out to touch him, but he rips his shoulder away. "Tzain—"

"What?" he yells, and I flinch. He pauses, releasing a deep sigh. "Sorry, I just—I can't do this. I'm done."

"What do you mean 'done'?"

Tzain wraps the leather straps around his back and pulls them tight. "I'm leaving. You can come with me if you want."

"Wait, what?"

Tzain doesn't pause to give me an answer. Before I can say anything else, he blows through the tent flaps, abandoning me for the brisk night.

"Tzain!"

I scramble after him, but he makes no attempt to wait. He storms past the campgrounds, leaving all traces of the festival in his wake. I can hear the faint roar of the Gombe River as he flies through the wild grass. He gets all the way to the next valley before I finally catch up.

"Tzain, *please*!"

He pauses, but his legs tense like he could take off at any moment.

"Can you just slow down?" I plead. "Just—just breathe! I know you hate Inan, but—"

"I don't give a damn about Inan. Everyone can do whatever the hell they want, just leave me out of it."

My chest freezes at the cruelty of his words, shattering all the warmth he put there before. Though my legs shake, I force them forward. "You're upset. I understand, but—"

"Upset?" Tzain narrows his eyes. "Amari, I'm tired of fighting for my life, I'm tired of paying for everyone's mistakes. I'm sick of doing everything I can to keep her safe when all she does is throw it away!" He lowers his head, shoulders slumping. For the first time since I've met him he appears small; it's disconcerting to see him this way. "I keep expecting her to grow up, but why would she when I'm always here? Why change when I stand by just waiting to clean up her mess?"

I step closer and grab his hands, lacing my fingers between his coarse ones. "I know their relationship is confusing . . . but I promise you, deep down my brother's intentions are pure. Zélie hated Inan more than anyone. If she feels this way about him now, it has to mean something."

"It means what it always does." Tzain slides out of my grasp. "Zélie's doing something stupid, and sooner or later it's going to blow up in her face. Wait for the explosion if you want, but I'm done." His voice breaks. "I never wanted to be a part of this anyway."

Tzain walks away again, cleaving something inside me. This is not the man I know, a man I have started to . . .

Love?

The word floats in my mind, but I can't call it that. Love is too strong, too intense for what I feel. For what I am allowed to feel. But even still . . .

"You never give up on her," I shout after him. "Never. Not once. Even when she cost you everything, you're always by her side."

Like Binta. My friend's playful smirk appears in my mind, lighting up the cold night. Tzain loves fiercely as she did, without condition—even when he shouldn't.

"Why now?" I continue. "After everything, why this?"

"Because he destroyed our home!" Tzain whips around. A vein bulges against his neck as he screams. "People drowned. Children *died*. And for what? That monster's been trying to kill us for weeks and now she wants to forgive him? Embrace him?" His voice strains and Tzain pauses, slowly clenching and unclenching his fists. "I can protect her from a lot of things, but if she's going to be this stupid, this reckless—she's going to get herself killed. I'm not sticking around to watch."

With that he turns, tightening his pack and walking farther into the darkness.

"Wait," I call, but this time Tzain does not slow. Each step he takes causes my heart to pound harder against my chest. He's really doing this.

He's really leaving.

"Tzain, please—"

A horn sounds, cutting through the night.

We freeze as more join in, silencing the drums of the festival.

I turn and my heart drops as the royal seal that has always haunted me comes into view, gleaming off suit after suit. The eyes of the snow leopanaires seem to flash in the darkness.

Father's men are here.

CHAPTER SIXTY-ONE

ZÉLIE

I INHALE SHARPLY as Inan's hands slide down to my thighs. His touch makes every part of my body explode; it's too hard to concentrate on kissing him back. But as my lips forget what to do, Inan's don't miss a beat. His electric kisses move from my mouth to my neck, so intense it's hard to breathe.

"Inan . . ."

My face flushes, but there's no point in hiding it. He knows what his kiss does to me, how his touch burns. If my emotions hit him like a tsunami, then he must know how much I want this. How my body aches to let his hands search and wander. . . .

Inan presses his forehead against mine and slides his hands to the small of my back. "Believe me, Zél. What I do to you is nothing compared to what you do to me."

My heart flutters and I close my eyes as Inan draws me in. He leans down for another kiss—

A loud horn blares. A crash rings through the air.

"What was that?" I ask. We jolt apart as another crash sounds.

Inan's grip on me tightens, a cold sweat breaking out. "We need to go."

"What's going on?"

"Zél, come on—"

I break free of his hold and run toward the edge of the festival grounds. The music of the celebration halts as everyone tries to figure out the cause of the sounds. A hushed hysteria erupts through the crowd, questions mounting as it spreads. But with time the source of the horns makes itself clear.

The legion of royal guards charges through the new wreckage of the gate and marches to the top of the hill overlooking the valley. They light up the black sky with red torch flames, blazing against the night.

Some soldiers position their arrows, others bare their sharpened blades. The most terrifying among them hold back a pack of wild panthenaires; the menacing beasts chomp and foam at their bits, desperate for a chase.

Inan catches up to me. He stalls when he sees the sight. The color drains from his cheeks. His fingers lace through mine.

The commander of the troops steps forward, distinguished by the golden lines carved into the iron of his armor. He raises a cone to his mouth so we can all hear his shouts.

"This is your only warning!" his voice booms through the silence. "If you do not comply, we will use force. Give up the scroll and the girl and no one here will get hurt."

The divîners break out in whispered conversations, fear and confusion spreading throughout the masses like a virus. Some people try to escape the crowd. A child begins to cry.

"Zél, we have to go," Inan repeats, gripping my arm once more. But I can't feel my legs. I can't even speak.

"I will not warn you again!" the commander shouts. "Give them up or we will take them by force!"

For a moment nothing happens.

Then a ripple breaks through the crowd.

Though the movement starts out small, in seconds waves of people split. They clear a path, allowing one person to walk through. Her small body steps forward. Her white mane dances.

"Zu . . . ," I breathe, fighting the urge to run and pull her back into the crowd.

She stands tall and strong, defiant beyond her young years. Her emerald-green kaftan blows in the wind, shimmering against her brown skin.

Though she is only thirteen, the entire legion readies their arms. Archers pull back against their bows. Swordsmen position the reins of their panthenaires.

"I don't know which girl you speak of," Zu shouts, her voice carried by the wind. "But I can assure you we don't have the scroll. This is a peaceful celebration. We only gathered here to honor our heritage."

The silence that follows is almost deafening. It brings a tremble to my hands I can't fight back.

"Please—" Zu steps forward.

"Don't move!" the commander shouts back, pulling out his sword.

"Search us if you must," Zu responds. "We will agree to an examination. But please, lower your weapons." She raises her hands in surrender. "I don't want anyone to get hur—"

It happens so fast. Too fast.

One moment Zu stands.

The next, an arrow pierces through her gut.

"*Zu!*" I scream.

But it doesn't sound like me.

I can't hear my voice. I can't feel anything.

Air dies inside my chest as Zu looks down, small hands gripping the arrow's shaft.

The young girl with a smile too wide for her face pulls against the weapon, speared with Orïsha's hate.

She strains, limbs shaking, somehow taking a step forward. Not back where we can protect her.

Forward, so she can protect us.

No . . .

Tears sear my vision, falling fast down my face. A Healer. A child.

Yet her last moments are stained with hate.

Blood spreads across the silk of her kaftan. The emerald darkens with red.

Her legs buckle and she hits the ground.

"Zu!" I race forward even though I know she can't be saved.

In that moment the entire world explodes.

Arrows fly and swords flash as the guards unleash their attack.

"Zél, come on!" Inan yanks on my arm, pulling me back. But as he tries to steer me away, one thought fills my mind. Oh gods.

Tzain.

Before Inan can object, I take off, stumbling more than once as I return to the valley. Screams of terror fill the night. Divîners run in all directions.

We sprint in vain, trying desperately to escape the archers striking from the sky. One by one divîners go down, pierced by an onslaught of arrows that never seems to end.

But the archers become a fear of the past as the suited seal of Orïsha spreads through the masses. Soldiers release the rabid panthenaires, allowing the ryders to sink their fangs straight through divîner flesh. Above them, armored guards push through the crowd, swords raised and sharpened. They show no mercy, no discretion, slashing through everyone in their path.

"Tzain!" I scream, another voice in the chorus of shouts. He can't die like Mama. He can't leave me and Baba.

But the farther I run, the more bodies fall to the ground, the more spirits bleed into the earth. Lost in the crowd, Salim howls, sharp screams rising above every other cry.

"Salim!" I scream, charging for the sweet boy I spun in my arms. A guard rides toward him on a rabid panthenaire. Salim raises his hands in surrender.

He has no magic. No weapon. No way to fight.

The guard doesn't care.

His sword slashes down.

"No!" I scream, insides aching at the sight. The blade rips straight through Salim's small body.

He dies before he even hits the ground.

His dead eyes chill my blood. My heart. My bones.

We cannot win. We cannot live. We never stood a chan—

The sensation strikes me in my core, deep, as powerful as my beating heart.

It rattles the magic in my blood. It pulls the air from my lungs.

Kwame brushes past me, running for the heart of the battle. He grips a dagger tight in his hands.

Then he slashes open his palm.

Blood magic.

Horror settles into my bones.

It's like the world slows to a stop, stretching the seconds between this moment and the last Kwame will ever have. His blood glows with a white light, splashing as it hits the ground.

In an instant the ivory light surrounds him, illuminating his dark skin like a god from above.

When it reaches the top of his head, it seals his fate.

A fire explodes from his skin.

Smoldering embers rain from his body. Flames blaze around his form. The fire erupts from every limb, shooting out of his mouth, his arms, his legs. The blast towers meters into the sky, a blaze so powerful it lights the horrors of the night. Shock stops the guards' attack just as Kwame's begins.

He punches his fists forward. Streams of fire crash through the settlement in smoldering waves. The flames incinerate everything in their path, blazing through the guards, destroying the camp.

The stench of burning flesh fills the air, mixed with the scent of blood.

Death strikes so quickly, soldiers don't even have a chance to scream.

"*Agh!*" Kwame's cries of agony rise above all else as he turns the night red. The blood magic tears through him, raw and unforgiving.

It's grander than any flame a maji could conjure on his own. He burns with the power of his god, but it burns through him.

His dark face flushes red, veins tearing from within. His skin bubbles and scalds from his flesh, revealing corded muscle and hard bone. He can't contain it. He can't outlast it.

The blood magic eats him alive, yet still he uses his last breath to fight.

"Kwame!" Folake screams from the edge of the valley. A strong divîner drags her back, keeping her from charging into the roaring fire.

A vortex of flames shoots from Kwame's throat, pushing the guards even farther back. As he sears through their attack with the last seconds of his life, the divîners react. My people flee in all directions, escaping through the flaming walls, leaving the wasteland in their path.

They live, fleeing the guards' senseless attack.

Because of Kwame, because of his magic, they survive.

Staring at the blaze, it's as if the entire world stops. The shouts and screams are muffled into nothingness. The festival fades to black. Inan's promises play out before my eyes, our Orïsha, a pact the world won't allow him to keep. *Peace.*

We will never have peace.

As long as we don't have magic, they will never treat us with respect. Baba's words simmer through my mind. *They need to know we can hit them back. If they burn our homes, we burn theirs, too.*

With one final cry, Kwame erupts like a dying star. Fire explodes in all directions, leaving the earth with the last remnants of himself.

As the final embers fall, my heart rips in my chest. I can't believe I ever denied Baba's truth. They'll never allow us to thrive.

We will always be afraid.

Our only hope is to fight. Fight and win.

And to win, we need our magic.

I need that scroll.

"Zélie!"

My head snaps up. I don't know how long I've stayed still. The world seems to travel in slow motion, weighed down by Kwame's sacrifice, dragging with all my pain and guilt.

Tzain and Amari approach from the distance, riding on Nailah's back. Tzain guides Nailah toward me through the chaos. Amari clutches my pack to her chest.

But as my name travels from his mouth, other guards take note. "*The girl*," they scream to one another. "*The girl! It's her!*"

Before I can take another step, hands wrap around my arms.

My chest.

My throat.

CHAPTER SIXTY-TWO

AMARI

As THE SUN RISES into the valley, a sob catches in my throat. The rays light the charred clearing where the procession occurred, the blackened remains of what was once a joyful place.

I stare at the scorched earth where Tzain and I danced, recalling how he twirled me, remembering the sound of his laugh.

All that remains now is blood. Hollow corpses. Ash.

I close my eyes and clasp my hand to my mouth, a futile attempt to block out the painful sight. Though it is silent, the cries of divîners still echo in my mind. The shouts of the soldiers who slaughtered them follow, the clash of swords striking into flesh. I cannot bear to look, but Tzain scans the destruction, searching for Zélie among every fallen face.

"I don't see her."

Tzain's voice is barely above a whisper, like if he speaks any louder, everything inside him will break: his rage, his pain, the heartache of having another family member ripped away.

Thoughts of Inan force their way into my mind: his promises, his potential lies. Though I can't bring myself to search the dead, I can feel it in my core.

Inan's corpse isn't on this ground.

No part of me wants to believe this was his doing, yet I don't know what to think. If this wasn't his betrayal, how did the guards find us? Where is my brother now?

Nailah whimpers behind us, and I stroke her snout the way I've seen Zélie do so many times before. A lump rises in my throat when she nuzzles my hand back.

"I think they took her," I say as delicately as I can. "It's what my father would've ordered. She's far too important to kill."

I hope this will give him hope, but Tzain's expression stays even. He stares at the bodies on the ground, his breaths escaping in short spurts.

"I promised." His voice cracks. "When Mama died, I promised. I said I'd always be there. I swore I'd take care of her."

"You have, Tzain. You always have."

But he's lost in his own world, a place far beyond where my words could go.

"And Baba . . ." His body seizes; he clenches his fists to try and stop the trembling. "I told Baba. I—I told him I would . . ."

I lay my hand on Tzain's back, but he retreats from my touch. It's as if every tear Tzain has ever fought back comes pouring out of his body at once. He crumples into the dirt, pressing clenched fists against his head so hard I worry he'll get hurt. His heartache bleeds raw, breaking through his every wall.

"You cannot give up." I drop to Tzain's side to wipe away his tears. Despite everything, he has always stayed strong. But this loss is too much to bear. "We still have the scroll, the stone, and the dagger. Until my father has retrieved the artifacts, his men will keep her alive. We can save her and get to the temple. We can still make this right."

"She won't talk," Tzain whispers. "Not if we're at risk. They'll torture her." His hands clench the earth. "She's as good as dead."

"Zélie is stronger than anyone I know. She'll survive. She'll fight."

But Tzain shakes his head, unconvinced no matter how hard I try. "She'll die." He squeezes his eyes shut. "She'll leave me all alone."

Nailah's whimpers grow as she nuzzles Tzain, attempting to lick his tears away. The sight crushes everything inside me, destroying the last fragments that were whole. It's like watching the magical light explode from Binta's palms only for Father's sword to rip through her chest. How many families has Father left like this, broken beyond repair, mourning their dead? How many times will I allow him to do it again?

I stand on the hill and turn toward the town of Gombe, a speck of pluming smoke before the Olasimbo Range. The map in Father's war room reappears inside my mind, crystallizing the *X*s that marked his military bases. As the layout forms in my head, a new plan falls into place. I cannot let Tzain endure this loss.

I will not let Father win.

"We need to move," I say.

"Amari—"

"Now."

Tzain lifts his head from the ground. I reach down and grab his hand, wiping the dirt sticking to the tearstains on his face.

"There is a guard fortress outside Gombe. That has to be where they took her. If we can get in, we can get her out."

We can bring Father's tyranny to an end.

Tzain stares at me with broken eyes, fighting the spark of hope that tries to light. "How would we get in?"

I turn back to the silhouette of Gombe against the night sky. "I have a plan."

"Will it work?"

I nod, for once not fearing the fight. I was the Lionaire once.

For Tzain and Zélie, I shall be her again.

CHAPTER SIXTY-THREE

ZÉLIE

MAJACITE CUFFS SCALD my skin, searing straight through my wrists and ankles. The black chains suspend me above the floor of my jail cell, making it impossible for me to cast an incantation. Sweat drips down my skin as another warm blast funnels through the vent. The heat must be intentional.

Heat will make the coming pain worse.

Live . . . Lekan's words echo, a taunt as I face my death.

I told him it was a mistake. I told him, I told everyone. I begged them not to waste this chance on me; now look what I've done. I laughed and spun and kissed as the king prepared our slaughter.

Metal-soled boots clank outside. I flinch as they near my door. It would be easier if my cell had bars. At least then I could prepare myself. But they've locked me in an iron box. Only two burning torches keep me from being left in the dark.

Whatever they plan to do, they intend to hide it even from the guards.

I swallow hard, a feeble attempt to quench my dry mouth. *You've done this before*, I remind myself, *more times than you can count*. For a moment I ponder whether Mama Agba's constant lashings weren't to punish, but to prepare. She beat me so often I got good at taking it, good at loosening my body to minimize the aches. Could she sense that my life would end this way?

Dammit. Tears sting my eyes at the shame of all the corpses I've left in my wake. Little Bisi. Lekan. Zulaikha.

Their sacrifice will never amount to anything.

This is all my fault. We never should have stayed. Somehow we must've led the army to that camp. Without us, they might still be alive. Zu could've survived. . . .

My thoughts slow.

Tzain's glare flashes into my mind. My heart seizes at the thought. Could Inan have done this?

No.

My throat burns with the fear I choke back like bile. He wouldn't. After everything we've been through, he couldn't. If he wanted to betray me, he had countless opportunities. He could've made off with the scroll without taking all those innocent lives away.

Amari's face overtakes Tzain's, her amber eyes dripping with pity. *Either he's about to betray us or something else is taking place.*

Inan's smile breaks through their hate, the soft gaze he gave me before we kissed. But it blackens and it twists and it burns until it wraps around my throat with the strength of his grip—

"No!" I close my eyes, remembering the way he held me in his arms *He saved me.* Twice. And he tried to save me again. He didn't do this. He couldn't have.

A clink sounds.

The first lock outside my door opens. I brace myself for pain, holding on to the last good things I have left.

At least Tzain is alive. At least he and Amari survived. With Nailah's speed, they had to have gotten away. I have to focus on that. One thing turned out alright. And Baba . . .

The threat of tears burns behind my eyes as I remember the crooked grin I prayed I would see once more. When he finds out about this, he'll never smile again.

I close my eyes as the tears fall, stinging like tiny knives. I hope he's dead.

I hope he never experiences that pain.

The final lock unhinges and the door groans open. I steel myself.

But when Inan fills the entryway, my every defense breaks.

My body jolts against the chains as the little prince walks in, flanked by two lieutenants. After days of seeing him in muted kaftans and borrowed dashikis, I forgot how cold he looks in a guard's uniform.

No . . .

I search him for any sign of the boy who promised me the world. The boy I almost gave up everything for.

But his eyes are distant. Tzain was right.

"*You liar!*" My scream echoes in the cell.

The words aren't enough. They can't cut the way I need them to, but I can barely think. I grip the metal chains so hard they rip through my skin. I need the pain to distract myself, otherwise nothing will stop my tears.

"Leave," Inan orders his lieutenants, looking at me as if I were nothing. Like I wasn't in his embrace just hours ago.

"She's dangerous, Your Highness. We can't—"

"That was an order, not a suggestion."

The guards exchange glances but reluctantly leave the room. Gods know they can't defy a direct order from their precious prince.

Clever. I shake my head. It's not hard to guess why Inan wants privacy. The white streak that shone so vibrantly in his hair hides under a new coat of black dye. Can't have anyone finding out the truth about their little prince.

Was this his plan all along?

I squeeze everything in me to keep my face even. He doesn't get to see my pain. He doesn't get to know how he's hurt me.

The door swings shut, leaving us alone. He looks at me as we hear the sounds of the guards retreating. It's only when we can't hear them anymore that his hardened face crumbles into the boy I know.

Inan's amber gaze fills with fear as he steps forward, eyes catching on the largest bloodstain on my dress. A warm rush of air fills my lungs—I don't know when I stopped breathing. I don't know when I started needing him this much.

I shake my head. "It's not my blood," I whisper. *Not yet.* "What happened? How did they find us?"

"The festival." Inan looks down. "Divîners went into Gombe to get supplies. A few guards got suspicious and tailed them."

Gods. I bite back a new wave of tears that wants to come forth. Slaughtered for a celebration. One we never should've had.

"Zél, we don't have much time," he rushes out, voice strained and hoarse. "I couldn't get to you until now, but a military caravan just docked. Someone's coming, and when they do . . ." Inan turns back to the door, hearing something that isn't there. "Zél, I need you to tell me how to destroy the scroll."

"What?" There's no way I heard him correctly. After everything, he can't think that's the answer.

"If you tell me how to destroy it, I can protect you. Father will kill you as long as the possibility of magic coming back is still a threat."

By the gods.

He doesn't even realize we've already lost. The scroll means nothing without someone to read it. But I can't let him know that.

They'll slaughter us all if they find out, erasing every man, woman, and child. They won't stop until we're gone, until they've wiped our existence from this world with their hate.

"—they're vicious, Zél." Inan swallows hard, bringing me back to the present. "If you don't give it up, you won't survive."

"Then I don't survive."

Inan's face twists. "If you don't talk, they'll cut it out of you!"

A lump forms in my throat; I guessed this much. I can't talk.

"So I'll bleed."

"Zél, please." He steps forward, putting his hands on my bruised face. "I know we had our plans, but you have to realize everything's changed—"

"Of course everything's changed!" I scream. "Your father's men killed Zu! Salim! All those children." I shake my head. "They couldn't even fight, and the guards murdered all of them!"

Inan grimaces, face splitting with pain. His soldiers. His men. Our undoing once again.

"Zélie, I know." His voice breaks. "I know. Every time I close my eyes, her body is all I can see."

I look away, fighting back fresh tears. Zu's bright smile fills my mind, her endless joy, her light. We should've been halfway to Zaria by now. She and Kwame should still be alive.

"They shouldn't have attacked," Inan whispers. "Zulaikha deserved a chance. But the soldiers thought you were using the scroll to create a maji army. And after what Kwame did . . ."

Inan's voice trails off. All the grief that filled him before seems to shrink, overpowered by fear.

"Kwame took out three platoons in seconds. Burned them alive. He incinerated that camp. We'd probably be dead if he hadn't burned out himself."

I rear back in disgust. What in gods' names is he talking about? "Kwame sacrificed himself to protect us!"

"But imagine how it looked to the guards." Inan speaks quickly. "I know Kwame's intentions were pure, but he took it too far. For years we've been warned about magic like that. What Kwame did was worse than anything Father's ever said!"

I blink, searching Inan's face. Where is the future king who was ready to save the maji? The prince who threw himself in front of flames to keep me safe? I don't know this boy, afraid, making excuses for everything he claimed to hate. Or maybe I know him too well.

Maybe this is the truth: the broken little prince.

"Make no mistake, the attack was an abomination. I know we'll have to deal with it. But right now we have to act. The soldiers are terrified a maji like Kwame will attack again."

"Good." I squeeze my chains to hide the tremor in my hands. "Let them be afraid."

Let them taste the terror they make us swallow.

"Zélie, please." Inan grits his teeth. "Don't choose this. We can still unite our people. Work *with* me and I'll find a way for you to return to Lagos. We'll save Orïsha with something safer, something without magic—"

"What's wrong with you?" My shout echoes against the walls. "There's nothing to save! After what they just did, there's nothing at all!"

Inan stares at me, a flash of tears in his eyes. "You think I want this? You think after planning a new kingdom with you I want *this*?" I see my own grief reflected in his eyes. The death of our dream. The future Orïsha will never see. "I thought things could be different. I *wanted* them to be different. But after what we just saw, we have no choice. We can't give people that kind of power."

"There's always a choice," I hiss. "And your guards made theirs. If they were scared of magic before, they should be terrified now."

"Zélie, don't add your body to the dead. That scroll is the only way I convinced them to keep you alive. If you don't tell us how to destroy it—"

Another click sounds through the door. Inan steps back just as it opens.

"Did I say you could ente—"

His voice falters. The color drains from his face.

"Father?" Inan's lips part in surprise.

Even without his crown, it's impossible not to recognize the king.

He enters like a storm, the air darkening in his presence. A wave of emotions hits me as the door swings shut. I forget how to breathe as I meet the soulless eyes of the man who murdered Mama.

Gods, help me.

I don't know if I'm in a dream or a nightmare. My skin heats with a rage like I've never known, yet my pulse thunders with fear. Since the early days after the Raid I've pictured this moment, imagined what it would be like to meet him face-to-face. I've orchestrated his death so many times in my mind I could fill a tome detailing all the ways he should die.

King Saran rests his hand on Inan's shoulder. His son flinches, as if waiting for a blow. Despite everything, the flash of terror in Inan's eyes pains me. I've seen him broken before, but this is a side of him I don't know.

"The guards tell me you tracked her to the uprising."

Inan stands up straight and clenches his jaw.

"Yes, sir. I'm in the middle of an interrogation. If you leave us, I'll get the answers we need."

Inan's voice stays so even I almost believe the lie. He's trying to keep me away from his father. He must know I'm about to die.

A shudder runs through me at the thought, but it's quickly met with an unearthly calm. The fear in Saran's presence is undeniable, yet it doesn't overwhelm my desire for vengeance.

In this man—this one wretched man—is an entire kingdom. An entire nation of hate and oppression, staring me in the face. It may have been the guards who broke down the doors in Ibadan that day, but they were simply his tools.

Here lies the heart.

"What of Admiral Kaea?" Saran lowers his voice. "Is this her killer?"

Inan's eyes widen and drift to me, but when Saran follows his gaze, Inan realizes his mistake. No matter what he says now, he can't stop the king of Orïsha from approaching me.

Even in the sweltering room, Saran's very presence chills my blood. The burning in my skin intensifies as he nears with his majacite blade. This close to him, I can make out the pockmarks in his deep brown skin, the gray hairs of old age speckled throughout his beard.

I wait for the slurs, but there's something worse about the way he looks at me. Distant. Removed. Like I'm some beast dragged from the mud.

"My son seems to think you know how the admiral died."

Inan's eyes bulge. It's written all over his face.

Someone died, his words from the festival come back to me. *Someone I loved.*

But it wasn't just someone . . .

It was Kaea.

"I asked you a question," Saran's voice breaks back in. "What happened to my admiral?"

Your maji son killed her.

Behind Saran, Inan jerks back, likely horrified at my thoughts. They're secrets I should scream to the world, secrets I should spill onto this floor. But something about Inan's terror makes it impossible for me to break.

I look away instead, unable to stomach the monster who ordered Mama's death. If Inan's truly on my side, then when I die, the little prince might be the divîners' only ho—

Saran's grip jerks my chin back to his face. My whole body flinches. The calm that sat in Saran's eyes before explodes with a violent rage.

"You would do well to answer me, child."

And I would. I would do well indeed.

It would be perfect to have Saran find out here, try to kill Inan himself. Then Inan would have no choice to attack back. Kill his father, take the throne, rid Orïsha of Saran's hate.

"Plotting, are we?" Saran asks. "Cooking up those precious incantations?" He digs into me so hard his nails draw blood from my chin. "Make any moves and I will personally rid your body of its wretched hands."

"F-Father." Inan's voice is faint, but he forces himself forward.

Saran glances back, wrath still burning in his eyes. Yet something about Inan reaches him. With a violent jerk, he releases my face. His lips curl as he wipes his fingers against his robe.

"I suppose I should be angry with myself," he muses quietly. "Pay attention, Inan. When I was your age, I thought the children of the maggots could live. I thought their blood needn't be spilled."

Saran grabs on to my chains, forcing me to meet his eyes.

"After the Raid you should've been desperate to keep magic away. You were supposed to be afraid. Obedient. Now I see there is no educating your kind. You maggots all crave the disease tainting your blood."

"You could've taken magic away without killing us. Without beating our bodies into the ground!"

He jumps as I pull against my chains, wild like a rabid lionaire. I itch to unleash magic fueled by the blackest part of my rage. A rage born because of everything he took away.

A new searing burns my flesh as I fight the majacite, doing everything I can to call forth my magic despite the power of the black chains. Smoke sizzles from my skin as I fight in vain.

Saran's eyes narrow, but I can't be silent. Not when my blood boils and my muscles shake to break free.

I will not let my fear silence the truth.

"You crushed us to build your monarchy on the backs of our blood and bone. Your mistake wasn't keeping us alive. It was thinking we'd never fight back!"

Inan steps forward, jaw taut, eyes traveling back and forth between us. The fury in Saran's gaze flares as he lets out a long, low chuckle.

"You know what intrigues me about your kind? You always start in the middle of the story. As if my father didn't fight for your rights. As if *you* maggots didn't burn my family alive."

"You can't enslave an entire people for the rebellion of a few."

Saran bares his teeth. "You can do whatever you want when you're the king."

"Your ignorance will be your downfall." I spit in Saran's face. "Magic or not, we won't give up. Magic or not, we *will* take back what's ours!"

Saran's lips curl back in a snarl. "Brave words for a maggot about to die."

Maggot.

Like Mama.

Like every brother and sister slaughtered by his command.

"You'd be wise to kill me now," I whisper. "Because you're not getting any of the artifacts."

Saran smiles slow and sinister like a jungle cat.

"Oh, child." He laughs. "I wouldn't be so sure of that."

CHAPTER SIXTY-FOUR

INAN

The walls of the cellar close in. I'm trapped in this hell. It takes everything in me to stand, not to buckle under Father's glare. But while I can barely breathe, Zélie rises. Defiant and fiery as ever.

No regard for her life.

No fear for her death.

Stop, I want to scream over her. *Don't talk!*

With each word, Father's desire to break her grows.

He pounds against the door. With two sharp knocks, the metal door flies open. The fortress physician walks in, flanked by three lieutenants; all fix their gazes on the floor.

"What's going on?" My voice comes out hoarse. It's hard to speak through the strain of suppressing my magic once more. Sweat pours down my skin as another blast of heated air funnels through the vent.

The physician glances at me. "Does Your Highness—"

"You're under my orders," Father interrupts. "Not his."

The physician scurries forward, drawing a sharp knife from his pocket. I stifle a cry as he slices into Zélie's neck.

"What're you doing?" I yell. Zélie grits her teeth as the physician digs with his blade.

"Stop!" I shout in panic. *Not now. Not here.*

I start forward, but Father presses his hand into my shoulder so hard I nearly stumble. I watch in horror as the physician cuts a shallow X into Zélie's neck. With an unsteady hand, he pushes a thick, hollowed-out needle into the exposed vein.

Zélie tries to jerk her head back, but a lieutenant holds it still. The physician removes a small vial of black liquid and prepares to pour the serum down the needle.

"Father, is this wise?" I turn to him. "She knows things. There are more artifacts. She can find them. She's the only person who understands the scroll—"

"Enough!" Father's grip on my shoulder tightens until it aches. I'm angering him now. If I keep going, he'll only cause Zélie more pain.

The physician looks back at me, as if looking for a reason to stop. But when Father pounds his fist against the wall, the physician pours the serum through an opening in the hollow needle, feeding it straight into her vein.

Zélie's body jerks and spasms. The serum releases under her skin. Her breaths go short and rapid. Her pupils grow large and dilated.

My own chest tightens as blood pounds inside my head.

And it's only an echo of what they're doing to her. . . .

"Don't worry." Father speaks, mistaking my grief for disappointment. "One way or another, she'll tell us what she knows."

Zélie's muscles seize, rattling the chains. I press against the wall as my own thighs shake. I struggle to keep my voice even. Keeping calm is my only chance of saving her.

"What'd you give her?"

"Something to keep our little maggot awake." Father smiles. "Can't have her passing out before we get what we need."

A lieutenant slides a dagger from his belt. Another rips Zélie's dress, exposing the smooth skin of her back. The soldier holds the blade in the heat of the torch flames. The metal warms. Smoldering red.

Father steps forward. Zélie's spasms intensify; so violent the two other lieutenants have to hold her down.

"I admire your defiance, child. It's impressive you've made it this far. But I wouldn't be doing my job as king if I didn't remind you what you are."

The knife sears into her skin with a fury so intense her agony leaks into me.

"*ARGH!*" A bloodcurdling scream rips from Zélie's throat. Rips straight through my being.

"No!" I cry out, and run forward, plunging straight for the lieutenant.

I knock one of the guards holding Zélie back.

I kick the other in the gut.

My fist collides with the lieutenant carving into her back, but before I can do more Father shouts.

"Restrain him!"

Instantly, two guards latch onto my arms. The entire world blazes in white. The scent of burning flesh fills my nose.

"I knew you wouldn't have the stomach for this." Somehow Father's disappointment cuts through the sound of Zélie's shrieks. "Remove him," he snaps. "Now!"

I feel Father's command more than I hear it. Though I struggle forward, I'm pushed back. All the while, Zélie's screams grow.

She only gets farther and farther away.

Her sobs and screams bounce against the metal walls. As her singed flesh cools, I make out the shape of an *M*.

And when Zélie's breathing grows shallow, the lieutenant starts on the *A*.

"No!"

They throw me into the hallway. The door slams shut.

I pound so hard my knuckles split and bleed, but no one comes out.

Think! I ram my head against the door, blood pounding as her screams grow. I can't get in.

I need to get her out.

I race along the corridor, but the distance does nothing to break the anguish. Concerned faces flash as I stumble past.

Lips move.

People speak.

I can't make out their sounds over Zélie's screams. Her shrieks ring through the door. They screech even louder in my head.

I crash into the nearest washroom and slam the door. Somehow, I latch the lock.

I can sense they've started on the *G* now; it's as if the curve is etched into my own back.

"Ugh!"

I grasp the porcelain sink's rim with shaking hands. Everything in me comes out. My throat stings from the burn of vomit.

The world spins around me, violent and thrashing. It's all I can do not to pass out. I have to power through.

I need to get Zélie out—

I WHEEZE.

Cool air hits me like a brick to the face. It pulls the scent of wet grass into my lungs. Wilted reeds tickle my feet.

The dreamscape.

The realization brings me to my knees.

But I have no time to waste. I have to save her. I need to bring her to this place.

I close my eyes and picture her face. The haunting silver of her eyes. What new letter have they carved into her back? Her heart? Her soul?

Within seconds, Zélie appears. Gasping. Half-naked.

Her hands grip the earth.

Her eyes hang empty in her head.

She stares at her shaking fingers with no recognition of where she is.

Who she is.

"Zélie?"

Something's missing. It takes me a second to realize what's wrong. Her spirit doesn't surge like the ocean tides.

The sea-salt scent of her soul is gone.

"Zél?"

The world seems to shrink around us, pulling in the blurred white borders. She's still—so still I don't know if she's heard me or not.

I reach out. When my fingers graze her skin, she shrieks and scrambles back.

"Zél—"

Her eyes flash something feral. Her trembling intensifies.

When I move toward her, she crawls back. Shattered. Broken.

I stop and put my hands up. My chest aches at the sight. There's no sign of the warrior I know. The fighter who spit in Father's face. I don't see Zél at all.

Only the shell Father left behind.

"You're safe," I whisper. "No one can hurt you here."

But her eyes fill with tears. "I can't feel it," she cries. "I can't feel anything."

"Feel what?"

I move toward her, but she shakes her head and pushes herself back through the reeds with her feet.

"It's gone." She says the same words again. "Gone."

She curls into the reeds, writhing with the pain she can't escape.

Duty before self.

I dig my fingers into the dirt.

Father's voice rings loud in my head. *Duty above all else.*

Kwame's flames come back to life behind my eyes, blazing through everything in their path. My duty is to prevent that.

My duty has to be keeping Orïsha alive.

But the creed rings hollow, carving a hole inside me like the knife that carved through Zélie's back.

Duty isn't enough when it means destroying the girl I love.

CHAPTER SIXTY-FIVE

AMARI

THIS WILL WORK.

By the skies, this has to work.

I hold on to this flickering hope as Tzain and I slip down the alleys between the rusted structures of Gombe, blending into the shadows and darkness.

A city of iron and foundry, Gombe's factories run late into the night. Erected by Welders before the Raid, metal structures rise and bend in impossible shapes.

Unlike the tiers dividing the classes of Lagos, Gombe is split into four quadrants, partitioning residential life from its iron exports. Through the dust-covered windows divîners work, forging Orïshan goods for the next day.

"Wait." Tzain holds me back as a patrol of armored guards clunk by. "Okay," he whispers when they pass, but his voice lacks its usual determination. *This will work*, I repeat in my head, wishing I could convince Tzain as well. *When this is over, Zélie will be alright.*

With time, the streets of cluttered, cramped mills transform into the towering iron domes of the downtown district. As bells ring, released workers swarm us, each covered in dust and ferrous metal burns. We follow the swell toward the music and drums pumping into the night.

As the aroma of liquor replaces the stench of smoke, a cluster of bars appears, each nestled under a small, rusted dome.

"Will he be here?" I ask as we walk up to a particularly shoddy structure that hums quieter than the rest.

"It's the best place to look. When I was in Gombe last year for the Orïshan Games, Kenyon and his team took me here every night."

"Good." I muster a smile for Tzain's sake. "That's all we need."

"Don't be so sure. Even if we find him, I doubt he'll want to help."

"He's a divîner. He won't have a choice."

"Divîners rarely have choices." Tzain raps his knuckles against the metal door. "When they do, they usually choose to look after themselves."

Before I can respond, a slit in the door slides open. A gruff voice barks out, "Password?"

"Lo-ïsh."

"That's old."

"Oh . . ." Tzain pauses, as if the right word might appear out of thin air. "That's the only one I know."

The man shrugs. "Password changes every quarter moon."

I push Tzain aside and climb onto my tiptoes, straining to reach the slit. "We do not live in Gombe, sir. Please, help us."

The man narrows his eyes and spits through the slit. I recoil in disgust. "No one gets in without a password," he seethes. "Especially not some noble."

"Sir, please—"

Tzain moves me aside. "If Kenyon's in there, can you let him know I'm here? Tzain Adebola, from Ilorin?"

The slit slams shut. I stare at the metal door in dismay. If we don't get inside, Zélie's as good as gone.

"Is there another way in?" I ask.

"No," Tzain groans. "This was never going to work. We're wasting time. While we stand here, Zél's probably de—" His voice catches and he closes his eyes, steeling everything inside. I unfold his clenched fists and reach for his face, placing my hands on his cheeks.

"Tzain, trust me. I will not let you down. If Kenyon isn't here, we can find someone else—"

"Gods." The door swings open and a large divîner appears, dark arms covered in sleeves of ornate tattoos. "I guess I owe Khani a gold piece."

His white hair clumps in long, tight locs, all piled atop a bun on his head. He wraps his arms around Tzain, somehow eclipsing his massive frame.

"Man, what're you doing here? I'm not supposed to beat your team for two weeks."

Tzain forces a laugh. "It's your team I'm worried about. Heard you twisted your knee?"

Kenyon pulls up the leg of his pants, revealing a metal brace anchored around his thigh. "Doctor says it'll heal before qualifiers, but I'm not worried. I could take you in my sleep." His eyes move to me, slow and indulging. "Please tell me a pretty little thing like you didn't come here just to see Tzain lose."

Tzain shoves Kenyon and he laughs, sliding his arm around Tzain's neck. It amazes me that Kenyon can't sense the desperation Tzain holds back.

"He's good, D." Kenyon turns to the bar's guard. "Promise. I can vouch for him."

The owner of the gruff voice peeks around the door. Though he appears to be only in his twenties, his face is marked with scars. "Even the girl?" He nods at me. Tzain slides his hand over mine.

"She's fine," Tzain vouches for me. "Won't say a word."

"D" hesitates but steps back, allowing Kenyon to lead us inside. Though he makes sure to glare at me until I disappear from his sight.

The thud of drums reverberates through my skin as we enter the ill-lit bar. The dome is packed, and the patrons are young; no one looks much older than Kenyon or Tzain.

Everyone shrinks in and out of shadows, shrouded by weak, flickering candlelight. Its glow illuminates the chipping paint and patches of rust marring the walls.

In the back corner, two men pound a soft beat on the canvas of their ashiko drums while another hits the wooden keys of a balafon. They play with a practiced ease, filling the iron walls with their lively sound.

"What is this place?" I whisper in Tzain's ear.

Though I have never stepped foot in a bar, I soon realize why this one requires a password. Among all the patrons, almost everyone's hair shines white, creating a sea overflowing with divîners. The few kosidán who made it inside are all visibly linked to the divîners who belong. The various couples sit hand in hand sharing kisses, closing the space between their hips.

"It's called a tóju," Tzain responds. "Divîners started them a few years ago. They have them in most cities. It's one of the only places divîners can go to gather in peace."

Suddenly the doorman's animosity doesn't feel as misplaced. I can only imagine how quickly the guards could dispatch a gathering like this.

"I've played against these guys for years," Tzain whispers as Kenyon leads us toward a table in the back. "They're loyal, but they're guarded. Let me do the talking. I'll ease them in."

"We don't have time for easing," I whisper back. "If we don't get them to fight—"

“There won’t be a fight if I can’t convince them to say yes.” Tzain gives me a gentle nudge. “I know we’re tight on time, but with them, we need to take it slow—”

“Tzain!”

A chorus of excitement erupts when we reach a table with the four divîners I can only assume complete Kenyon’s agbön team. Each player is bigger than the last. Even the twin girls Tzain calls Imani and Khani almost match his height.

Tzain’s presence incites smiles and laughter. Everyone rises, slapping his hand, patting his back, teasing Tzain about the coming agbön tournament. Tzain’s instructions to take it slow buzz in my mind, but his friends are so consumed with games, they do not even realize Tzain’s world is falling apart.

“We need your help.” I break through the noise, the first sentence I manage to get in. The team pauses to stare at me, as if noticing me for the first time.

Kenyon sips on his bright orange drink and turns to Tzain. “Talk. What do you need?”

They sit in silence as Tzain explains our precarious situation, hushed when they hear about the fall of the divîner settlement. He tells them everything from the origin of the scroll to the impending ritual, ending with Zélie’s capture.

“The solstice is in two days,” I add. “If we’re going to make it, we need to act fast.”

“Damn,” Ife sighs, his shaved head reflecting the candlelight. “I’m sorry. But if she’s in there, there’s no getting her out.”

“There has to be something we can do!” Tzain points to Femi, a broad divîner with a cropped beard. “Can’t your father help? Isn’t he still bribing the guards?”

Femi's face darkens. Without a word, he jerks back, rising so fast he almost knocks over the table.

"They took his father a few moons ago." Khani drops her voice. "It started as a tax mix-up, but . . ."

"Three days later they found his body," Imani finishes.

Skies. I stare after Femi as he makes his way through the crowd. Another victim of Father's power. One more reason we must act now.

Tzain's face falls. He reaches out and grips someone's metal cup so hard it dents under his touch.

"It's not over," I speak up. "If we can't bribe our way in, we can break her out."

Kenyon snorts and takes another long swig of his drink. "We're big, not dumb."

"How is this dumb?" I ask. "You don't need your size, you just need your magic."

At *magic*, the whole table freezes, as if I've hissed a hurtful slur. Everyone turns to look at one another, but Kenyon fixes a sharp glare on me.

"We don't have magic."

"Not yet." I pull out the scroll from my pack. "But we can give you your powers back. The fortress was designed to hold back men, not maji."

I expect at least one of them to take a closer look, but everyone stares at the scroll as if it's a fuse about to blow. Kenyon backs up from the table.

"It's time for you to go."

In an instant, Imani and Khani rise, each gripping one of my arms.

"Hey!" Tzain yells. He struggles as Ife and Kenyon hold him back.

"Let go!"

The bar stops, not wanting to miss out on the entertainment. Though I kick and shout, the girls do not relent, instead rushing to the doors as if their very lives depend on it. But as Imani's breath comes out in short rasps and Khani's grip on me tightens, the realization sinks in.

They are not angry . . .

They're afraid.

I twist out of their grasp with a maneuver Inan taught me moons ago. I grab the hilt of my sword, releasing the blade with a sharp flick.

"I am not here to hurt you." I keep my voice low. "My only desire is to bring your magic back."

"Who the hell are you?" Imani asks.

Tzain finally breaks free of Kenyon's and Ife's grasp. He pushes through divîners and the twins to get to my side.

"She's with me." He forces Imani to back up. "That's all you need to know."

"It's alright." I step out of Tzain's shadow, leaving the circle of his protection. Every eye in the bar pierces through me, but for once I do not shrink away. I picture Mother before a crowd of oloyes, able to command a room with just the slightest arch of her brow. I must call on that power now.

"I am Princess Amari, daughter of King Saran, and . . ." Though the words have never left my lips, I now realize there is no other choice. I cannot let the line of succession stand in my way. "And I am the future queen of Orïsha."

Tzain's brows knit in surprise, but he doesn't let himself rest in his shock for too long. The bar erupts in an unyielding chatter that takes forever to quiet down. Eventually he manages to silence the crowd.

"Eleven years ago my father took your magic away. If we don't act now, we'll lose the only chance we will ever have to bring it back."

I look around the tóju, waiting for someone to challenge me or try to throw me out again. A few of the divîners leave, but most stay, hungry for more.

I unclench the scroll and hold it up so they can see its ancient script.

A divîner leans in to touch it and yelps when a burst of air shoots from his hands. The accidental display gives me all the proof I need.

"There's a sacred ritual, one that will restore your connection to the gods. If my friends and I don't complete it during the centennial solstice in two days, magic will disappear forever." *And my father will run through the streets, slaughtering your people again. He will stab you in the heart. He'll kill you like he killed my friend.*

I look around the room, locking eyes with each divîner. "There is more than your magic at risk. Your very survival is on the line."

The mutters continue until someone from the crowd shouts, "What do we have to do?"

I step forward, resheathing my blade and lifting my chin. "There is a girl trapped in the guard fortress outside Gombe. She is the key. I need your magic to get her out. If you save her, you save yourselves."

The room remains silent for a long moment. Everyone stands still. But Kenyon leans back, crossing his arms with an expression I can't discern.

"Even if we wanted to help, whatever magic that scroll gave us wouldn't be strong enough."

"Do not worry." I reach into Zélie's leather pack and pull out the sunstone. "If you agree to help, I will take care of that."

CHAPTER SIXTY-SIX

INAN

ZÉLIE'S SCREAMS HAUNT ME long after they end.

Shrill.

Piercing.

Though her broken consciousness rests in the dreamscape, my physical connection to her body remains. Echoes of her anguish burn my skin. At times, the ache is so severe it hurts to draw breath. I fight to mask the pain as I knock on Father's door.

Magic or not, I have to save her. I've already failed Zélie once.

I'll never forgive myself if I allow her to perish here.

"Enter."

I open the door and push my magic down, stepping into the commander quarters that Father's commandeered. He stands in his velvet night robes, scanning a faded map. No sign of hatred. Not even a hint of disgust.

For him, carving MAGGOT into a girl's back is just another day's work.

"You wanted to see me."

Father chooses not to answer for a long moment. He picks up the map and holds it to the light. A red *X* marks the divîner valley.

In that instant it hits me: Zulaikha's death. Zélie's screams. They don't mean a thing to him. Because they're maji, they're nothing.

He preaches duty before self, but his Orïsha doesn't include them. It never has.

He doesn't just want to erase magic.

He wants to erase them.

"You disgraced me." He finally speaks. "That's no way to conduct yourself during an interrogation."

"I wouldn't call that an interrogation."

Father sets the map down. "Excuse me?"

Nothing.

That's what he expects me to say.

But Zélie sobs and shakes in the corners of my mind.

I won't call "torture" by another name.

"I didn't learn anything of use, Father. Did you?" My voice crescendos. "The only information I received was how loud you can make a girl scream."

To my surprise, Father smiles. But his smile is more dangerous than his fury.

"Your travels have fortified you." He nods. "Good. But do not waste your energy defending that—"

Maggot.

I know long before the slur leaves Father's lips. It's how he sees them all.

How he would see me.

I shift, moving until I can check my reflection in the mirror. Once again the streak is covered under a coat of black dye, but skies only know how long that'll stay.

"We are not the first to bear this burden. To go to these lengths to keep our kingdom safe. The Bratonians, the Pörltöganés—all crushed because they didn't fight magic hard enough. You would have me spare the maggot and allow Orïsha to suffer the same fate?"

"That is not what I proposed, but—"

"A maggot like that is like a wild ryder," Father continues. "It won't just give you answers. You have to break its will, demonstrate a new command." He turns his gaze back to the parchment. He marks another *X* over Ilorin. "You'd understand that if you'd had the disposition to stay. By the end, the maggot told me everything I needed to know."

A bead of sweat runs down my back. I clench my fists. "Everything?"

Father nods. "The scroll can only be destroyed with magic. I suspected this much after Admiral Ebele's failure, but the girl confirmed it. With her in our grasp, we finally have everything we need. Once we retrieve the scroll, we'll have her do the deed."

My heartbeat pulses into my throat. I have to close my eyes to keep calm. "So she'll live?"

"For now." Father runs his finger over the *X* marking the divîner valley. The red ink runs thick. Dripping like blood.

"Perhaps it's for the best," he sighs. "She killed Kaea. A quick death would be a gift."

My body goes rigid.

I blink hard. Too hard.

"W-what?" I stammer. "She said that?"

I struggle to say more, but every word dries in my throat. Kaea's hatred flashes back into my eyes. *Maggot.*

"She confessed to being at the temple." Father speaks as if the answer was obvious. "That's where they recovered Kaea's body."

He picks up a small turquoise crystal, stained with blood. My stomach twists as he holds it up to the light.

"What's that?" I ask, though I already know the answer.

"Some kind of residue." Father's lips curl. "The maggot left these in Kaea's hair."

Father crushes the remnant of my magic until it crumbles into dust. As it breaks, the smell of iron and wine hits me.

The scent of Kaea's soul.

"When you find your sister, end her." Father speaks more to himself than to me. "There's no shortage of people I would eradicate to keep you both safe, but I cannot forgive her for whatever role she played in Kaea's demise."

I grip the hilt of the sword and force a nod. I can almost feel the knife carving TRAITOR into my back.

"I'm sorry. I know—" *She was your sun.* "I know . . . how much she meant to you."

Father twists his ring, lost in his emotions. "She didn't want to go. She feared something like this would happen."

"I think she feared disappointing you more than her own death."

We all do. We always have.

No one more than me.

"What will you do with her?" I ask.

"With who?"

"Zélie."

Father blinks at me.

He's forgotten she has a name.

"The physician is tending to her now. We believe her brother has the scroll. Tomorrow we'll use her as leverage to retrieve it. After it's in our hands, she'll destroy it for good."

"And after that," I press, "after it's gone, what then?"

"She dies." Father turns back to his map, charting a course. "We'll parade her corpse around Orïsha, remind everyone what happens if they defy us. If there's even a whiff of rebellion, we'll wipe them all out. Then and there."

"What if there's another way?" I speak up. I glance at the cities on the map. "What if we could hear their complaints—use the girl as an ambassador? There are people . . . people she loves. We could use them to keep her in line. A maji we control." Each word feels like a betrayal, but when Father doesn't interrupt, I keep going. I don't have a choice. I have to save her at all costs. "I've seen things on these travels, Father. I understand the divîners now. If we can improve their situation, we'll quell the possibility of rebellions altogether."

"My father thought the same thing."

I suck in a quick breath.

Father never speaks of his family.

The little I know about them comes from gossip and whispers around the palace.

"He thought we could end their oppression, build a better kingdom. I thought so, too, but then they killed him. Him and every other person I loved." Father places a cold hand on my neck. "Believe me when I say there's no other way. You saw what that Burner did to their camp."

I nod, although I wish I hadn't. There's no fighting Father now that I've seen humans incinerated so fast they couldn't even scream.

Father's grip tightens. Almost to the point of pain. "Heed my word and learn this lesson now. Before it's too late."

Father steps forward and embraces me. A touch so foreign my body flinches in shock. The last time his arms were wrapped around me was when I was young. After I cut Amari.

A man who can cut his own sister is a man who can be a great king.

For a second I allowed myself to feel proud.

I was happy as my sister bled.

"I didn't believe in you." He pulls back. "I didn't think you would succeed. But you've kept Orïsha safe. All of this will make you a great king."

Unable to speak, I nod. Father turns back to his maps. He's done with me now. With nothing more to say, I leave the room.

Feel, I command myself. Feel *something*. Father's given me everything I've ever wanted. After all this time, he finally believes I will be a great king.

But when the door slams shut, my legs buckle. I slide to the ground.

With Zélie locked in chains, it doesn't mean a thing.

CHAPTER SIXTY-SEVEN

INAN

I WAIT TILL FATHER SLUMBERS.

Until the guards leave their post.

I sit in the shadows. Watching. The iron door moans when the physician exits her cell.

His face is blanched with strain, his clothes stained with her blood. The sight of him fortifies my desires.

Find her. Save her.

I zip across the floor and slide in my key. As the door groans open, I brace myself for the sight.

Nothing can prepare me.

Zélie hangs limp, her body nearly lifeless, her torn dress soaked through with blood. The sight rips a new hole inside of me.

And Father thinks the maji are the animals.

Shame and rage thrash within me as I select the right key. This isn't about magic. For once it has to be about her.

I unlock the shackles binding her wrists and ankles, freeing Zélie from their hold. I catch her in my arms and cover her mouth. As she wakes, I muffle the sound of her screams.

Her pain ripples through me. Already the physician's stitches are splitting. Her blood seeps out.

"I can't feel it," she whimpers against my skin. I adjust my arms to put pressure on the bandages around her back.

"You will," I try to soothe her. *What in skies' name does she mean?*

Her mind is a wall, running her torture on a constant loop.

There's no ocean, no spirit. No scent of the sea. I can't see beyond the anguish. She lives in the prison of her pain.

"Don't do this." Her nails claw into my shoulder as we ascend an empty stairwell. "I'm already bleeding out. Just leave me."

The heat of her blood leaks through my fingers. I press harder against her back.

"We'll find a Healer."

Guards' boots clank around the corner. I duck into an empty room as I wait for them to pass by. She cringes and fights back a scream. I press her even tighter to my chest.

When the corridor clears, I ascend another set of stairs. My heart pounds with every step.

"They'll kill you," she whispers as I run. "He'll kill you."

I steel myself against her words.

I can't think about that now. All that matters is this. I need to get Zélie ou—

The shouts ring first.

The heat comes next.

We crash to the ground as a blast from above shatters through the fortress wall.

CHAPTER SIXTY-EIGHT

AMARI

THE FORTRESS TOWERS over Gombe's horizon like an iron palace, casting its shadow through the night. Troops man every corner, leaving no meter unprotected for more than a few moments. My heart beats in my throat as we wait for the guards patrolling the southern wall to pass. Thirty seconds is all we shall have. I pray to the gods above that thirty seconds is all we need.

"Can you do this?" I whisper to Femi, stepping away from the overgrown kenkiliba bushes granting us cover. Since touching the sunstone, his hands do not remain still, running over his fingers, his beard, his crooked nose.

"I'm ready." He nods. "It's hard to explain, but I can feel it."

"Alright." I turn my attention back to the patrol. "Next time they pass, we go."

The instant the guards round the corner, Femi and I dash across the manicured wild grass. Tzain, Kenyon, and Imani follow fast behind, sticking to the shadows to avoid being spotted by those above. Though many divîners from the tóju agreed to help, only Kenyon and his team were willing to touch the scroll and awaken their magic. I hoped they would be enough to take the fortress down, but not even all five of them could fight.

Khani turned out to be a Healer, and Ife awakened his powers as a Tamer. Without magic that could strike quickly, it wasn't safe for them to enter. Thankfully, Kenyon turned out to be a Burner, Femi a Welder, Imani a Cancer. Not the maji army I had hoped for, but with the sunstone's surge, they could be the only soldiers we need.

"Fifteen seconds," I hiss, panting as we reach the southern wall. Femi places his hands against the cold iron, moving over the grooves and plates with the grace of an enlightened Welder. He feels around for something I can't see, painfully slow as our time aches by.

"Ten seconds."

Femi closes his eyes and presses harder into the metal wall. My chest clenches as time ticks away.

"Five seconds!"

Suddenly, the air tightens. A green light glows in Femi's hand. The metal wall ripples open like water.

We all rush through the emerging tear, sneaking into the fortress as quietly as we can. Hard footsteps pound outside just as Femi slips in. He manages to close up the wall moments before the next patrol marches past.

Thank the skies.

I let out a long, slow breath, savoring the small victory before the next battle commences. We're in.

But now the hard part begins.

Polished swords adorn the walls around us, reflecting our anxious faces. *This must be the armory. . . .* If this fortress's structure mirrors the one in Lagos, we must be near the commander quarters on the upper level. That means the prison cells have to be below—

The door handle twists. I hold up a hand, signaling everyone to duck out of sight as the armory door groans open. I hear the sounds of a guard approaching and catch his reflection in the glinting swords as he enters.

I watch the guard, waiting, counting each step he takes. He's close. One more step and we can—

"Go!" I hiss.

Tzain and Kenyon strike, tackling the guard to the ground. As they shove a rag into his mouth, I run and close the door before any sound leaks out. By the time I return, the soldier's screams are muffled. I crouch down and release my blade, pressing the cold metal into his neck.

"Scream and I'll slit your throat."

The venom in my words surprises me. I've only heard this poison in Father's voice. But it does the trick.

The soldier swallows hard as I rip the gag from his mouth.

"The maji prisoner," I bark. "Where is she?"

"Th-the what?"

Tzain whips out his ax and holds it above the guard's head, daring him to feign ignorance again.

"The cell is at the base! Down all the stairs, the farthest one to the right!"

Femi kicks the guard in the forehead, knocking him out cold. The guard hits the floor with a heavy thud as we run toward the door.

"Now what?" Tzain asks me.

"We wait."

"For how long?"

I study the hourglass timepiece hanging around Kenyon's neck, reading the grains as they fall past the quarter mark. *Where is the second wave?*

"They should've already hit—"

A blast thunders and booms, reverberating through the iron under our feet. We press against the wall as the fortress quakes, shielding our heads from the swords that rain from the walls. More blasts ring from outside, followed by the yells of running guards. I open the door a crack, watching soldiers fly by. They sprint toward a fight I pray they'll never find.

The divîners who weren't willing to awaken their powers agreed to fight from afar. Using the bar's alcohol, we managed to make nearly fifty firebombs, building while others constructed the slingshots they would use to launch the explosives. With the distance, the divîners should be able to strike and flee on their ryders before the guards get close. And while the guards are distracted, we'll make our escape.

We wait till the thundering footsteps are silenced before fleeing the armory and heading down the stairwell in the center of the fortress. We sprint down flight after flight of stairs, descending the floors of the iron tower. Just a few more levels until we can set Zélie free. We shall head straight for the sacred island. With two days left, we'll make it just in time for the ritual.

But as we descend another stairwell, a group of soldiers blocks our path. When they raise their blades to strike, I have no choice but to scream.

"Attack!"

Kenyon strikes first, sending a prickle of fear through my skin as his heat warms the air. A powerful red glow swirls around his fist; with a punch, a stream of flame erupts, knocking three guards into the wall.

Femi lunges forward next, using his metal magic to liquefy the blades of the guards' swords. As they skid to a halt, Imani steps forward. Our Cancer, perhaps the most terrifying one of all.

She leaks dark green energy from her hands, trapping the men in a malignant cloud. The moment it touches the guards, they crumble, skin yellowing as disease rages through them.

Although more guards filter in, the maji's powers flourish, unlocked with threatening strength. They run on raw instinct, fueled by the unbreakable swell of the sunstone's surge.

"Let's go," I say.

Tzain takes advantage of the hysteria, pressing against the walls to slip through the battle. I follow his lead and join him on the other side, racing down another stairwell to rescue Zélie. With this power, no one can stop us. Not one soldier will stand in our way. We can defeat the army. We can even face—

Father?

The guards flank Father on all sides, shielding him from attack while he runs along the upper level. As he surveys the uproar, his dark brown eyes find mine, zeroing in like a hunter targeting his prey. He stumbles in shock, but only for an instant. As my involvement in the attack sinks in, Father's rage breaks free.

"Amari!"

His glare freezes my blood. But this time I have my sword. This time I am not afraid to strike.

Be brave, Amari.

Binta's voice rings loud. The sight of her blood fills my head. I can avenge her *now.* I can cut Father down. While the maji take out the guards, my sword can free Father of his head. Retribution for all his massacres, every poor soul he has ever killed . . .

"Amari?"

Tzain pulls my attention, allowing Father to disappear behind an iron door at the end of his hallway. *A door Femi could easily melt . . .*

"What're you doing?"

I blink at Tzain and keep my mouth shut. There is no time to explain. One day, I shall fight Father.

Today I must fight for Zélie.

CHAPTER SIXTY-NINE

INAN

I CLUTCH ZÉLIE to my chest as another blast rings. The fortress shakes. Black smoke fills the air. Screams echo against the iron walls. Cries break through the charred door.

I run into a chamber and look out the barred windows; though flames blast the walls of the fortress, no enemy appears. Instead troops scream as they catch fire. Panthenaires run rabid in fear.

It's a chaos unmatched, bringing back all the horrors of Kwame's blaze. Maji attack again. My soldiers fall as they reign.

"No!"

I run away from the window and look out the iron door as a mangled scream rings from the floor above me. Fire and metal and disease wage war, ravishing an endless stream of soldiers.

The men who charge are incinerated by a Burner's flames. Those who shoot arrows are struck by a Welder—the bearded maji reverses each arrowhead, sending the sharp metal straight through the shooter's armor.

But worst of all is the freckled girl. A Cancer. A harbinger of death. Dark green clouds of disease spew from her hands. With one breath, the soldiers' bodies seize.

A slaughter . . .

A slaughter, not a fight.

Only three maji battle, yet the soldiers crumble beneath their power.

It's worse than the destruction of the divîner camp. At least then, the soldiers were the first to strike. But now their premature fear seems justified.

Father was right. . . .

There's no denying it now. No matter what I desire, if magic returns, this is how my kingdom will burn.

"Inan . . . ," Zélie whimpers. Her warm blood leaks down my hands. The key to Orïsha's future. Bleeding in my arms.

The pull of duty weighs down my step, but I can't listen to it now. No matter what, Zélie must live. I can find a way to stop magic after she's safe.

I race through the empty hallway as the battle rages. I ascend another stairwell. Another blast rings.

The fortress quakes, knocking me off the steps. I clutch Zélie as we fall; this time she can't muffle her screams.

I brace us against a wall when another blast hits. At this rate, Zélie will bleed out before she escapes.

Think.

I close my eyes and press Zélie's head against my neck. The schematics of the fortress run through my mind. I search for a way out. Between the guards and maji and firebombs, there's no way we can escape. But we don't need to . . . they're coming for her. She doesn't need to get out.

They need to get in.

The cell! I rise. That has to be where they're headed. Zélie screams as we rush down a stairwell. Her cries join the agony of the night.

"We're close," I whisper when we take the last corridor. "Just hold on. They're coming. We'll get back to the cell. Then Tzain will . . ."

Amari?

I don't recognize my sister at first. The Amari I know hides from her sword.

This woman looks ready to kill.

Amari sprints down the hallway toward us with Tzain following close behind. When a guard charges her with his blade outstretched, she's quick to slice him in the thigh. Tzain follows up with a blow to the head that knocks the soldier out cold.

"Amari!" I shout.

She skids to a halt. When she spots Zélie in my arms, her jaw drops. She and Tzain rush to meet us. That's when they see all the blood.

Amari's hand shoots to her mouth. But her horror is nothing compared to Tzain's. A strangled noise escapes his lips—something between a whimper and a moan. He shrinks. It's strange to see someone his size appear so small.

Zélie peels her head from my neck. "Tzain?"

He drops his ax and races to her. As I hand Zélie over, I see that the gauze pressed to her back runs red.

"Zél?" Tzain whispers. The loose bandages reveal the full extent of her wounds. I should've warned them.

But nothing could prepare anyone for the bleeding MAGGOT carved into Zélie's back.

The sight shatters my heart. I can only imagine what it does to Tzain. He holds her. Too tight. But there's no time to criticize.

"Go," I urge them. "Father's here. More guards will come. The longer you wait, the more impossible it'll be to escape."

"Come with us?"

The hope in Amari's voice cuts me. The thought of leaving Zélie makes my chest tight. But this isn't my fight. I can't be on their side.

Zélie turns back to me; fear floods her tearstained eyes. I lay a hand on her forehead. Her skin scorches hot against my palm.

"I'll find you," I whisper.

"But your father—"

Another blast. The hall fills with smoke.

"Go!" I shout as the fortress shakes. "Get out while you still can!"

Tzain rushes off, carrying Zélie through the smoke-filled hysteria. Amari starts after him but hesitates. "I won't leave you behind."

"Go," I press. "Father doesn't know what I've done. If I stay behind, I can try to protect you from the inside."

Amari nods and follows Tzain, accepting my lie with her sword raised. I collapse into the wall as I watch them disappear up the stairwells, crushing the desire to follow. Their battle is won. Their duty fulfilled.

My fight to save Orïsha has only begun.

CHAPTER SEVENTY

ZÉLIE

Escaping the fortress is a blur, a painting of madness and pain.

Through it all, my back rips open; with each tear the agony burns raw. My vision goes black, but I know we've escaped when the heat of the fortress opens into the cool night air. It whips against the gashes carved into my skin as Nailah carries us to safety.

All these people . . .

All these maji come to save me. What will they do when they learn the truth? That I'm broken. Useless.

Through the blackness, I try something, anything to feel magic's rush. But no warmth runs through my veins, no surge erupts in my heart. All I feel is the searing slash of the soldier's knife. All I see are Saran's black eyes.

I faint before my fears reach their full fruition, not knowing how much time has passed or where we've gone. When I wake from the haze, calloused hands wrap around my body and lift me from Nailah's saddle.

Tzain . . .

I'll never forget the despair carved into his face when he saw me. The only time I've seen that look was after the Raid, when he discovered Mama's body in chains. After everything he's done, I can't give him a reason to make that face again.

"Hold on, Zél," Tzain whispers. "We're close." He lays me down on my stomach, exposing the horrors of my back. The wounds draw a crowd of gasps; one boy begins to cry.

"Just try," a girl coaxes.

"I—I've only done cuts, some bruises. This—"

I spasm at the woman's touch, seizing up as the pain rips through my back.

"I can't—"

"Dammit, Khani," Tzain cries. "Do something before she bleeds out!"

"It's alright," Amari soothes. "Here. Touch the stone."

Once again I flinch as the woman's hands press down, but this time they're warm, heating me like the tidal pools surrounding Ilorin. The warmth travels through my body, soothing the pain and aches.

As it weaves under my skin, I get my first breath of relief. With it, my body jumps, snatching the chance for sleep.

THE SOFT EARTH FLATTENS beneath my feet, and I instantly know where I am. The reeds brush against my bare legs as the roar of rushing water falls nearby. On another day, the falls would beckon me closer.

Today they sound wrong. Sharp, like my screams.

"Zélie?"

Inan comes into view, eyes wide with worry. He takes a step forward but stops, like if he gets any closer I'll shatter.

I want to.

To crack.

Crumble into the dirt and cry.

But more than anything, I don't want him to know how his father's broken me.

Tears well in Inan's eyes and he shifts his gaze to the ground. My toes curl into the soft earth as I follow his lead.

"I'm sorry," he apologizes; I don't think he'll ever stop. "I know I should let you rest, but I had to see if you were . . ."

"Okay?" I finish for him, though I know why he doesn't speak the word.

After everything that's happened, I don't know if I'm capable of feeling okay again.

"Did you find a Healer?" he asks.

I shrug. Yes. I'm healed. Here in our dreamscape, the world's hatred isn't carved into my back. I can pretend my magic still flows through my veins. I don't struggle to speak. To feel. To *breathe*.

"I . . ."

In that instant I see a face that cuts like another scar in my back.

Since the day I met Inan, I've seen so much in his amber eyes. Hatred, fear. Remorse. I've seen everything. *Everything*.

But never this.

Never pity.

No. Fury grips me. I won't let Saran take this, too. I want the eyes that stared at me like I was the only girl in Orïsha. The eyes that told me we could change the world. Not the eyes that see I'm broken.

That I'll never be whole again.

"Zél—"

He stops when I pull his face to mine. With his touch, I can push away the pain. With his kiss, I can be the girl from the festival.

The girl who doesn't have MAGGOT etched into her back.

I pull away. Inan's eyes stay closed like they did after our first kiss. Except this time he winces.

As if our kiss causes him pain.

Though our lips touch, the embrace isn't the same. He doesn't run his fingers through my hair, graze my lip with his thumb. His hands hang in the air, afraid to move, to feel.

"You can touch me," I whisper, fighting to keep my voice from cracking.

The lines in his forehead crease. "Zél, you don't want this."

I pull his lips to mine again and he breathes in, muscles softening under my kiss. When we pull apart, I press my forehead to his nose. "You don't know what I want."

His eyes flutter open, and this time there's a glimmer of the look I crave. I see the boy who wants to take me back to his tent, the gaze that lets me pretend we could be okay.

His fingers brush against my lips and I close my eyes, testing his restraint. His knuckles graze my chin and—

—Saran's grip jerks my chin back to his face with violent force. My whole body flinches. The calm in his eyes explodes with rage as my breath withers in my throat. It takes everything in me not to cry out, to swallow my terror as his nails draw blood from my skin.

"You would do well to answer me, child—"

"Zél?"

My nails dig into Inan's neck. I need the grip to stop my hands from shaking; I need it to keep from crying out.

"Zél, what's wrong?"

Concern creeps back into his voice like a spider crawling across the grass. The look I need is falling apart.

Just.

Like.

Me.

"Zél—"

I kiss him with so much force it breaks through his hesitation, his contempt, his shame. Tears fall from my eyes as I press into his touch, desperate to feel the way we felt before. He pulls me close, fighting to be tender, yet holding me tight. It's like he knows that if he lets go, it's over. There's no denying what awaits us on the other side.

A gasp catches in my throat as his hands clutch my back, grip the slope of my thighs. Each kiss takes me to a new place, each stroke pulls me from the pain.

His hands slide up my back and I wrap my legs around his waist, following his silent command. He lowers me onto a bed of reeds, laying me down with a gentle ease.

"Zél . . ." Inan breathes.

We're moving fast, too fast, but we can't slow down. Because when the dream ends, it's over. Reality will hit, sharp and cruel and unforgiving.

I'll never be able to look at Inan's face without seeing Saran's again.

So we kiss and we clutch each other until it all goes away. Everything fades; every scar, every ache. In this instant, I only exist in his arms. I live in the peace of his embrace.

Inan pulls away, pain and love swirling behind his amber eyes. Something else. Something harder. Maybe a good-bye.

It's then I realize that I want this.

After everything, I need this.

"Keep going," I whisper, making Inan's breath hitch. His eyes drink in my body, yet I can still feel his restraint.

"Are you sure?"

I pull his lips to mine, silencing him with a slow kiss.

"I want this." I nod. "I need you."

I close my eyes as he draws me close, letting his touch drown out the pain. Even if it's only for a moment.

CHAPTER SEVENTY-ONE

ZÉLIE

My body wakes before my mind. Though there's an improvement from the searing agony, a throbbing ache still runs through my back. It stings as I rise; I flinch from the pain. *What is this? Where am I?*

I gaze at the canvas tent erected around my cot. Everything in my mind sits in a haze except the echo of Inan's embrace. My heart flutters at the thought, taking me back to his arms. Parts of him still feel so close—the softness of his lips, the strong grip of his hands. But other parts already feel so far away, as if they happened a lifetime ago. Words he said, tears we wept. The way the reeds tickled my back, reeds I'll never see again—

—Saran's black eyes watch as the lieutenant carves into my back.

"I wouldn't be doing my job as king if I didn't remind you what you are—"

I grip the rough sheets. Pain ripples through my skin. I stifle a groan as someone enters the tent.

"You're up!"

A large, freckled maji with light brown skin and a head full of white braids walks to my side. I flinch at her touch at first, but when heat travels through my cotton tunic, I breathe a sigh of relief.

"Khani," she introduces herself. "It's nice to see you awake."

I glance at her again. The vague memory of watching two girls who looked like her compete in an agbön match surfaces. "You have a sister?"

She nods. "A twin, but I'm the cuter one."

I try to smile at her joke, but the joy doesn't come.

"How bad is it?"

My voice doesn't sound like my own. Not anymore. It's small. Empty. A well run dry.

"Oh, it's . . . I'm sure with time . . ."

I close my eyes, bracing myself for the truth.

"I managed to stitch the wounds, but I . . . I think the scars are there to stay."

I wouldn't be doing my job as king if I didn't remind you what you are.

And there are Saran's eyes again. Cold.

Soulless.

"But I'm so new at this," Khani rushes out. "I'm sure a better Healer can take them away."

I nod, but it doesn't matter. Even if they wipe away the MAGGOT, the pain will always stay. I rub my wrist, discolored and scaly, indented where the majacite cuffs burned through my skin.

More scars that will never heal.

The tent flaps open again and I turn. I'm not ready to face anyone else. But then I hear it.

"Zél?"

His voice is delicate. Not the voice of my brother. It's the voice of someone who's scared, someone who feels ashamed.

As I turn, he shrinks into the corner of the tent. I slip down from the cot. For Tzain, I can swallow my fears. I can hold back every tear.

"Hey," he calls out.

Stings sear my back as I wrap my arms around Tzain's chest. He pulls me close and the ache intensifies, but I let him squeeze as hard as he needs to see I'm okay.

"I left." His voice shrinks. "I got angry and I left the celebration. I wasn't thinking . . . I didn't know—"

I pull back from Tzain and paste a smile on my face. "The wounds looked a lot worse than they were."

"But your back—"

"It's fine. After Khani's done, there won't even be a scar."

Tzain glances at Khani; thankfully, she manages to smile back. He searches me, desperate to believe my lie.

"I promised Baba," he whispers. "I promised Mama—"

"You've kept your promise. Every single day. Don't blame yourself for this, Tzain. I don't."

His jaw clenches tight, but he hugs me again and I breathe as his muscles relax under my arms.

"You're awake."

It takes me a few seconds to place Amari; rid of her usual braid, her black hair cascades down her back. It swishes from side to side as she enters the tent with the sunstone in hand. The stone bathes her with its glorious light, but nothing inside me stirs.

The sight almost breaks me. *What happened?*

The last time I held the sunstone, the wrath of Oya lit every cell of my being on fire. I felt like a goddess. Now I hardly feel alive.

Though I don't want to think about Saran, my mind takes me back to the cellar.

It's like that bastard cut the magic out of my back.

"How are you feeling?"

Amari's voice pulls me from my thoughts, amber eyes piercing. I sit on the cot again to buy time.

"I'm okay."

"Zélie . . ." Amari tries to meet my gaze, but I look away. She's not Inan or Tzain. If she pries, I won't fool her.

The flap opens as Khani exits; the sun begins to set behind the mountains. It dips under a jagged peak, sliding off the orange horizon.

"What day is it?" I interrupt. "How long was I out?"

Amari and Tzain make eye contact. My stomach drops so hard it must lie at my feet. *That's why I can't feel my magic. . . .*

"We missed the solstice?"

Tzain looks to the ground as Amari chews on her lower lip. Her voice comes out in a whisper. "It's tomorrow."

My heart jumps in my throat and I hide my head in my hands. How are we going to get to the island? How am I going to do the ritual? Though I can't feel the chill of the dead, I whisper the incantation in my mind. "*Ẹ̀mí àwọn tí ó ti sùn, mo ké pè yín ní òní—*"

—with a lurch the soldier finishes the A. Bile spews from my lips. I scream. I scream. *But the pain never ends—*

My palms burn and I look down; my fingernails have cut red crescents into my own skin. I unclench my fists and wipe the blood on the cot, praying no one sees.

I try the incantation again, but no spirits rise from the dirt ground. My magic is gone.

And I don't know how to get it back.

The realization reopens a gaping hole inside of me, a pit I haven't felt since the Raid. Since the moment I saw Baba crumble in the streets of Ibadan and knew things would never be the same. I think back to my first incantation in the sand dunes of Ibeji, back to the ethereal rush of holding the sunstone and grazing Oya's hand. The ache that cuts through me is sharper than the blade that cut through my back.

It's like losing Mama all over again.

Amari sits on the corner of my bed and sets the sunstone down. I wish its golden waves would speak to me once more.

"What do we do?" If we're this close to the Olasimbo Range, Zaria's at least a three days' ride away. Even if I had my magic, we wouldn't get to Zaria in time, let alone be able to set sail for the sacred islands.

Tzain looks at me like I've slapped him in the face. "We run. We find Baba and get the hell out of Orïsha."

"He's right." Amari nods. "I don't want to retreat, but my father has to know you're still alive. If we can't make it to the island, we need to get to safety and regroup. Figure out another way to fight—"

"The hell are you talking about?"

I whip my head around as a boy nearly as big as Tzain charges through the tent flaps. Though it takes me a moment, I remember the white locs of a player who once faced Tzain on the agbön court.

"Kenyon?" I ask.

His eyes flick to me, but there's no nostalgia in his glare. "Good to see you've decided to wake up."

"Good to see you're still an ass."

He glares before turning back to Amari. "You *said* she was going to bring magic back. Now you're trying to cut and run?"

"We're out of time," Tzain shouts. "It'd take three days to get to Zaria—"

"And only half a day to go through Jimeta!"

"Skies, not this again—"

"People died for this," Kenyon yells. "For her. Now you want to run away because you're afraid of the risk?"

Amari glowers with an intensity that could melt stone. "You have no idea what we have risked, so I advise you to keep your mouth shut!"

"You little—"

"He's right," I speak up, a new desperation bubbling to the surface.

This can't be it. After everything, I can't lose my magic again. "We have a night. If we can get to Jimeta, find a boat—" If I can get my magic back . . . find some way to communicate with the gods . . .

"Zél, no." Tzain bends to my eye level, the same way he does with Baba. Because Baba is delicate. Broken. And now so am I. "Jimeta's too dangerous. We're more likely to be killed than to find help. You need to rest."

"She needs to get off her ass."

Tzain gets in Kenyon's face so quickly I'm surprised he doesn't take the tent down with him.

"Stop it." Amari wedges herself between them. "There's no time for us to fight. If we cannot get through, we need to get out."

As they erupt in arguments, I stare at the sunstone, within arm's reach. If I could touch it . . . just a graze . . .

Please, Oya, I lift up the silent prayer, *don't let this be it*.

I take a deep breath, preparing for the rush of Sky Mother's soul, the fire of Oya's spirit. My fingers brush the smooth stone—

Hope shrivels inside my chest.

Nothing.

Not even a spark.

The sunstone is cool to the touch.

It's worse than before my awakening, before I ever touched the scroll. It's like all the magic has bled out of my body, left on that cellar's floor.

Only a maji tethered to Sky Mother's spirit can perform the sacred act. Lekan's words echo back into my mind. Without him, no other maji can be connected to Sky Mother before the ritual.

Without me, there's no ritual at all.

"Zélie?"

I look up to find everyone staring at me, waiting for the final answer.

It's over. I should tell them now.

But as I open my mouth to deliver the news, the right words don't come out. This can't be it. Not after everything we've lost.

Everything they did.

"Let's go." The words are weak. By the gods, I wish I could make them sound strong. This has to work. I won't *let* this be the end.

Sky Mother chose me. Used me. Took me away from everything I loved. She can't abandon me like this.

She can't throw me away with nothing but scars.

"Zél—"

"They cut 'maggot' into my back," I hiss. "We're going. I don't care what it takes. I won't let them win."

CHAPTER SEVENTY-TWO

ZÉLIE

After hours of traveling through the forest surrounding the Olasimbo Range, Jimeta makes its way onto the horizon. Sharp and jagged like its rumored inhabitants, its sand cliffs and rocky bluffs jut out over the Lokoja Sea. Waves crash against the base of its cliffs, creating a familiar song I know all too well. Though the crashing waves pound and rumble like thunder, just being near the water again sets me at ease.

"Remember when you wanted to live here?" Tzain whispers to me, and I nod, a half smile rising to my lips. It's nice to feel something else, to *think* of something besides all the ways our plans could fail.

After the Raid, I insisted we go to Jimeta. I thought its lawless borders were the only place we'd be safe. Though I'd heard stories of the mercenaries and criminals who filled its streets, in my young eyes that danger paled in comparison to the joy of living in a city without guards. At least the people trying to kill us here wouldn't wear the Orïshan seal.

As we pass by the small homes nestled within the towering cliffs, I wonder how different our lives would've been. Wooden doors and window frames stick out of the rock, protruding as if they were grown inside the stone. Bathed in the moonlight, the criminal city almost appears peaceful. I might even think it beautiful if not for the mercenaries lurking at every corner.

I keep my face hard as we pass a group of masked men, wondering where their specialties lie. From what I've heard of Jimeta, anyone we pass could run the gamut from common thievery to assassination requests. Rumor has it the only true way to get out of the stocks is to hire a mercenary to break you free; they're the only ones strong and sneaky enough to defy the army and live.

Nailah growls as we pass another band of masked men, a mix of kosidán and divîners, men and women, Orïshans and foreigners. Their eyes comb over her mane, likely calculating her cost. I snarl as a man dares to step forward.

Try me, I threaten him with my eyes. I pity the poor soul who tries to mess with me tonight.

"Is this it?" I ask Kenyon when we stop before a large cave at the base of the cliffs. Its mouth is shrouded in darkness, making it impossible to peer inside.

He nods. "They call him the silver-eyed foxer. I heard he took out Gombe's general with his bare hands."

"And he's got a boat?"

"The fastest. Wind-powered, last I heard."

"Alright." I grasp Nailah's reins. "Let's go."

"Wait." Kenyon puts a hand out, stopping us before we take another step. "You can't just enter a clan's dwelling with a crew of your own. Only one of us can go."

We all hesitate for a moment. *Dammit*. I'm not ready for this.

Tzain reaches for his ax. "I'll go."

"Why?" Kenyon asks. "This whole plan revolves around Zélie. If anyone goes, it should be her."

"Are you crazy? I'm not sending her in there alone."

"It's not like she's defenseless," Kenyon scoffs. "With her magic she's more powerful than any of us."

"He's right." Amari places her hand on Tzain's arm. "They might be more likely to help if they see her magic at work."

This is where I agree. Where I tell them I'm not scared. Convincing these fighters should be easy. My magic should be stronger than ever.

My stomach churns with the truth, guilt gnawing away at me. It would all feel so much better if just one person knew we're not relying on me at all.

Whether or not we get magic back is completely up to the gods.

"No." Tzain shakes his head. "It's too much of a risk."

"I can do it." I hand Tzain Nailah's reins. This has to work. Whatever's going on, it *has* to be Sky Mother's plan.

"Zél—"

"He's right. I have the best chance of convincing them."

Tzain steps forward. "I'm not letting you go in there alone."

"Tzain, we need their fighters. We need their boat. And we have nothing to offer in return. If we want to get to the temple, it's best not to start the conversation with breaking their rules." I hand Amari my pack with the three sacred artifacts, keeping only my staff. I run my fingers along the etchings and force a deep breath into my chest.

"Don't worry." I send a silent prayer up to Oya with my thoughts. "If I need help, you'll hear me scream."

I walk through the mouth of the cave. The air hangs wet and cold. I move to the nearest wall and slide my hands along the slick ridges, using the stone as a guide. Each step is slow and tentative, but it feels good to move, good to do something besides reread that damn scroll with a ritual I might not be able to do.

As I travel, giant blue crystals drip from the ceiling like icicles, hanging so low they almost brush the cave floor. They provide a faint light, illuminating the two-tailed batters gathered around their glowing cores. The batters seem to watch me as I move through the cave. Their chorus of squeaks is the only sound I hear until it's drowned beneath the chatter of men and women gathered around a fire.

I pause, taking in their surprisingly vast domain. The ground beneath them dips into a depression, coated with a light moss that the mercenaries fashion into cushions. Rays of light peek through cracks in the ceiling, illuminating hand-carved steps that travel farther down the cliff.

I take a few more steps forward and a hush falls over the crowd.

Gods, help me.

I make my way through their gathering. Dozens of masked mercenaries clad in black leer at me as I pass, each sitting on a rock structure that juts out of the ground. Some reach for their weapons, some shift into a fighting stance. Half stare like they want to kill, others like they want to devour.

I ignore their hostility as I search for gray eyes amid a sea of ambers and browns. The man they belong to emerges from the front of the cavern, the only unmasked mercenary in sight. Though he's covered in black like the rest of the fighters, a dark red scarf wraps around his throat.

"You?" I breathe out in confusion. I can't hide my shock. The sandstone complexion, the striking, storm-gray eyes. *The pickpocket . . .* the thief from the divîner settlement. Though only a short time has passed, it feels like a lifetime ago now.

Roën takes a long drag off a hand-rolled cigarette as his angular eyes slide up my form. He sits down, resting against a circular rock structure reminiscent of a throne. His foxer-like smile spreads wide against his lips.

"I told you we'd meet again." He takes another drag off his cigarette and is slow to exhale. "But unfortunately, these aren't the right circumstances. Not unless you're here to join me and my men."

"Your men?" Roën looks only a few years older than Tzain. Though he has a fighter's build, the men he commands are twice his size.

"You find that amusing?" A crooked grin rises to his thin lips, and he leans forward on his stone throne. "Do you know what amuses me? A little maji. Stumbling into my cave unarmed."

"Who says I'm unarmed?"

"You don't look like you know your way around a sword. Of course, if that's what you're here to learn, I'd be more than happy to teach."

His crudeness elicits laughter from his crew, and my cheeks grow hot. I'm a game to him. Another mark he can pickpocket with ease.

I survey the cave, taking stock of his mercenaries. If this is going to work, I need his respect.

"How kind." I keep my face even. "But it's me who's here to teach you."

Roën lets out a hearty laugh that bounces along the cave walls. "Go on."

"I need you and your men for a job that could change Orïsha."

Again the men jeer, but this time the pickpocket doesn't laugh. He leans farther out of his seat.

"There's a sacred island north of Jimeta," I continue, "a full night's sail away. I need you to take us there before tomorrow's sun rises."

He leans back against his stone throne. "The only island in the Lokoja Sea is Kaduna."

"This island only appears every hundred years."

More taunts erupt, but Roën silences them with a sharp hand.

"What's on this island, mysterious little maji?"

"A way to bring magic back for good. For every maji in Orïsha's lands."

The mercenaries explode in laughter and taunts, yelling at me to go away. A stocky man steps out of the fray. His muscles bulge beneath his black fatigues. "Stop wasting our time with these lies," he growls. "Roën, get this girl out of here or I wi—"

He lays his hand on my back; his touch sends spasms through my wounds. The pain takes me away, locking me inside the cell—

—rusted cuffs rip against my wrists as I pull. My screams echo against the metal walls.

And during it all, Saran stands calm, watching them tear me apart—

"Agh!"

I throw the man over my shoulder, slapping him against the rock floor with a loud smack. As he recoils, I ram my staff into his sternum, letting up just before I hear anything crack. His screams are loud, but not louder than the ones still ringing in my head.

The cave seems to hold its breath as I bend down, placing the end of my staff above the mercenary's throat.

"Touch me again." I bare my teeth. "See what happens."

He flinches as I release my hold, giving him the chance to crawl away. With his retreat there's no more laughter.

They understand my staff.

Roën's stormy eyes dance, filled with even more amusement than before. He puts out his cigarette and walks forward, stopping only a finger's breadth away from my face. The scent of his smoke engulfs me, sweet like milk and honey.

"You're not the first to attempt this, love. Kwame already tried to bring magic back. From what I hear, it didn't go so well."

Kwame's name sends a pang through my heart, reminding me of the meeting he took with Roën in the divîner camp. Even back then, he must have been preparing. Deep down, he always knew we'd have to fight.

"This is different. I have a way to give all the maji back their gifts at once."

"What kind of payment are we talking?"

"No coin," I say. "But you'll earn the favor of the gods."

"How do you figure?" he snorts. "Just general goodwill?"

He needs more. I rack my mind, searching for a better lie. "The gods sent me to you. Twice. It's no accident we're meeting again. They've chosen you because they want your help."

The crooked smile drops off his face and he's solemn for the first time. I can't read the expression behind his eyes when it's not amusement or mischief.

"That may be enough for me, love, but my men are going to need a little more than divine intervention."

"Then let them know that if we succeed, you'll be employed by the future queen of Orïsha." The words tumble out of me before I can even assess whether or not they're true. Tzain told me of Amari's intention to claim the throne, but with everything going on, I haven't thought of it since.

Yet now I hold on to it, using my only leverage. If Roën and his men don't help us, we won't get anywhere near that island.

"The queen's mercenaries," he muses. "It has a ring to it, no?"

"It does." I nod. "One that sounds a lot like gold."

A smirk tugs at the corners of his lips. His gaze slides over me once more.

Finally, he holds out his hand and I hide a smile, keeping my grip firm as we shake.

"When do we leave?" I ask. "We have to hit the island by daybreak."

"Right now." Roën smiles. "But our boat's small. You'll have to sit next to me."

CHAPTER SEVENTY-THREE

ZÉLIE

WIND FILLS THE SILENCE as we ride across the Lokoja Sea on Roën's boat. Unlike the vast vessels of Ibeji's arena, Roën's ship is sleek and angular, only a few meters longer than Nailah. Instead of sails, metal turbines harness the blowing wind. They propel us through the choppy waters as they hum and rotate.

I brace myself against Tzain and Amari as another large wave crashes against the iron boat. Unlike the Warri Sea off the coast of Ilorin, the Lokoja Sea is phosphorescent; beneath the water plankton glow bright blue, making the sea sparkle like the stars in the sky. It would be an incredible sight if we weren't packed into the boat so tightly. Between Kenyon's team and a dozen of Roën's crew, we're forced to squeeze in side by side with men we can't trust.

Ignore them, I coach myself turning to the ocean to revel in the familiarity of sea-salt spray on my skin. Closing my eyes, I can almost imagine myself back in Ilorin, back with the fish. With Baba. Before all of this began, back when my biggest worry was a graduation match.

I stare at my hands, thinking of everything that's passed since then. I thought this close to the solstice I would feel something again, but still no magic runs through my veins.

Oya, please. I clench my fists and pray. *Sky Mother. Everyone. I'm trusting you.*

Don't let me be wrong.

"Are you alright?" Amari whispers. Though her voice is gentle, her amber eyes are knowing.

"Just cold."

Amari tilts her head, but she doesn't pry. Instead, she laces her fingers through mine and looks back out at the sea. Her touch is kind. Forgiving. Like she already knows the truth.

"We've got company, boss."

I whip around to find the silhouettes of large, three-masted warships on the horizon. There's far too many to count. The wooden beasts cut through the water, metal plates marking the cannons lining their decks. Though they fade into the sea's mist, the moonlight illuminates Orïsha's seal. My chest tightens at the sight and I close my eyes, willing the image away—

—the heat intensifies my pain as the knife rips through my back. No matter how much I scream, the darkness never comes. I taste my own blood—

"Zél?"

Amari's face swims through the blackness. I squeeze her hand so hard her knuckles crack. I open my mouth to apologize, but I can't form the words. A sob threatens to creep up my throat.

Amari puts her other hand around me and turns to Roën. "Can we avoid them?"

Roën pulls a collapsible telescope from his pocket and presses it against his eye. "That one's easy, but not the fleet behind it."

He hands me the telescope, but Amari comes to my rescue and snatches it away. Her body goes rigid as she takes in the sight.

"Skies," she curses. "Father's battleships."

Saran's cold eyes flash into my mind and I whip around, gripping the wooden ledge of Roën's boat to stare out at the sea.

I wouldn't be doing my job as king if I didn't remind you what you are.

"How many?" I manage to croak, but that isn't what I want to ask.

How many of his lieutenants are on the ships?

How many wait to scar me again?

"At least a dozen," Amari answers.

"Let's take another path," Tzain offers.

"Don't be foolish." The mischievous glint in Roën's gray eyes reignites. "Let's take the closest ship."

"No," Amari objects. "That will give us away."

"They're in our way. And by the looks of it, they're headed to this island, too. What better way to get there than on one of their own warships?"

I stare at the colossal vessels in the crashing sea. Where's Inan? If Saran's aboard one of those ships, is Inan with him?

The thought is too hard to speak out loud. I lift up another silent prayer. If any god above cares for me, I'll never have to face Inan again.

"Let's do it." Dozens of faces turn to me, but I keep my gaze on the sea. "If all those ships are headed to the island, we have to be smarter, efficient."

"Exactly." Roën tilts his head in my direction. "Käto, head for the nearest ship."

As the boat speeds up, my heart beats with enough force to break free of my rib cage. How will I face Saran again? What good will I be without my magic?

I grab my staff with shaking hands and flick to expand it.

"What're you doing?"

I look up to find Roën at my side.

"We need to take the warship."

"Love, that's not how this works. You hired us for a job. Sit back and let us do it."

Amari and I glance at each other before turning to the monstrous battleship.

"You really believe you can accomplish this without our help?" Amari asks.

"Taking it is easy. The only question is how fast we can do it."

He gives a hand signal to two men. They withdraw a crossbow with a hook and rope. Roën raises a fist, presumably to release the arrows, but pauses and turns to me. "What's your limit?"

"What?"

"What are we allowed to do? Personally, I prefer a clean throat slit, but with the sea, drowning could be efficient, too."

The ease with which he speaks of ending human life sends a chill through my skin. It's the calm of a man who fears nothing. The calm that sits in Saran's eyes. Though I can't sense the spirits of the dead right now, I don't want to imagine how many spirits would swarm around Roën.

"No killing." The order surprises me, but as soon as it leaves my lips, it feels right. So much blood has already been spilled. Whether we win or lose tomorrow, these soldiers don't need to die.

"You're no fun," Roën groans before turning to his men. "You heard her—take them out, but keep them breathing."

A few mercenaries grumble and my heart shivers; how often is death their first answer? Before I get a chance to ask, Roën flicks out two sharp fingers.

The crossbow releases and hooks through the wooden hull of the ship.

Roën's biggest man ties the end of the rope around his massive frame to keep it secure.

The mercenary Roën calls Käto rises from the boat's steering wheel and makes his way to the newly taut rope.

"Pardon," Käto mutters in Orïshan as he brushes past. Though a mask obscures much of his face, he shares Roën's coloring and angular eyes. But where Roën has been brash and taunting, Käto has only been cordial and serious.

Käto reaches the other side of the boat and pulls on the rope to test its hold; satisfied, he jumps on and wraps his legs around it. My lips part in surprise as he shimmies up with the speed of a bat-eared foxer. Within seconds, Käto disappears over the railing, fading into the blackness of the other ship.

A weak grunt sounds, followed by another; a few moments later Käto reappears to give the go-ahead. As the last of his men board the ship, Roën beckons to me.

"Level with me, my mysterious maji. What will the gods give me if I take down this boat? Do I get to say what I'm interested in, or do they already know?"

"It doesn't work like that—"

"Or maybe I need to impress them?" Roën talks over me, pulling his mask over the bridge of his nose. "What do you think I'll get if I clear this boat in five minutes?"

"You won't get anything if you don't shut your mouth and go."

His eyes crinkle through the holes of the mask; I have no doubt his foxer smile shines behind it. With a wink, he climbs up and we're left to wait with only the mercenary anchoring the rope as company.

"Ridiculous." I click my tongue. Five minutes for a boat of that size? The deck alone looks like it could support the whole army. They'll be lucky to take it at all.

We sit in the night, cringing at the faint screams and grunts from above. But after the initial skirmish, the sounds fade into silence.

"There's only a dozen of them," Tzain mutters. "You really think they can take a whole shi—"

We stop as a shadowy figure slides down the rope. Roën lands on the boat with a thud and removes his mask, revealing his crooked smile.

"You did it?" I ask.

"No," he sighs, and shows me the colored crystals of the hourglass in his timepiece. "Six minutes. Seven, if we're rounding up. But if you'd let me kill, it would've been under five!"

"No way." Tzain crosses his arms.

"See for yourself, brother. Ladder!"

A ladder flies over the side of the ship and I grab on, ignoring the pain in my back as I climb up the rungs. *He's joking.* More games, more lies.

But when I hit the deck, I can hardly believe my eyes: dozens of royal guards lie unconscious, bound from head to toe in rope. Each is stripped of his uniform and their bodies are strewn across the deck like litter.

I release a breath I didn't realize I was holding when I see that Inan and Saran aren't among the new captives. Yet somehow I doubt they'd fall so easily to Roën and his men.

"There's more below deck," Roën whispers in my ear, and even I can't help but smile. I quickly roll my eyes, but Roën shines at this small hint of approval.

He shrugs and brushes nonexistent dirt off his shoulders. "I suppose it's to be expected when you're chosen by the gods."

His smile lingers before he steps forward, a captain taking charge.

"Get these men in the brig. Sweep for any tools they can use to escape. Rehema, keep this ship on track. Käto, sail behind us in our boat. At this speed, we hit the island's coordinates at daybreak."

CHAPTER SEVENTY-FOUR

INAN

TWO DAYS HAVE PASSED.

Two days without her.

In her absence, the ocean air hangs heavy.

Every breath whispers her name.

Staring over the railing of the warship, I see Zélie in everything. A mirror I can't escape. Her smile shines through the moon, her spirit blows with the ocean wind. Without her, the world is a living memory.

A ledger of all the things I'll never enjoy again.

I close my eyes, reliving the sensation of Zélie against the reeds of the dreamscape. I didn't know it was possible to fit so perfectly inside someone else's arms.

In that moment—that one, perfect moment—she was beautiful. *Magic* was beautiful. Not a curse, but a gift.

With Zélie, it always is.

I wrap my hand around the bronze piece she gave me, holding it tight as if it's the last piece of her heart. Something inside tempts me to throw it into the ocean, but I can't bear to let the last part of her go.

If I could've stayed in that dreamscape forever, I would have. Given everything up. Never looked back.

But I woke up.

When my eyes opened, I knew it'd never be the same again.

"Scouting?"

I jump. Father appears beside me. His eyes look as black as the night. They feel as cold.

I turn away, as if that could hide the longings buried deep in my heart. Father may not be a Connector, but his retaliation will be swift if he senses anything less than steadfast resolve.

"I thought you were asleep," I manage.

"Never." Father shakes his head. "I don't sleep before battle. Neither should you."

Of course. Every second is a chance. An opportunity, a strategized counterattack. All things that would be so easy to concern myself with if I was positive I was doing the right thing.

I squeeze the bronze piece tighter, allowing its ridges to dig into my skin. I've already let Zélie down once before. I don't know if I have the stomach to betray her again.

I look up to the sky, wishing I could see Orí peering through the clouds. *Even in the darkest times the gods are always there.* Zélie's voice runs through my mind. *They always have a plan.*

Is this your plan? I ache to shout, desperate for a sign. Our promises, our Orïsha—however distant, there's a world in which our dream still lies in our grasp. Am I making a huge mistake? Is there still a chance for me to turn back?

"You waver," Father says.

A statement, not a question. He can probably smell the weakness leaking through the sweat on my skin.

"I'm sorry," I mutter, and brace for his fist. But instead he pats my back and turns out to sea.

"I wavered, once. Back before I became king. When I was just a simple prince and got to follow my own naïveté."

I remain still, worried that any movement will interrupt this rare peek at Father's past. A glimpse of the man he might have been.

"There was a referendum going through the monarchy, a proposal that would integrate leaders of the ten maji clans into the nobility of our royal courts. It was my father's dream to unify the kosidán and the maji, build an Orïsha like history had never seen."

Unable to stop myself, I look up at Father, eyes wide at the thought. An act like that would be monumental. It would shift our kingdom's foundation forever.

"Was it met with favor?"

"Skies, no." Father chuckles. "Everyone but your grandfather was against it. But as king, he didn't need their permission. He could make the final decree."

"Why did you waver?"

Father's lips press into a tight line. "My first wife," he finally answers. "Alika. She was too softhearted for her own good. She wanted me to be someone who could create change."

Alika . . .

I picture the face that might've accompanied that name. From the way Father talks about her, she must have been a kind woman, one with an even kinder face.

"For her, I supported my father. I chose love over duty. I knew the maji were dangerous, yet I convinced myself that with the right show of faith, we could work together. I thought the maji wanted to unify, but all they've ever craved is a desire to conquer us."

Though he speaks no more, I hear the end of the story within his silence. The king who perished trying to help the maji. The wife Father would never hold again.

The realization brings back the horrible images of the Gombe fortress: metal melted to guards' skeletons; bodies yellowed and ravished by horrible disease. It was a wasteland. An abomination. And all by magic's hand.

After Zélie escaped, there was a carpet of corpses piled on top of one another. We couldn't see the floor.

"You waver now because that is what it means to be king," Father says. "You have your duty and your heart. To choose one means the other must suffer."

Father removes his black majacite blade from its sheath and points to an inscription on the tip that I have never seen:

Duty Before Self.

Kingdom Before King.

"When Alika died, I had this blade forged, inscribed so that I would always remember my mistake. Because I chose my heart, I will never be with my one true love again."

Father extends his sword to me and my stomach clenches, unable to believe the gesture. All my life, I've never seen my father without this blade strapped to his side.

"To sacrifice your heart for your kingdom is noble, son. It is everything. It's what it means to be king."

I stare at the blade; the inscription gleams in the moonlight. Its words simplify my mission, creating space for my pain. A soldier. A great king. That's all I've ever wanted to be.

Duty over self.

Orïsha over Zélie.

I wrap my hand around the hilt of the majacite sword, ignoring the way it blisters my skin.

"Father, I know how we can get the scroll back."

CHAPTER SEVENTY-FIVE

ZÉLIE

When I settle into the captain's quarters below deck, I expect sleep to come easily. My eyes scream for it, my body cries even louder. Nestled between the cotton sheets and velvet panthenaire furs, I don't know if I've ever slept in a softer bed. I close my eyes and wait to be pulled into blackness, but the moment unconsciousness takes hold, I'm thrown back into chains—

"I wouldn't be doing my job as king if I didn't remind you what you are."

"I wouldn't be doing my job as king unless—"

"Agh!"

My sheets are soaked in sweat, so drenched the captain's bed might as well be in the sea. Though I'm awake, it feels like the metal walls keep closing in around me.

In an instant, I'm on my feet, running out the door. When I make it to the outside deck, the cool air hits me with a welcome gust of wind. The moon hangs so low in the sky its roundness kisses the sea. Its pale light illuminates me as I inhale the ocean air.

Breathe, I coach myself. Gods, I long for the days when the only thing I had to worry about when I closed my eyes was the dreamscape. Though the nightmare is more than past, I can still feel the knife cutting through my back.

"Enjoying the view?"

I whip around to find Roën leaning against the helm, teeth gleaming even in the dark. "The moon didn't want to rise tonight, but I convinced her you were worth the trip."

"Does everything have to be a joke with you?" My words are harsher than I intend, but Roën's grin only widens.

"Not everything." He shrugs. "But life's a lot more fun that way."

He shifts his stance, and the moonlight hits the splatters of blood on his fatigues and bandaged knuckles.

"All in a good day's work." Roën wriggles his bloodstained fingers. "Had to get those soldiers talking about your magical island somehow."

Nausea rises to my throat at the sight of the blood on his hand. I gulp to keep it down. *Ignore him.* I turn back to the sea, grasping on to the calm it brings.

I don't want to picture the mess he made of those men. I've seen enough blood. I'll stay here, within the crashing waves, where it's soft and safe. Here, I can think of swimming. Of Baba. Of freedom—

"The scars." Roën's voice cuts into my thoughts. "Are they new?"

I glare at him like he's an Orïshan honeybee begging to be smashed. "They're none of your damn business."

"If you're looking for some advice, they could be." Roën pulls back his sleeve, and all the venom I want to spit evaporates. Crooked tallies mar his wrist, traveling up his arm, disappearing underneath his shirt.

"Twenty-three," he answers my unasked question. "And yes, I remember each mark. They killed one of my crew members in front of me each time they carved a new one."

He runs his finger down one crooked line in particular, face hardening with the memory. Watching him, my own scars prickle. "The king's guards?"

"Nope. These kind and gracious men were from my home. A land across the sea."

I stare at the horizon, imagining a different ship route, a place away from the ritual, from magic, from Saran. A land where the Raid never happened at all.

"What's it called?"

"Sutōrī." Roën's gaze grows distant. "You'd like it there."

"If it's full of tally marks and scoundrels like you, I can assure you that's one kingdom I'll never see."

Roën smiles again. A nice smile. Warmer than I expect. But knowing what I know so far, this smile could appear when he tells a joke or slits another man's throat.

"Level with me." He steps closer, looking me straight in the eye. "In my humble experience, the nightmares and scars take time to heal. Right now your wounds are a bit too fresh for my comfort."

"What're you trying to say?"

Roën puts a hand on my shoulder; it's so close to the scars I flinch out of instinct.

"If you can't do this, I need to know. Don't—" He stops me before I interject. "This isn't about you. I couldn't speak for weeks after I got my scars. I certainly couldn't fight."

It's like he's in my head, like he knows my magic's run dry. *I can't do this*, I scream inside. *If an army's waiting, we're sailing to our deaths.*

But the words stay in my mouth, burrowing back down. I have to trust the gods. I need to believe that if they took me this far, they won't turn their backs on me now.

"Well?" Roën presses.

"The people who gave me my scars are the ones on those ships."

"I'm not putting my men in danger so you can get revenge."

"I could skin Saran alive and I still wouldn't have my revenge." I shrug off his hand. "It's not about him. It's not even about me. If I don't stop him tomorrow, he'll destroy my people like he destroyed me."

For the first time since the torture, I feel a hint of the old fire that used to roar louder than my fear. But its flame is weak now; as soon as it flickers, it's blown out by the wind.

"Fine. But if we go in there tomorrow, you better stay strong. My men are the best, but we're going against a fleet. I can't afford for you to freeze up."

"Why do you even care?"

Roën's hand flies to his heart, feigning a wound. "I'm a professional, love. I don't like to disappoint my clients, especially when I've been chosen by the gods."

"They're not *your* gods." I shake my head. "They didn't choose you."

"Are you sure?" Roën's smile turns dangerous as he leans against the railing. "There are over fifty mercenary clans in Jimeta, love. Fifty caverns you and your staff could've stumbled into. Just because the gods didn't blast through the ceiling of my cave doesn't mean they didn't choose me."

I search Roën's eyes for mischief, but I find none. "That's all you need to face an army? A belief in divine intervention?"

"It's not a belief, love, it's insurance. I can't read the gods, and in my line of work it's best not to mess with things I can't read." He turns to the sky and shouts, "But I prefer to be paid in gold!"

I burst out laughing, and it feels foreign—I never thought I would laugh again.

"I wouldn't wait on that gold."

"I don't know about that." Roën reaches out and cups my chin. "They did send a mysterious little maji into my cavern. I'm sure more treasure will follow."

He walks away, pausing only to call back, "You should talk to someone. The jokes don't help much, but talking does." His foxer smile returns, mischief lighting in his steel-colored gaze. "If you're interested, my room's next to yours. I've been told I'm an excellent listener."

He winks, and I roll my eyes as he walks away. It's as if he can't stomach being serious for more than five seconds.

I force myself to turn back to the sea, but the longer I stare into the moon, the more I realize he's right. I don't want to be alone. Not when tonight could be my last night. Blind faith in the gods may have taken me this far, but if I'm going to get on that island tomorrow, I need more.

I fight my hesitation and walk through the ship's narrow hallway, passing Tzain's door, then my own. I need to be with someone.

I need to tell someone the truth.

When I come to the right room I knock softly, heart pounding when the door swings open.

"Hey," I whisper.

"Hi." Amari smiles.

CHAPTER SEVENTY-SIX

AMARI

ZÉLIE FLINCHES as I comb through the final section of her hair. The way she squirms and writhes under my touch, you would think I'm stabbing her scalp with my sword.

"Sorry," I apologize for the tenth time.

"Someone has to do it."

"If you just combed it every few days—"

"Amari, if you ever see me combing my hair, please call a Healer."

My laughter bounces against the metal walls as I separate her hair into three parts. Although it's difficult to comb, a twitch of envy runs through me when I start the last braid. Once smooth as silk, Zélie's white hair is now coarse and thick, framing her beautiful face like a lionaire's mane. She doesn't seem to notice the way Roën and his men stare at her when she looks the other way.

"Before magic went away, my hair looked like this." Zélie speaks more to herself than to me. "Mama had to hold me down with animations to get a comb through my hair."

I laugh again, picturing stone animations chasing after her for this simple task. "I think my mother would've loved those. There weren't enough nannies to keep me from streaking through the palace."

"Why were you always naked?" Zélie smiles.

"I don't know," I giggle. "When I was young, my skin felt so much better without clothes."

Zélie clenches her teeth as the braid reaches the nape of her neck. The easiness between us falls away, something that keeps happening again and again. It's like I can see the wall building up around her, bricks built from unspoken words and cemented with painful memories. I release the braid and rest my chin on her scalp.

"Whatever it is, you can talk to me."

Zélie's head drops; she wraps her hands around her thighs and pulls her knees to her chest. I squeeze her shoulder before finishing the last braid.

"I used to think you were weak," she whispers.

I pause; I wasn't expecting that. Of all the things Zélie probably used to think of me, "weak" could be the nicest.

"Because of my father?"

She nods, but I sense her reluctance. "Every time you thought about him, you shrank. I didn't understand how someone could wield a sword the way you do and still hold so much fear."

I run my fingers along her braids, trailing the lines in her scalp. "And now?"

Zélie closes her eyes, muscles tensing. But when I wrap my hands around her, it's like I can feel the cracks in her dam.

The pressure builds, pushing against all her emotions, all her pain. When she can bear it no longer, the sob I know she's been holding back breaks free.

"I can't get him out of my head." She squeezes me as hot tears fall onto my shoulder. "It's like every time I close my eyes, he's wrapping a chain around my neck."

I hold Zélie close as she sobs into my arms, releasing everything she's been trying to hide. My own throat chokes up with her cries; it's my family who's caused her all this pain. Holding Zélie makes me wonder about Binta and all the days she probably needed this. She was there for me in all my struggles, yet I never got to be there for her in the same way.

"I'm sorry," I whisper. "For what my father did. For what he's done. I'm sorry Inan couldn't stop it. I'm sorry it took us both so long to try to right Father's wrongs."

Zélie leans into me, letting my words sink in. *I'm sorry, Binta*, I think to her spirit. *I'm sorry I didn't do more.*

"The first night we escaped, I couldn't fall asleep in that forest no matter how hard I tried." I speak softly. "I was barely conscious, but each time I closed my eyes I saw Father's black blade ready to cut me down." I pull back and wipe away her tears, staring straight into her silver eyes. "I thought if he ever found me I would shatter, but do you know what happened when I saw him in the fortress?"

Zélie shakes her head and the moment returns, making my pulse quicken. The memory of Father's rage flares, yet what I remember is the weight of my sword in my hand.

"Zélie, I grabbed my blade. I almost ran after *him*!"

She smiles at me and for a moment, I see Binta in the way it softens her features. "I expect nothing less of the Lionaire," Zélie teases.

"I can recall a day where the Lionaire was told to get herself together and stop being such a scared little princess."

"You're lying." Zélie laughs through her tears. "I was probably a lot meaner."

"If it makes you feel better, you *did* push me into the sand before you said it."

"So is it my turn?" Zélie asks. "Is this where you push me?"

I shake my head. "I needed to hear that. I needed *you*. After Binta died, you were the first person to treat me like more than some silly princess. I know you may not see it, but you believed I could be the

Lionaire before anyone ever uttered that name." I wipe away the remainder of her tears and place my hand on her cheek. I couldn't be there for Binta, yet being with Zélie, I feel the hole in my heart closing. Binta would've told me to be brave. With Zélie, I already am.

"No matter what he did, no matter what you see, believe me when I tell you it is not forever," I say. "If you broke me free, you will find a way to save yourself."

Zélie smiles, but it only lasts an instant. She closes her eyes and clenches her fist, the way she always does when practicing an incantation.

"What's wrong?" I ask.

"I can't . . ." She looks down at her hands. "I can't do magic anymore."

My heart seems to stop, sluggish, heavy in my chest. I clasp Zélie's arms tight. "What are you talking about?"

"It's gone." Zélie grips her braids, pain etched into her face. "I'm not a Reaper anymore. I'm not anything."

The weight Zélie bears on her shoulders threatens to break her back. All I want to do is comfort her, yet this new reality makes my arms feel like lead.

"When did it happen?"

Zélie closes her eyes and shrugs. "When they cut me, it was like they cut the magic out of my back. I haven't been able to feel anything since."

"What of the ritual?"

"I don't know." She takes a deep, shuddering breath. "I can't do it. No one can."

Her words rip the floor out from under me. I can almost feel myself falling through the hole. Lekan said only a maji tethered to Sky Mother's spirit could perform the ritual. Without another sêntaro to awaken others, no one else can take Zélie's place.

"Perhaps you just need the sunstone—"

"I tried that."

"And?"

"Nothing. It doesn't even feel warm."

I chew on my bottom lip, brows furrowed as I try to figure out something else. If the sunstone isn't helping her, I doubt the scroll will.

"Didn't this happen in Ibeji?" I ask. "After the arena battle? You said your magic felt blocked."

"Blocked, not gone. It felt stuck, but it was still there. Now I feel nothing."

Hopelessness builds inside me, making my legs go numb. *We should turn back.* We should wake one of Roën's men and redirect the ship.

But through it all Binta's face shines through, overpowering my fear, Father's wrath. I'm taken back to that fateful day a moon ago, standing in Kaea's quarters, holding the scroll. The odds were against us then. Reality told us we would fail. But again and again, we fought. We persevered. We rose.

"You can do it," I whisper, feeling it even more when I say it aloud. "The gods chose you. They don't make mistakes."

"Amari—"

"I've watched you do the impossible since the first day we met. You've taken on the world for the people you love. I know you can do the same to save the maji."

Zélie tries to look away, but I grab her face and force her to meet my eyes. If only she could see the person I see now, the champion prevailing inside.

"You're that sure?" she asks.

"I have never been more sure of anything in my life. Besides, just look at you—if you cannot do magic, no one can."

I hold up a mirror, showing Zélie the six thick plaits that fall to the small of her back. Her hair's grown so curly over the past moon I forgot its former length.

"I look strong. . . ." She fingers her braids.

I smile and put the mirror down. "You should look like the warrior you are when you bring magic back."

Zélie squeezes my hand, something sad still leaking through her grip. "Thank you, Amari. For everything."

I rest my forehead against hers, and we sit in a comfortable silence, translating our love through touch. *The Princess and the Warrior*, I decide in my head. When they tell the story of tomorrow, that is what they shall call it.

"Will you stay?" I pull back to look at Zélie's face. "I don't want to be alone."

"Of course." She smiles. "Something tells me I might actually fall asleep in this bed."

I roll over to make space and she climbs in, nestling under the panthenaire covers. I lean over to put out the torchlight, but Zélie grabs my wrist.

"You really think this will work?"

My smile falters for a moment, but I hide it.

"I think no matter what, we have to try."

CHAPTER SEVENTY-SEVEN

ZÉLIE

THE SKY LIGHTENS to pinks and tangerines as sunrise nears. Soft clouds move across the colors with ease, almost peaceful despite what today could bring. I'm eternally grateful for the navy's armor when I grab the helmet that obscures my face. I put it on and tuck in my braids as Roën approaches with his mischievous grin.

"I'm sorry we didn't get a chance to chat last night." A fake pout fills his face. "If this was about your hair, you should know I'm an excellent braider, too."

I narrow my eyes, hating that the uniform suits him. He wears the armor with confidence; if I didn't know better, I would think it was actually his.

"Nice to see a day of impending death hasn't dampened your spirits."

Roën's smile widens. "You look good," he whispers as he fastens his helmet. "Ready."

With a sharp whistle he rallies our crew and everyone huddles up. Amari and Tzain push their way to the front, followed by Kenyon and the four members of his team. Tzain gives me an encouraging nod. I force myself to nod back.

"I interrogated Saran's soldiers last night." Roën's voice rises above the sea wind. "They'll be stationed around the perimeter of the island

and within the temple itself. There's no way to avoid them when we dock, but if we don't draw attention to ourselves, we shouldn't arouse suspicion. They're expecting Zélie to storm in with a maji army, so as long as we're in their armor, we'll maintain the element of surprise."

"But what about when we get inside the temple?" Amari asks. "Father will order his soldiers to shoot at the first sign of a disturbance. Unless we divert their forces, they'll attack the moment they see us with the sacred artifacts."

"When we're near the temple, we'll stage a distant assault to divert their forces. That should free Zélie up for the ritual."

Roën turns to me and gestures, giving me the floor. I step back, but Amari pushes me forward; I stumble into the center of the crowd. I swallow hard and clasp my hands behind my back, desperate to sound strong.

"Just stick to the plan. As long as we don't call attention to ourselves, we should make it to the temple alright."

And that's when you'll see I can't do it. That the gods have abandoned me once again. That's when Saran's men will attack.

That's when we'll all die.

I swallow again, shaking away the doubts that make me want to run away. *This has to work. Sky Mother has to have a plan.* But the prodding eyes and anxious mutters tell me my words aren't enough. They want a rousing speech. But I need one myself.

"Gods . . . ," Tzain curses.

We whip around to the small fleet anchored around the island coordinates. As the sun peeks over the horizon, the island materializes before our eyes. At first it's transparent like a mirage out at sea. But as the sun rises, the island solidifies into a large mass of fog and lifeless trees.

A warmth spreads through my chest, strong like when Mama Agba cast magic again for the first time. In that moment I felt so much hope. After all these years, I stopped feeling so alone.

Magic is here. Alive. Closer than it's ever been. Even if I can't feel it now, I have to believe I will feel it again.

I entertain the thought, pretending magic swirls through my veins, stronger than ever before. It would blister today, burning as hot as my rage.

"I know you're scared." Everyone turns back to me. "I'm scared, too. But I know your reason for fighting is stronger than your fear, because it's led you here. Each of us has been wronged by the guards, by this monarchy that's sworn to protect us. Today we strike back for us all. Today we make them pay!"

The shouts of agreement ring through the air; even the mercenaries join in. Their cries bolster my spirits, unlocking the words trapped within. "They may have a thousand men in their army, but not one of them has the support of the gods. We have magic on our side, so stay strong, stay confident."

"And if everything goes to hell?" Roën asks when the cheers die down.

"Strike," I answer. "Fight with everything you've got."

CHAPTER SEVENTY-EIGHT

ZÉLIE

My throat dries as I watch an endless sea of soldiers patrol the perimeter of the island. It's like every soldier in Orïsha has come to stand guard.

Behind them a forest of blackened trees rises, shrouded in mist and twisting smoke. The energy surrounding the forest bends the air above it, a sign of the spiritual power hiding within its trees.

When the last of our disguised troop makes it off the rowboat, Roën leads us toward the temple. "Look alive," he says. "We need to move."

The moment we set foot on the eastern shoreline, I instantly feel the spiritual energy at work. Even without the hum of magic in my bones, it radiates from the ground, flows from the burnt trees. As Roën's eyes widen, I know he realizes it, too.

We walk among the gods.

A strange thrum fills me at the thought, not quite the rush of magic, but the surge of something greater. Walking through the island, I can almost feel Oya's breath in the way the air chills around us. If they're here, with me, then maybe I was right to trust them. Maybe we actually have a shot.

But to do that, we have to get past the guards.

My heart slams against my chest as we pass through the endless rows of patrolling soldiers. With each step I'm convinced they can see through our helmets, but wearing the seal of Orïsha shields us from their gaze. Roën leads with a convincing strut, wearing the commander's armor with ease. With his sandstone skin and confident gait, even real commanding officers step out of his way.

Almost there, I think, stiffening when a soldier eyes us a moment too long. Each step toward the forest stretches into a breathless eternity. Tzain carries the bone dagger, while Amari's grip tightens on the leather bag she uses to hide the sunstone and scroll; I keep my hand readied on my staff. But even when we pass the last of the perimeter troops, the soldiers barely spare us a glance. They keep their focus on the sea, waiting for a maji army that will never come.

"My gods," I breathe to myself when we make it past the soldiers' earshot. My fragile calm explodes into nerves. I force air into my lungs.

"We made it." Amari grips my arm, skin paling beneath her helmet. Our first battle is over.

Now another one begins.

A cold fog rolls in as we travel into the forest, mist licking the trees. By the time we've journeyed a few kilometers, the fog is so thick it blocks out the sun and makes it hard to see.

"Strange," Amari whispers into my ear, arms outstretched to avoid hitting a tree. "Do you think it is always like this?"

"I don't know." Something tells me the fog is a gift from the gods.

They're on our side. . . .

They want us to win.

I cling to the words of my speech, praying that they're true. The gods wouldn't abandon us now; they wouldn't fail me here. But as we near the temple, no warmth pulses through my veins. There'll be no hiding in the fog soon.

I'll be exposed for the world to see.

"How'd you know?" I whisper as the temple looms through the fog, thinking back to that fateful day in the market. "In Lagos, why'd you come to me?"

Amari turns, amber gaze bright through the white fog. "Because of Binta," she answers softly. "She had silver eyes. Just like yours."

With her words, something clicks—a sign of the greater hand. We've been led to this moment, pushed in the tiniest, most obscure ways. No matter how this day ends, we're doing what the gods intend. But what could be their purpose when no magic flows from my veins?

I open my mouth to respond but stop when the spiritual energy thickens. It weighs us down like gravity, pushing against every step.

"Do you feel that?" Tzain whispers.

"It's impossible not to."

"What's going on?" Roën calls back.

"It can only be—"

The temple . . .

No words can describe the sheer magnificence of the pyramid before us. It towers into the sky, each section carved from translucent gold. Like Chândomblé, intricate sênbaría decree the will of the gods. The symbols shine in the absence of light, but now that we're here, the real battle begins.

"Rehema," Roën orders. "Take your team to the edge of the southern shoreline. Raise hell on the beach and disappear into the fog. Follow Asha's lead to get away."

Rehema nods, pulling up her helmet until we can only see her light brown eyes. She bumps Roën's fist before leading two men and two women into the fog.

"What do we do?" I ask.

"We wait," Roën answers. "They should divert the army's attention, freeing up the temple."

Minutes stretch into hours, an eternity that drags like death. Each second that passes is another second my mind tumbles in guilt. What if they're captured? What if they die? I can't have any more people perish for this.

I can't have more blood stain my hands.

A black plume rises in the distance. Rehema's distraction. It pushes through the fog, reaching high into the sky. Within seconds, a sharp horn pierces through the air.

Guards stream out of the temple, taking off toward the southern shoreline. So many men race out that I quickly realize I can't fathom the temple's true size.

When the first flood of soldiers passes, Roën leads us in, pushing against the heavy air. We ascend the golden steps as fast as we can, not pausing until we reach the ground floor and enter the temple.

Vibrant jewels decorate every inch of the walls, exquisite in their design. Around us, Yemọja's breathtaking image dots the golden walls in topaz and blue sapphire; waves of shimmering diamonds flow from each fingertip in light. Above us, the bright emeralds of Ògún glow, paying homage to his power over the earth. Through the crystal ceilings, I glimpse each plane—all ten floors dedicated to the gods.

"You guys . . ." Amari nears a stairwell in the center of the floor traveling underground, and the sunstone glows in her hand.

This is it. . . . I clench my clammy fists.

This is where we're supposed to go.

"You ready?" Amari asks.

No. It's written all over my face. But with her nudge, I take the first step, leading us down the cold stairwell.

Traveling through the narrow space, I'm pulled back to our time in Chândomblé. Like that temple, torchlight illuminates the tapered path, glowing against the stone walls. It brings me back to when we still had a chance.

Back to when I still had magic.

I touch my hand to the walls, sending a silent prayer to the gods. *Please . . . if you can help me, I need it now.* I bide my time as we descend farther and farther; sweat drips down my back though the air cools to a chill. *Please, Sky Mother*, I pray again. *If you can fix this, fix it now.*

I wait for a glimpse of her silver eyes, for her electric touch through my bones. But as I begin to pray again, the magnificence of the ritual ground silences all words.

Eleven golden statues line the hallowed dome, each towering into the sky. They rise above us with devastating height, looming like the mountains of the Olasimbo Range. In the precious metal, the gods and goddesses are carved with exquisite detail; from the wrinkles in Sky Mother's skin to the individual coils of her hair, no line or curve is spared.

Each deity's gaze focuses on the ten-pointed star of stone gleaming below. Every point is marked by a sharp stone pillar, sênbaría carvings etched into all four of its sides.

In the center, a single gold column is raised. Atop it, a circle is carved out. Round and smooth—the exact shape of the sunstone.

"My gods," Kenyon breathes as we step into the stale air.

"My gods" is right.

It's like walking into the heavens.

With each stride, I feel mighty under the gods' watch, protected under their ethereal gaze.

"You can do this." Amari hands me the parchment and the sunstone. She takes the bone dagger from Tzain and slips it into the waist of my uniform.

I nod and take the two sacred objects. *You can do this*, I repeat. *Just try.*

I step forward, prepared to bring this journey to an end. But then a figure moves in the distance.

"Ambush!" I cry out.

I flick open my staff as hidden men emerge. They move like shadows, crawling out from behind every statue, every pillar. In the frenzy we all bare our blades, eyes darting to find the next attack. But when the blurs settle, I see Saran, a smirk of satisfaction on his face. Then I see Inan, face pained, majacite blade in his hand.

The sight rips straight through me; a betrayal colder than ice. He promised.

He swore he wouldn't get in my way.

But before I can truly break, I see the worst of it. A sight so alarming, it doesn't even seem real.

My heart stops as they bring him forward.

"Baba?"

CHAPTER SEVENTY-NINE

ZÉLIE

He's supposed to be safe.

This one thought keeps me from accepting the truth. I scan the guards for Mama Agba's wrinkled form, waiting for her attack. If Baba's with the guards, where is she? What did they do to her? After everything, she can't be dead. Baba can't be standing here.

Yet he trembles under Inan's grip . . . ripped clothes, gagged, bloodied face. They've beaten him for my mistakes. And now they'll take him.

Just like they took Mama.

Inan's amber eyes trap me in the truth of his betrayal, but it isn't the gaze I know. He's a stranger. A soldier. The shell of the little prince.

"I assume the situation speaks for itself, but since your people are daft, I'll break it down. Relinquish the artifacts, and you can take your father back."

Just the sound of Saran's voice closes the metal chains against my wrists—

I wouldn't be doing my job as king if I didn't remind you what you are.

He stands clothed in rich purple robes, defiance in his snarl. But even he looks small against the statues of gods staring him down.

"We can take 'em," Kenyon whispers from behind. "We have our magic. They only have guards."

"We can't risk it." Tzain's voice cracks.

Baba gives the slightest shake of his head. He doesn't want to be saved.

No.

I step forward but Kenyon grips my arm, whipping me around. "You can't surrender!"

"Let me go—"

"Think of someone other than yourself! Without the ritual all the divîners will die—"

"We're already dead!" I shriek. My voice echoes against the dome, revealing the truth I wish I could change. *Gods, please!* I plead one last time, but nothing happens.

They've abandoned me once again.

"My magic's gone. I thought it would come back, but it hasn't. . . ." My voice shrivels and I stare at the floor, biting back the shame. The anger. The pain. How dare the gods force themselves back into my life only to break me this way.

Against everything, I try once more, searching for any remnant of ashê that might remain. But they've discarded me.

I won't let them take anything else away.

"I'm sorry." The words are hollow, but they're all I have. "But if I can't do the ritual, I'm not going to lose my father."

Kenyon unhands me. Hatred doesn't begin to describe the looks I receive from the gathered men. Only Amari's eyes are sympathetic; even Roën looks taken aback.

I step forward, clutching the sunstone and scroll to my chest. The bone dagger presses into my skin, almost cutting with every step. I'm halfway across the floor when Kenyon yells, "We saved you!" His screams bounce against the walls. "People died for this! People died for *you*!"

His words dig into my soul, into everyone I've left behind. Bisi. Lekan. Zulaikha. Maybe even Mama Agba.

All dead.

Because they dared to believe in me.

They dared to think we could win.

As I approach Inan, Baba's shaking grows frantic. I can't let him break my resolve. *I don't want them to win, Baba.*

But I can't let you die.

I clench the stone and scroll as Inan moves forward, gently guiding Baba ahead. The apology is stark in his amber eyes. Eyes I'll never trust again.

Why? I itch to scream, but it withers in my throat. With each step, the echo of his kiss presses against my lips and travels down my neck. I stare at his hands on Baba's shoulders, hands I should've crushed. I swore I'd die before I let a guard have his way with me, yet I gave their captain free rein?

I know we're meant to work together. We're meant to be together.

His pretty lies play in my ear, each new one drawing more tears.

We'd be unstoppable. A team Orïsha has never seen.

Without him, Ilorin would still stand. Lekan would be alive. I would be here saving my people, not sealing their fate.

As my tears burn, my insides rip raw. It's worse than the searing of Saran's knife. Despite everything, I let him in.

I let him win.

Baba shakes his head one last time, my last chance to run away. But it's over now. It ended before it even began.

I pull Baba out of Inan's grip, dropping the parchment and stone on the floor. I almost reach for the bone dagger, but then I remember Inan has never seen it. I toss out Tzain's rusted knife instead, keeping the true bone dagger hidden in my waistband. I can hold on to this one thing. This one artifact now that he's taken everything else from me.

"Zélie—"

Before Inan can mutter another treacherous word, I take off Baba's gag and walk away. As my footsteps echo against the ritual ground, I focus on the statues instead of the hateful glares.

"Why?" Baba sighs. His voice is weak but rough. "Why when you were so close?"

"I was never close." I choke down a sob. "Never. Not even once."

You tried, I console myself. *You did more than your best.*

It wasn't meant to be. The gods chose wrong.

At least it's over. At least you're alive. You can leave on that boat, find a new—

"No!"

I freeze as Inan's cries ring against the dome walls in a deafening timbre. Baba throws me to the ground as a *swoosh!* flies through the air.

I move to shield Baba, but it's too late.

The arrowhead pierces my father's chest.

His blood leaks onto the ground.

CHAPTER EIGHTY

ZÉLIE

When they came for Mama, I couldn't breathe. I didn't think I would ever breathe again. I thought our lives were connected by a string. That if she died, I would, too.

I hid like a coward as they bludgeoned Baba half to death, relying on Tzain to be my strength. But when they wrapped the chain around Mama's neck, something in me snapped. As frightened as the guards made me, nothing compared to the terror of them taking Mama away.

I chased her through the chaos of Ibadan, blood and dirt splattering against my small knees. I followed her as far as I could until I saw it.

All of it.

She hung from a tree like an ornament of death in the center of our mountain village. Her and every other maji, every threat to the monarchy crushed.

That day I swore I'd never feel that way again; I promised they'd never take another member of my family. But as I lie paralyzed now, blood drips down Baba's lips. I promised.

And now I'm too late.

"Baba?"

Nothing.

Not even a blink.

His dark brown eyes are empty. Broken. Hollow.

"Baba," I whisper again. *"Baba!"*

As his blood spreads onto my fingers, the world goes black and my body grows warm. In the darkness I see everything—I see him.

He runs through the streets of Calabrar, kicking an agbön ball through the mud with his younger brother. The child in him has a smile Baba never had, a grin ignorant of the world's pain. With a hearty kick, the ball bounces away and Mama's young face appears. She's stunning. Radiant. She takes his breath away.

Her face fades to the magic of their first kiss, the awe of their first-born son. The awe blurs as he rocks his baby daughter to sleep, running his hands over my white hair.

In his blood, I feel the moment he woke after the Raid, the heart-break that never ceased.

In his blood, I feel everything.

In his blood, I feel him.

Baba's spirit tears through my being like the earth ripping in half. Every sound rings louder, every color shines brighter. His soul digs deeper into me than any magic I've ever felt, deeper than magic at all. It's not incantations that run through my veins.

It's his blood.

It's him.

The ultimate sacrifice.

The greatest blood magic I could wield.

"Kill her!"

The first two guards charge at me, swords pointed and raised. They run with a vengeance.

The last mistake they will ever make.

As they near, Baba's spirit tears from my body as two sharp, twisting shadows. The darkness wields the power of death, commands the power of blood. They pierce through the soldiers' breastplates, skewering them like meat. Blood splatters into the air as dark matter spills from the holes in their chests.

The men choke on their last breaths, eyes bulging in defeat. They wheeze as their bodies crumble into ash.

More.

More death. More blood.

The blackest part of my rage finally has the power it's always craved, the chance to avenge Mama. Now Baba. I'll take these shadows of death and end them.

Each and every one.

No. Baba's voice rings in my head, steady and strong. *Revenge is meaningless. There's still time to make this right.*

"How?"

I peer through the frenzy as Roën's crew and Kenyon's team lunge into battle. *Revenge is meaningless*, I repeat to myself. *Revenge is meaningless. . . .*

As the words settle, I see it, the one person running away from the fight. Inan scrambles for the rolling sunstone through the madness, dodging the blades of Roën's men.

As long as we don't have magic, they will never treat us with respect, Baba's spirit booms. *They need to know we can hit them back. If they burn our homes—*

I burn theirs, too.

CHAPTER EIGHTY-ONE

INAN

THE GIRL I HELD in my sleep is nowhere to be seen.

In her place a monster rages.

It bares fangs of death.

Two black shadows shoot from Zélie's hands and hurtle forward like venomous snakes, hungry for blood. Vengeance. They pierce through the first two guards. Then something in Zélie's silver eyes clicks.

Her gaze homes in on me. The sunstone glows in my hand. I barely have time to draw my sword before the first shadow attacks.

Pointed like a saber, it clashes against my sword, recoiling through the air. The next attack comes in fast. Too fast for me to block—

"Prince Inan!"

A guard lunges forward. He trades his life for mine. The shadow pierces through his body—he wheezes before turning to ash.

Skies!

I retreat into the insanity. Her shadows rear back for another attack. As I run, she chases after me. Her sea-salt soul rages like an ocean storm.

Even with the sunstone's surge, I can't stop her. No one can. I'm dead.

I died the moment her father hit the ground.

Skies. I fight my own tears back. Zélie's heartbreak still throbs in my core. A sorrow so strong it could shake the earth. He was supposed to live. She was supposed to be saved. I was going to keep my promises to her. I was going to make Orïsha a better place—

Focus, Inan. I force out a deep, long breath and count to ten. I can't give up. Magic is still a threat. One only I can end.

I race across the dome to Orí's statue. The outcomes run through my mind. If Zél performs the ritual, she'll wipe us out. And then all of Orïsha will burn. I can't let that happen. No matter what, my plan remains the same: take the stone; take the scroll.

Take magic away.

I hurl the sunstone toward the ground with all my might. *For skies' sake, please shatter.* But it rolls away untouched. If anything's to be destroyed, it has to be the scroll.

I tear it from my pocket and dart into the frenzy. Zélie dashes after the stone. With the few seconds of life I have left, the gears in my head turn. Father's old words ring. *The scroll can only be destroyed with magic.*

Magic . . .

What about my magic?

I focus the energy of my mind onto the parchment, losing track of Zélie in the turmoil. A turquoise glow wraps around the weathered scroll. The scent of sage and spearmint fills my nose as a strange memory takes hold of my mind.

The hysteria of the temple fades out. A sêntaro's consciousness flashes in: generations of women with elaborate white ink tattooed into their skin. All chant in a language I cannot comprehend.

The memory only lasts an instant, but the attempt is no good. My magic won't do it.

The scroll remains unharmed.

"Help!"

I spin as shouts ring; Zélie's shadows skewer more men. Dark matter consumes their bodies as they're bucked from the black arrowheads.

Before they crash into the ground, the soldiers disintegrate into ash. In that instant everything clicks—the answer hidden in plain sight.

Perhaps if I was a Burner, my flames could incinerate the parchment, but my Connector magic is of no use. The scroll has no mind for me to control, no body for my magic to paralyze. My magic can't eliminate the scroll.

But Zélie's magic can.

I've never seen her powers wielded this way. Her magic destroys everything in its path, vicious and twisting, howling as it tears through the sacred temple like a tornado. Its black arrowheads strike with the vengeance of spears, impaling armor, ripping straight through flesh. Anyone unfortunate enough to encounter them crumbles into ash.

If I do this right, the scroll shall crumble, too.

I take a deep breath. One that'll probably be my last. Zélie's fatal arrowheads shoot through the guts of four soldiers, leaving ruptures through their cores. Their bodies crumble into nothing but dust as they fall to the ground.

As Zélie rips through more soldiers, I run forward.

"This is all your fault!" I yell.

Zélie skids to a halt. I don't think I will ever hate myself more than I do now. But I need to draw this pain out of her. It can't be about us.

It never could.

"Your father didn't have to die!" I shout. It's a line that shouldn't be crossed. But I have to unlock her fury. I need a lethal blow.

"Don't speak of him!" Her eyes flash. All grief and hate and rage. Her anguish fills me with shame. Yet, I press on.

"You didn't have to come here. I would've taken him back to Lagos!"

Shadows spin around her like a sharp wind sweeping into a tornado.

She's close now.

My life is nearing its end.

"If you trusted me, worked *with* me, he'd still be alive. Him." I swallow. "Mama Agba—"

The shadows charge me with a speed that takes my breath away. It's all I can do to hold the scroll before my chest. In that instant, she realizes her mistake—the trap I've baited her into.

She screams and jerks her hand back, but it's too late.

The shadows rip through the parchment as they arc.

"No!" Zélie's shrieks reverberate through the hallowed dome. The ash of the destroyed parchment falls through the air. The shadows wither and fade, disappearing as particles leak through her hands.

You did it. . . .

The fact doesn't sink in. It's over. I won.

Orïsha is finally safe.

Magic will die for good.

"Son!"

Father runs to me from the outskirts of the battle. A smile like I've never seen beams on his face. I try to smile back, but a guard closes in behind him. He raises his sword, targeting Father's back. *A mutiny?*

No.

One of the mercenaries.

"Father!" I shout. My warning won't reach him in time.

Without thinking, I draw on the surge of power left from the sunstone's touch. Blue energy flies from my hands.

Like in Chândomblé, my magic pierces through the mercenary's head, paralyzing him in place. I freeze him long enough for a guard to cut through his heart. It saves Father from the attack.

But the sight of my magic turns Father to stone.

"It's not what you think—" I start.

Father jerks back, recoiling like I'm a monster he can't trust. His lips curl back in disgust. Everything in me shrivels.

"It doesn't matter." I speak so quickly it all blurs together. "I was infected, but it's going away. I did it. I killed magic."

Father kicks the mercenary over with his feet. He claws at the turquoise crystals left in the assailant's hair. He stares down at his hands, and his face twists. I can see him putting the pieces together. These are the same crystals he held in the fortress.

The same crystals they plucked from Kaea's corpse.

Father's eyes flash. He grips the hilt of his sword.

"Wait—"

His blade rips into me.

Father's eyes pound red with rage. My hands clutch at the sword, but I'm too weak to pull it out.

"Father, I'm sorry—"

He pulls out his sword with a mangled scream. I drop to my knees, clutching the gushing wound.

Warm blood spills from the cracks between my fingers.

Father brings his sword up again, this time for the final blow. There's no love in his eyes. No hint of the pride that flashed just moments ago.

The same fear and hatred that burned in Kaea's final gaze stains Father's now. I'm a stranger to him. *No.* I've given up everything to be his son.

"Father, please," I wheeze. I beg for his forgiveness as I pant. My vision blacks out—for a moment, all of Zélie's pain leaks in. The destroyed fate of the maji. The death of her father. Her heartache mixes with my own; a sickening reminder of everything I've lost.

I've sacrificed too much for it to end this way. All the pain I caused in his name.

I reach out to him with a shaking hand. A hand covered in my own blood. It can't be for nothing.

It can't end like this.

Before I touch him, Father crushes my hand under the heel of his metal boot. His dark eyes narrow.

"You are no son of mine."

CHAPTER EIGHTY-TWO

AMARI

THOUGH A DOZEN MEN barrel forward, they are no match for the vengeance of my blade. By my side, Tzain tears through the guards with his ax, fighting though tears stream down his face. It is through his pain I fight, through his, through Binta's, through every poor soul ended by Father's life. All this blood and death—an endless stain on every breath.

I rip through the guards with my blade, striking first with a debilitating attack.

A guard tumbles when I slice through a tendon.

Another falls as I slash at his thigh.

Fight, Amari. I spur myself onward, forcing myself to see past the Orïshan seals that adorn their armor, past the faces that fall from my sword. These soldiers are sworn to protect Orïsha and its crown, yet they betray their sacred vow. They come for my head.

One swings a sword at me. I duck and it plunges into his fellow soldier instead. I prepare to strike the next when—

"No!"

Zélie's cries from across the temple force me to pivot just as my blade pierces another soldier. She falls on her knees, shaking, ash spilling between her fingers. I run to help her but skid to a halt as Father raises his sword and plunges it into the stomach of one of his own soldiers. As the boy falls to his knees, his helmet slips off. Not a soldier.

Inan.

Everything inside me runs cold as blood spills from my brother's lips.

It is a sword through my own gut. It is *my* blood that spills. The brother who carried me through the palace halls on his shoulders. The brother who snuck me honey cakes from the kitchen when Mother took my dessert away.

The brother Father forced me to fight.

The brother who cut me in the back.

It can't be. I blink, waiting for the image to correct itself. *Not him . . .*

Not the child who gave up everything to be everything Father wanted.

But as I watch, Father raises his sword again, prepared to remove Inan's head. He's taking him away.

Just like he took Binta.

"Father, please," Inan cries, reaching out with his dying breath.

But Father steps on his hand and crushes it. "You are no son of mine."

"Father!"

My voice does not sound like my own as I dash forward. When Father spots me, his rage explodes.

"The gods have cursed me with you children," he spits. "Traitors who stink of my blood."

"Your blood is the true curse," I snap back. "It ends today."

CHAPTER EIGHTY-THREE

AMARI

FATHER'S FIRST CHILDREN were loved, but they were frail and weak. When Inan and I were born, Father would not allow us to be the same.

For years he forced Inan and me to trade blows and bruises under his watchful eye, never relenting, no matter how hard we cried. Every battle was a chance to correct his mistakes, to bring his first family back to life. If we got strong enough, no sword could take us down, no maji could burn our flesh. We fought for his approval, stuck in a battle for his love neither of us would ever win.

We raised our swords against each other because neither of us had the courage to raise one against him.

Now, as I lift my blade to his rage-fueled eyes, I see Mother and Tzain. I see my dear Binta. I find everyone who ever tried to fight back, every innocent soul cut down by his blade.

"You raised me to fight monsters," I mutter, stepping forward with my sword. "It took far too long to understand that the real monster was you."

I lunge forward and catch him by surprise. I cannot hold back with him; if I do, I know how this battle ends.

Though he raises his sword to parry, I overpower him, slicing dangerously close to his neck. He arches, but I rush him again. *Strike, Amari. Fight!*

I swing my sword in a swift arc, cutting into his thigh. He stumbles back in pain, unprepared for a lethal blow from my sword. I am not the little girl he knows. I am a princess. A queen.

I am the Lionaire.

I push forward, blocking one of Father's jabs at my heart. His strikes are merciless now that he's no longer caught off guard by my attacks.

The clinks and clashes of our blades ring above the madness as more guards filter down the stairs. Having slain the men on the ritual ground, Roën's men fend off the new wave. But as they fight, Tzain runs toward me from across the room, only moments away.

"Amari—"

"Go!" I urge him, striking back against Father's blade. Tzain cannot help me here, not in the fight I have trained for all my life. It is only the king and me now. Only one of us shall live.

Father trips. This is my moment, a chance to end our endless dance.

Do it now!

Blood pounds against my ears as I lunge forward, raising my blade. I can rid Orïsha of its greatest monster. Abolish the source of its pain.

But at the last moment, I hesitate, angling my blade up. Our swords collide head-on.

Curse the skies.

I cannot end it like this. If I do that, I'm no better than him.

Orïsha will not survive by employing his tactics. Father must be taken down, but it is too much to drive my sword through his heart—

Father pulls back his blade. Momentum carries me forward.

Before I can pivot, Father swings his sword around and the blade rips across my back.

"Amari!"

Tzain's scream sounds distant as I stumble into a sacred pillar. My skin burns red-hot, searing with the same agony Inan inflicted upon me as a child.

Veins bulge from Father's neck as he charges forward, no hesitation as he angles for a killing blow.

He does not cringe at the thought of slaughtering his own daughter, his own flesh and blood. He's made his decision.

Now it's time for mine.

I whip out of harm's way as his sword strikes the pillar, chipping into the stone. Before he can rally, I plunge my sword forward without hesitation.

Father's eyes bulge.

Hot blood leaks from his heart onto my hands. He wheezes, crimson spurting from his lips as the rest spills across the stone.

Though my hand shakes, I plunge the blade in deeper. Tears blur my vision.

"Do not worry," I whisper as he takes his last breath. "I will make a far better queen."

CHAPTER EIGHTY-FOUR

ZÉLIE

"Come on." I channel all my energy into the dust of the destroyed parchment. This can't be happening. Not when we're this close.

Baba's energy surges into my arms, bursting through my fingertips as twisting shadows. But no parchment rises from the ashes. It's over. . . .

We lost.

The horror hits so hard I can hardly breathe.

The one thing we need, destroyed by my hand.

"No, no, no, no!" I close my eyes and try to remember the incantation. I read that scroll dozens of times. How did that damn ritual start?

Ìya awọ̀n ọ̀run, àwa ọmọ képè ọ́ lọ́nì—No. I shake my head, combing through fragments of remembered words. It was *àwa ọmọ́ ò* ***re*** *képè ọ̀ lọni. And then . . .*

Oh gods.

What came next?

A sharp clap rings through the dome, rumbling like thunder. As it pounds, the entire temple shakes. Everyone freezes as stone and dust rain from the ceiling.

Yemọja's statue begins to glow, blinding in its shine. The light starts at her bare feet, travels up the curves and folds of her carved robes. When it reaches her eyes, her golden sockets glow bright blue, bathing the dome in its soft color.

Ògún's statue shimmers to life next, eyes glowing in dark greens; Sàngó's comes in fiery reds; Ochumare's in bright yellows.

"A chain . . . ," I breathe, following the path to Sky Mother. "Oh my gods . . ."

The solstice.

It's happening now!

I paw at the ashes, looking for anything. Everything. The ancient ritual was painted on this scroll. Shouldn't the spirits of the sêntaros who painted it be here as well?

But as I wait for the chill of the dead to overcome me, I realize the number of corpses there are strung across the dome. I didn't feel their deaths pass through me, I didn't feel anything at all.

All I felt was Baba.

The magic in my blood.

"A connection . . ." The realization hits me like ice. A connection I share with him because of blood. The scroll's incantation was supposed to tether us to Sky Mother through magic, but what if there was another way to reach her instead?

My mind spins, trying to calculate the possibilities. Could I draw on the connection with my ancestors through our blood? Could we reach back, forging a new connection to Sky Mother and her gifts through our spirits?

Amari dives past, fending a soldier away from the ritual ground. Though blood drips from her back, her blows are ferocious, almost feral against the coming guards. And even as the entire army pours in, Roën and his men don't relent.

They fight against all odds.

If they haven't given up, neither can I.

My heart slams against my chest as I scramble to my feet. The next statue illuminates, bathing the dome in blue light. Only a few dark gods stand in Sky Mother's way. The end of the solstice is near.

I grab the fallen sunstone, and it scalds under my touch. Instead of Sky Mother, I see blood. I see bone.

I see Mama.

It's that image I hold on to as I drop the sunstone in the single golden column in the center of the dome. If her blood surges through my veins, why not the blood of other ancestors, too?

I whip out the true bone dagger from the waistline of my pants and slice through both my palms. With bleeding hands, I press onto the sunstone, releasing the binding blood for the ultimate sacrifice.

"*Help!*" I scream out loud, drawing on their strength. "*Please! Lend me your hand!*"

Like an erupting volcano, the power of my ancestors flows through me, maji and kosidán alike. Each grips onto our connection, onto the very heart of our blood. Their spirits twirl with mine, with Mama's, with Baba's. We pour ourselves forward, our souls fighting into the stone.

"More!" I scream to them, calling on all spirits linked by our blood. I dig through our lineage, clawing all the way back to those who first received Sky Mother's gifts. As each new ancestor surges forward, my body screams. My skin tears like it's being pulled apart. But I need it.

I need them.

Their voices begin to ring, a chorus of the living dead. I wait to hear the words inked onto the destroyed scroll, but they chant an incantation I've never read. Their strange words echo through my head, through my heart, through my soul. They fight their way onto my lips, though I don't know what the incantation will do.

"Àwa ni ọmọ rẹ nínú ẹ̀jẹ̀ àti egungun!"

Spiritual pathways explode within me. I fight through my screams to get the words out as the sunstone buzzes beneath my hands. The light travels up Sky Mother's chest, over the hand holding her horn. It's almost over.

The solstice is almost at an end.

"A ti dé! Ìkan ni wá! Dà wá pọ̀ Mama! Kí ìtànná wa tàn pẹ̀lú ẹ̀bùn àìníye rẹ lẹ́ẹ̀kan síi!"

My throat closes up, making it hard to breathe, let alone speak. But I force myself to continue, channeling everything I have left.

"*Jẹ́ kí agbára idán wa tàn kárí*," I shout as the light zips up Sky Mother's collarbone.

The voices sing so loud in my mind that the whole world must be able to hear. They push for the last of the incantation, desperate as the glow crosses the bridge of Sky Mother's nose. With their blood, I can finish this.

With their blood, I am unstoppable.

"Tan ìmọ́lẹ̀ ayé lẹ́ẹ̀kan sii!"

The light reaches Sky Mother's eyes and bursts with a white glow as the last of my incantation rings. The sunstone shatters in my hands. Its yellow light explodes through the room. I can't tell what's happening. I don't know what I've done. But as the light invades every fiber of my being, the whole world shines.

Creation swirls before my eyes, the birth of man, the origin of the gods. Their magic crashes into the room in waves, a rainbow of every vibrant hue.

Magic shatters through every heart, every soul, every being. It connects us all, threading through the shell of humanity.

The power sears into my skin. Its ecstasy and agony flow at once, indistinguishable from pleasure and pain.

As it fades, I see the truth—in plain sight, yet hidden all along.

We are all children of blood and bone.

All instruments of vengeance and virtue.

This truth holds me close, rocking me like a child in a mother's arms. It binds me in its love as death swallows me into its grasp.

CHAPTER EIGHTY-FIVE

ZÉLIE

I ALWAYS PICTURED DEATH as a winter wind, but heat surrounds me like the oceans of Ilorin.

A gift, I think into the peace and darkness of alâfia. Payment for my sacrifice.

What other reward could there be but an end to an endless fight?

"Mama, Òrìsà Mama, Òrìsà Mama, àwá ún dúpẹ̀ pé egbọ́ igbe wa—"

Voices hum through my skin as the rich sound rings through the blackness. Silver shrouds of light swirl into the darkness, bathing me in their beautiful notes. As the song continues, a snowflake of light falls through the darkness with a voice that sings louder than the others. It leads them in worship and praise, ringing through the shrouds.

"Mama, Mama, Mama—"

The light's voice is smooth like silk, soft like velvet. It wraps itself around my form, drawing me to its warmth. And though I can't feel my body, I float through the blackness toward it.

I've heard this sound before.

I know this voice. This love.

The song grows louder and louder, fueling the light. It evolves from a snowflake, taking shape before my eyes.

Her feet emerge first, skin black as the night sky. It's radiant against her red silk robes, rich and flowing on her unearthly form. Gold jewelry drips from her wrists, her ankles, her neck; all highlight the shimmering headdress hanging from her forehead.

I bow as the chorus rings, unable to believe I lie at Oya's feet. But when the goddess lifts the headdress embedded in her thick mane of white hair, her dark brown eyes make my heart stop.

The last time I saw these eyes they were empty, void of the woman I loved. Now they dance, shimmering tears falling from their lids.

"Mama?"

It can't be.

Though my mother wore the face of the sun, she was human. She was a part of me.

But when this spirit touches my face, the familiar love spreads through my body. Tears fall from her beautiful brown eyes as she whispers, "Hello, my little Zél."

Hot tears sting my eyes as I collapse into her spiritual embrace. Her warmth soaks into my being, making every crack whole. I feel all the tears I've cried, every prayer I've ever sent. I see every time I looked up in our ahéré and wished she sat there, looking back.

"I thought you were gone," I croak.

"You are a sister of Oya, my love. You know our spirits never die." She pulls me back and wipes my tears with her soft robes. "I have always been with you, always by your side."

I clutch at her, as if at any moment her spirit might slip through my fingers. If I'd known she waited for me in death, I would have embraced it, run toward it. With her is everything I ever wanted, the peace she took with her when she died. With her, I'm finally safe.

After all this time, I'm home.

She runs her hands over my braids before kissing my forehead. "You will never know how proud we are of everything you've done."

"We?"

She smiles. "Baba's here now."

"He's okay?" I ask.

"Yes, my love. He's at peace."

I can't blink away the new tears fast enough. I know few men who deserve peace more. Did he know his spirit would end in this grace, beside the woman he loved?

"Mama, Mama, Mama—"

The voices sing louder. Mama holds me again and I breathe in her scent. After all this time, she still smells of warm spices and sauces, the mixtures she brewed in her jollof rice.

"What you did in the temple is unlike anything the spirits have ever seen."

"I didn't recognize the incantation." I shake my head. "I don't know what I did."

Mama takes my face in her hands and kisses my forehead. "You will learn soon, my mighty Zél. And through it all, I will never leave your side. No matter what you feel, what you face when you think you're alone—"

"Tzain . . . ," I realize. First Mama, then Baba, now me? "We can't leave him," I gasp. "How do we bring him here?"

"Mama, Òrìsà Mama, Òrìsà Mama—"

Mama's grip on me tightens as the voices grow louder, almost deafening now. Creases wrinkle across her smooth forehead.

"He doesn't belong here, my love. Not yet."

"But Mama—"

"Neither do you."

The singing voices blare so loudly I can't tell if they're praises or screams. My insides twist as Mama's words hit.

"Mama, no . . . please!"

"Zél—"

I cling to her again, fear choking my throat. "I want this. I want to stay here with you and Baba!"

I can't go back to that world. I won't survive that pain.

"Zél, Orïsha still needs you."

"I don't care. I need *you*!"

Her words grow hurried as her light begins to fade with the chorus of heavenly voices. All around us the blackness brightens, drowning in a wave of light.

"Mama, don't leave me—Please, Mama! Not again!"

Her dark eyes sparkle as tears fall, their warmth landing on my face.

"It's not over, little Zél. It's only just begun."

EPILOGUE

When I open my eyes, I want them to close. I want to see my mother. I want to be wrapped in the warm blackness of death, not gazing at the purple hues staining the open sky.

The air above me seems to sway back and forth, gently rocking my form. It's a glide I'd know anywhere. The ebb and flow of the sea.

As realization takes hold, burns and aches sear into every cell of my body. The pain is stark. The pain that accompanies life.

A moan escapes my lips and footsteps pound.

"She's alive!"

In an instant, faces crowd my sight: Amari's hope, Tzain's relief. When they pull away, Roën and his smirk remain.

"Kenyon?" I manage to speak. "Käto? Rehema—"

"They're alive," Roën assures me. "They're waiting on the ship."

With his help, I sit up against the cold wood of the rowboat we used to dock on the sacred island. The sun dips below the horizon, masking us in the shadow of night.

A flash of the sacred temple surges through my mind, and I brace myself for the question I'm too terrified to ask. I lock onto Tzain's dark brown eyes; failure will sting the least from his lips.

"Did we do it? Is magic back?"

He stills. His silence sinks my heart in my chest. After all that. After Inan. After Baba.

"It didn't work?" I force out, but Amari shakes her head. She holds up a bleeding hand, and in the darkness it swirls with vibrant blue light. A white streak crackles like lightning in her black hair.

For a moment, I don't know what to make of the sight.

Then my blood chills to ice.

AUTHOR'S NOTE

I SHED MANY TEARS before I wrote this book. Many tears as I revised it. And even as it sits in your hands now, I know that I will shed tears again.

Although riding giant lionaires and performing sacred rituals might be in the realm of fantasy, all the pain, fear, sorrow, and loss in this book is real.

Children of Blood and Bone was written during a time where I kept turning on the news and seeing stories of unarmed black men, women, and children being shot by the police. I felt afraid and angry and helpless, but this book was the one thing that made me feel like I could do something about it.

I told myself that if just one person could read it and have their hearts or minds changed, then I would've done something meaningful against a problem that often feels so much bigger than myself.

Now this book exists and *you* are reading it.

From the bottom of my heart, thank you.

But if this story affected you in any way, all I ask is that you don't let it stop within the pages of this text.

If you cried for Zulaikha and Salim, cry for innocent children like Jordan Edwards, Tamir Rice, and Aiyana Stanley-Jones. They were fifteen, twelve, and seven when they were shot and killed by police.[1]

If your heart broke for Zélie's grief over the death of her mother, then let it break for all the survivors of police brutality who've had to witness their loved ones taken firsthand. Survivors like Diamond Reynolds and her four-year-old daughter, who were in the car when Philando Castile was pulled over, shot, and killed.[2]

Jeronimo Yanez, the officer who killed him, was acquitted of all charges.[3]

These are just a few tragic names in a long list of black lives taken too soon. Mothers ripped from daughters, fathers ripped from sons, and parents who will live the rest of their lives with a grief no parent should have to know.

This is just one of the many problems plaguing our world and there are so many days when these problems still feel bigger than us, but let this book be proof to you that we can always do *something* to fight back.

As Zélie says in the ritual, "*Abogbo wa ni ọmọ rẹ̀ẹ̀ nínú ẹ̀jẹ̀ àti egungun.*"

We are all children of blood and bone.

And just like Zélie and Amari, we have the power to change the evils in the world.

We've been knocked down for far too long.

Now let's rise.

---

1 VELEZ, ASHLEY. "I Made It to 21. Mike Brown Didn't." *The Root*, 2017.

2 PARK, MADISON. "After Cop Shot Castile, 4-Year-Old Worried Her Mom Would Be Next." *CNN*, 2017.

3 SMITH, MITCH. "Minnesota Officer Acquitted in Killing of Philando Castile." *The New York Times*, 2017.

ACKNOWLEDGMENTS

I'VE BEEN BLESSED to know and work with some of the best human beings the world has to offer and I believe that's only possible because God put them in my life. Thank you, God, for everything You've done and all that You've blessed me with.

Mom and Dad, thank you for sacrificing everything you knew and loved to give us all the opportunities in the world. I'm forever grateful for your support when I embarked on this dream. Dad, you taught me to never settle and always pushed me to do my best. I love you and I know Grandma's watching over us every day. Mom, I think my characters lose their moms young because you did and that's always been my worst fear. Thank you for loving and supporting me in so many ways I can't even list them all. Also thank you to the aunties and uncles who helped with the Yoruba translations!

Tobi Lou, if you hadn't been so incredible when we were growing up, my spiteful childhood self wouldn't have been motivated to be the best I could be. Thank you for pursuing your dreams so relentlessly that I knew it was possible for me to do the same. Toni, you were my mortal enemy for the first fifteen years of your existence and you were so mean to me on 11/25/17. (I told you you'd be sorry!) *Nevertheless*, I love you dearly, I'm proud of you, and I know you'll be the most famous Adeyemi.

Jackson, my bae and my beta reader. You've believed in me and my book from *before* the beginning. Thank you for being my number one fan and supporter, and for pushing me when I was too scared to believe in myself. Marc, Deb, and Clay, *thank* you for accepting me into your family with open arms and grilled cheeses. I love you all, and Clay, I'm proud to call you my little bro.

DJ Michelle "Meesh" Estrella, you are an incredible person and an incredible artist. Thank you for the beautiful symbols in this book!

Brenda Drake, thank you for making such a selfless sacrifice to help so many writers achieve our dreams. Ashley Hearn, you poured your heart and your brilliant mind into this manuscript and you helped me tell the story I wanted to tell the entire time. I love you and I'm so lucky to have been mentored by you!

Hillary Jacobson and Alexandra Machinist, you both defy the term "dream agents" because you're above and beyond anything I could've ever dreamed. You're brilliant and fierce and I'm so blessed to work with you. Thank you for making the impossible possible.

To Josie Freedman, the most epic film agent ever, thank you for taking me from dreaming of working on *a* movie to talking with some of the coolest people in Hollywood about *my* movie. Hana Murrell, Alice Dill, Mairi Friesen-Escandell, and Roxane Edouard, thank you for making my story global. It literally means the world.

Jon Yaged and Jean Feiwel, *thank* you for believing in me and this series in a way that's never been done before. You've made Macmillan such a wonderful home, and I'm blessed to publish this book with you guys.

DEAREST CHRISTIAN TRIMMER! You're my Mama Agba: the badass, magical, impeccably dressed elder who gives me tea, a metal staff, and sage wisdom when I need it the most. Thank you for being an incredible champion for me and this book!

DEAREST QUEEN EMPRESS TIFFANY LIAO! You are my Amari. You got down and dirty and stabbed the arena captain to save my life, and you braided my hair on the boat and told me that you believed in me even when I didn't believe in myself. Tiff, you are everything and I am blessed to work with such an incredible and brilliant woman. Rich Deas, every line, stroke, and letter in this book is nothing short of brilliant. Thank you for putting the most stunning cover on the book of my heart.

To my Macmillan publicity and marketing team, YOU GUYS ARE INCREDIBLE! Thanks for everything you've poured into introducing this book to the world. To my wonderful publicist Molly Ellis, the best days are the ones where I get to email you ten times. I feel so lucky to work with you. Kathryn Little, you're a brilliant, badass director, and I've loved every moment I've gotten to interact with you. Mary Van Akin, I can't type your name without thinking "AND YOU ARE A RENEGADE!" and laughing. You're the BEST hype woman in publishing. #BBs for life. Mariel Dawson, you're a goddess and everything you've done for this book has been as beautiful and epic as you are. Ashley Woodfolk, you wonderful writer, marketer, and friend. I love you and eternal happy book birthday to *The Beauty That Remains*! Allison Verost, I know that none of this incredible campaign could've happened without your guidance and support. And special thanks to the rest of my amazing team, including Brittany Pearlman, Teresa Ferraiolo, Lucy Del Priore, Katie Halata, Morgan Dubin, Robert Brown, and Jeremy Ross.

Thank you to the Macmillan sales team for your love and support of the book, with special thanks to Jennifer Gonzalez, Jessica Brigman, Jennifer Edwards, Claire

Taylor, Mark Von Bargen, Jennifer Golding, Sofrina Hinton, Jaime Ariza, and AJ Murphy. To Tom Nau and everyone in Production who worked with our deadlines to turn this into a real thing! To Melinda Ackell, Valerie Shea, and the copyeditors for your hard work. To Patrick Collins, who made the inside of this book as beautiful as the outside. To Laura Wilson, Brisa Robinson, and Borana Greku at Macmillan Audio. And to every single person in that wonderful building who has done anything for this book, thank you from the bottom of my heart.

To the CBB Film Team, there are no words to describe what it means to me to have you behind this movie. Thank you for your enthusiasm and passion for this story. Patrik Medley and Clare Reeth, you are wonderful humans with the most wonderful smiles. Thank you for loving this book and helping it find an amazing home. Elizabeth Gabler, Gillian Bohrer, and Jiao Chen, thank you for *giving* this book an incredible home with a studio that's made so many of my favorite movies. I've loved every minute spent getting to know you, and I can't wait for everything to come. Karen Rosenfelt, thank you for bringing your brilliance into producing this movie. Wyck Godfrey, thank you for bringing your love and enthusiasm to this project for as long as you could! Marty Bowen, John Fischer, and Temple Hill Productions, thank you for making the movies I've loved since I was a teen, and for adding CBB to your epic list. David Magee and Luke Durett, thank you for creating the brilliant script.

Barry Haldeman, Joel Schoff, Neil Erickson, thank you for working so hard to guide me through this crazy process!

Romina Garber, you're a light to the universe and a blazing sun in my own life. Thank you for being such a wonderful friend and support. Marissa Lee, you're talented beyond words and you've made me a better person and a better writer. Thank you for all the love and joy you've brought into my life! Kristen Ciccarelli, I'm forever grateful for all the times you've helped me work through this story and through my own struggles. My life, my book, and my heart are better because I have you. Kester "Kit" Grant, my darling writing wife! You're a beautiful person inside and out, and I can't wait for the world to meet *A Court of Miracles*. Hillary's Angelz, thank you for the endless source of love, support, and laughs!

Shea Standefer, you are the most compassionate human I've ever met, and your talent knows no bounds. Adalyn Taylor Grace, LOLOLOLOMG! You're my eternal partner in crime *and* you let me send you so many pictures of BTS and other random men and that makes you a *true* friend. Thank you both for always being there for me and this book.

Daniel José Older, Sabaa Tahir, Michael Dante DiMartino, and Bryan Konietzko, thank you for creating the stories that made me want to create this book. Dhonielle Clayton, Zoraida Cordova, and DJO, thank you for helping me make CBB into a story I'm proud to put into the world. Angie Thomas, Leigh Bardugo, Nic Stone, Renée Ahdieh, Marie Lu, and Jason Reynolds, thank you for the love, support, guidance, and inspiration you've each given me at different points throughout my journey. I'm proud to be writing in a time when incredible authors like you are putting stories into the world.

Morgan Sherlock and Allie Stratis, I don't know what I did to get such wonderful best friends, but I'm so glad that I had you growing up and that I still have you both now. I love you, I'm so proud of the women you've become, and I will never, ever forgive you for letting me get bangs. Shannon Janico, you have always been an unbelievable friend and you've grown into an amazing woman. I love you, and every kid you teach is one of the luckiest kids in the world. Mandi Nyambi, you're the most intelligent, passionate, and hardworking woman that I know. Thank you for being a sister to me. I love you, I'm proud of you, and keep taking over the world. Yasmeen Audi, Elise Baranouski, and Juliet Bailin, you have always loved, supported, and pushed me to achieve my dreams. I love you and I'm blessed to have you in my life and am so proud of everything you've done, and everything you're going to do. Also Elise, you can use this text as proof whenever someone doubts how close we actually are.

To my friends at TITLE Boxing and Cody Montarbo, thank you for keeping me sane! Lin-Manuel Miranda, thank you for creating such an inspiring work of art that kept me company during my all-nighters. Brilliant Black People, thank you for inspiring and motivating me. Special shout-out to Michelle and Barack Obama, Chance the Rapper, Viola Davis, Kerry Washington, Shonda Rhimes, Lupita Nyong'o, Ava DuVernay, Zulaikha Patel, Kheris Rogers, Patrisse Cullors, Alicia Garza, and Opal Tometi.

To my teachers, thank you for helping me discover who I am and what I want to say. Special shout-out to Mr. Friebel, Mrs. Colianni, Mr. McCloud, Mr. Woods, Mr. Wilbur, Joey McMullen, Maria Tartar, Christina Phillips Mattson, Amy Hempel, and John Stauffer.

And last but *certainly* not least: to my readers. None of this would be possible without you. Thank you for taking a journey into Orïsha. I can't wait to continue the adventure with you.

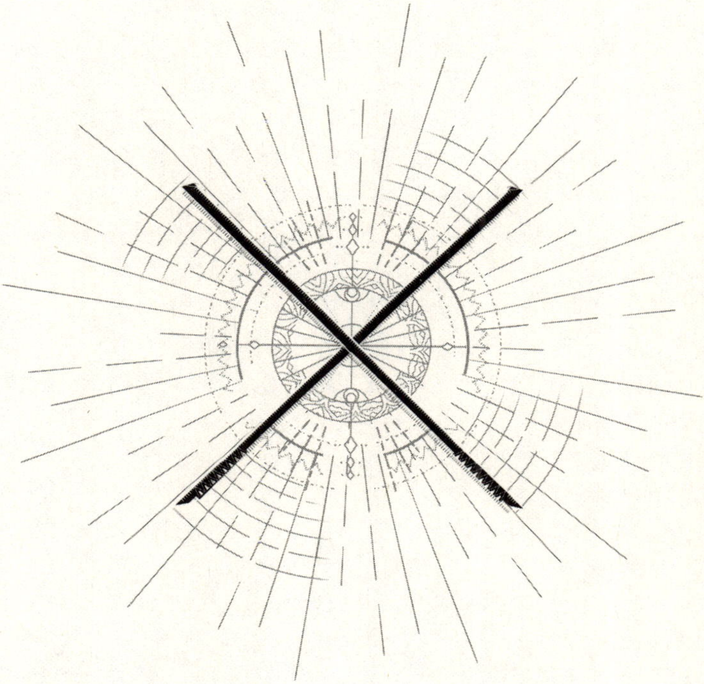

KANO
MAKURDI
DUTSE
ZARIA
IBADAN
GUSAU
ROYAL PALACE
ILORIN
LAGOS
SOKOTO
CHÂNDOMBLÉ
CALABRAR
IBEJI
MINNA
WARRI
IKOYI
OR